FAULT TOLERANCE

FAULT TOLERANCE

A NOVEL

Valerie Valdes

HARPER Voyager
An Imprint of HarperCollins*Publishers*

HarperCollins books may be purchased for educational, business, or sales promotional use. For information, please email the Special Markets Department at SPsales@harpercollins.com.

Harper Voyager and design are trademarks of HarperCollins Publishers LLC.

FIRST EDITION

Designed by Joy O'Meara
Chapter opener art © happy_fox_art/Shutterstock.com

Library of Congress Cataloging-in-Publication Data has been applied for.

ISBN 978-0-06-308589-3

22 23 24 25 26   LSC   10 9 8 7 6 5 4 3 2 1

To all who dare to believe they can survive
You hold the future in your hand

FAULT TOLERANCE

Chapter 1

NO SHIT, THERE I WAS

Captain Eva Innocente stifled a yawn as the doors at the far end of the green room slid open, allowing the screaming, whistling, and feet-pounding of thousands of audience members to wash over her like a coronal mass ejection. Other competitors lined up in front of her, fidgeting with nervous excitement or stoically awaiting further orders from the production assistants, who communicated via silent commlink messages. Indistinct blue, pink, and yellow lights slowly illuminated a massive arena with platforms floating in midair above an enormous stage. Exuberant music rose in volume, the rhythmic thump of bass vibrating in Eva's chest. An announcer's voice emanated from the wristband an employee had strapped onto Eva earlier.

"Welcome, persons of all persuasions, to the *Crash Sisters* Grand Melee!" the voice said, dragging out the final syllable. The crowd's roar increased in intensity.

Record scratch, freeze-frame, Eva thought. Yup, that's me. You're probably wondering how I ended up in this situation.

"I'm really sorry, Captain," Leroy said. He tugged on his neat orange beard, an old nervous habit, stranger now that his facial hair was neatly trimmed rather than scraggly and unkempt.

"No te preocupes," Eva said, propping her face up with one hand as she leaned on the table in the mess. A half-finished cafecito sat in front of her, doing little to sweeten her bitter mood.

She was worried. Most of the sizable paycheck she'd just collected from The Forge—with a hefty bonus for the whole "destroying a huge enemy ship and possibly saving the universe" thing—was supposed to go toward ship repairs, supplies, and upgrades, not this impromptu vacation.

But this was Brodevis, the Planet of a Million Microclimates, home to about that many overpriced tourist traps scattered across the various landscapes. It was also a prime location for memvid production facilities, including *Crash Sisters*, the competitive combat reality show in which Leroy starred. The docking fees alone were more expensive than most hotels in any other part of the universe.

"I was so sure I'd be able to swing something, but all the hotels are packed." Leroy's holo crackled a bit from lag, as the heavy traffic on the local quantumnet relays reinforced what he'd just said.

"It's not your fault," Eva said. "I should have waited to come until you confirmed." Everyone had been so excited, and desperate to leave the Forge base after weeks of sporadic repairs. It was hard to get ship parts when your secret space station was days away from the nearest Gate. And between the Forge people treating them like pets who did an impressive trick and the Fridge refugees from the battle being salty about losing and trying to take advantage to lurk and spy, the place was a reactor core leaking radiation, waiting to explode.

An orange striped cat wandered in, tail primly raised and slightly curved at the end. Same color as Leroy's hair, more or less. It was pursued a few moments later by a black-and-white spotted cat.

"I couldn't even get your docking fees waived, there are so many people here for the Grand Melee. I even tried to, uh, ask some other people for help, but it's a total mess." Leroy lifted his chin in greeting at someone offscreen, probably his girlfriend, Momoko, who also starred in the show. "Hold on a sec, I'll be right back." The holo flickered and switched to a still of Leroy's face, frozen in a dramatic scowl more reminiscent of his villainous *Crash Sisters* persona, The King.

Leroy had sworn that, with his relative fame and connections, he'd be able to get them a swank room, free parking, even some meal coupons for the fancy replicators—the kind that could make complex meals instead of patties and cubes and liquids that tasted almost like they saw flavor once across a crowded room. Instead, *La Sirena Negra* was crammed into the spaceship equivalent of a sleeping pod, and her crew was getting increasingly antsy. They'd been promised beaches, window shopping, fancy shore excursions, and maybe even a foot massage or two. But they couldn't even get a reservation at the cheapest sidewalk food vendor stall. The last place Eva had tried to order takeout from wasn't taking requests for the next twenty cycles.

The black-and-white cat sidled up to the orange one, rubbing its head under the other's chin. Apparently the orange one didn't appreciate this, because it hissed and sent out a psychic wave of irritation that made Eva scowl.

They weren't the only ones fighting on the ship right now.

Her sister Mari had tagged along, after her superiors at The Forge had gently but firmly encouraged her to recuperate from her injuries somewhere besides their damaged base. Agent Elus wanted to recruit Eva's crew to work for The Forge, an offer Eva hadn't rejected yet, so this might be a plot to convince them it would be a good idea. If so, Mari had been the wrongest possible woman for the job. Still, Eva had thought this might be a good opportunity to reconnect, heal their relationship along with their physical injuries.

Qué bobería. Min and Sue were surviving because they had each other, but Pink was ready to surgically extract the stick from Mari's ass and beat her to death with it. The only thing keeping the good doctor from going bad was the promise of that foot massage at the end of the long flight. This might finally break her.

As if on cue, Mari hobbled in and went straight for the cafetera. Her broken leg was on the mend but still encased in a latticed cast, and she leaned on Eva's cane, affectionately called Fuácata. She'd pulled her brown hair back into a neat ponytail, and she scowled when she noticed Eva had left the coffee grounds in the filter basket.

Cue the nagging, Eva thought. Three, two . . .

"You know you should empty this out when it's still hot," Mari said.

"I didn't want to burn my fingers," Eva replied.

"You can use a towel," Mari said.

Eva smiled humorlessly, her facial scar pulling at the skin around it. "Or I could wait for it to cool down first."

"It gets all sludgy if you wait," Mari insisted. "It's disgusting."

Eva slurped her own coffee and stared at Leroy's frozen face while Mari made frustrated noises. She'd have to deliver the bad news to her crew, which sucked. They deserved a real break. They'd been dragged through a huge pile of mierda and the stink hadn't washed off yet. Now they were out a bunch of credits, refueling would cost an arm and a half dozen tentacles, and she'd maybe have to encourage her sister to catch a ride with someone else or face Pink's wrath. Healing was a nice dream, but Pink was reality, and much more important.

I wish Vakar were here, Eva thought miserably, then quickly pushed that thought away like a baby shunning peas.

"We should have gone to Neos," Eva muttered. "It's a hot mess, but at least it's cheap and quiet." Pink had vetoed that option last time Eva had brought it up, though. Which, fair, because Pink would be the one working to pay for their stay.

"My agent did have a suggestion," Leroy said.

"Dímelo," Eva said.

"You could enter the Grand Melee, if you wanted to."

Eva's eyebrows climbed her forehead. "I could do what now? The Grand qué?" Mari paused in her coffee preparations, now actively eavesdropping.

"The Grand Melee," Leroy continued. "It's a big free-for-all fight, you know? Dump a ton of people in a room, there can be only one? One of the contestants got a nasty concussion trying to do the latest q-net dare, so a slot opened up."

"What's the dare?" Mari asked.

Leroy gave a surprisingly evil laugh. "Okay, so, first you need twenty cans of coconut cream and a box of sparklers—"

"Shouldn't that slot go to someone on a waiting list or something?" Eva interrupted. "How do you even qualify for this?"

"Oh, it's all good. You just have to beat a Challenge Room. You already did that at Evercon, remember?" He grinned, clearly into the idea. "My agent said all I have to do is get you bumped to the top of the list, and you're in."

Eva took another sip of coffee. "So I kick ass, ignore names, and I get what? A prize?"

"If you win, you get a trophy!" Leroy exclaimed.

"A trophy?" Eva blinked. How would that solve their problems? What would she even do with a trophy?

"Cap!" Min yelled over the speakers. The pilot had been eavesdropping as well, apparently. "You have to do this! The Grand Melee trophy is a super-big deal. I need that trophy. I need it more than I need to live."

Eva hid her snort-laugh behind another sip of coffee. Min had always loved *Crash Sisters* as much as Leroy. Of course she would want this to happen. That didn't make it a good idea.

"Do I have to fight you?" Eva asked.

Leroy shook his head. "It's just noobs like you. None of us from the roster. Doesn't mean it will be easy, but you're tough."

Min giggled. "You called her a noob."

"I'm extremely insulted," Eva deadpanned, rolling her eyes. "Are medical costs covered if I'm injured?"

"Um, not exactly," Leroy said.

"That sounds like a no," Pink said, sauntering into the mess. Her black hair was longer than it had been for a while, arranged in tiny braids thanks to the combined efforts of Min and Sue over their long Forge stay. She hadn't dressed for work yet, still wearing her cozy pajamas and the slippers Eva had bought for her last birthday. "Y'all think casts grow on trees?" she continued. She glared at Mari, then pointedly ignored her, sliding into the seat next to Eva.

Sue ran in from the direction of the cargo bay, slightly out of breath. Her face and jumpsuit were streaked with grease from whatever she'd been working on, safety goggles perched on top of her head. One of her tiny robots peeked out from inside a pocket in her pants and made a squealing sound that startled the two cats, who had retreated to opposite corners of the room. They both chased each other out of the room in a burst of indignation.

"Uh, hi," Sue said. "Min told me to come, um, you know."

"Make sure Cap says she'll get the trophy!" Min exclaimed through the speakers.

Someone said something behind Leroy, and he added, "It's not only a trophy. You also get a seven-cycle stay in a luxury resort."

"Now, that," said Pink, "is what I'm talking about. Foot massages?"

"It's all-inclusive," Leroy said. "Full resort privileges, including the spa. Free food, free booze, and all the memvids you can physically tolerate."

Eva looked around the room at her assembled crewmates, all of them staring at her like cats waiting to be fed. Mala sauntered in to join them, her tail swishing in amusement at the tension in the air, thicker than the scent of Mari's fresh coffee percolating.

"Miau," said Mala, slowly blinking her hazel eyes.

"No empieces," Eva muttered.

Leroy's cocky grin returned. "So? What do you say?"

Eva heaved a sigh. "Me cago en diez," she said.

Focus, Eva told herself. If you don't win this, Pink will kill your sister and Min will kill you.

The announcer continued. "A massive sixty-four challengers will enter the proving grounds tonight, but only four will reach the Final Four-for-All! Who will our winning warriors be? Who has the strength, the speed, the stamina, and the sex organs of steel to stand atop the stunned remains of their feisty fellow fighters?"

Another voice cut in. "Sparks will fly, my friends, make no mistake! And as you know, Bob, sparks are not the only thing up in the air tonight."

"That's right, Xyzzkh," Bob said. "Which of these contestants will earn the coveted *Crash Sisters* trophy?"

Eva tried not to zone out as the two hosts bantered, stretching her arms in front of her. A glowing display popped up on her wristband, reading 0%. Her injury counter. If it reached 100%, her weight would decrease, making her easier to knock off the stage, so she could be hauled away by attendants waiting below.

After everything they'd been through in the past few weeks—all the times she'd come close to actually dying while looking for Sue's brother, Josh, or afterward when she got spaced in an unknown galaxy, or when she was almost murdered by mysterious sentient robots and their massive dreadnought—she snickered at the absurdity of a machine tallying up some fake measure of the damage she took.

"Looks like it's time to meet our contestants!" Xyzzkh exclaimed. "Could one of them be up to the task of dethroning The King at the end of this season?"

"Anything is possible," Bob replied. "The King himself was a complete unknown before exploding onto the scene after winning his Grand Melee, taking down Sergeant Eagle despite his unbeatable Eagle Kick."

"That's right, Bob, what a fierce battle that was. But the Eagle has landed, and The King rules the roost. Here come the challengers now!"

Eva checked that her holo-mask disguise still ran smoothly. Anyone more than a few centimeters away would see a pale person with blue eyes and spiky blond hair, instead of her usual light-brown skin, dark-brown eyes, and black hair. Didn't want any of her enemies recognizing her, since she was about to be broadcast to a few billion people across the universe.

She wasn't the only person in a costume. Some wore masks or face paint, others had wild hair, but most looked like they belonged at Evercon with their elaborate gloves and capes and fancy attire. Also like Evercon, outside weapons were banned, even though the official *Crash Sisters* fighters had signature ones they used regularly.

Two recording devices hovered just beyond the door to the arena. The lines started to move, staggered so that as one person said their stage name, the person in the line next to them stepped up to the other recorder. Despite there being so many people, things moved quickly. Next thing Eva knew, the person in front of her said their name was Poo and she choked down a laugh, which turned into a cough, which turned into her missing her cue and getting shoved forward by someone behind her.

"Vendetta," Eva said, her voice modulated to sound deeper. She stepped onto her assigned hover disc and stared over her shoulder at the person who had pushed her.

"Sniper," he said. The top of his face was covered by a holo-mask as well, made to look like a red helmet. Also like Eva, he wore a simple gray jumpsuit—spacesuits could double as armor, so they weren't allowed. He strutted away from the line toward his disc, whistling softly.

Sniper, huh? Eva thought. I'll be sure to kick his ass first. That tune was weirdly familiar, though.

As the introductions ended, one of the announcers said, "Let's get ready to melee!" and the hover disc Eva stood on shot into the air.

A winding flight ended with her positioned above a fellow challenger—a boxer, given his taped hands. Some of the fighters leaped off their discs onto the stage below, which consisted of a long, broad main platform and three smaller ones floating above it at different heights. Around them, a black field of recording nanobots obscured the crowds that screamed and whistled and hooted in their seats.

Without warning, Eva's disc slipped out from under her and zoomed away. She fell to the floor, rolling to her feet and narrowly avoiding a flurry of punches from a human in a cape. Who wears a cape to a brawl? she thought, grabbing the fabric and twining it around the wrist of the boxer as he charged her from the other side. She danced away from the entangled people, looking for a new target.

A dark-furred rani launched a kick at her, their foxlike snout baring small, sharp teeth. No time to dodge. Eva blocked with her forearms, protecting her head and torso. The rani tried another leaping kick, and this time she stepped inside it and caught their leg, spinning the fighter around with their own momentum and tossing them into a guy whose costume looked like Leroy's. The band on Eva's wrist flashed: 5%.

"Wow, Xyzzkh," Bob said. "Kroko has wasted no time crushing Bogado under his enormous body. Packun used her floral head maw to swallow the pizkee Ramilo and spit him over the side of the platform, while Margarida is squaring off against a young human in a sports hat. I think his name was Poo?"

Someone hit Eva from behind and she stumbled. Sniper grinned at her.

"Jódete, cabrón," she said, sliding her leg back into a fighting stance. Her crew needed her to get that fancy hotel package. And, she grudgingly admitted, the trophy would look good in the mess.

Sniper charged. They exchanged a series of fast strikes before returning to neutral positions, each breathing more heavily. He was good. Annoyingly good. She couldn't see his damage counter, but hers now read 24%.

A strange canister fell to the ground between them. Reflexively, Eva kicked it toward Sniper. She didn't want to get blown up or gassed. Then she remembered the training module and groaned.

"Things are about to get interesting, Bob," said Xyzzkh. "The Crash Cans are in play! I wonder what surprises we have in store this time?"

Hard to unlearn years of training at avoiding mysterious projectiles. Meanwhile, Sniper grabbed the container and twisted the top. It opened with a hiss, and he pulled out a small metal cylinder, pressing the button on the side so it flared to life.

Maybe he doesn't know how to use it? she thought. He twirled it in his fingers, popping that hope bubble.

"Sniper got his hands on a glow knife!" Bob exclaimed. "Those things can wreak havoc on the battlefield. His opponent, Vendetta, doesn't seem so eager to tangle with him now. And Canela has pulled a proximity mine from her Crash Can—"

An explosion reminded Eva that this was a brawl, not a duel. She glanced over her shoulder in time to avoid a tackle from a truateg. He skidded to a halt and laughed at her, covering his bulldog face with a large, furry hand. She kicked his knee out and elbowed him in the throat, then pushed him into Sniper, who made quick use of his new glow knife.

"Looks like Kroko is about to drop Poo, Bob."

A human in a baseball cap fell right in front of Eva. He was unconscious, blood streaming from his nose, and his wristband flashed 100%. She lifted him—light as a balloon—and gently tossed him away from the fighting.

A crash behind her, another taunting roar. Kroko was wrecking shit. He was a todyk, about three meters tall, with green feathers under his flashy gold robes. Few of the other fighters were interested in engaging him; most tagged each other, pairing off in their own little battles, occasionally interrupted by a third party.

Sniper reappeared, glow knife gone, wristband flashing 37%. He charged Eva again, and she spun sideways like a matador to avoid being grappled. Unfortunately, she spun directly into a tall dark-haired woman, who smiled sweetly and pulled Eva against the front of her orange dress, slipping her arm under Eva's chin and tightening her grip.

"Uh-oh, Margarida has caught up with Vendetta," Bob said. "Vendetta and Sniper had a rivalry from the start, but that may be over now."

It had been a while since anyone but Vakar had put her in a rear choke hold. Eva's breath came in ragged sips through her nose, and worse, the woman lifted her off the floor, leaving Eva's feet dangling. Her vision edged to black, her wristband ticking up like a clock: 31% . . . 43% . . .

Eva kicked her legs forward, the momentum enough to bring Margarida down with her. Eva jammed her thumbs into the woman's forearms and slid sideways, scrambling free.

"Here comes another round of mystery items, Xyzzkh! What will the challengers find to help them this time?"

A Crash Can fell right next to Margarida, who grinned and grabbed it.

Instead of unleashing a new toy, the canister exploded.

Margarida tumbled backward. Eva rolled away and got to her feet, her wristband flashing 57%. Not great.

Eva barely raised her arms in time to block a vicious punch that would have hit her solar plexus. Sniper was back. She wouldn't be safe for long. Sniper swung again, then again. Too many more hits and she'd be flushed like Poo.

When she saw an opening, Eva lunged forward. She'd learned plenty of tricks from her old boss, Tito Santiago, who only fought clean if he'd just taken a shower, and for whom the best defense was a brutal offense. But as she feinted a straight punch, hoping to draw Sniper into a block she could turn to her

advantage, he sidestepped and brought his fist around for a vicious right hook.

Eva's body moved on its own thanks to years of practice
drills. She angled to take the hit on her shoulder as she rushed
her opponent, grabbing him around the waist and tackling him
to the floor. A series of grappling counters ended with Sniper's
face pressed to the metallic surface of the stage. Even so, he positioned his arms to break Eva's hold, so she released him and
backed away quickly.

Her damage meter read 69% now. Nice.

"Who the fuck are you?" she shouted at him. That whole
back-and-forth was textbook Tito. Where had this guy picked
up those skills?

"Here we go, Bob," Xyzzkh said. "Kroko is out for blood
again. He's personally taken down four challengers already. Will
Vendetta be his fifth?"

The floor trembled from rhythmic thuds behind her. Eva
didn't bother looking; she leaped sideways into a roll. Kroko
passed in a rush of wind, his attention immediately shifting to
Sniper.

Good, she thought. Maybe they could soften each other up
for her to take them down.

The number of challengers had dwindled substantially, but
the audience remained as engaged as ever. Hopefully Min and
Sue were still enjoying the show. Pink and Mari might be united
in disdain for a change.

"I can't believe what I'm seeing, Xyzzkh," Bob said. "Looks
like Sniper is holding his own against Kroko, but barely."

And Margarida was about to cut in. Eva grinned. Couldn't
let those three have all the fun. Besides, she wanted another
shot at Sniper; if he worked for Tito, she might know him, and

more important, might want to punch him more than she had already.

Eva waited, and watched, and took her chance when Sniper kicked Margarida in the gut, doubling her over in pain.

"Peekaboo!" Eva shouted, planting a hand on Margarida's back and vaulting over her to kick Kroko in the eye.

"What a tense match, Bob," Xyzzkh said. "Some unorthodox methods by the fighters, but the crowd is loving it!"

As Kroko's hands flew to his injury, Eva grabbed his bicep and swung on it to land behind him. He tried to clothesline her, but she ducked, then jumped over his tail as he spun. Margarida didn't avoid the appendage, however, and ate the floor.

Sniper stepped in, finishing Margarida with a few quick strikes, then shoving the now-buoyant beauty off the platform. Kroko tried to body-slam Eva, but she darted out of his way, which put Sniper on the opposite side of the large todyk. They shared a glance that felt like it lasted longer than the moment it did, their respective identities hidden behind their holo-masks.

"We're down to four challengers now, Xyzzkh," Bob said. "Flameor is hanging back on an upper platform, while Vendetta, Sniper, and Kroko engage in a triple showdown. The suspense is so thick you could cut it with a glow knife."

As much as Eva wanted to know who Sniper was, the important thing was winning. For the vacation, for the trophy, and especially for Min, who was hopefully losing her shit with delight. She stretched her aching hands, then clenched them into fists and prepared for her next assault.

The omnipresent background music suddenly cut out. The audience shrieks and cheers and whistles turned to confused chatter, sprinkled with shouts that translated to "What the fuck" in a plethora of languages. Eva backed away from the other fighters and scanned the arena, but couldn't see through the thick black cloud of memvid nanobots.

"Everyone, please remain calm and stay in your seats until further notice," Bob the announcer said, his voice unusually strained.

Confusion turned to panic. The production assistants were conspicuously absent, the door to the green room closed and no other exits visible. There was no smoke, no vibrations to suggest an earthquake, no explosion or projectile-weapon sounds, just the agitated crowd and the neon glow of the stage lights. Eva tried to message Pink on her commlink, but comms were blocked inside the nanobot cloud. She couldn't even attempt to access the q-net to see if whatever it was had hit the feeds. Unless . . .

"Sniper," she said.

The helmeted man gave a slight nod.

"I need you to hit me," Eva continued.

Sniper's mouth quirked up in a half grin. "What?" he asked.

"If you get me to 100%, I can try to jump past the nanobots and figure out what's happening," Eva said. A foolish idea, maybe, but the alternatives were diving off the platform or doing nothing.

Sniper's grin expanded. "You don't want to wait? More information could be coming."

"Whatever is happening, it's not something they're prepared for." Eva gestured around the arena as she ticked off the options on her fingers. "That means it can't be a natural disaster, internal accident, or facility attack." It has to be an even bigger arroz con mango than any of that, Eva thought grimly, or they wouldn't be cagando in their bloomers. They'd either be evacuating people in an orderly fashion or they would never have interrupted the Grand Melee in the first place.

Was her crew safe? Was Leroy? She had to know.

Warily, Sniper approached her. "You had better not be tricking me."

"I'm not, trust me."

Sniper paused a few meters away. "Your name is Alvarez, isn't it? You fight like her, and you talk like her."

She knew his fighting style was familiar. So was hers, apparently. Or her cussing. "I don't go by that name anymore," she said quietly.

As if he understood something implicitly, maybe a sentiment he shared, Sniper walked up to her without hesitation. "Let me know when to stop," he said, and started to punch her shoulder—not gently, but not so hard that bruising would be swift.

Eva kept an eye on her damage counter as it ticked up, slowly but steadily. 74% . . . 79% . . . 84% . . . The crowd continued their combination of anger and hysterics, but the nanobot cloud didn't shift a centimeter, and the elusive Bob and Xyzzkh didn't return to make more announcements. Her anxiety level rose like that fake-ass injury number, and she tried to stifle the whiny thought that even on a vacation she couldn't catch a cabrón break.

Finally the counter hit 104%, and Eva held up a hand to stop Sniper. She rolled her shoulder experimentally; stiff, but no worse than a sparring session with Vakar.

Oh, Vakar. She sighed, putting those feelings away for later with everything else.

As promised, her wristband created a field that made her extremely light. She gave an experimental jump, passing the middle level of platforms before drifting back down.

"Let's get up to the top platform," she told Sniper. "Think you can toss me from there?"

Sniper nodded. "Will it be enough?"

Eva shrugged. Wouldn't know until they tried.

The two of them climbed to the highest platform, Eva practically floating. After some arguing about technique, Sniper made a basket with his hands for her to step on and tried to launch her into the air. Eva managed to achieve a decent amount of height, but not enough to clear the cloud. Next, they moved to the edge of the platform and he grabbed her by the ankles, then spun her like a figure skater to get momentum and threw her as hard as he could. She went higher this time, but also farther off the stage, and she had to execute an awkward series of aerial jumps to get back. The longer this took, the more frustrated and worried Eva felt, and the more desperate she was to find out what had happened. They were arguing about whether she should make him bouncy, too, and try to use each other as springboards somehow when a polite chirp interrupted them.

Kroko advanced, hands folded in a todyk gesture of nonaggression. "Greetings, esteemed colleagues," he said, his voice a pleasant tenor. "Do I hear correctly that you intend to seek information about our current predicament?"

Eva had forgotten how formal todyk were. "Em, sí," she replied. "We are investigating the situation . . . verily?"

Kroko, who had until now been the picture of unrestrained rage, nodded sagely. "If my services may assist this endeavor in any way, please do not hesitate to call upon me, and I shall be pleased to oblige you."

Eva pursed her lips, examining him. "I think you could help," she said. "You could probably toss me much higher than him, if you used your leg muscles."

Kroko lay down on his back, tail stretched out along the floor, and Sniper helped Eva climb onto his feet and get in position to jump.

"Shall we count simultaneously?" Kroko asked.

"On three," Eva replied, taking a deep breath to steady herself. "One . . . two . . . three!"

Kroko kicked, hard enough that Eva felt herself accelerate. Up and up she flew, and before she could worry that she wouldn't clear the nanobot cloud, she went through it. Her commlink came online in a rush as it reconnected with the local relays, messages rapidly filling her queue. She hovered for a few long moments, then drifted back down, gently as a fart on a breeze, silently cagando en la mierda the entire time.

"What's happening?" Sniper asked.

"Did you learn anything of merit or interest?" Kroko added.

Eva touched down on the platform and bounced a few times, then turned to them with a sour expression.

"Bueno," she said, extending the second syllable. "The short answer is, no one knows qué coño está pasando."

"And the long answer?" Sniper asked.

"Hundreds of weird monoliths just appeared all over the universe, right next to Gates." Eva stared up at the ceiling as if she could see through the nanobots all the way out into space, but they stayed frustratingly dark. "They're all broadcasting the same message: 'All recipients of this transmission, prepare to surrender or be exterminated.'"

Chapter 2

DUTY CALLS

After a few more todyk-assisted jumps to get further information, Eva and the others were abruptly separated and released from the *Crash Sisters* arena in a flurry of polite nonapologies and additional legal forms. Eva never got to grill Sniper about his history with Tito, though she and Kroko did exchange q-mail codes so they could stay in touch. She also got a call from Leroy asking her for a ride if she planned to leave the system. She told him to start packing.

By the time she made it back to *La Sirena Negra*, Eva knew both a lot more and frustratingly little about the situation unfolding across the known universe.

The monoliths were metallic, dull gray, and apparently inert, about four meters long by two meters wide. There was one within a hundred meters of every Gate, two in the handful of systems that had two Gates. No one knew where they came from, how they got there, or what they could do, and they couldn't be moved from their paths.

They were also immune to every weapon anyone tried to use on them.

The vague but threatening message they broadcast was in hundreds of languages, so its potential source was uncertain, and various fingers and appendages were rapidly pointed in many directions at once. Most Gate usage ground to a halt—temporarily, anyway, until commerce and law enforcement could agree on acceptable risk levels. Experts debated the various translations, what constituted surrender or extermination, whether they were expected to destroy their arms and defenses or just not retaliate whenever the message sender arrived . . .

If information was the grease that kept the wheels of civilization turning, then this mystery was a bag of wrenches in the gears. But some people had more information than others, and Eva was fortunate to be related to one of those people. Possibly three, but only one of them was speaking to her at the moment. Her father was off doing whatever bullshit he did now that his criminal empire had been yoinked away from him by The Fridge, and her mother was still cleaning up the mess Eva had left behind in Garilia. She did send an encrypted message asking Eva to go hide in a BOFA safe house with her abuelos, which was a step up from the silent treatment.

Eva stalked up the open cargo hatch of *La Sirena Negra*, waving absently at the camera in the corner when Min greeted her. A glance at the cats slowed her stride; they weren't splayed about the room as usual, sleeping or eating or licking themselves. Instead, they all sat in a circle, their flanks almost touching, looking straight ahead as if each was having a staring contest with the one across from them. It was, frankly, creepy as hell, but Eva wasn't going to ask.

Within moments Eva puttered around the mess, making coffee as she absently whistled, massaging her aching neck, and pinging the rest of the crew to pause their preparations for departure and convene for a meeting. Mari had refused to fill her in while Eva was en route, citing security concerns, which meant she knew more than the q-net feeds and various official BOFA and governmental announcements were sharing with the public. And while Mari had been reluctant to let Eva see her dominoes in the past, this time Eva was going to flip the table if that's what it took to get a look at what her sister was hiding.

Pink arrived first, sliding into a seat and slouching. She wore what Eva called her "doctor suit," a stiff white lab coat over a white button-down shirt with a maroon bow tie. Her makeup was impeccable, her lipstick a neutral red, her visible eye perfectly lined with mascara emphasized by a fake eyelash. From the waist up, she was the picture of professionalism.

From the waist down, she wore light-brown shorts and fluffy socks. Business in the penthouse, party in the basement.

"The hell are you whistling?" Pink asked.

"Was I whistling?" Eva asked.

"Yeah, it sounds familiar."

Eva shrugged. She'd been so focused on her coffee that she hadn't noticed. "You still on the clock?" she asked.

"Nope," Pink said, popping the *p* so the word had two syllables. "My teledoc queue is closed until further notice. All appointments to be rescheduled or rerouted to local docs. Techs are doing mandatory unscheduled maintenance because they're worried the message is some kind of virus, installing spyware to steal patient data."

Eva paused with her spoon in her taza. "No me diga."

"Yeah, I know." Pink waved her hand dismissively. "The

whole universe is on fire, and these chumps think it's all about them. Meanwhile, I'm sitting on my thumb not getting paid."

Sue wandered in next, from the direction of the bridge. While she might have been in the head, or in the crew quarters, it was safe to assume she'd been doing something with Min. Her black hair and jumpsuit were disheveled, which wasn't unusual; the pink flush on her pale cheeks, however, was.

"Captains," Sue mumbled, sliding into a chair.

"Engineer," Eva replied solemnly. "Have you been engaging in unscheduled maintenance, too?"

"Cap!" Min exclaimed through the ship's speakers. "Don't tease her." Sue's pink blush turned red as a ripe pitanga all the way down her neck.

"You and Vakar were a pain when you started getting your groove on," Pink added. "Whole damn ship smelled like licorice for weeks." She paused, leaning back in her chair and crossing her arms. "Have you been able to get ahold of him yet?"

Eva finished pouring the last of her espresso into its tiny cup, her hand trembling just enough that she spilled a few drops on the counter.

"Not yet," Eva replied.

Pink frowned, then shrugged. "Not unexpected, at least, but still. Stinks like a sack of shit."

"Yeah." The sweet, frothy layer of espumita on Eva's coffee covered the inky blackness underneath, which felt like a metaphor for something she couldn't put her finger on. So she gave up trying and took a sip instead, savoring the sugary bitterness that washed over her tongue.

She turned around to find Mala sitting in her chair, tail wrapped around her feet primly. For all the jokes Eva made about the cat's uncertain language abilities, there was no doubt that Mala was intelligent enough to steal someone's seat at the most annoying time possible, and sinvergüenza enough to feel no remorse about it whatsoever. Eva stuck her tongue out, earning a slow, disinterested blink, followed by a paw lick.

Mari took that moment to appear finally, limping in like a grizzled, cane-wielding flight instructor about to lecture a room full of raw recruits. She'd swapped her ponytail for a severe bun, the lapel of her black-and-gray suit drawing a straight line down the left side of her body. Why had she even packed a suit to go on vacation? Eva wondered. Without greeting anyone, she went to a cabinet, grabbed a cup, and filled it with water. She then stepped up next to the table, put her glass down, and stood there waiting, stiff with suppressed energy.

Normally, Eva would torment her sister a little, drag things out until Mari snapped at her in frustration, but since Eva had specifically requested this briefing session and Mari was cooperating, she decided business should come before pleasure for once. She leaned against the counter, drink in hand.

"Cuéntamelo," Eva said. "And skip the stuff everyone knows already."

Mari paused and took a deep breath as if recalibrating, then gestured, and a hologram of a monolith appeared above the surface of the table.

"This is the device near this system's Gate," Mari said. "It's broadcasting the same message as every other device, repeated on a loop roughly every forty-two seconds."

Roughly? Eva thought, suppressing a smirk.

"We have not yet determined the device's locational origin," Mari continued. "However, its chemical composition and other technological markers strongly suggest it was created by the Proarkhe."

"What?" Sue squeaked, her hands flying to her face. A small yellow robot wriggled out of her jumpsuit, making tinny whining noises.

"Someone is using Proarkhe tech to spam the whole universe?" Pink asked. "How did they even get it when BOFA locks that shit down as soon as they hear about it?"

"Is it The Fridge?" Min asked through the speakers.

Mari held up a hand and inhaled slowly through her nose, a stalling tactic she'd used on Eva many times. "Our investigations are ongoing," she replied. "But we don't think it's The Fridge."

"This isn't their style," Eva said. They preferred to work in the dark, out of sight, and let most people believe they were a myth. That made it harder for anyone they harmed to get help and made it easier for them to retaliate without attracting unwanted attention. Besides, they'd blown a lot of their load on the attack against the Fridge base.

Pink asked quietly, "Does this have something to do with the hornet's nest you and your buddies kicked? The one shaped like a big-ass ship that almost blew all y'all to kingdom come?"

Eva had spent the past three weeks trying to forget that dreadnought, at least enough to avoid the surge of nightmares that came every time she let it linger in her thoughts. It had been huge, and its weapons had been intense, and she had almost died stopping it from getting any farther into the known universe from its weird starless corner of the black.

Mari didn't answer Pink's questions right away, doing her slow exhale again instead.

"She does think this is connected," Eva said, watching her sister. "But she doesn't want to say anything, because she's afraid of being wrong, but she's more afraid of being right."

Mari opened her mouth, then closed it, her lips curling slightly at the corners. "That was surprisingly insightful for you, Eva-Benita," she said.

"I'm maturing like a ron añejo," Eva replied. "Complex, spicy, and full-bodied."

Pink gave a brief, throaty laugh, while Mari failed to suppress an eye roll.

Eva squinted down at her mostly empty taza. "So what does The Forge plan to do about—"

"Uh, Cap," Min interrupted. "There's a message coming through on your private channel."

Eva and Mari exchanged a look. The only ones who used that channel were them and their parents, and since they were together right now . . .

"Let's have it," Eva said, dismissing Mari's holographic presentation with a wave. Hopefully it wasn't bad news, but knowing Pete and Regina, it could be anything.

But instead of her parents' faces and voices, nothing happened. Eva waited, raising her eyebrows after a moment and glancing at the camera in the corner of the room.

"Is it—" *playing*, she started to ask just as Mala hissed and yowled in dismay.

Eva's vision went dark like the blood had rushed to her feet, and her mouth filled with the taste of copper and ozone. Her hand spasmed shut, breaking her coffee cup with a quiet crunch, and then Eva fell on her ass, limbs seizing as her eyesight slowly returned.

Pink knelt at her side, eye patch flipped up so her mechanical eye could scan Eva. "The hell was that?" Pink asked. "Mercy, your blood pressure is all over the place. I hope your artificial heart wasn't damaged."

Eva swallowed uncomfortably, flexing her hand. Tiny cuts began to throb and weep red around slivers of cheap ceramic material.

"I was, uh, getting a message, I think," Eva said. It sat in her mind like a poorly constructed memvid, hard-edged and unfamiliar, as if she'd simultaneously read and heard it all at once instead of in some normal linear way. Creepy, and unpleasantly similar to a recent experience she'd rather forget.

"The good news is, you don't have a concussion," Pink said. "And whatever happened, it wasn't a stroke."

Eva let Mala rub against her arm as she rubbed her forehead with her uninjured hand. "Nobody else just got their brains cracked open and scrambled like an egg?"

"No," Mari said. "Qué te pasa?"

"No sé," Eva said. "But there's a message in my head that wasn't there before, and it says, 'Captain Eva Innocente, meet us at the following Gate coordinates to obtain the information and tools that may prevent the coming war.'"

Everyone in the room fell silent and stared at Eva like she'd grown an extra head. She certainly felt like she had.

"Rusty buckets," Sue whispered.

"Cap, that is so extra," Min added.

Pink dabbed Eva's hand with a towel, gently removing the largest pieces of broken cup.

Eva bit her lip, ignoring the sting in her palm. She was used to being on people's shit lists for various reasons, but honestly, she was more used to being nobody. One random person in a universe with trillions of people scattered across thousands of planets. For someone to explicitly contact her like this, to single her out as someone who should be involved in stopping some war she knew nothing about, was as unbelievable as the situation itself.

"What are the coordinates?" Mari asked, her tone carefully neutral.

Eva rattled them off, unable to recall the last time she'd had to verbalize such a long string of numbers. Certainly she'd never had to memorize them; that's what computer logs and navigation software were for. And this wasn't even a real memory, just some strange neural equivalent of a noisy ad popping up in her personal feed.

When she finished, Min said, "Cap, those don't match any known Gates."

"That's ten kilos of weird in a two-kilo bag," Pink added, stopping her wound cleaning to shine a light directly into Eva's eyes. Eva blinked away the dark spots left behind, then obediently opened her mouth when Pink pushed a thumb down on her chin.

Only Mari looked more interested than worried. "Another lost Gate," she murmured. "Incredible. But why would they contact you? What could they want?"

"Who are you talking about, Agent Virgo?" Sue asked.

"Yeah, Agent Virgo," Pink added, flicking her light off.

Mari frowned. "Whoever sent the message, obviously. It could be someone from The Fridge, I suppose, some spy or defector, though we had thought we obtained all their intelligence on Gates in our various raids of their facilities."

"Why wouldn't they send a regular message, though?" Pink asked. "None of this makes any damn sense."

Mari shrugged and stared down at Eva, who stayed on the floor and rested her arms on her bent knees. She had her own ideas about who might be sending weird brain messages, and they weren't comforting. Mala approached her, patting her leg until Eva reached out her uninjured hand and rubbed the cat's head.

"Let me guess, Mari," Eva said. "You want to see what's on the other side of the mystery Gate?"

Mari's eyes widened even as her brow furrowed. "I . . . You . . . Sí," she sputtered. "If it's not in any of our records, that means it likely predates them."

"Or someone wiped the data intentionally," Eva muttered.

Mari glared at her. "This could be an opportunity to explore a sector that hasn't been visited in all of recorded history!"

Pink snorted. "It could be an ambush."

"Exactly," Eva said. "We don't know who sent the message, so we have no reason to trust them. I want to know more about the monoliths, same as you, but this seems risky." Then again, she thought, it would be a strangely elaborate way to trap Eva personally, and for what? Anyone dangling "prevent war" as an incentive clearly didn't know her very well. As bait went, it wasn't the most enticing.

Mari's careful mask slid back into place. "The Forge could deploy assets to explore the sector," she said. "They would arrive quickly and send me regular updates on the situation. It would be as safe as we can make it."

Eva and Pink shared a look and burst into laughter.

"Alabao, you're hilarious," Eva said. "And anyway, this person went to a lot of trouble to send this to me secretly, so having your Forge people going full metiche is probably a bad idea."

Mari's brow furrowed, but she didn't respond.

"Okay, okay," Eva said, getting to her feet slowly, still holding the towel. "So some mystery person says a war is coming and wants me to go to an unexplored system to find out more. I can go by myself or we can go together, or we can ignore it and make our own plans." She met her crew's eyes one by one: Sue looked down at the table, Pink raised her eyebrow, and Min . . . was just a camera, as far as eyes went, since her body lounged on the bridge. Eva's gaze fell on Mala last, and the feisty feline blinked back.

"Miau," Mala said.

"Of course we're going to take a vote," Eva replied. "We always vote."

"Eva, you're talking to the cat again," Mari said, exasperated.

Mala glared at Mari, who winced as if pinched.

"All right," Eva said. "All those in favor of finding out whether this exciting new Crash Can has a fun prize or a bomb inside, say 'Carajo.'"

Silence replied, stretching out long enough for Mari's neutral expression to transition to a furrowed brow. Finally, Sue spoke.

"Um, Captain?" Sue asked. "Why do you want us to say 'crow's nest'?"

A banging noise came from the cargo bay door. Sue shrieked and fell out of her chair, while Mari produced a pistol from somewhere so fast Eva didn't see her move.

"Sorry, Cap," Min said over the speakers. "Didn't want to interrupt. It's Leroy and his girlfriend, Momoko."

"Let them in," Eva said. "But that ride I promised them just got a lot more complicated."

La Sirena Negra approached the Gate cautiously, skirting the halfhearted blockade the authorities from Brodevis had implemented, as well as the monolith. Pink sat at the controls for the weapons systems while Sue waited in the bowels of the ship with her tiny bots in case sudden repairs or modifications were necessary to the shields or drives. Leroy and Momoko strapped into safety seats in the cargo bay, keeping an eye on the cats, who had retreated into their container. Min remained in her pilot's chair, Mala snug on her lap, and Eva slouched in the seldom-used captain's chair. They all wore their spacesuits, por si las moscas.

Mari hovered at the back of the bridge, watching them all work. Eva resisted the urge to snap at her to go back to the passenger cabin; since she was their resident expert on Proarkhe tech, it seemed prudent to have her nearby, in case the monolith got aggressive or something.

"Activating the Gate now," Min said.

The Gate's pinkish lights didn't change, the metal ring continuing its serene transit through space. But inside it shifted from the starfield behind it to an entirely different view, as if it had gone from a window to a holovid in the blink of an eye.

"Security is hailing us, Cap," Min said. "What do I tell them?"

"Just get us through before they override," Eva said. Brodevis had enough rich-ass residents and visitors that she had no doubt plenty of folks were quietly leaving the system while the local cops looked the other way.

Min pushed *La Sirena Negra* through the hole in space, emerging on the other side only to have the Gate close behind them. Eva scowled; getting back shouldn't be a problem, but it felt like an ominous sign.

With a sigh, she turned her attention to the scanners. Nothing showed up in their vicinity, so she fiddled with the sensitivity and range to see what she could find.

"The sector is empty," Mari said.

Eva looked over her shoulder at her sister. "And you know this because?"

"My people arrived a few minutes ago," Mari said. "They've already done substantial reconnaissance."

Dozens of thoughts raced through Eva's mind, most of them involving words like "me cago en diez" and "resingado comemierda" and so on.

"Que coño, Mari?" Eva asked, anger flaring up in her chest.

"Your people," Pink said slowly. "The ones you weren't supposed to tell about this secret message."

"My sister's safety is more important," Mari said primly.

Eva snorted in derision. "Ay, jódete," she said.

"And the horse you rode in on," Pink added without turning around.

"It's safer than the alternative," Mari retorted. "Anyway, they're still running scans and sending out probes, but they haven't been able to find any . . ." She trailed off, staring at nothing as her brows drew together.

"Sounds like they found something now," Pink said. Eva threw her hands in the air and then crossed her arms and waited. Not like she could stop them.

"It's not, that is—" Mari swallowed and cleared her throat. "They've located the system's star."

"What kind?" Eva asked. "Is it stable?"

"It's a black dwarf."

The room fell silent. A black dwarf star was a theory, a possible end state for a white dwarf star billions or trillions of years in the future, not something a mere Gate trip away. There shouldn't be anything like it in the universe, so either this wasn't in their universe—Eva couldn't begin to wrap her head around that one—or something had happened to massively speed up the star's breakdown.

That option wasn't better, and any bravado Eva might have mustered for this expedition started to sublimate.

"There's still time to back out," Pink murmured. "You don't have to show up at every party you're invited to."

"I'm the only one who got an invite," Eva said. "So far as we know. And if someone else did, it might be worth seeing who's on the guest list."

"Don't worry," Mari said. "My people are continuing to sweep the area. If they find anything, we'll know."

"Chaperoned like a fucking quinceañera," Eva muttered. Mala gave a soft chirp of irritation, as if in agreement.

They continued in silence, Eva monitoring the scanners and contemplating whether to waste some of their precious probes to expand the reach of their systems. They couldn't exactly fly in a random direction and hope they eventually found whatever they were meant to find here—the message sender? Something else? Mierda, mojón y porquería, this had probably been a bad idea all around. They should just get back to charted territories and worry about their own damn selves instead of the universe.

"Cap, there's another message on the private channel," Min said suddenly.

Pink leaned sideways in her chair to wag her finger at Eva. "If that thing gives you an aneurysm, I swear," she said.

"Swear you'll fix me?" Eva asked. Her injured hand throbbed slightly under the bandages Pink had wrapped around it earlier. "Let me have it, Min."

She braced herself this time, unsure of what to expect. The message came through in the same awful jolt as the first, but the series of terrible sensations seemed to pass more quickly, though the coppery taste stayed in her mouth again.

"I do not like this," Pink said quietly, once again scrutinizing Eva with her mechanical eye. "So?"

"Specific coordinates within this system," Eva said. She glanced over her shoulder at Mari and raised an eyebrow.

"What?" Mari asked innocently. "Don't you want backup if something goes wrong?"

"No me busques," Eva said. "If you tell your buddies where we're going, I'm tossing your culo into the cat box."

"Bueno," Mari said, drawing out the second syllable. She sounded so much like their mother that Eva groaned.

Instead of telling Min where they were going, Eva fed the coordinates directly into the nav systems. She then shifted her attention to the scanners and hull cameras, to see what might be waiting for them in this strange, dead-star place.

As they approached their destination, what they found was even more confusing: a small debris field, as if pieces of something had exploded outward and then been somehow recaptured by a gravity source before they could continue their endless trajectory out into space. Instead, they spun lazily in the black, barely visible since the system's star didn't give off any light. At the epicenter of their strange orbit was absolutely nothing, and that nothing was where *La Sirena Negra* was supposed to go.

It made no sense. Maybe a ship would meet them there? But why not somewhere closer to the Gate, or hell, literally anywhere else in the universe?

As Eva pondered the continued weirdness they entered the debris field, and the nothing suddenly became something.

Eva leaned back in her chair, squinting at the fore hull cameras' display and the scrolling feed of data picked up by their instruments. Most of what it said was UNKNOWN, which also conveniently described what her own eyes and brain were reporting.

"The fuck is that?" Pink asked.

"Madre de dios," Mari whispered.

Eva had seen a lot of weird shit in her life, but this was definitely the first time she'd seen a tiny island inside a lavender bubble floating serenely in space.

Chapter 3

SECOND CONTACT

Min flew them in slowly as they all fell silent, no other vessels appearing on scanners. *La Sirena Negra* landed on the surface of the space island, softly as a cat, and nobody moved for several long moments, as if waiting for some inevitable, terrible surprise.

"Miau," Mala said. Mari jumped with a yelp.

Eva chuckled and rose from her chair, heading for the emergency-access hatch. She and Pink had agreed that she would explore the strange island with Mari while everyone else stayed on board, ready to take off at the first sign of trouble. They both strapped on weapons, Eva opting for her standard pistol and vibroblade, Mari nestling a nasty little submachine gun in the small of her back and strapping a pistol to each thigh.

Eva raised an eyebrow. "You seem to be expecting a lot of trouble."

"You seem underprepared, as usual," Mari replied coolly.

With a snort, Eva activated her isohelmet and climbed down the access ladder, waiting until Mari secured herself inside before opening the exterior hatch and exiting the craft.

A field of grasslike vegetation with clusters of purplish flowers stretched out in front of her, the ankle-high stalks rustling in a gentle breeze she couldn't feel through her spacesuit. Above her, the sky was a deep lavender despite the dark local star. Sensors indicated the air was breathable, if a bit high in oxygen content, with a temperature of 16.4 degrees Celsius. Cool, but not dangerous. Gravity was a hair below Terran standard, hardly enough to notice.

At the center of the field stood an enormous building that looked, unbelievably, like a castle made entirely of rose-colored stone or clouded glass. Its spires rose at least ten stories into the sky, its walls shining faintly from within, or possibly glowing from phosphorescent paint. The structure had been visible on approach, but seeing it up close made it even more surreal.

"This is astonishing," Mari said. "The technology required to create and maintain—"

"The coordinates would put us over there," Eva said, gesturing toward the right. She began to walk toward a small outcropping of gray rocks a dozen meters away.

Mari gave a huff of indignation before hobbling to catch up. "How can you not have a shred of curiosity?"

"Trying to keep my cats alive," Eva replied.

Together they reached the designated spot, and together they waited for whatever would happen now that they had arrived. Eva took in the flat expanse of plants and the strange sky and the fairy-tale fucking castle, shaking her head slightly. If she'd been alone, she would have assumed she was hallucinating. She wished Vakar were there to see it with her.

"Incredible," Mari whispered. "This is nothing like any known Proarkhe sites."

"That's because it's Ithorian," said a voice behind them.

Eva and Mari both spun and drew their weapons simultaneously.

The speaker was a giant robot. Specifically, the robot that had helped Eva destroy the dreadnought from another galaxy by turning into a skybike with wheels.

Calling them a robot seemed crude, like saying a star was a big space fire, but Eva couldn't summon up a word that fit better. Their body was at least three meters tall and composed of overlapping blue, black, and pink metallic plates and panels that formed a lanky humanoid figure with spikes flaring from the wrists, elbows, and knees. They stared at Eva and Mari, their glowing blue eyes appearing to widen and contract like the iris on a camera lens. Their face was white and flat, with only a slit where a mouth would be, and they wore a helmet with another spike pointing up—or was that their head? Eva had no idea.

They waited patiently while she and Mari appraised the situation, making no effort to move or speak. As startled as she was, Eva decided they had earned at least a minimum level of trust by helping her before. And given the circumstances, she guessed they had sent the message that brought her here in the first place. After all, the last time Eva had experienced a similar headache and brain-scrambling sensation had been when she first met this very robot on the Forge's homemade Gate.

With a sharp exhale, Eva lowered her weapon. "Hola," she said. "Again."

"Who are the Ithorians?" Mari asked simultaneously, and Eva shot her a dirty look.

The robot raised their hand as if waving hello. "Captain Eva

Innocente," they said, their voice a rough contralto, somewhere between lounge singer and disasterpunk. "Me entiendes?"

"Yes," Eva replied, drawing out the word. "You speak Spanish?"

"Sí," they said. Their mouth opened and closed as they spoke, but Eva couldn't tell whether it was an orifice or a digital contrivance. "I got your primary languages from your mind when I found you during our last encounter. It took some time to pull everything else out of your civilization's translators afterward, but we have that now, too. We also used your memory imprint to figure out how to contact you securely, using the private channel to your ship."

"Gave me a damn migraine about it," Eva said.

"Ah," they said, eyes dimming briefly. "Sorry. Our information-delivery methods are different from yours. We'll find something less . . . invasive?"

"Who's 'we'?" Mari asked, glancing around.

"The rest of my team is in orbit," they said. "This place isn't safe for our kind, but we need you to—"

"Espérate," Eva interrupted, then took a deep breath. "Who are you, qué coño está pasando aquí, and why am I here?"

"Who are your kind?" Mari added. She had also lowered her weapon, her grip still tight.

"That too," Eva said.

The robot's eyes narrowed and widened again as they appeared to think. "You can call me Antimatter, pronoun she. I am one of the people you call the Proarkhe. Our enemies are the Artificers, and they're the ones broadcasting their intent to conquer all the systems in this Gate network. We need you to go inside that building to retrieve part of a weapon that can stop them."

Eva blinked. She wasn't used to people just answering her when she asked things. Worse, she now had at least a dozen more questions, and if she asked those, things would probably expand exponentially.

"A Proarkhe," Mari exhaled, almost reverently. "Where did you come from? Who are the Artificers, and—"

"What is the weapon?" Eva asked, holstering her pistol. Better to focus on the immediate problem and get to the rest later.

"It's a group of soulless bipedal constructs, 'mechs' I believe you would call them." Antimatter paused. "I admit, we're not entirely sure how they work, but we'll share what we know as soon as you have them in your possession. We should hurry, though—we may have been tracked here, and we're fairly sure the enemy knows the locations of the weapon components. I can't get any closer because of the automated defenses, but you should be safe."

"Automated defenses?" Eva asked. She crossed her arms, jutting out her hip. "I'm not walking into a laser party without a date."

"Sorry, I don't get that reference," Antimatter said. "Pero you should be fine. The Ithorian defenses are to stop my kind from approaching, not other life forms. Unfortunately, the Artificers may also be working through agents for the same reason."

"But who are the Ithorians!" Mari exclaimed. "Are the Artificers also Proarkhe? Why are you at war? You still haven't explained anything!"

Antimatter turned her attention to Mari, who took a step backward. "I've explained plenty," she said. They stared each other down for a moment, and Eva huffed in exasperation.

"So just to be clear," Eva said, "if I get all these mechs, I can somehow use them to take down the Artificers, who I assume were the ones who attacked the Forge base, and are also the ones sending the threatening message to everyone across the universe?"

"Sí," Antimatter replied. "You may not defeat them entirely, but you can at least make them retreat, like the Ithorians did before. The weapon is the primary reason this front in the war was abandoned millions of your Earth-years ago. This Gate network should be safe so long as the Artificers believe it to be protected. But you do need these keys to make the constructs function." She held out three crystalline objects, each a vaguely different color and shape.

Eva stepped back and held up her hands in front of her, palms out. "Okay, I know I've been going along with this so far because it's been happening really fast, but all this—" She gestured at the strange castle, at the sky with its huge space platform, and then turned back to Antimatter. "This is a lot at once, and I haven't actually agreed to help you."

Silence dropped like the bass at a club. More questions burst into Eva's mind, one after the other like a chain reaction—she could only imagine what Mari was thinking—but before she could start asking them, Antimatter spoke.

"Around this chunk of rock is a gravitational shield, holding what's left of this planet together." Antimatter paused as if carefully considering her next words. "The rest is gone. Blown apart."

"Gone?" Eva asked, aware of how ridiculous she sounded.

"How did, that—" Mari sputtered. "A whole planet can't just explode."

"Yes," Antimatter said, her voice muted. "Yes, it can. Anything can be nullified if you have the right tools."

The monoliths had been bad enough when they were a vague threat, a mystery to be unraveled before the consequences could be tested. But unless this was all some elaborate hoax, the extermination being promised by the repeated message was extremely, terrifyingly literal. Blowing up a planet was beyond anything BOFA could achieve, even with a whole fleet of dread-noughts attacking a place at once. How could anyone stop an enemy who could do that?

With the mechs Antimatter was promising, apparently. If, again, this wasn't a big lie orchestrated to—what? If she wanted Eva dead, there were much easier ways to do it. If the mechs weren't real, she'd know soon enough by going into the castle and finding nothing. If the mechs were real but weren't the promised superweapon, the universe would be no less jodido than before.

But if they were real, and did work as promised, then Eva would have a chance of stopping whatever had happened to this place. All she had to do was take the keys and find out. Her hand closed into a fist and she inhaled sharply.

"Why her?" Mari asked.

Eva blinked at her sister, who still clutched her submachine gun in white-knuckled hands.

"There are trillions of people you could have asked to do this," Mari continued. "Politicians. Soldiers. Scientists. I can think of a dozen better options without trying."

"Gracias, muy amable," Eva muttered.

Mari continued. "Eva is just . . . the captain of an old cargo ship. Why her?" She looked up at Antimatter, whose glowing blue eyes seemed to brighten.

"Because I believe she can do it," Antimatter replied.

Eva gave an incredulous huff, and Mari wrinkled her nose. Antimatter hunkered down next to Eva, her face a meter away.

"You were one of many sentient organics involved in the re-cent battle," Antimatter said. "When I found you sabotaging the traverse, I figured you would attack me. But you didn't. You let me help you, then you faced down Kilonova—one of my tough-est enemies—without flinching. You threw a boot at his head!"

She made a trilling sound almost like a laugh. "Smelt me to slag, he was furious. And after that, you single-handedly crippled the *Ruination*. We haven't taken down any of their fleetbreakers for petacycles, and you just up and did it. I nearly rebooted on the spot."

She made it sound much more impressive than it had felt at the time. Eva had mostly been trying to escape from the system, but things got tangled up, as they seemed to keep doing for her in the past year and a half. She and her crew had a choice between taking down the ship—*Ruination*, ño, what a name—or taking their chances by making a run for it. Eva still wasn't sure whether they'd made the right choice, but it sounded better and better the more Antimatter talked.

"I wasn't working alone," Eva said awkwardly.

"You don't have to work alone," Antimatter said, gesturing at Mari, whose mouth had fallen half-open. "Like I said before, we don't have a lot of time. The Artificers or their agents will be here any microtik, and if you don't get the weapon, they will. Assuming they don't destroy it instead." Her bright eyes bored into Eva's. "Will you help us stop them?"

Eva's breath caught in her throat. She should contact her crew. This wasn't a choice she could make alone. It was too big, too important, too—

"Frag me," Antimatter said. "Time's up. They're here."

A shadow passed far overhead, marring the uniformity of the lavender sky like a bug on a paper lantern. Eva's stomach tried to crawl up into her throat, so she swallowed heavily.

"Eva, let me handle this," Mari said, putting her gun away finally. "I can get my people to—"

"No," Antimatter said. "Captain Eva Innocente gets the keys, or I take them and find another way." She held out her hand again, those strange crystals glinting in the diffuse light.

"She could just take them and give them to me," Mari said sourly.

"She could," Antimatter agreed, blue eyes blazing. "Still not giving them to you, though."

Eva snorted a laugh, but any humor at the situation quickly fled. She had to decide.

She could walk. Let someone else figure out how to deal with this. It wouldn't be the first time, and if she was lucky, it wouldn't be the last. Maybe the universe would be destroyed by these Artificers, or maybe BOFA and everyone else would get their shit together and stop whatever was coming.

Or she could take the crystals and give them to Mari, let The Forge sort this all out. They had the resources and the personnel, certainly. Even Vakar's people might . . . Well, maybe not them. They were on her shit list right now.

Or she could handle this herself. With her crew. She didn't trust anyone else farther than she could throw them. But with the stakes so high, were they really the best people for the job? Could they possibly stop an entire war by themselves?

"Last chance," Antimatter said. Her previous words rang in Eva's ears: *I believe she can do it.*

Eva wished she had that much belief in herself. Wish in one hand and shit in the other, and see which one gets full first, she thought.

With a sigh, she grabbed the crystals and shoved them into a secure pocket in her suit. Three crystals. Three mechs, out there somewhere, scattered across the universe, waiting to be found. "I can't promise anything," Eva said. "But I'll do my best."

"That's all anyone can do," Antimatter replied, already walking away. "We'll hold the Artificers off as long as we can. One of those keys belongs to the construct here, and the other two will show you the way."

"What does that mean?" Mari asked.

But the Proarkhe had already opened one of her strange miniature Gates and stepped through, leaving Eva and Mari alone again.

"Give me those keys," Mari said immediately, resting a hand on Eva's shoulder. "My people will be here any minute, so they can—"

"They can what?" Eva snapped, pushing Mari's hand away. "This was supposed to be a secret, comemierda!"

"We needed backup, clearly, if—"

"Jódete, cabrona!"

A shadow passed overhead again, and without wasting another moment, Eva messaged Pink to take evasive maneuvers and stand by for a possible extraction. Then, she began to run.

Eva wasn't the best sprinter, but she stayed in shape, and her artificial heart helped when it came to exertion. She pumped her arms and pushed herself as fast as she could, focusing intently on the building growing larger and larger with every step. Mari trailed behind her, stims and painkillers attempting to compensate for her still-healing leg.

Eva hoped Antimatter was right about the defenses not perceiving her as a threat. If she was wrong, well, hopefully Eva would have time to retreat before she was turned into a scorch mark or a wisp of vapor.

She had almost reached the front door when the familiar whine of a ship's engines streaked past. She slowed just enough to glance in the direction of the sound. It was a Coleman-class sublight vessel, squat and black, its hull thick and its shields probably overclocked in the front. A human ship—the Artificer agents Antimatter had mentioned? Not The Forge, since Mari was still fleeing with her.

The arroz con mango was getting more asopao by the minute.

As Eva wondered how they'd get into the castle, a small door slid open in front of them, revealing a dimly lit room beyond. Mari had outpaced her by a few meters now and would be safely inside in moments. Unfortunately, the whine of the pursuing ship's proton cannons suggested Eva wouldn't be so lucky. With a quick prayer to the Virgin, she slid like a baseball player and activated her gravboots, hoping they'd catch on something inside.

They did, and Eva was yanked forward, the first blasts from the ship's weapons hitting the building barely a meter above her as she flew through the doorway.

The door dropped closed behind her. About five meters in, she reached the object her gravboots had been attracted to. A pillar too wide for her arms to encircle rose up and up within the vast atrium she now lay inside. Several other pillars were arranged at intervals in the room, all glowing a dim pink color like a guayaba. Each featured small platforms, about a meter on each side, circling the pillars like steps, but they were positioned much too far apart to be functional stairs. The walls appeared to be thin sheets of stone, either translucent enough to allow light to pass through, or somehow luminescent themselves. The floor was made of another material, pale as marble and polished to a mirror sheen despite what must have been eons of neglect, and the ceiling was some kind of force field that showed the lavender sky above, or a projection meant to look that way.

With a thought, Eva deactivated her gravboots and stood, her chest heaving as she sucked air into her burning lungs. She had no idea where the mech was, or whether her pursuers would send someone in after her, but at least she and Mari were temporarily safe.

Mari stood nearby, staring at everything with undisguised awe like a kid at an amusement park. Well, she would; she'd always wanted to explore ancient places and discover things and write super boring essays about them. Eva suppressed a smile, reminding herself that this same comemierda kept violating her fucking trust by doing things like calling her Forge friends when she'd been told not to.

"We need to find that mech," Eva said. Her voice sounded extra loud in the empty space, echoing up to the strange ceiling.

"Right, of course," Mari said. "I'll set my commlink to track us so we can make a map of the building."

Eva nodded and did the same, so she wouldn't have to rely on Mari. She also attached a small proximity sensor to the pillar facing the doorway; it would warn her if anyone followed them inside. The large room branched out into multiple hallways, so Eva chose one at random and started walking.

"We should go to the left!" Mari called behind her. "We need to be systematic about this."

Eva rolled her eyes and kept going.

The gentle pink glow made everything bright enough that she didn't have to turn on her spacesuit's light. All the surfaces were smooth and seamless, no protrusions to catch her arms or trip her. She wondered why there were no decorations, not even paint or etchings to break the monotony of the corridor, but maybe some inactive tech would have done that job in the past. The fact that any tech here still worked was frankly incredible.

"This isn't how one typically explores a place like this," Mari whispered angrily.

"Sorry I don't have special archaeologist training, Agent Virgo, but I have done this before," Eva whispered back.

"Well, you could just listen to me instead of wandering off, Captain Innocente."

Eva snorted. "Why are we whispering when there's no one here and we're talking through helmet comms?"

Mari huffed sullenly and didn't reply.

At the end of the hallway they found another room, smaller than the atrium at the entrance but still fairly large and equally empty and clean. No furniture, no random objects to suggest anyone had lived in this place. Like a house that had been built but never occupied. At least it didn't seem dangerous so far.

Eva's proximity alarm flashed a notification and trilled quietly. Someone had entered the atrium. Now she had something dangerous to worry about. She had to find the mech before these people did. Where the hell was the cabrón thing?

Antimatter had said something about the keys leading her to the mechs. She pulled the small crystals out of her pocket and examined them.

One was glowing. A dark aquamarine, shaped like a ring. Should she put it on? It didn't seem to be doing anything else. How would it tell her where to go if all it did was light up?

"Cuídate," Mari said.

Eva slid the crystal onto the ring finger of her left hand. Immediately, the ring expanded from her knuckles to her wrist—no, it was just a projection, like how some commlinks had a holographic interface. But when she touched it, the light felt solid enough, like the hard light furniture some fancy places could afford. Now she had to figure out how it worked.

"Incredible," Mari said, grabbing Eva's arm to examine her hand.

"Hey!" Eva pulled her arm back and glared.

The trill of her proximity sensor suddenly cut out. Whoever was in the castle with them had found it. Mierda, mojón y porquería. They had to find that mech, and fast.

As if the thought were enough, the ring's projection darkened, replaced by a single pulsing dot, like an old radar display. It seemed to be suggesting the mech was up ahead somewhere.

Mari gasped, and Eva rotated to test it; sure enough, the dot moved depending on which direction she was facing.

I hate tech that's indistinguishable from magic, she thought, pursing her lips like she'd sucked on a naranja agria.

Eva proceeded in what she hoped was the right direction, speeding up as much as she could without making a ton of noise. Her spacesuit could avoid most sensors, and Mari could go invisible briefly with her own fancy tech. Even so, depending on the building's construction and shielding levels, they might be easy to track, since they were the only things moving inside.

The dot on her hand shifted minutely. Eva decided haste was more important than quiet, so she started running again, her lungs protesting that they hadn't rested enough from the last sprint. Mari followed, keeping pace despite her injured leg. Corridors became rooms became more corridors—how many hallways did one building need? Surely they should have gotten to the end of the place by now; it wasn't that big.

They reached a long room with a narrow half pillar atop a platform at the other end and a vast window behind it, that wide lavender sky as pretty as a holovid. Except it wasn't really a sky, was it? It was the only thing keeping the void out and the planetary fragment in.

Eva approached the window, striding up the incline to reach the platform and its odd protrusion. The pillar reached just above her waist, narrow enough that she could link her arms around it without touching it. She walked to the far side, examining its surface. Flat, slightly shiny, no distinguishing marks, like everything else in this place. Unless she was misreading it, the blinking dot on the back of her hand seemed to indicate the mech was nearby.

"What are we even looking for?" Mari mused, standing next

to Eva. "What did a mech look like to ancient people? We could already be standing on top of it and we wouldn't know. Or maybe it's above us?" She looked up intently.

Eva did the same, but the ceiling was just a ceiling, the floor was a floor, and the people standing in the doorway were aiming weapons at her—oh mierda.

Before she could grab her own pistol, the floor opened up and Eva fell in.

Chapter 4

A LOT OF NERVE

No, Eva wasn't falling—she was sliding. Through a dark tube or tunnel that sloped downward and curved occasionally, moving fast enough that she worried about hurting herself if she tried to stop. The dot had vanished from her hand, and her commlink's mapping function no longer gave her useful information. The light on her suit illuminated only a few meters in front of her, and the longer she slid, the more time she had to wonder what she'd find at the end of the ride.

Her suit's sensors registered a change in air pressure and temperature, and moments later an antigrav mechanism kicked in to slow her descent. She was dumped awkwardly into a room that managed to feel cavernous before Eva could get her bearings to confirm its size. Once she did, it reminded her of the hangars her dad, Pete, used to store spaceships; however, unlike those, this one seemed to be completely empty.

Eva cranked up the intensity of her suit's light, trying to get a better look around. The thud of her gravboots echoed, rebounding over and over until it sounded as if a dozen other people walked ahead of her. After a few steps into the room, something in the distance began to glow, dimly at first, then more brightly the closer she got. By the time she was twenty meters away, there was no doubting what it was.

"Alabao," she murmured. "Absolute unit."

A massive mech stood like a statue waiting for a pilgrim to make some offering at its feet. It was bipedal, with a broad torso tapering to a thinner waist, its arms and legs slightly longer than human proportions. Its head rested on a surprisingly graceful neck, but the head itself was sharp-edged, angular, like the skull of some enormous animal stripped of all but the shadow of flesh and muscle. It was a uniform bone-white color, with brown horizontal stripes wrapping around its back and legs, though they were soft rather than crisp.

When Antimatter had talked about it, Eva had pictured something more like an exosuit, or the mechs some military or merc outfits used—five meters, maybe, certainly no more than ten. Big enough for the pilot to rest snugly inside while still doubling or even tripling their own height.

If her sensors were correct, this damn thing was easily forty meters tall. There was no way it could fit inside *La Sirena Negra*. Her cargo bay wouldn't even hold one of the bigger todyk, and this was way beyond that.

Bueno, she thought. I have to get it out of here before I can figure out where to stick it. Up my ass and around the corner, as Mami would say.

((Found it,)) Eva pinged at Mari. No response, which either meant Mari was busy or the signal couldn't reach her. Neither thought was pleasant.

Still, the proverbial clock ticked. She'd fallen down that chute and ended up here, but she didn't know what happened to Mari and the others up above. They might be stuck up there, or they might be on their way down already. She had to hurry.

A quick jog brought her to the mech's giant feet. But how would she get inside to activate it?

As if in answer, the turquoise crystal thing on her hand lit up. The mech's eyes began to glow a bright white, and it bent at the waist while reaching down with its large four-fingered hand. It rested the hand, palm-up, just above the ground, where it would be easy enough for Eva to climb on and—what? Be lifted to the cockpit entrance? How did this thing even know what she wanted?

Was this an invitation or a trap?

Over the past few weeks, Eva had tried to forget her near-death experience over the far-off planet in a starless corner of the universe, tried to shove the notion of impossible shapeshifting robots and impending doom into some cargo container in her mind so she could go about the business of living her normal life. She'd accepted whatever medications Pink had offered to manage her bouts of insomnia and the frigid terror that accompanied them, so she wouldn't wake up shaking and thrashing and screaming. She'd told herself that her part in the drama of the universe was over and she could go back to doing literally anything else, as long as it kept her crew safe and fed.

And now here she was, once again caught between the devil and the void, between known dangers and uncertain salvation.

Eva glanced back at the darkness behind her, the tunnel that had dumped her into this room already too far away to see. She looked up at the glowing eyes of the mech, at its strange face and outstretched hand. Not for the first time in the past several weeks, she desperately wished Vakar were with her; he would know what to do, what to say, to make her choice clear.

But she'd had a life before him, so for all that his presence was a help and a comfort, she could and would get by on her own.

"Bueno," she muttered. "El que quiera su celeste que le cueste."

Grabbing one of the fingers for leverage, Eva hoisted herself onto the hand and crouched, waiting for whatever would come next.

The mech lifted her up, fast enough that she almost activated her gravboots so she wouldn't take an accidental tumble to the increasingly distant floor. It stopped just above waist level, at what would have been the notch below a human's ribs. A small door appeared, leaving an opening about three by four meters. The hand pressed against the mech's body to allow her to easily step inside.

The room was less a cockpit and more a bridge, large enough that it seemed to occupy most of the space at the mech's core, and dimly lit by round ceiling and wall fixtures. The ceiling was easily twice Eva's height, but everything was a disconcertingly organic pink, making it feel less spacious, more confined. The only piece of furniture or equipment was a broad, clear tube that ran from floor to ceiling, fixed in place by more pink stuff that reminded her of a giant wad of used chewing gum.

Eva approached the tube, circling it, looking for controls. Nothing there, or anywhere else. Maybe the interface was holographic? Her commlink couldn't find anything to sync with, which didn't surprise her; this thing was much, much older than commlinks, and even modern tech had its limitations.

With a soft hiss, an opening appeared in the tube. It began to glow softly, and a strange gel-like fluid bubbled up from the floor inside. Should she put something in there? Eva looked around, but the room was as empty as she'd found it.

There is one thing here, she thought. Me.

Slowly, cautiously, Eva stepped into the tube and examined

the interior, turning in a circle. Her boots squelched in the goop on the floor, but otherwise there was nothing much to see.

The tube opening vanished, trapping her inside. She raised a fist to bang on the glass—or whatever it was—then forced herself to look around instead. Above her, a series of twinkling lights appeared, and her suit's sensors told her gas flooded the chamber—oxygen, specifically, and nitrogen, and other reassuringly familiar stuff. No, not just familiar . . . Earth-standard. But why? So she could breathe without her helmet?

Well, she'd already taken enough chances this cycle; what was one more?

Eva deactivated her helmet and took a deep breath. The air smelled sickly sweet, like mangos just past ripe but not yet rotten. The pattern of the lights above her changed from seemingly random dots to ordered clusters marching in rows. Then the fluid at her feet began to rise.

"Qué coño?" Eva yelped, reactivating her helmet. The fluid stopped just below her knees, and the lights went back to their random blinking.

Ah, wait, Eva had heard of this type of interface, assuming it was what she thought. A few species used it, rarely, but not humans, who had opted for the arguably more invasive method of spinal jacks. For some reason, anyone old enough to pilot a ship was also old enough to have a primal fear of drowning that made surgery more appealing than submersion in the equivalent of amniotic fluid.

Even now, just thinking about it, Eva had to fight to breathe calmly. If she was wrong, she'd die here, alone and suffocated by ancient technology she didn't understand. Mari might never find her body, might never—

Not the time to panic, she told herself sternly. For all you know, Mari has been captured by those mercs upstairs and you need to save her. So get your culo in gear.

Eva deactivated her helmet, and the fluid once again started to fill the tube. When it reached her chin, she reflexively kicked her legs like she was treading water, keeping her head in the rapidly shrinking air-filled portion of the chamber. Her face moved closer and closer to the panel of blinking lights above her, and she knew that in moments she'd have to let herself go and take a chance, or give up and get out somehow.

Praying to the Virgin for strength, Eva stopped kicking, sinking into the liquid and exhaling a stream of bubbles. It was murky, tinged pink like everything else in the mech so far. With a monumental, soul-clenching effort, Eva inhaled, letting the fluid fill her lungs and desperately hoping she hadn't made the wrong choice.

Everything went dark. Eva stifled a scream. The fluid was warmer than body temperature and smelled metallic, blood-tinged. Her breath came in ragged gasps, anxious and shallow, until she realized she wasn't drowning and her inability to see had nothing to do with her eyes failing. The lights above her still moved, faster now, and after a few moments the whole panel lit up, a solid pink. Something snaked up to cradle her head and back, almost like a restraint, but it didn't impede her movement.

Then, instead of the inside of the mech, Eva found herself looking at the room outside. The whole thing was visible now, as if dim lights had been turned on. The view was from much higher up—the mech's eye level, presumably, so it was equally likely to assume the place was just as dark as she'd left it, and the mech itself had better-than-human sensors. A series of translucent overlays offered her data she had no means of understanding, possibly about the mech's various systems.

How was she supposed to operate the thing when she had no clue how to control it?

Well, maybe it was like jacking into a ship, but with limbs instead of engines. Eva took a tentative step forward, as if the mech's legs were her own.

She misjudged basically everything and stumbled, utterly failing to catch herself despite reflexively raising her arms to stop her fall. The mech faceplanted with its arms half-bent, the impact shaking the ground. Eva didn't feel any pain, so either no damage was sustained or this machine wasn't the type to pass along that kind of biofeedback. The readouts hovering in her view didn't seem to indicate anything alarming, but she still had no idea what any of them meant.

"Guess we'll do literal baby steps," Eva muttered. She flexed all the mech's limbs and appendages one by one, trying to get a feel for how they worked, how they differed from her own body. The arms and legs were longer, and so were the fingers, and even the neck and head. She wondered whether the joints might bend more than her own, but decided she didn't have the guts to find out. Certainly the knees and elbows moved like hers, and for now that was good enough. Further experiments could wait until she was somewhere safe.

Slowly, she moved the mech's arms until they were under the body, then bent its knees and slid them under its belly. She pushed up carefully until she was on all fours, in crawling position, then paused. Patience was not one of her virtues—she'd never been able to manage Tai Chi—but she forced herself to take this in stages. Why did this have to be so hard, when it was just using all the same parts she herself had? It was worse than when she'd first jacked into a regular spaceship; she had flown those manually beforehand, but she would have thought that being a biped would count for something here.

At least you didn't drown in a tube of ancient goo, Eva told herself. You got the mech, you're piloting it . . . Everything else is details. Take your time.

And then the first mercenary appeared at the bottom of the tunnel-slide, quickly followed by a second, and her time ran out.

"Mierda, mojón y porquería," Eva said. She had to make like a flea and jump, except she still couldn't even stand.

The mercs were fully decked out in armor, complete with helmets obscuring their appearances. Weapons stuck out of different portions of their anatomy, but the ones they held were unfamiliar—like assault rifles, but larger and boxier, with multiple barrels in a single chunky casing. Worse, a telltale pinkish-purple glow emanated from them, suggesting they weren't simple projectile weapons.

Whatever they were, they were probably Proarkhe tech, and that meant they were likely way more dangerous than anything in Eva's arsenal.

Both mercs raised their weapons and aimed them at Eva—at the mech, that is, and she couldn't tell which part they were planning to shoot because the thing was so damn big. But they didn't fire, maybe because they didn't want to cause any damage. Another pair of mercs joined them, carrying the same strange guns, and then one final merc strolled out, graceful as a cat and just as relaxed.

Eva knew that swagger. She hadn't seen it in over a year and a half, and she'd sworn to herself that next time they crossed paths, she'd see how he liked being tossed in a freezer like a chuleta de puerco.

"You in there, Beni?" came the careless, cocky voice of Tito Santiago, patron saint of smug assholes. "Looks like you're having a little trouble with the controls."

"Me cago en tí," Eva said. She had no idea whether he could

hear her, and she didn't especially care. The prospect of stepping on him was simultaneously appealing and revolting.

"Tranquilízate," Tito continued, approaching her slowly. "We're here for that fancy machine, and it would be nice if you'd stop scuffing the paint job. Why don't you come out and we can have a little chat, eh? Face-to-face?"

There were things she wanted to do to his face, and none of them involved chatting. Eva struggled to her feet as the visualizations expanded to include outlines of each merc, including Tito. She wasn't sure what the mech was tracking or doing, but she faintly hoped there were at least some robust defensive measures that would kick in without her explicit commands. The last thing she needed was for the mech to get blown up before she even left.

"Come on, Beni," Tito continued. "You don't want to get mixed up in this. Get out of there, go back to your ship, and forget this place exists." She almost missed the quick flick of his fingers, though what he signaled she didn't know. He had multiple systems of signs and codes and comm protocols, and he switched between them on missions to trip up anyone who might have intel on him and his people.

Another outline appeared behind the mercs, at the mouth of the tunnel. This one wasn't immediately visible as anything but an overlay—cloaked? Another merc, or . . .

((Status?)) Mari pinged.

((Splendid,)) Eva pinged back.

"Who's your friend?" Tito asked, pausing in his lazy stroll. His stance was relaxed, but Eva knew that was a trick. He could execute at least a half dozen attacks from that position without telegraphing anything. And he was monitoring comms traffic if he'd heard their exchange.

"Jódete, cabrón," Eva replied.

Tito's hand flew to his heart as if he were wounded. "I

thought we were tight, Beni," he replied. "You still mad about the whole cryo thing? That was just business. Ya tu sabe."

"Claro," Eva said bitterly. That was the difference between her and Tito. Once upon a time she had shared his attitude, more or less, but a few swift kicks in the conscience had cured her of that. "Just business" was a mantra meant to absolve mercenaries of any responsibility for their actions, but mercs were people, not mechs without pilots. Mercs could choose which jobs to take and which to ignore, and those choices had meaning.

Might didn't make right, and neither did money.

Mari was a few dozen meters away and moving as fast as her stealth suit and injury allowed. Eva hunkered down, trying to keep the mech from overbalancing and falling forward or backward, and ending up with one hand on the floor. If she could get Mari into the chamber with the tube, they might both have a chance of escaping. Mari was the ancient-tech specialist; maybe she'd know how to make the machine work properly.

Is there no instruction manual for this damn thing? Eva thought.

A moment later, her vision went black again, without even the overhead blinking lights this time. Had she broken something? Turned the mech off? Madre de dios, would Tito make a run for it and try to take it from her?

Before she could chase the cat's tail of her thoughts, she blinked, and suddenly she knew how everything worked. Just like that. Apparently ancient species had a thing for direct-brain infodumps, or maybe time passed differently in neurospace and she'd gone through a whole tutorial without realizing it. Distantly, she had the sense that her body was spasming uncontrollably, that something hadn't gone precisely as intended and she'd have to deal with it later, but for now she could at least pilot the damn mech. She could get it away from Tito, get back to *La Sirena Negra*, and proceed on her impossible universe-saving mission.

The mech's sensors kicked in again, and now all the readouts were intelligible. She still had no idea how some of the underlying fundamentals came together—there was a big difference between knowing how to pilot a ship and how to disassemble one—but she could at least understand the data she was being fed.

"—is your last chance, Beni," Tito was saying. He'd gotten much closer, but so had Mari; she was only a few meters away.

"Okay, Tito," Eva said. "I'll make you a deal." She rested the mech's hand on the floor, palm-up, the same way it had done for her earlier, trying to make it seem casual. Hoping Mari got the gist, because she couldn't risk a ping.

"Cuéntamelo," Tito said, hip cocked again like an old rifle.

"Bueno, here are my terms." Eva paused, ostensibly for effect or to gather her thoughts, but really to give Mari an extra few seconds to pick up what she was putting down.

Mari didn't. She slowed to a stop just in front of the mech and began to circle it, as if looking for a way in. Eva suppressed the urge to facepalm.

"Your terms?" Tito nudged. Behind him, four weapons targeted different parts of the mech.

"First, you go fuck yourself," Eva said. "Second, the rest of your team eats a bag of spicy farts. Last, but not least, you do the entire universe a favor and take a spacewalk without a suit."

Someone else might have gotten angry or insulted, but Tito just laughed. "You always did talk a lot of shit," Tito said. "I used to think it was because of your dad being the big boss, but nah, you're just like that."

Mari was somewhere behind the mech, which sucked for escape purposes, but at least Eva could keep her shielded if the shit hit the air filters.

"Maybe I wouldn't have eaten so much shit if you didn't keep dishing it out," Eva said. "Are you going to talk for the rest of the cycle, or are your muñecos over there going to start something?" She kept the mech hunkered down but raised the other hand and extended its middle finger.

"A la orden," Tito said. In a fluid motion, he aimed his own weapon.

Eva raised the mech's shield before the first high-pitched shot reached her. Energy weapons, not projectiles, pinkish-purple streaks that hit with something between a splash and a spray of sparks. She wasn't sure how much of that was the shield, but it didn't matter. The most important things, in order, were getting Mari inside the mech and getting the mech outside and away.

Mari struggled to climb up the back of the mech's leg, so Eva reached around with her free hand and gently grabbed her sister. Thankfully, she now knew how to do so without accidentally gripping too hard and crushing her, using just a thumb and forefinger. Mari kicked wildly for a moment before relaxing, and Eva opened the entrance to the bridge and carefully shoved Mari inside.

"Eva, are you okay?" Mari asked, her voice weirdly disembodied since Eva's senses were merged with the mech's.

"Bueno, aquí," Eva replied. She also knew how to manifest a place for Mari to sit now, thanks to the bizarre instantaneous instruction manual download, so she did. "Strap in and get ready to go."

Tito and his mercs paused their attack, realizing it was having no effect. Two moved to flank while the other two were somehow merging their weapons together into a larger one as Tito supervised. He also seemed to be having a conversation with someone not present; the mech had an overlay that showed comms were being used, though it didn't have the capacity to hack them. Ancient tech had its limitations.

"Beni, I'll cut you a deal," Tito shouted. "Two million credits, immediate deposit, and you walk out of here clean."

Eva paused. That was a hell of a lot of money. Tito didn't toss that out lightly; he hated cutting anyone in on his profits. Not only did he really want this mech, he had decided he couldn't get it more easily some other way. And that many credits would keep her crew fed and happy for a very, very long time.

Then again, hard to be happy in a universe where no one was safe. If Antimatter wasn't bullshitting, this mech was vital to making that happen. And he might also be bluffing for time, a trick she'd learned from him.

"Counteroffer," Eva said. "Jódete." She wondered if her lips were curling into a smile as she floated in the tube.

The mech crouched, then launched into the air, straight up into an access tunnel. After a few dozen meters it slanted, and she knew from internal sensors and maps that she'd be coming out the back side of the island where the castle floated. The entrance wasn't merely hidden from outside view, it was blocked entirely, but she was piloting a wrecking ball. In less than a minute, she punched through layers of rock and dirt like they were paper, emerging into the void of space.

Eva hovered for a moment, turning back to examine the strange castle, the drifting chunk of what had once been a planet. People had lived there, dreamed and died there, and now that she'd taken the mech hidden inside, it was finally, truly empty. Maybe she'd come back someday to pay her respects to whoever had left the legacy that was now in her hands.

With a silent prayer to the Virgin for those who came before, Eva flew toward the system's Gate, and whatever awaited her beyond it.

Chapter 5

OPEN HAND, CLOSED FIST

Because it was too big to fit in the cargo bay, and because Eva didn't feel like staying stuck in a tube forever, the mech had to be tethered to *La Sirena Negra* with the same tech they normally used for Vakar's ship when he couldn't stash it somewhere convenient. Thinking of Vakar again soured the victory Eva was trying to enjoy.

Tito would come after them, certainly, but telling him to fuck off and depriving him of the thing he wanted had been supremely satisfying. He'd had more ships waiting for her out in space, but before she could try out the mech's offensive capabilities, the Forge people reappeared to cover her escape. Eva refused to be grateful for it, and it reminded her that she'd have to deal with Mari's well-meaning betrayal.

In the meantime, they emerged from the Gate in Scood, a system abandoned by its original occupants thousands of years earlier, thanks to the accidental spread of a particularly aggressive plant that still made a nuisance of itself on every habitable planet nearby. Mostly the place served as a layover for smugglers who wanted to lie low or do a quick Gate-skip to avoid pursuit. Nobody bothered to land, certainly, and risk the plant getting them.

La Sirena Negra wasn't the only ship lingering there, but everyone gave each other the courtesy of space. One of the useful bits of intel that had somehow spread was a list of systems that didn't have monoliths hovering near the Gates, so plenty of paranoid or secretive individuals and factions had moved their operations as best they could. The strange devices were still a mystery to them, and mysteries were bad for business.

Everyone settled in the mess for a meeting once Eva and Mari boarded and went through full decontamination procedures. There was a lot to talk about, time was money, and they were running out of it fast.

Pink leaned back in her chair, arms crossed over her chest, while Mari leaned on Fuácata next to the counter. Leroy and Momoko sat next to each other, hands clasped, though Leroy also sported a cat on each of his legs that he alternated petting with his free hand. Min and Sue sat on the floor, Min in Sue's lap, Sue's arms draped lazily around her shoulders. A pair of cats curled up together in a corner, and two of Sue's tiny yellow bots chittered to each other as they played something that reminded Eva of slapjack.

All these damn happy couples, Eva thought sullenly. Give me strength.

Eva and Mari launched into the story of what had happened, alternating and filling in each other's gaps as needed. Once they finished, stunned silence fell. Pink broke it first, her uncovered eye narrowed.

"You shouldn't have taken this on without talking to the rest of us," Pink said. Before Eva could object, she raised her hand. "I get it, but it still stinks to high heaven. We have to hope this person isn't lying, that the mech really can do something against whatever's coming like a storm, and that it was worth pissing off Tito over."

"No me diga," Eva said. "I'm happy to piss him off for free."

Pink's stern expression broke into a grin. "Yeah, you're right, fuck that asshole. Too bad you couldn't flick him into a wall or something."

"Amen," Eva said, chugging more water. She'd already drunk a full glass trying to get the bloody taste of mech fluid out of her mouth, but it wasn't working.

Min leaned forward eagerly. "When can I fly it? I wanna fly it!"

"Tranquilízate," Eva said. "It's easy enough to learn, sort of, but it's jarring. I do think we should all take turns so we aren't relying on one person to be the pilot."

"Sensible," Mari said. Eva raised an eyebrow at her but said nothing.

"Does that include us?" Leroy asked. "It may not be Pro-arkhe tech, but it's still ancient, and that's extremely awesome." He'd always had a soft spot for ancient stuff, a trait he and Mari shared. Though where Mari had gotten advanced degrees and gone on archaeological digs, Leroy had mostly surfed the q-net soaking up conspiracy theories.

Eva and Pink shared a look, and Pink nodded. "Yeah," Eva said. "I know you didn't come on board to join the crew again, but you're always welcome, and so's your partner."

"Thank you, Captain Innocente," Momoko said politely. "Your trust is extremely appreciated."

Leroy, meanwhile, flushed red from his orange hair down to his beard. "Thanks, boss," he murmured. For a moment, he was the lost soldier she'd pulled from a shitty cycle of rage and unemployment. Then he recovered his dignity and sat taller—no more hunching, not for him, not again. Momoko patted his hand, and he grinned at her.

Ah, life had its moments, even when everything was going to shit in a shipping container.

"Do you think I can maybe dig into its guts to see how it works?" Sue asked, eyes bright and wide despite the perpetual faint grease smudges on her forehead and cheeks.

"Absolutely not," Pink said. "Maybe when this is all over and we've kicked the ass of whoever is threatening the whole damn universe, but right now we're not taking any chances."

"What she said," Eva added. She leaned forward, palms on the table. "We know we can't go around trusting random strangers, even if they did help us out before. But if Antimatter is right, if these mechs really do have a weapon that can keep some massive invasion from going down, we go along with this whole retrieval business but we stay looking out. We treat it like a job, like we've been hired to pick them up. We do our part and take no shit. Agree?"

Nods from around the room answered her. Eva swallowed, because she had one more tough thing to put out there, and damn it all, she still tasted that bloody mech fluid.

"Last chance to back out," she added. "And really think about it before you answer. What we're doing may be the most dangerous thing in the universe right now. Tito, at the very least, wants this mech. If he knows about it, other people might, too. He didn't say who he was working for, but given his fancy new weapons, it's fair to assume the Artificers figured out how to hire local mercs to do their dirty work." She inhaled, then exhaled slowly. "There's still time to be dropped off somewhere, with family or friends or wherever we can manage. You're not a coward if you don't want to be part of this. Just say the word, and we'll get you to safety."

Silence fell as the others processed what she'd said. Surprisingly, this time, Sue spoke up first.

"There won't be any safety if the whole universe gets invaded," Sue said quietly. "No matter where we go." Min pulled Sue's arms more tightly around her, her expression flickering between worry and resolve.

"War is—" Leroy began, then stopped, dropping his gaze to the table for a few moments before he collected himself. "I wouldn't wish it on anyone. If we can stop it, I want to help."

Momoko touched his face gently, and he smiled at her like she was a star—which she was, technically, of the memvid variety. On his lap, the cats began to purr loudly enough to be audible from across the room.

"If that's settled," Mari said, "we should discuss how we plan to proceed with acquiring the remaining mechs." She moved away from the counter and toward the table, standing stiffly at attention with her hands clasped on the cane.

"First things first," Eva said, smiling so cheerfully she knew her sister would recognize the venom in it. "Where would you like to be dropped off, Mari?"

Mari's eyes widened in surprise. Pink snickered and nodded at Eva in approval.

"What part of 'don't tell your Forge amigos about our secret meeting' did you not understand?" Eva continued. "Don't answer that, because I don't care. We trusted you, y la cagaste, so your vacation here is over."

Mari furrowed her brow, but the rest of her demeanor went rigidly professional. "Without me, you won't have access to any Forge resources going forward. I know you were offered the chance to work with us officially. Now, with so much at stake, this would be an excellent time to—"

Eva made a loud fart noise with her mouth. "All your help is conditional, Marisleysis. If you really gave a shit about our mission and making it work, you'd be offering intel with no strings attached."

"You're one to talk, Captain Págame," Mari shot back. "All you care about is money. You only helped us because we hired you, not for the greater good."

"You don't get to decide what the greater good is for everyone, cabrona," Eva snapped. "And I was helping Sue find her missing brother. You high-and-mighty paragons of virtue were just using her to get to him. How is that better?"

"We needed him to get our Gate working so we could locate the missing Proarkhe tech," Mari said, "which, as you have conveniently forgotten, was lost when you ruined our plans to steal it back from the Fridge base."

"I was there because Dad stole my ship!" Eva exclaimed. "He stole it while I was in cryo because of you, because you fucking lied to me about being kidnapped and then let Tito ambush me while I was trying to save you."

"I didn't let him do anything," Mari replied. "And I made sure you were safe the entire time."

"You left me in a closet for a year!"

"I monitored your movements and made sure the Glorious Apotheosis didn't get his hands on you."

"He wouldn't even have known who I was if it weren't for you, comemierda!"

Mari smiled grimly. "Nobody made you punch him, Eva-Benita."

"Kick him."

"Whatever. And don't pretend you raced to my rescue out of the goodness of your heart, either. I heard how you asked Pholise about being paid for all the Fridge work you were expected to do."

Eva's jaw dropped. "Because how else was I going to feed my crew and fuel my ship? Magic? Fairy farts? Exposure? Or maybe I was supposed to fire everyone and pay off the enormous ransom all by myself somehow? What exactly was your brilliant plan for making that make sense? Maybe if you'd told me what you were doing—"

"Your reactions had to be natural, and the whole point—"

"The whole point," Eva interrupted, "is fuck you. Everyone in this room, except Momoko and the cats, was a piece in your stupid game. You're just like Dad, with his fucking Reversi logic."

Eva stopped, swallowing whatever else had been on the tip of her tongue. Mari and Pete had never had a good relationship at the best of times, and when Eva had left to work for him, Mari had been furious. It had probably ground Mari's gears to ask him for help with the Fridge raid; The Forge must have been desperate, or decided his crew's skills and experience were more important than Mari's grudge. And even if the comparison was valid, even if it wasn't the anger talking, she shouldn't have said that.

Before Eva could apologize, Mari retorted, "If I'm as bad as Dad, then you're as bad as Tito."

The silence in the mess was profound, as if they'd all suddenly been dropped into the vacuum outside.

"Oh, honey," Pink said softly. "You really stepped in it."

A lot of responses flickered through Eva's head at once. That if she were as bad as Tito, if all she cared about was making money, she would still be part of his crew, and making a hell of a lot more than she was now. That if it weren't for Tito, she would never have murdered hundreds of people on Garilia, on top of all the others she'd killed under his orders, and if she were like him she wouldn't have cared so much that she would have nightmares about it for the rest of her life. That for the last eight years she had desperately attempted not to be like Tito, ever, in any way, because he was a vile, lying, manipulative, backstabbing, "it's just business, don't take it personally" resingado hijo de la gran mierda. But ultimately, none of those responses came out of her mouth.

Instead, Eva punched Mari in the face. So hard, her sister flew into the cabinets, bounced off, and landed on the floor in a heap. She didn't move.

A distant part of Eva knew that was bad, that concussions were real and could cause long-term damage, that her own fist would be swelling up soon and she should wrap it and ice it, that poor Pink would have more work to do and that wasn't fair to her, that she'd lost her temper in front of her crew and Momoko and that wasn't acceptable because she was one of the captains and she had to keep a level head.

Another part of her was sorry she didn't have her sonic knuckles on, and that part scared Eva enough to temper the rage boiling inside her like water in a cafetera.

"Pink," Eva said, "I'm going to pick a drop-off point while you take care of Agent Virgo. Is that okay?"

"Fine by me," Pink replied, standing up and stretching her arms to the ceiling. "Let's see how bad her eggs are scrambled, then we'll move her to the med bay." She ambled over to Mari, which comforted Eva slightly; if Pink had been worried, she wouldn't be taking her time about this.

Eva turned around and walked out, down the hall to her quarters. Once inside, she took a deep breath and exhaled slowly, several times, for all the good it did. She wanted to go to the cargo bay, to where her heavy bag waited, and keep punching and punching until her muscles turned to jelly. She wanted to scream herself hoarse. She wanted a lot of things, but what she had was a sore hand, a shitty sister, and a mission more important than any she'd ever had before.

Her collection of fish swam obliviously in the tank above her bed. The automatic feeder went off, and several of them darted toward the flakes and pellets drifting in the water while others continued to hide in their rock caves or among the plants. The flashes of color and movement had once been a balm to her senses, despite being a sometimes-painful reminder of her family and how they were scattered across the universe instead of together in one place. Now the quiet burbling of the air pump was worse than the grinding of unlubricated gears.

Maybe she would go down to the cargo bay after all. She just needed Pink to finish getting Mari out of the mess and then she could pass through quickly and blow off steam. But first . . .

Eva sat on the corner of her bed and crafted a brief q-mail on her commlink. She'd refrained from sending a similar message so many times in the past three weeks, each time feeling as if she'd won some battle against an invisible foe. This one she agonized over, debating the pros and cons of breaking her silence, then trying to keep the wording as neutral and vague as possible in case it was intercepted.

"Please send update on your status re: monoliths," she wrote. No salutation, no signature. No desperation or flowery language. Just a simple, straightforward request.

Any response would immediately ping her on arrival, but she spent a few minutes refreshing her feed anyway. One of the reasons she hadn't sent a message before now was because she knew herself well enough to anticipate not only her own impatience, but also the dread of not receiving a reply.

Oh, Vakar, she thought, where the hell are you?

· · · · · · · ·

Pink was thoughtful enough to ping Eva before releasing Mari from the med bay, which gave Eva time to get into the sonic shower after spending a solid hour punching and kicking the shit out of her heavy bag. Despite wrapping her hand, the knuckles were still swollen and sore enough to give off twinges of pain every time they connected with the firm vinyl, even through the padding of her light gloves.

They arrived at their destination an hour later. Eva had chosen a trade outpost on the fringe that saw enough traffic to have a permanent population, but not large enough to warrant a monolith at the Gate. She assumed someone would be along to pick Mari up eventually, though at this point if her sister stayed there for the next year, it would be about what she deserved.

The rest of the crew made themselves scarce as Eva escorted a silent Mari to the cargo bay door. Even the cats were absent, except Mala, who nonchalantly sat next to Sue's mech, Gustavo. Her hazel eyes followed Mari's limping progress, and the twitch of her tail practically said "good riddance" despite her making no vocalizations whatsoever.

Outside, the rock-strewn field that passed for a spaceport was surprisingly crowded. Thankfully, the mech had a cloaking function, so she parked it behind the ship without anyone noticing. Makeshift tables were set up for bartering various goods, from food to ship parts to other random necessities, all of them suddenly rarer and more valuable since commerce across the universe had slowed to a trickle. The longer supply lines were down, the harder life would get for anyone in a star system that wasn't self-sufficient. So, pretty much everyone.

All the more reason Eva needed to find the other two mechs

and deal with the Artificers quickly. The universe didn't need any more black dwarfs or blown-up planets.

Mari paused at the end of the ramp and spoke without looking back at Eva. The left side of her face was swollen, especially at her temple and around her eye. Eva hadn't broken the skin, though she'd definitely rung her sister's bell; Pink had given Mari some anti-inflammatories, but hadn't parted with any of their more expensive and limited quick-heal nanites.

"I'm sorry I compared you to Tito," Mari said.

"I'm sorry I compared you to Dad," Eva replied. "I'm sorry I forgot to send you a bill when Vakar saved your ass from the Proarkhe. And I'm sorry I didn't charge you room and board for your trip to Brodevis. I'm almost sorry I didn't leave you on that rock with Tito, given where I ended up last time he and I were in a room together."

Mari flinched. Good, Eva thought.

"Please rethink this," Mari said. "The Forge needs those mechs to protect the universe, if your contact is telling the truth. We could do a lot of good with them, with you and your crew, all of us working together."

"You had your chance," Eva said. "You blew it."

Mari turned sideways, looking at Eva with her good eye. "We could pay you."

"Vete pa'l carajo." After what she'd said, now Mari offered her money?

Mari inhaled, and Eva could practically hear her mentally counting to ten before she exhaled.

"I could tell you where Vakar is," she said.

Eva's hands curled into fists. "How long have you known?" she asked quietly.

Perhaps sensing there was no right answer to the question, Mari remained silent.

Eva closed her eyes, smelling the mingled fumes of the various ships nearby, the grunge of unwashed bodies and pheromones and perfumes and everything in between. The only thing she wanted to smell was licorice, and that was far away somewhere, on a secret mission, and without a doubt she would do some truly unscrupulous things to get the information Mari dangled in front of her like so much fish bait.

What is he doing? Eva wanted to ask. Is he okay? Is he safe?

Instead, she flipped Mari off, turned around and walked away. She didn't trust herself to speak, because no matter what she said, she knew her voice would break. And if that happened, her sister's neck might be next.

After a few Gate-hops to a relatively empty system, they began taking turns with the mech. They randomly chose and Sue won first chance, but she immediately ceded her turn to Min, to the pilot's delight and an excess of jumping. So romantic. Pink stayed on the ship to keep an eye on things, while Eva guided Min through the ring-key activation and the unnerving tube situation, and prepped her on how to access the instructions, so at least that went faster and more easily.

From the outside, it was clear when the connection and information transfer occurred; Min's body jerked as if being electrocuted, and a mist of blood drifted from her nose into the fluid. Eva wondered how safe this was after all, and resolved to have Pink examine both her and Min thoroughly before anyone else took their turn.

In the meantime, Eva helmed *La Sirena Negra* while Min flitted around in the mech, immediately more graceful than Eva had been when she tried it. How much of that was because of the lack of gravity, and how much was Min's innate skill and years of piloting ships and training with other mechs, was hard to suss out. But Min not only managed to execute bursts of speed and physics-defying stops and turns, she also cycled through all the available shield and weapon systems as if pulling them up on a menu—which is what she must be doing, now that Eva thought of it.

The mech instructions sat in Eva's head like a lump of dry protein powder that hadn't been properly mixed into a liquid. Except it was a lot of smaller lumps, spread throughout her memory, strange bubbles of data that occasionally popped when she poked them. Even her muscles reacted when Min performed some of her maneuvers, as if Eva's body remembered doing them, though she knew she hadn't.

Humans had worked on developing those kinds of training methods for a long time, but they'd never gotten them to work. Usually you couldn't just drop knowledge in someone's head and expect it to incorporate properly, and sometimes you ended up with a violent rejection, like how some people's bodies used to reject organ transplants before those became tailor-made.

Then again, humans hadn't figured out how to make Gates, either, until they deciphered recovered Proarkhe plans. A human had figured out how to make robots that got larger or smaller, despite that being physically impossible, but he'd used Proarkhe tech to do it. There was enough tech out there being indistinguishable from magic that Eva was ready to go back to lighting prayer candles on the chance that it would make a difference.

One thing that wasn't different, though, was the monoliths. They still drifted along near their respective Gates, broadcasting their message of surrender or death, with no clear timeline and no instructions on who anyone should be surrendering to or how. Civil and political unrest had rippled through the universe as different places argued about whether to bulk up their defenses or wave the cultural equivalent of white flags. BOFA was currently taking a neutral stance, claiming they were waiting for more information before making a determination, while managing relief efforts in places already struggling to provide basics like food.

Thankfully, BOFA regulations included provisions for other catastrophes that helped now, though whether anyone had ever foreseen this kind of mass-threat situation was questionable. Eva had no idea of the inner workings of that stuff, and she wasn't about to ask her mom, who might know.

Speaking of her mother, Eva sent her another terse rejection of an offer to shelter at some BOFA facility in Casa Carajo. She wasn't about to say anything about this mech mission, on the off chance that Regina Alvarez the loyal BOFA employee decided to share with her bosses, who would almost certainly want to confiscate the mech for their own purposes. Eva trusted BOFA about as much as she trusted anyone: not at all.

Mari knows where Vakar is, the tiny voice in Eva's head whispered.

Mari can eat nails and shit blood, Eva told herself. She was still hurting, and that wasn't going anywhere soon.

After Min finished her mech shift, Pink checked her out from stem to stern. Everything seemed fine, despite the nosebleed, which she thought might have been due to a sudden increase in blood pressure.

"I'll monitor the next person who goes in," Pink said grimly. "Should have been there the first time, but live and learn."

Sue went next, then Momoko. Sue mostly flew around La Sirena Negra, even hugged it a few times, and practiced with the mech's shield. Momoko, who neither confirmed nor denied having previous experience with piloting or mechs or anything similar, nonetheless took to it quickly, her style involving a lot more spinning and strafing, often leading with her hips. If she did that in her regular fights, Eva mused, it was understandable that she'd caught Leroy's eye. And his other parts, eventually.

Though Eva knew this was all important and necessary, as the hours slipped past, her patience dwindled. They needed to move on to the next mech's location and get it before Tito did. She didn't know how he'd found the first one, but thankfully, she had the two remaining keys Antimatter had given her. Once she'd gotten the instructions out of the first mech, she'd learned how to use them to do more than just point in the right direction. Now she could extract coordinates, down to the system, planet, and specific location.

One of the remaining mechs was on a planet called Aplionus, while the other was on Yastroth. Their systems were nowhere near where the first mech had been hidden, and the planets were nothing alike: one was a gas giant with an active mining company as well as some radiation flux manufacturing, and the other featured oceans of lava on one side and smaller lava lakes with vaporized rock for rain on the other. Neither place sounded particularly appealing, and certainly neither was as hospitable as the mysterious castle on its tiny island. The mission parameters were clear, though, so they had to get the mechs no matter where they were. If that meant wading through lava, so be it.

Eva's spacesuit was rated to handle extreme temperatures and pressures, but she had never been eager to test those limits. What was life without a little extreme testing, though?

Safe, she thought. Easy. Relaxing. Foot massages. Even the notion of fistfighting dozens of other strangers for a fancier vacation sounded reasonable compared to this.

Given her current mood, she was ready to fistfight anyone

who crossed her. She almost wished she would run into Tito again just so she could vent some of her steam buildup.

Then again, running into him was a complication her mission could do without. Instead, she'd hope for safe, easy, and relaxing, and deal with him later.

Sadly, later had a tendency to come at her fast.

Chapter 6

SNIPER, NO SNIPING

Aplionus was, as expected, enormous and gassy, blue veined with brown and rust-red. The clouds were layered like a serving of tres leches, except where they were a swirling mass of storms, streaked with lightning flashes big and bright enough to be visible from orbit. *La Sirena Negra* docked at the mining colony, whose residents were curious about the small cargo ship randomly appearing amid all the strangeness happening in the wider universe. Eva's cover story was that their Gate transponder had malfunctioned and they didn't want to use it again until their engineer had examined it thoroughly, and in the meantime they needed to refuel.

The system's Gate had its own monolith, floating serenely like some unmarked coffin, continually sending out the same message as everywhere else. Production had stopped once they hit capacity and couldn't offload any of the gas and manufactured items; Eva tried to strike a deal to deliver some of their locally made heat-exchanger tubing for a tidy profit, but the co-op spokesman brushed her off. There were already contracts in place, the co-op would have to take a vote . . . Eva happily accepted their excuses, because all she really cared about was finding the mech.

Their existing mech waited a ways off, cloaked and piloted by Sue. While Eva didn't expect Tito to literally have spies everywhere, for all she knew, his employers had some sophisticated algorithms monitoring various transmissions on a massive scale, and might pick out a random report of someone seeing a weird giant robot in the company of a particular vessel. She wouldn't put it past Tito to at least be aware of some of her fake ship credentials after all this time, and she couldn't buy or fabricate new ones on such short notice.

According to the key, the second mech was somewhere within a persistent anticyclonic storm north of the equator. The mine had air tunnels set up to allow access to the center of the storm, where an aerostat collected ethylene and stored it in tanks. Mostly, machines loaded the tanks into remotely controlled vehicles and ferried them out to the processing facility, where some would go to the propellant depot and others were loaded onto cargo ships for delivery. But some vehicles were designated for people to use, in case they had to inspect the aerostat or make repairs or adjustments on-site instead of from a distance.

"So," Eva said, "all we have to do is hijack one of those vehicles, follow the tunnels to the eye of that big hurricane, find the mech, and get out." She tried to toss a piece of popcorn into her mouth, missed, then picked it off her shirt and ate it. "Easy."

Pink, Leroy, and Momoko sat around the table in the mess, staring at Eva with eerily similar blank expressions.

"And which part of that is easy, exactly?" Pink drawled.

"Min and Sue already got us the manufacturer's override codes for the vehicles," Eva said. "Min should have the tunnel maps soon, and then it's all over but the celebration." If Vakar had been there, he and Min could probably have found the information faster, but he wasn't, and anyway Eva wasn't going to think about him right now because it hurt, and hurting was bad, and she was sick of it.

"Are there no security guards?" Momoko asked. "No one to control access to the vehicles themselves?"

Eva shrugged. "Why would they need guards? If there are guards, they're hanging around the full gas tanks, the stuff that's already been processed and packed up. Much easier to steal." She tried to toss another kernel into her mouth and it bounced off her cheek and to the floor. One of the cats immediately pounced, batting it around the mess like wounded prey.

"Let me get this right in my head," Pink said slowly. "Your plan is to walk in like we own the place, go right for the vehicles, slide on in and take one to where the mech is, then what . . . Fly the damn thing up and out like some avenging angel going back to heaven?"

Eva nodded, threw a piece of popcorn into the air, and neatly caught it. She grinned at Pink as she chewed, then coughed as a bit got stuck in her throat.

"You okay, boss?" Leroy asked.

Eva gave him a thumbs-up, then left to get ready for this mission, which would definitely go better than her attempts at fancy snacking.

"Are they still behind us?" Eva asked, trying to stay focused on the controls as they flew along the air tunnel.

"Yup," Pink replied. "Not gaining, but still there."

"Me cago en la mierda," Eva said.

They sat in the mining transport vehicle, which comfortably fit six passengers, or three harried smugglers and Leroy, who was extremely tall and broad. Eva occupied the single pilot seat while everyone else sat on two long benches facing each other. Behind them, the back of the cargo bed stretched about triple the length of the cab. Instead of a ceiling, which would have been sensible and good, the damn thing was open to the elements, with a force field that could be turned on and off at will.

The notion that some of these miners wanted to zip around with the wind whipping through their hair or other head parts was, frankly, unbelievable, but so were a lot of things in the universe.

Around them, illuminated by the dim lights of the transport, red-orange and blue eddies intermingled with swirling beige clouds, streaks of lightning forking at intervals short enough to fray Eva's nerves. The corridor around them should have been sufficient to protect them from the various planetary elements, but all it took was one glitch, one sufficiently strong gust or shock, to bring the whole system down and leave them entirely exposed to brutal temperatures and even worse pressures.

Their spacesuits would protect them to a point, but massive electrical shock wasn't on the safe parameters list. Neither was plummeting for a few thousand kilometers and impacting an extremely hard surface.

Farther back in the tunnel, a group of miners in another vehicle pursued them. They were armed with short-range stun rounds, which they periodically fired at the intruders. While Eva had been right about the lack of security near the tunnels, she'd been extremely overconfident about their ability to saunter in and act natural enough to fool the random employees they encountered. It hadn't taken long for security to be summoned, and Eva and the others were presumed to be saboteurs from a rival mining company based on the comms chatter Min was feeding them.

"Where's the next tunnel change?" Eva asked, looking over her shoulder periodically.

"A few thousand meters ahead," Leroy said, checking their stolen map.

"Hopefully we can lose them by shifting to another route." The changeover should be simple enough; at every junction, a switch controlled which air tunnel was open and which was closed, allowing the vehicle to smoothly move between them without stopping. If they could switch it back behind them before they were caught, it would be like Gate-hopping, and they could hopefully get the rest of the way to the storm's eye unimpeded.

An alarm on the control panel chirped annoyingly. The vehicle began slowing down on its own—were the miners controlling it? No, she'd locked them out, that shouldn't be possible.

Once again, Vakar would have been extremely fucking handy, she thought bitterly.

But it wasn't the miners; it was a safety override. As they approached the tunnel fork, the switch floating in the air blinked red. Both paths were closed, turning their route into a dead end.

"Me cago en diez," Eva said. "They've shut down the tunnels."

Pink flipped up her eye patch, revealing her cybernetic eye. Squinting slightly, she stared down the path ahead.

"There must be some way to manually override it," she said.

"I definitely don't want to take on a bunch of angry security guards," Eva said. She could probably beat them, especially with Leroy and Momoko as backup, but it would be ugly. And she didn't like the odds if they got a clear shot with their stun rounds.

"I see something on the panel," Pink said. "Looks like a pair of buttons, one for each track. We just need to push the one we want and the tunnel should open again."

"But we would be forced to stop to do so," Momoko said. "That seems disadvantageous."

Leroy grinned at her. "I love when you use big words." Momoko flushed in response, trying to suppress her own smile.

Eva rolled her eyes. According to Pink, she and Vakar were equally insufferable, but she found it hard to believe.

"I've got an idea," Pink said. She shifted the pack she wore on her back to her lap and opened it, methodically removing items one by one.

"You brought your sniper rifle?" Eva asked incredulously.

"I brought both of them," Pink replied, her hands moving almost automatically as she reassembled one. "And a bunch of different rounds. If I hit the button with a low-impact shot, it might activate the switch and get us through."

Eva laughed. "Genius," she said. "Dale. Worst case, we have Leroy jump up and slap it, then shoot the people behind us instead."

"I don't wanna hurt them," Pink said tartly. "Low-impact isn't painless. They're just collecting their paychecks; they ain't Fridge."

"We're not breaking any eggs," Eva said, "we're just rattling the carton."

Pink made a dismissive noise and finished putting her weapon together. Within moments she had loaded the shot pack, activated the heat sink, and rested the barrel on the front of the vehicle for extra stability.

"You'll have to drop the force field," Pink said.

"Just tell me when," Eva replied. "Is the wind gonna be a problem?"

"Your face is gonna be a problem if you ask me another fool-ass question like that."

Leroy laughed. "I missed you two. This is just like old times!"

Momoko smiled nervously. "You weren't joking when you said your work used to be interesting."

"It wasn't always like this," Eva said. "Sometimes we'd go a whole week without getting shot at."

The vehicle turned a corner. In the distance, Eva could barely make out the switch at the end of a long, straight section of tunnel, softly backlit by a red light, with a blinking indicator to show it was deactivated. The clouds outside that area swirled, tinted that same red.

"Hold your breath, y'all," Pink said, and they all did. Eva flicked the force field off, and the wind of their motion pushed through the vehicle like an invisible hand stroking a cat. It roared like a lion, though.

Two things happened at once. Pink fired her sniper rifle, the concussive boom echoing through the tunnel a scant moment later as she hit her target. The switch spun in the air from the impact, but the blinking red light turned to green, and the tunnel on the right irised open.

Another shot rang out, the boom reaching Eva's ears just after Leroy yelped behind her.

Eva couldn't check on him right away, instead trusting that someone else had it handled while she turned the force field back on, eased the vehicle into the tunnel, and sped up. She hadn't realized their pursuers had gotten close enough to shoot at them, but she wouldn't let it happen again if she could help it.

The vehicle speed topped out at about fifty kilometers per hour, a snail's pace compared to what Eva wanted. She tried a trick her dad had shown her once and, sure enough, found a speed limiter locking down the controls for "safety purposes" or whatever. With a few quick taps, she switched that off and juiced the motor up to one hundred and twenty, grinning. Still slower than she was used to, but better.

"How's Leroy?" Eva called over her shoulder.

"Not stunned," Pink answered grimly. "He took an SW-RV round through the arm."

"Mierda, mojón y porquería," Eva muttered. That wasn't civilian-issue, and it wasn't short-range either. Those fuckers could curve, though they couldn't penetrate the vehicle's force shield. She hadn't seen one since—

Tito. He'd caught up to them, el muy cabrón. And he had a sniper with him.

"I'm getting him stable," Pink said. "Bullet went straight through and out into the wind. Leroy, sugar, do you remember if there are any more switches we need to hit?"

"Two," Leroy replied through gritted teeth.

Eva bit back a curse. Pink couldn't shoot the switches and help Leroy, and if they slowed down they'd be easy targets for Tito. He definitely knew the same limiter-override trick she did, so he'd be up their asses in a hurry.

Think, Eva, think, she told herself. We have to make this work. We need to get to the mech first, and maybe take out Tito in the process.

"Momoko, are you better at driving or first aid?" Eva asked.

Momoko hesitated before answering, "Driving."

That surprised Eva; she would have expected someone who got beaten up professionally to know her way around bandages and painkillers.

"You sure?" Eva asked, glancing over her shoulder.

"I used to race draggers," Momoko said coolly.

"The big turbine-towed ones?"

"Yes."

Eva whistled. Lady had unexplored depths, but then, didn't everyone?

"Get up here and take over," Eva said. "Pink, walk me through what Leroy needs, and get back to sniping. We need those switches popped, and we need Tito to go for a ride on the storm. We'll drop the shields, hopefully lure him into dropping his and see what happens."

Pink gave a low laugh. "Sure, make me multitask."

"You can handle it," Eva said. "And we both know you're a better shot than I am."

Eva quickly showed Momoko the controls, and sure enough, the vehicle was in safe hands. Staying low in case Tito had some shield-penetrating trick up his sleeve, Eva hunkered down next to Leroy and examined his injury. It was more than a flesh wound, but it had hit the outside of his arm between biceps and shoulder. If it had been a few centimeters to the side, or worse, a bit higher . . . Eva put the brakes on that train of thought. Pink had stripped Leroy's spacesuit off, baring his chest and the injured arm, and had finished stopping the bleeding with a dusting of clotting crystals and a pressure wrap. She passed her bag to Eva and retreated to the end of the vehicle, rifle in one hand.

"There's an injector in there," Pink said as she set up her weapon. "It's preloaded with a combo sterilizer, painkiller, and shock-treater."

"Neck or arm?" Eva asked.

"Neck. Under the jaw." She made minute adjustments as she peered through the scope, then swore softly, so softly Eva almost didn't hear it.

"Something wrong?" Eva asked, the injector in her hand, poised to be triggered.

"Nope," Pink replied. Then, after a moment, she added, "Tito has Joe over there."

Eva felt like she'd already done enough swearing in the last ten minutes for a whole cycle, but she threw in another "coño carajo" for good measure. She and Pink had worked with Joe back when they were on Tito's crew. He was a hell of a fighter, but more than that, he was as good a sniper as Pink, if not better. Then the full weight of the implication sank in.

"He's Jei's brother," Eva said. They'd teamed up with Jei on Garilia, working together to bring down the corrupt government and stop a plan to send tiny mind-controlling spy robots all over the universe. Later, Jei had confessed that he was looking for his brother, Buruusu, who he seemed to think was coerced into working for Tito somehow, but who had gone missing at some point. Turned out that Buruusu and Joe were one and the same.

And apparently, he was missing no longer and was back to his old job.

"Wait a minute," Eva said slowly, sifting through more recent memories. "That Sniper guy I was fighting in the *Crash Sisters* melee. Do you think—"

"I thought it as soon as I saw you fighting him," Pink said. "He always did love blades. Check Leroy's vitals and let me focus."

Pink usually used her cybernetic eye for that, but she always stashed a backup scanner in her bag in case she was the one who got hurt. Eva tapped it on and swung the wand around Leroy. His heart rate and blood pressure were up, but not dangerously so; the meds were probably working, and the bleeding had stopped.

"You okay, King Cooper?" Eva asked.

Leroy gave her a weak grin. "I've had worse. Probably ruined my tattoos, though."

"We'll get you some new ones, really bring out the coolness of the scar," Eva said. She knew enough about injuries from her own experiences to know he needed to keep that arm immobile, so she fished around in the bag for a sling. Nada nada, limonada, but there were more wraps she could use to at least improvise for now.

Something nagged at her though. Pink had said she thought of Joe as soon as she saw him fighting Eva. It wasn't like Pink sparred with the rest of Tito's crew that much. Her interactions with him would have been mostly doctor and patient, so identifying him by fighting style was odd. It was possible she'd done hand-to-hand with Joe, but she also knew he liked using bladed weapons . . .

"I need the shields down to take a shot," Pink said. "Get Leroy's suit back on and get his isohelmet up, and let me know when we're ready." She continued to tweak her aim as Eva followed her instructions, shelving her thoughts for another time.

"On my mark," Eva said. "Shield's coming down in three, two, one, go!"

The wind rushed back in, stronger than last time since they were moving faster. It didn't take long for Pink's sniper rifle to kick, the bullet's sonic boom following soon afterward. Tito must have had Joe watching them, too, but instead of hitting someone inside the vehicle this time, he hit the vehicle itself.

Momoko wrestled the controls as the impact knocked them off-center in the tunnel. The magnetic fields created by the machines that kept the tunnels open also worked to stabilize the transports, so they wouldn't accidentally spin out into the storm beyond. Eva wondered what had happened to the security guards who had been trailing them initially; were they working with Tito, or had he taken a separate vehicle and knocked them out of the way?

"Did you get him?" Eva asked.

"No, but I hit Tito in the shoulder," Pink replied coolly.

Eva frowned. Their motion and the wind and magnetic fields made any sniping an enormous challenge, but Pink had said she was up to it, and Eva trusted her word on that. So how had she missed that badly?

Unless she hadn't. But why aim for Tito instead of Joe? And why the shoulder? Petty revenge? A warning?

"The switch," Momoko reminded them. The next tunnel split was coming right up.

"Pink, get to the front," Eva said. "Momoko, can you bring us closer to the top of the tunnel to narrow their target?"

"Yes," Momoko replied, "but I can't keep us there for long."

More careful timing. Not Eva's favorite. The difficulty multiplier was getting outrageous. "I'll try to give them an alternate target," Eva said. She pulled Pink's other sniper rifle out of the bag and assembled it—not as quickly as Pink had, because she was out of practice, but her muscles remembered more than she'd expected. And anyway, she wasn't planning to shoot, because she wasn't nearly as good as Pink and Joe; she'd just be wasting precious ammo.

No, all she wanted was to lure Joe into aiming at her instead of Pink or the vehicle, which would be even more dangerous with them riding high.

This was all supposed to be easy, Eva thought bitterly. Why can't anything ever be easy?

"I'm set up," Pink told Momoko. "I'll have to fix my aim when we move, so don't drop the shields until I say."

Momoko brought the vehicle to the top of the tunnel. Lightning flashed above them, close enough to bathe them all in brilliant blue light. Leroy yelped, then laughed nervously. Eva flinched, but finished her work with steady hands.

On a whim, she peered through the scope. All she could see were the swirling clouds, and then the tunnel straightened and Tito's transport came into view. None of the security guards were visible, so either they were hiding, knocked out, or dead.

Or, as she'd thought before, their vehicle had been spun out into the storm. Or Tito had somehow managed to get his transport in front of theirs and they were way back in the tunnel somewhere, which Eva hoped was what had happened.

She was so tired of leaving a trail of bodies in her wake, even if they weren't directly her fault.

"Ready," Pink said. "Drop the shields on three."

Eva tightened her grip on the sniper rifle and prepared to duck.

Momoko counted down, fighting the controls to keep them stable, then lowered the shields.

Once again, the wind whipped through, but this time a boom came before Pink did anything.

"Shit on a shingle," Pink said. "Keep the shields down!" She took her shot after a few seconds, cussing smoothly the entire time.

A sound like crunching and breaking glass, followed instantly by a loud ping behind her, startled Eva as shards of something rained on her face. Another boom came right after. The scope she'd been looking through earlier had disintegrated, she realized, pieces of it now littered all over the floor as well as on her.

That was too fucking close.

"Shields back up," Pink shouted over the wind. A moment later, they careened into the new tunnel, once again centered, so Momoko didn't have to worry about the magnetic fields.

Eva shook herself out of her own shock. "What happened?" she asked.

"Joe shot the fucking switch," Pink said. "Tried to send us into the wrong tunnel. I got it."

"He shot me, too," Eva said. "He's fast as fuck, to re-aim that quickly."

"Yeah," Pink replied. She didn't elaborate. Her cybernetic eye swept over Eva. "Check Leroy's vitals and wipe up your face. You have seven lacerations on your cheek, and one on your forehead that's gonna sting."

Eva frowned again. Pink was juggling a lot right now, certainly, but she was being more brusque than usual. Something was wrong, and it wasn't just the situation.

Cold sweat beaded on Leroy's forehead, his freckled skin a shade paler than usual, but he maintained his weak smile as Eva examined him.

"How's the pain?" Eva asked.

"Could be better, could be worse," he said. "Is Momoko okay?"

"She's great," Eva said, smirking. "Any other secret talents of hers we should know about?"

Leroy barked out a laugh, then winced. "A lot. Her family is real competitive. She can kick my ass in just about every sport ever invented, and she can cook, too."

"Best way to a lover's heart," Eva said. She couldn't see the woman sitting in the pilot's chair, but she smiled at her anyway. As she did, she noticed Pink staring into space, her cybernetic eye still uncovered.

Eva scooted closer. "Qué te pasa?" she asked.

"Nothing," Pink said. "Where's the next switch?"

A few minutes away at their current speed. "Far enough," Eva said. "I'm not going to make you talk if you don't want to, but something's got you messed up. Spill the tea."

"I don't . . . I think . . ." Pink fell silent again, her lips pursed and puckered. Eva couldn't remember the last time she'd seen her friend like this, if ever. It shook her more than she wanted to admit.

"I think Joe is missing his shots on purpose," Pink said finally. "He's better than I am, and I'm managing fine."

So Pink had hit Tito in the shoulder on purpose before

instead of taking him out, or aiming at Joe instead? Eva raised an eyebrow. Choices were being made, and she didn't understand them.

"Why would he miss on purpose?" Eva asked.

"Joe and I . . ." Pink sighed and lowered her gaze to the floor. "We used to be a thing."

Eva stared at her, speechless. "Pink," she said finally. "Are you telling me your secret ex-boyfriend is over there with Tito, purposely fucking up so he doesn't get you killed?"

Pink shrugged, then nodded, then shrugged again. "Maybe. I don't know."

Lightning forked around them, throwing Pink's face into alternating light and shadow. Her furrowed brow and pursed lips said she was upset, worried, confused even. Eva didn't know what terms the two of them had parted on, but Pink had clearly hesitated to shoot Joe, so they couldn't have been too bad. And she seemed to care what happened to him now.

This was so much less complicated when I was trying to beat Joe's ass for a vacation, Eva thought.

Chapter 7

STORMING THE EYE

Eva shook free of her dark thoughts as the storm roiled around them. More than anything, they had to get to the mech before Tito, and get it to safety. A whole universe of people depended on it, not just one. She had no idea what weapons Tito might have brought along this time, so she didn't know whether they'd get blasted to hell before ever reaching their goal.

Then again, even if Joe was missing shots on purpose as Pink suspected, why hadn't Tito himself done something? He wasn't as good a sniper—even Eva had been better—but surely some Artificer weapon might have more destructive potential that could take care of Eva and the others easily.

Unless maybe he needed them for something . . . Of course. The keys. He couldn't steal the mechs unless he had them. Antimatter had said the Artificers knew where the mechs were, so Tito could have come straight here after Eva ditched him and been gone before she ever arrived. Except without the keys, he probably only knew the mechs' general locations, and even if he did find them, he'd need a way to extract them without pilots. Assuming their automated defenses didn't kick in first and disintegrate him. And he couldn't risk trying to get the keys off *La Sirena Negra* with the other mech standing by as protection, so he had to wait for Eva to come out and play.

So if Tito was harrying them instead of actually trying to kill them, that might mean Joe wasn't being as precious about Pink as she thought. He could be following orders precisely, no messy feelings, no lingering tenderness. Eva had gotten the impression during the *Crash Sisters* fight that something had happened to change whatever he'd been, like what had happened to her, but she might have been wrong. She'd misread people before.

This was a lot of maybe in one place. Another thought occurred to her: if Joe was on their side and she could save him from the wrath of Tito, she'd be doing him—and Pink—a big favor. If he wasn't, finding a way to nab him for interrogation might instead give her insight into Tito's employers and intentions, or at least deny him access to a hell of a sniper. Either way, winner-winner, chicken dinner.

Plans raced through Eva's head, elements retained or discarded like tunnels through a mine that led to dead ends, sorted as quickly as she could manage until she had some semblance of a path forward.

"How's this?" Eva told Pink. "We get the mech, grab Joe out of Tito's car, and salpica."

Pink raised an eyebrow. "Seriously? That's what you've got?"

Eva shrugged. "It's simple. Simple beats fancy most of the time."

"Says the lady who once planned an elaborate cruise-ship caper just to get laid," Pink replied.

Eva flushed, but smirked when Pink's doomed expression shifted to determination.

"No plan survives contact with the enemy," Pink said. "The mech is more important."

"It is," Eva said, "but we'll see what we can manifest. We've got one more tunnel switch to deal with, and then the eye of the storm."

Pink nodded and started setting up her next shot. If her movements were sharper than usual, more clipped and precise, well, that was Pink. In a crisis, some people panicked, and some people overclocked their competence until they were running hot enough to burn.

Momoko once again brought them high to lower their profile. If Tito didn't try to shoot them into a spinout, it might prove one way or the other whether he did indeed need someone on Eva's team to get to the mech, and was just keeping up appearances to throw off their suspicions. Or maybe he was tired of wasting ammo and would wait until they got to the eye to go all out, where there was an easier target and less wind to get in the way.

Sure enough, Pink took her shot at the switch unimpeded, and Tito did nothing. They flew into the final tunnel, which curved and angled down, and Eva was left to continue wondering what exactly Tito planned.

A minute later, they were expelled from the confines of the corridor into open air, which was briefly disorienting. The eye was massive, far too large to see any of its edges except the ones receding behind them, and even those churning walls of cloud were illuminated only by the dim glow of the vehicle's rear indicators. Above them, lightning continued to flash in the distance, the air incredibly hot compared to this area. Ahead, darkness loomed, periodically broken by the blinking warning lights of the aerostat, whose ethylene collection had been halted until the existing supplies could be off-worlded.

Eva had come in knowing where the second mech would be based on the key tucked into a pocket of her spacesuit, but she was shocked to find she could sense it calling to her like a beacon. It was closer than she expected, thankfully; her plan had included a fair amount of travel time to reach it, given the sheer size of the storm and her limited knowledge of the tunnels, but it wouldn't be necessary.

"Momoko—" Eva began.

"I feel it," Momoko said. She sped up the vehicle, cranking it well past the sad initial speed the limiter had permitted, going straight for the target.

"No, no," Eva said, "you have to plot a curve, or two even. If we take a direct trajectory, Tito may try to pass us and get there first. Best if we point him wrong, or he thinks we aren't totally sure ourselves."

"Understood," Momoko replied. She shifted her approach, angling about ten degrees off.

Behind them, a row of bright lights appeared—Tito, no doubt, emerging from the tunnel entrance. He'd been farther away than she expected. But just as they had, he pushed the vehicle faster, no longer inhibited by the uncertain curves of the corridors they'd left.

"Pink, you wanna give him some trouble?" Eva asked.

Pink frowned and shook her head. "It might be easier to hit him now, but that would make us easier targets, too. Better to keep the force field up."

That still meant Tito could shoot at the vehicle itself, which wasn't shielded. Eva didn't like that, didn't want to fully test her theories about him not wanting them dead, given the price of being wrong. If Joe was innocent and they hit him now, that would also suck.

"How good are you at evasive maneuvers?" Eva asked Momoko.

Momoko shrugged. "I'm better at racing."

"Let me take over, then. Go check on Leroy."

In a quick motion, Momoko vacated the pilot's seat and let Eva slide in. Eva had always been Min's backup on *La Sirena Negra*—had, in fact, been the original pilot before Min was hired on—and she may have been rusty but she still knew how to handle a little number like this one. Her dad had let her pilot anything on his lot, anytime, as long as she put it back where she found it and didn't ding it up too badly.

She put all those skills to good use now. Back and forth she weaved, up and down, on a random count that she kept running in her head. A few times, the sonic boom of a sniper shot sounded nearby, but they didn't take any hits. Unfortunately, Leroy seemed to be having the worst time of it, groaning in pain behind her. Pink had retreated to the rear of the vehicle, keeping an eye on their pursuers even if she wasn't actively trying to shoot them.

"Brace yourselves," Eva called over her shoulder. She counted to four, then took a hard right that would put them on a course to pass the mech. It was unsettling how she could feel it, like a limb that wasn't attached to her body. She'd never remotely piloted things the way Min had, always either did it manually or used the jack in her neck, but she imagined it must be something like what Min felt when she walked around *La Sirena Negra* in her human body while still controlling its various systems.

Lightning continued to fork above them, sending brief flashes of illumination into the darkness along with echoes of thunder.

Within minutes they'd reach their destination, and then it was a matter of getting into the mech before Tito could stop them.

But how to get Joe? There had to be a way to win the damn chicken dinner.

Chicken. Of course.

"Pink," Eva yelled. A few moments later, Pink was at her side. Her eyepatch was still up; she'd probably been using her cybernetic eye to watch Tito, or Joe.

"What do you need?" Pink asked.

"You think Momoko can get Leroy in the mech by herself?" Eva asked. "Or will you need to help?"

Pink narrowed her eyes. "Why?"

Eva explained, and Pink pursed her lips.

"Momoko can handle him," Pink said. "His legs work fine, he's just lost enough blood to be weak."

"Get your rifle ready then," Eva said. "As soon as we stop at the mech, open fire on their transport."

Pink hesitated, then asked, "And you?"

"If Momoko pilots the mech, and you and Leroy get inside, I can make some trouble until you get settled." Eva pulled the key out of her pocket and handed it over to Pink. This one was bright orange and larger than a ring—a bracelet, she assumed, though she hadn't tested it. "I'll try to grab Joe, and we'll sort him out later. And if it doesn't work . . . I'm just one person, right? The mission will go on."

"Don't be a martyr," Pink said.

"I'm not." Eva glanced at her friend, her best friend in the universe for the past decade, and smiled. "How many times have you saved Vakar for me, eh? This is the least I can do."

"I saved him for himself, jackass. He's my friend, too."

"And so is Joe. Maybe." Eva raised a hand to stave off any

other arguments. "I'm coming back, so stop planning my fucking funeral. We good?"

"Yeah, we good," Pink replied. She bumped Eva's hip with her own and moved away.

Eva continued weaving, angling so they'd end up behind their target as Pink set up her sniper rifle one more time. The silence that fell was eerie, too calm, an eye within an eye that would turn to destruction soon enough. No matter what happened, they would almost assuredly get the mech, but whether she'd be able to steal a sniper out of his moving nest surrounded by vultures was much more debatable.

"Coming around fast," Eva warned as they were about to pass the mech. It still wasn't visible, presumably cloaked, and she realized it was bobbing slightly, carried along by the storm like a leaf in a stream.

A moment after they passed it, Eva jerked the transport controls hard, drifting into a sharp turn that brought them toward the front of the mech. Whatever cloaking had hidden it from them stopped, and the giant machine coruscated into view. Its eyes glowed bright white like the first one, but the transport's lights showed a stripey orange paint color rather than the first one's bone white. The design was otherwise similar—bipedal, four-fingered hands, animal-skull-shaped head—though of course Eva couldn't be sure it was identical without syncing up with it the way she had with the first one.

The door in the mech's midsection opened when she slid up next to it. Eva had to drop the transport's force field so Leroy and Momoko could cross over; as soon as she did, Pink began to fire at Tito's vehicle. One shot after another cracked and boomed in the vast darkness, echoed by the thunder of the storm itself. She shifted her aim between rounds to account for the evasive maneuvers Tito's driver was taking, but Eva couldn't tell whether she hit anything. Hopefully she missed Joe, at least.

Behind them, Momoko helped Leroy to his feet and waited until just after Pink fired, then hauled him through the doorway as quickly as she could. Eva held her breath, bracing for a cry of pain or the sick thud of a bullet impacting meat.

None came. They were safely inside. Eva exhaled, despite her guts still being clenched in fear for Pink and her own damn self. Now came the hard part.

"Your turn," Eva told Pink. "Don't forget your bag. Get Leroy settled so we can get the fuck off this giant fart planet already."

Pink took one more shot, then grabbed her bag and leaped into the mech. As soon as she was clear, Eva pushed the vehicle as fast as it would go, on a collision course with Tito's own rapidly approaching transport.

She didn't need to hit him, she just needed to distract him by playing chicken long enough for Momoko to take control of the mech. Then either she could swap to bumper cars and knock Joe overboard, plucking him out of the sky as he fell, or the mech could tip Tito's transport over like a kettle and pour Joe out.

Unfortunately, Eva had underestimated the number of shits Tito might give about one weaponless truck barreling toward him. Especially since she clearly no longer had the key to the mech.

A sizzling blast knocked her transport sideways and sent it careening into the darkness. She wrestled with the steering to get it back under control, then tried to figure out where Tito had ended up. There was so much space to cover, it took her longer than she'd hoped, more than enough time for him to line up another brutal shot. She dropped her vehicle into a dive, and a ball of plasma exploded above her with a sound like a live wire hitting water, pushing the vehicle's nose down harder.

Tito had to be using one of his fancy new Artificer toys. Malcriado. She hoped it backfired in his face.

Not before she got Joe or got away, though. She once again pointed her vehicle toward Tito and gunned it, hoping Momoko did something before Eva got herself blown out of the sky.

Unfortunately, her luck ran out.

The next blast hit the rear of the vehicle squarely, vaporizing it and sending the front—and Eva—spinning wildly downward. The emergency stabilizers blew apart, and the force field protecting her from the elements and projectiles vanished. The safety buoy tucked under the pilot's seat also didn't work, so she couldn't eject and hover in the air to wait for a pickup. Not that she'd want to make herself such an extremely visible and easy target for Tito. She wasn't wearing an antigrav belt, only her gravboots, and there was nothing around to aim for in the hopes of stopping her descent. Even if some other life-preserving method for passengers hid in a side compartment, she'd have to get out of her restraints to find it.

A wave of energy above her distracted her from the imminent shittiness of her situation: the mech, fully powered, glowing a soft red occasionally backlit by lightning. She didn't know whether it or Tito had fired, but neither seemed damaged. Not that it was easy to tell while being flung around like a demented children's toy.

Eva sent a location ping to Pink, along with a terse ((Falling, help)) addendum. The bottom of the storm was far enough away that she still had hope, but close enough that she didn't want to find out the hard way whether her suit could handle the combination of pressure, temperature, and lightning surges.

And then the transport caught fire, so staying put was no longer an option.

Her restraints had locked, so she pulled her vibroblade off

her belt and swiped it on, then sliced through the straps keeping her in the pilot's chair. As soon as those were off, she started to rise. She bent her knees and pushed up and away from the flaming wreck, trying to move far enough that if the worst happened, she wouldn't be—

The vehicle exploded, tossing her farther up and setting the air around her ablaze.

Oh no, Eva thought, not again.

Then she was falling like a meteor through the atmosphere. Part of her wondered how many times a person could almost fall to their death in one lifetime, another part wondered why she kept getting set on fire, and yet another was busy screaming in terror.

Her breath whooshed out of her as she hit something: the mech's giant hand. Its other hand closed around her, almost squishing her. A sense of immense speed pressed her harder into the smooth material of the palm, and within moments the fire swirling around her had vanished, whether left behind or snuffed out, she didn't know. She was shoved unceremoniously into the machine's door, where she slid across the floor and into Pink's outstretched foot.

"Glad you could join us," Pink said dryly. "Pull up a chair."

Another seat rose from the floor next to Pink's. Eva picked herself up and staggered toward it, her legs trembling with adrenaline. Inside the pilot tube, Momoko floated, eyes open but seeing the outside rather than the mech's interior.

Across from her, next to Leroy, Joe sat in his own chair. He'd abandoned his flashy holographic *Crash Sisters* helmet for a plain isohelmet, currently translucent. Now that Eva saw his face, she recognized him immediately: the mop of dark-brown hair, the big brown eyes under thick brows, the pale skin, the perpetual smirk. His gray spacesuit had a few smudges that suggested fire residue, possibly from blasts similar to the one Eva had survived. He gripped his sniper rifle in one hand, but the other could be swapped for an arm cannon, she knew, though now it was a prosthetic arm with a five-fingered hand.

She resisted the urge to wave. As it was, he stared at the floor like it might open up and swallow him whole.

"We have company," Momoko said, her voice resonating eerily throughout the room, coming from both her mouth and the mech.

Eva mentally summoned up an image of what the mech saw, and it floated in front of her like a holographic projection, overlaid with different visualizations of things like infrared and ultraviolet and motion sensors where necessary. They had already passed through the superhot upper layer of the storm and were rising beyond, out of the atmosphere and into outer space. As they reached the black, Eva searched the image for a sign of the mining station's security forces, the tiny flash of drones or some larger ship in the distance.

Instead, one of the Artificers hovered in front of them. The very one Eva had faced at the Gate weeks earlier. Kilonova, Antimatter had called them.

They were bipedal but stocky, red with pale legs and large winglike fins rising from their back. Compared to the mech Eva sat in, they were tiny, only about nine meters tall instead of more than quadruple that. Their red eyes glowed like a warning, and as Eva watched, they transformed into something like a spaceship and vanished into the black.

Well, that was anticlimactic, Eva thought. But after everything else, I'll take it.

"We need to get out of here before Tito catches up," Eva said. "Let's make like a flea and jump."

She looked over at Pink, who nodded, her expression serious.

Eva couldn't imagine what her friend was thinking right now, and she wasn't about to push, but her own mind suddenly filled with questions.

How had Pink kept this secret for so long? Why had she never told Eva? Was there still something between her and Joe? Did Pink even want there to be something, or did she feel bad that Joe might have the wrong idea and be risking himself for her over a dead flame? Would Joe be able to give them any useful intel about Tito's plans and employer, or was he a literal hired gun along for a single mission?

Worst of all, what if Pink had misread the situation entirely, and they'd just picked up someone from the opposing team who would stab them in the back at the first chance?

Chapter 8

CADA VEZ QUE PIENSO EN TÍ

On returning to *La Sirena Negra*, the crew's mood was a mix of celebratory and awkward. They'd picked up the second mech of three, which theoretically meant they were on the verge of fulfilling their mission and, if Antimatter was to be trusted, possibly helping to save the universe from their unknown enemy.

But Leroy was in the med bay getting his arm wound properly attended to, and with the monoliths halting most free movement and trade, their medical supplies were limited to whatever they had on hand and needed to be rationed carefully. Likewise their food, which they'd restocked before leaving for Brodevis. And now they had an extra mouth to feed.

Joe, aka Sniper, aka Buruusu Rokku, sat cuffed to a chair in the cargo bay being watched by tiny robots and cats, a confinement he had agreed to without protest, which unfortunately made Eva more suspicious rather than less. Some people were excellent manipulators, and a lot of them worked for Tito, who was the king of finding buttons and pushing them at the most opportune times for him.

The cats, at least, had taken a liking to Joe, which was a point in his favor. His natural smirk was constant, but when a cat brushed against his leg, it seemed to expand into a more genuine smile. Eva had even caught him whispering to them a few times when they deigned to settle in his lap, purring regally like he was a new piece of furniture to be used for their comfort and pleasure.

They couldn't just leave him like that forever. They'd taken a chance based on Pink's history with him, Eva's recent interactions, and some circumstantial evidence that would make a lawyer like Pink's brother snicker. Joe could be a strong ally even if he had no intel, but he was dangerous if he was loyal to Tito, so they needed to figure it out fast, or their mission could be compromised.

As soon as Leroy was resting, with everyone alternately keeping an eye on him and practicing with both mechs, Eva summoned Pink to her quarters for a debrief. She hoped by calling it that she could manage to keep her mouth from saying something incredibly foolish before her brain caught up.

Pink settled into a chair while Eva leaned against her closet door, looking at her fish so it wouldn't seem like she was scrutinizing Pink too harshly.

"How are your hormones and whatnot?" Eva asked, then winced. "Wait, that's not what I—"

"I assume," Pink interrupted, "you're asking about medical supplies. I can synthesize enough hormones for a little less than a month."

"Oh, good. Cool. And, em, your secret stash?"

"Two and a half bottles left. I can make that stretch if I have to." Her eye narrowed as she scrutinized Eva's face. "I need to clean those cuts."

"Ay, what's a few more scars?" Eva asked. "They'll be fine. I'll wash up in the head."

"Tito got it worse," Pink said smugly.

"You love to see it," Eva said.

The fish tank whirred, releasing a burst of bubbles like an underwater fart. Eva's brain did the same, more or less.

"So," Eva said, "Joe."

"Yup," Pink replied, giving the last letter its own loud popping syllable.

When no further explanation came, Eva said, "We talked about your other flings all the time. Why not Joe?" She risked a glance at Pink, who was looking at her hands.

Pink sighed heavily. "My other flings weren't with crewmates. I shouldn't have . . . I was the ship's doc. I crossed a line."

"I hate lines," Eva said, trying to keep her tone light. "Standing in them, coloring inside them . . . lines have always been a pain in my ass."

Pink chuckled, but it was bitter. "Yeah, you've done your fair share of redrawing them, too. You can get away with it. I can't."

It was true. Hell, Pink had lectured Eva about the rules when it came to Vakar, back when the two of them were dancing around each other, pretending not to notice how badly they both wanted to make something happen. They'd made it work, but it hadn't been easy, and on a crew like Tito's? It was one thing to mess around with someone on your level, but you never went above or below your rank to have your fun. The power imbalance made for ugly situations, if not right from jump then certainly further down the flight path.

And the ship's doctor, while not necessarily outranking everyone, was by nature a keeper of secrets. Pink didn't know everything about every crew member—Tito was the one who usually sat on that information, for his own purposes—but she knew enough to make her job awkward if she ever got busy with one of her patients. And on the ship, everyone was her patient.

Pink had to maintain trust, so that people would come to her with their problems and believe she would take care of them. She couldn't play favorites, and she couldn't turn anyone away. The success of their jobs depended on her keeping everyone healthy, mentally and physically.

Eva had known it was lonely work, but the enormity of it hit her all at once. Pink had always been a little aloof, a little quiet, watching more than participating. She took care of everyone else, but she wouldn't let anyone take care of her. At the time, Eva had assumed that was by choice. Now she wondered.

"You want to tell me how you two hooked up?" Eva asked.

Pink rested her face in her hands for a moment, then looked up. "It started during that one mission where we had to wait around in the ass end of nowhere for four months. You remember that one?"

"Yeah, that sucked plutonium exhaust. By the end, a bunch of us were ready to fuck or fight anything that moved."

"Pain in my ass, keeping all you non-aces from doing exactly that. But I was riled up, too." She shook her head at the memory. "It was fine at first, you know? He was hot, we were both into long guns . . . We swore to keep it chill. No feelings, just fun. No special treatment on either end."

"What happened?"

Smirking, Pink looked down again. "Feelings. Special treatment. I should have backed off—I told myself I would, over and over again. No piece of ass is worth that much. But it's so rare I get to have anything that's just for me. I don't get to be selfish like that."

Eva nodded, listening for a change instead of opening her big mouth.

"I'm tired, Bee," Pink continued. "I'm tired of being a load-bearing wall. I'm tired of fixing problems. I'm tired of being patient, and kind, and watching all y'all like a mama bear. I'm tired of staying strong when I just want to get drunk as a lord and let the universe go to hell."

Eva knelt down in front of Pink, put a hand on her friend's knee. Pink took it, holding it tightly.

"Things weren't perfect when we left Tito," Pink said. "But they were better, even when we were eating nutrient bricks and trading favors for fuel. And now, everything is one big fucking trash fire, and we're trying to put it out by pissing on it. Even messing with The Fridge, which was at least a righteous pleasure, was hard and constant and so damn exhausting. This whole mech business, the monoliths . . ." She squeezed Eva's hand harder.

"And now Joe, on top of it," Eva said.

"Yeah." Pink scowled, her jaw moving like she was holding back tears. "We said our goodbyes and agreed it was for the best and moved on. Because he wasn't ready to tell Tito to fuck all the way off, and I couldn't keep my mouth shut anymore. I thought I'd never see him again. That I wouldn't have to worry about all this shit, wouldn't have to feel some kind of way about it."

"Life comes at you fast," Eva said.

"I'm tired of dodging," Pink replied. "And I'm tired of getting whacked when I'm too slow."

Eva nodded in agreement, and they sat together in silence, still holding hands. The quiet hum of the fish tank's machinery, the occasional groan and creak of the hull, even the hush of the air cyclers soothed her nerves a little. The sounds were familiar, comforting. Home.

"So wait," Eva said. "Am I the daddy bear in this scenario?"

Pink stared at her incredulously, then barked out a laugh. "You are the smallest bear that ever lived. And you ain't nobody's daddy. Lord, woman, the things that come out of your mouth."

"Made you laugh, though."

"That's my secret," Pink said. "I'm always laughing."

Otherwise you'll cry, Eva thought, but she didn't say as much. She released Pink's hand and stood, huffing out a breath. "We still have to decide what to do with Joe. Do you want to talk to him alone first?"

With pursed lips, Pink slowly nodded. "We don't have a lot of time, and we need to make that call quick like a bunny. I'll holler at you if I need backup."

"Good cop, bad cop?" Eva asked.

"All cops are bad," Pink replied. "But we can be bad at him together."

Pink was still interrogating Joe when Eva received another message from Antimatter. This one, as promised, wasn't a painful blast of psychic information but a perfectly normal audio transmission using standard encryption methods. The Proarkhe were learning fast, it seemed, which gave Eva little comfort.

If they were figuring these things out, the Artificers probably were, too.

"We need to meet immediately," the message indicated. It didn't have a location or a time, and Eva wasn't sure how to reply, since it didn't have a proper sender code. As she tried to figure this out, a loud clanging sound echoed throughout the ship, coming from the cargo bay door.

"Qué coño?" Eva muttered. The rear cameras didn't show anything, and Min and Sue were off training in the mechs. She sprinted from the bridge and nearly collided with Momoko, who had emerged from the med bay.

"What is that?" Momoko asked.

"No sé," Eva replied, though she had a suspicion. "Sit tight."

She grabbed a pistol from her room and ran for the cargo bay. Pink had flipped up her eyepatch and squinted at the door, while Joe sat in the same place Eva had left him, still cuffed to the chair. His thick eyebrows were up near his hair; he didn't look like he expected anyone, certainly.

"If that's Tito . . ." Eva let her tone carry the promise of retaliation, even as her brain insisted it was nonsense.

"If that were Tito, he'd have blown your ship to pieces," Joe said. "Come on, Alvarez, you know that."

Hearing her old name used so casually threw her off for a moment, so she just said, "Yeah."

"There's something out there," Pink said. "About three meters tall, nonorganic, but it's putting off enough heat to be visible in the infrared."

"Back up," Eva said. "I think I know what's happening." Eva stalked over to the door controls and prepped to open it, making sure the energy curtain was in place to keep the void from trying to come in along with their surprise guest.

"The hell are you—" Pink began, then stopped as soon as the door opened.

Antimatter waited outside, hovering in the rear cameras' blind spot. For some reason, Eva thought of vampires needing to be invited inside before they could enter a building, and she repressed a giggle. The giant robot person looked nothing like a vampire, though until a few weeks ago, Eva would have been convinced that the Proarkhe were equally mythical.

Silently as space, Antimatter floated inside, stumbling

slightly when her feet were pulled down by the ship's artificial gravity. That brief moment of imperfection was strangely endearing; it was hard to be completely intimidated by someone who could still stub a toe.

"Captain," Antimatter said cordially. "I've come to—" Before she finished her sentence, she suddenly retreated back out into space, her eyes blazing brightly and arm spikes extended, her stance promising violence.

"Qué rayo?" Eva asked, raising her own weapon and aiming it, first at Antimatter, then at Joe. He just sat there, his mouth open in disbelief. A cat had been resting under his chair, but now it stood on all fours, ears back, hackles up, fully bristled tail swishing around dramatically. It loosed a low growl, and a wave of psychic aggression flowed out of it.

The hair on Eva's arms stood up in response. She'd never seen one of the cats this furious, not even with each other in their petty territorial disputes around the ship. Worse, more of them appeared, posturing, emitting hisses and yowls and other threatening noises, as if they were defending their territory against an intruder.

Not just any intruder: a dangerous one.

They'd taken down Fridge agents before, and done so like assassins, with wiles rather than tooth and claw. Eva hadn't considered it at the time, but in retrospect that suggested a certain arrogance, cockiness, that those agents were easy prey and didn't warrant more effort. This, though . . . The more she thought about it, the more this looked like fear.

But then, what did that make Antimatter's reaction? The Proarkhe hovered outside, silent, her own stance alert and defensive. Like Eva's mom when a bug surprised her, except to her knowledge, Regina Alvarez didn't have hand-to-hand-combat training.

Mala sauntered in, no more than three or four kilos of calico cat, her hazel eyes trained on Antimatter. Unlike the other cats, she didn't bristle or hiss, she only watched. Instead of aggression, she exuded confidence, and what Eva would have called the cat equivalent of a raised eyebrow. Every other feline in the vicinity quieted as if waiting for her verdict, though their fur was still raised.

After a few tense moments, Mala said, "Miau." She then sat down and primly curled her tail around her paws.

"We good here?" Eva asked.

"Miau," Mala replied. She yawned, showing her sharp teeth and pink tongue. Around her, the other cats relaxed and returned to whatever they had been doing before.

Eva walked toward the energy curtain separating the cargo bay from space, then gave Antimatter a thumbs-up and waved her back in. Hesitantly at first, the Proarkhe moved toward the door, then stepped inside again, arm spikes gone.

"Sorry about that," Eva said. "I don't know what got into them."

"What are they?" Antimatter asked, her tone wary.

"Cats," Eva replied. "You haven't come across them in your . . . studies?" It felt like the wrong word, given that the Proarkhe had seemed to somehow pull things out of Eva's head psychically before, but she had no idea how the lot of them were educating themselves on the ins and outs of civilization otherwise.

Antimatter regarded Eva with her glowing blue eyes, less blazing than they had been before. "I have located them in my memories. These specimens are modified somehow?"

"Psychic, yeah."

"I . . ." Antimatter's arm spikes extended slightly, then retracted fully again. "I confess that I experienced a strangely primitive and instinctual reaction that overcame my judgment."

Eva blinked. "You what?"

"They scared the ozone right out of my vaporizers."

Mala stood up and Antimatter flinched—or the equivalent thereof, a rippling movement in all her surface components.

"Miau," Mala said, and sauntered over to the cats' container, tail raised as if she didn't have a care in the world.

"I'm not going to say they're harmless," Eva said, "but they're definitely much more squishable than you are. I don't think you have anything to worry about." Still, she thought of her mom again, of how easy it was to deal with tiny insects, and yet how people might still climb on a chair to get away from them.

Instincts were weird.

Antimatter seemed to collect herself, rising to her full height and adjusting the components of her face. Her head nearly brushed the catwalks attached to the ceiling. "Apologies. I came here to discuss the situation further." She looked at Pink and Joe as if they'd just appeared, instead of being there the entire time. "Ah, greetings. We should be formally introduced? I'm called Antimatter."

"Dr. Rebecca Jones," Pink said. "Co-captain and ship's doctor. You can call me Dr. Jones."

"Joe," Joe said. "Call me Joe." Eva raised an eyebrow but didn't speak.

"Joe is restrained?" Antimatter asked Eva. "Is he a prisoner?"

Eva shrugged. "It's complicated. Pink—Dr. Jones, you should probably—"

"I got it," Pink said. She removed Joe's leg restraints and stood him up, guiding him toward the mess. Her grasp on his elbow seemed gentle rather than hard; Eva hoped that was a good sign. After everything, she didn't want Pink to have to deal with an even more painful separation than the first had probably been. Joe coming back to her after all this time was a blow to the gut, but her misjudging his intentions would be a pair of kidney punches and a roundhouse to the face.

Once they were gone, Antimatter said, "You've made remarkable progress in little time."

Eva grinned, resisting the urge to preen. "It wasn't easy, but we're almost there."

"I'm glad," Antimatter said. "I know you had concerns about our asking you to do this, concerns that your associate shared when we met previously."

The thought of Mari soured Eva's expression immediately. "I still have concerns," Eva said. "I'm just doing the job anyway. Sometimes you have to work through the worry."

"Sensible," Antimatter said. "While you've been doing that, my people and I have been attempting to find more information about the Artificers' plans."

"What have you got?"

"Not nearly enough." Antimatter took two steps, then halted, as if she'd wanted to pace and then realized it was impossible in such a small space. "Our usual back-and-forth with them has stopped, and they've withdrawn somewhere, but we haven't found the bulk of their forces yet. There's been activity on our homeworld—you've seen that one—but it's mostly hidden from sight. No ships, and they're using traverses—smaller versions of what you call Gates—to move in and out."

Probably like the ones Eva had seen Fridge scientists developing way back when she and her crew raided their main facility—or one of them anyway. She still had those guns squirreled away, though they had both been depowered so they didn't work anymore. But maybe Antimatter would know how to fix them?

"But you still believe they're planning some kind of coordinated attack, right?" Eva asked.

"Sí," Antimatter said. "It's the most logical explanation

for this tactic, and we've found evidence of them trying this in the past."

Eva furrowed her brow. "What do you mean? I thought you were really old. Don't you remember what they've done?"

Antimatter's eyes brightened, then faded back to normal. "For us, memories are not as clear as you might think. You see me and I'm probably an elaborate machine to you, given your experiences?"

Eva flushed with embarrassment at the assumption but nodded in acknowledgment.

"And you look like a furless—well, they're extinct, so never mind. The point is, our memories are long, but they degrade. Sometimes we wipe them on purpose, you know, clear the cache." Antimatter tapped her leg idly. "It can be kind of nice, actually. Reliving experiences from a long time ago, picking which ones we want to keep . . ."

"Decluttering," Eva said.

Antimatter's irises narrowed, then widened. "Ah, sí, like that. 'Out with the old,' as your saying goes. You can keep and honor some historical artifacts without ascribing equal value to all of them."

"But your point is, you don't remember the last time the Artificers pulled this trick."

"Exactly." Antimatter's tapping stopped and she rested a hand on her hip-equivalent. "Even our leaders—the Radices—had to consult the archives, and their memories are often more thorough than most. Though almost all of us still maintain our own individual experiences of the Cataclysm." Antimatter paused. "We very much hope that is not what they are planning."

Cataclysm sounded bad, but before Eva could ask, Antimatter had moved on.

"The monoliths are beacons," she explained. "They transmit

as well as monitor traffic between the traverses—at least, we believe they might have that capacity, because otherwise they've found some way to access traverse logs."

"Gates, you mean," Eva said.

"Yes, Gates. The point is, the monoliths are mysterious, and indestructible, so it gets the targeted systems worried. They scare people into submission without the Artificers having to actually fight."

"So it's all a bluff?" Eva asked.

"No, no," Antimatter said. "They definitely have the planet destroyer, on top of the fleetbreakers and other forces. But better to deploy their assets strategically rather than risk losing them."

Eva remembered the complete and utter blackness of the space around that planet, the one Antimatter said was their homeworld. How many stars had the Artificers destroyed? How was such a thing even physically possible? And how could anyone, any member of any sentient species with that kind of power, ever make the conscious choice to wield it?

War was bad enough, but that level of annihilation was utterly evil. She wanted to believe even someone as shitty as Tito would never go so far.

Then again, maybe he would, if he had the power to do so. The thought that he was working with these Artificers made her skin prickly.

"So the plan stays the same," Eva said. "We get the last mech, we figure out how to use them against the Artificers, and then everything goes back to normal."

Antimatter's face did that odd shifting thing again. "I don't think your 'normal' is ever coming back, but at least you'll be defended. Once you use the weapon, the Artificers will crawl back into whatever black hole they've been hiding in, fix their damage, and hopefully turn their attention to less difficult targets."

"I'll take it." Eva folded her arms over her chest. "How do I contact you once I have all the mechs?"

"I'll contact you again soon," Antimatter replied. "I think my people should bring you on board our ship for safety, but our leaders don't all agree."

"I'd rather stay on my own ship, gracias," Eva said. Then again, having extra protection around in case Tito or his buddies came knocking might be good. She resolved to talk that over with Pink as soon as they handled all the other problems on their ever-growing list.

"I'll be going, then. Until next we meet." Antimatter gestured at Eva and turned away, then launched herself out into space and disappeared from view.

Eva blinked. Did she just shoot finger guns at me? she thought. Shaking her head and chuckling, she headed for the mess to let Pink know the cargo bay was hers again.

After that, she continued to the bridge and sank down into the pilot's chair, still empty while Min and Sue played with the mechs. A quick search through the system alerts showed she'd had a call come in on the private channel while she was busy. That meant it was one of four people: Mari, Pete, Regina, or . . .

Artificial heart in her throat, Eva queued up the message. No, it wasn't Vakar, it was just Mari. Her heart sank, then set her whole chest on fire as she remembered what her sister had tried to pull right before she was dropped off. Sinvergüenza. She almost deleted the damn thing but decided to wait until after she heard the contents before unleashing her full rage. With a finger flick, she set it to play, and Mari's voice filled her ears.

"I hope this message finds you safe and that you're . . . enjoying success in your mission. I've thought about what you said, and you were right. I made poor choices for what I thought were good reasons, but I violated your trust, and then I tried to make a very hurtful deal."

Ay, jódete, Eva thought.

"I want to make it up to you," Mari continued. "So: Vakar is in the Trabbert System, between the fourth and fifth planets, on an asteroid at the attached coordinates. I'm not entirely sure of the nature of his mission, but he hasn't communicated with anyone since before he passed through the Gate to get there. I can confirm there is a small Fridge operation of some kind that he may be monitoring, so in all likelihood he's undercover and trying to maintain secrecy. I'm sorry again for what I did, and for not being able to confirm for you that Vakar is safe and well. I also hope you don't do something rash like rushing off to find him, since you're doing much more important work right now, but maybe the knowledge of his location will at least be a comfort to you." After a pause, she said, "I do love you, you know, whatever you may think. I'm not very good at it, but I'll try to be better."

The message ended there, and Eva stared at the consoles in front of her, considering the notion that the one thing Mari wasn't good at was the most important thing in the universe. Funny how that happened.

She knew where Vakar was. Or at least, where he was supposed to be, assuming nothing had happened to him. His superiors must not have been worried—or were they? The message hadn't been clear on that. Mari had only said Vakar wasn't communicating with others, and that he was at a known Fridge base. But she also hadn't mentioned anything about anyone trying to save him or pull him out of the mission, even with the whole monolith business going on. They couldn't have forgotten about him, could they? Or was it possible he couldn't be contacted for some reason?

Mari was wrong about one thing, at least: knowing where Vakar was didn't comfort Eva in the slightest. It made her stomach hurt, her chest tighten, her skin burn like she'd just walked out into the full sun of a desert with no protection. Her imagination churned with scenarios where Vakar was lying alone on that asteroid, dying, dead, ignored because he was only one person in a universe where bigger problems were occupying everyone who could potentially help him.

At that moment, Min and Sue bounced in, giddy from their turn with the mechs. They chattered excitedly to each other in that special language people developed when they were on the same wavelength, half sentences and allusions to things only they knew. They trailed off when they noticed Eva.

"You okay, Cap?" Min asked. Her dark eyes peered into Eva's. "I came to take over the ship again so you could sync with the new mech, but you look sick."

"I'm okay," Eva said. She held out a hand and accepted the mech keys from Sue, then gave a friendly salute and left the bridge. Almost on autopilot, she entered her room, dressed in her spacesuit, and loaded up on a full complement of weapons, ammo, and other useful toys.

Some part of her screamed warnings, but she let them wash over her, through her, as if they weren't there at all.

"What are you doing?" Pink asked as soon as Eva stepped into the cargo bay.

"Getting Vakar," Eva replied.

"He called you?"

"No, Mari told me where he is. Top secret mission on a Fridge base."

"Fuck me to tears." Pink put a hand on Eva's shoulder. "Are you sure we should go get him? What if you break his cover?"

Eva looked up at her friend, wondering why everything was

slightly blurred. She tasted salt, ran a hand over her face to remove the sudden moisture. Then she growled.

"Me cago en diez!" Eva yelled. "Me cago en ella, me cago en la mierda, y me cago en la hora que yo nací, carajo!" She lurched over to the punching bag and launched a kick at it that tore the vinyl. A steady stream of pellets trickled out, piling up on the floor.

"Hey," Pink said quietly. "Easy. You came in here with a plan. What were you gonna do?"

Eva sat on the floor and buried her head in her hands. "I was going to take a mech," she murmured. "I was going to use its stealth mode to sneak in and scope the place out, and I was going to find Vakar and pull him out of whatever fucking hole he's in and drag him back here."

Silence fell. A moment later, Joe whistled. Eva glanced up sharply, barely catching the annoyed look Pink directed at him.

"Sounds legit," Pink said. "Do it. Go get him."

"I can't," Eva said, her voice strained with misery. "I can't risk the mech like that."

"What's the risk?" Pink said. "Does that system have a monolith?"

"No."

"So the Artificers don't have eyes there. And no one can steal the mech without the key. Plus, I doubt any random Fridge flunkies are gonna be able to take it in a fight if they try to start shit. As rescues go, it's probably worth a try."

It was tempting. So, so tempting. All Eva had wanted for weeks was to know Vakar was okay, and now she might be able to find out. He was Schrödinger's cat, and Mari had just taken the lid off the box and dared Eva to look inside.

"Cap," Min said over the speakers. "We all want Vakar to be safe. Go find him."

Sue stood in the entrance to the cargo bay, her face pink. "I'd do it for Min," she said.

Momoko came up behind Sue and nodded. "And I for Leroy."

Pink and Joe pointedly looked away from each other, Pink at the wall and Joe at the floor.

"We all need some sleep anyway," Pink said. "Unlike Vakar."

Eva's vision blurred again. "Thanks," she whispered.

Relief and fear warred inside her. Pink was right. The mech was a powerhouse, and this was a small operation, not the main Fridge facility. She wasn't storming Nuvesta with a pistol. She could do this, come back, and get the final mech before Tito could go fuck himself twice.

The heavy bag's contents continued to leak out with a gentle hiss, like sands in an hourglass warning her that she was running out of time. She only hoped she wasn't already too late.

Chapter 9

A PAIR OF RAGGED CLAWS

The Trabbert System had asteroids like a crehnisk had parasites, and the one that supposedly contained Vakar wasn't even the largest. It was about ten kilometers long and eight wide, pockmarked and uneven, bulbous like an inflated gas sac. Based on the readings the mech was picking up, something was strange about the interior, but it was difficult to detect anything specific through the layers of rock and metal and other elements. No security drones patrolled the area, no satellites orbited this particular chunk of detritus . . . Nothing at all indicated the place was worth a second look, or even a first one.

Eva wondered if Mari had tricked her, used reverse psychology or some other manipulative tactic to get her to come all the way here by herself for no good reason. But then, Mari couldn't have known Eva would do this, risk one of the mechs this way. Eva herself hadn't known until she did it, and she'd almost turned back more than once with a sick feeling in the pit of her stomach.

Get in, get Vakar, get out. Nothing fancy. The mech could stealth, it was easier to maneuver than *La Sirena Negra*, and even if this was all a trap to get Eva alone so Mari could steal the mech, Eva could take anyone in a fight. Or run away before they even realized she was there.

Still, one paranoid thought after another rolled around in Eva's head, and not for the first time, she was tired of a long history of people lying to her and making her second-guess the smallest things.

Then she found the tunnel, and at least she knew this couldn't be a total bust.

"Why'd it have to be tunnels?" she muttered to herself as she brought the mech in for a landing. She'd seen enough of the damn things in the past few days for an entire lifetime.

The tunnel wasn't closed off, merely sealed with an energy curtain like the one on her own spaceship. Did it have an atmosphere inside that needed to be kept in? Was this even a real asteroid?

One thing was for sure: the small tunnel wouldn't accommodate the mech, so she had to either give up or leave it outside. Mierda. She drifted for a few minutes, scanning the area and pondering her predicament. Eventually she found a big cavity and hid the crouched mech inside, tucking its key into a pocket of her spacesuit so she wouldn't lose it.

The asteroid had no gravity, so Eva activated her gravboots and moved slowly toward the tunnel entrance, scanning the area for any signs of life. Nothing. No guards, no workers, not a soul in sight. Not even automated defenses. The lack of security surprised her. Was this place so low-priority for The Fridge that they didn't care if strangers came knocking? Or was this a whole other level of mind trick to keep anyone from noticing it was here in the first place?

Staying as low as possible, Eva crept all the way to the tunnel and peered inside. Dim red lights jutted from the ceiling, barely enough to show her the way forward. The shape of the opening and the roughness of the walls and ground suggested this was a natural rather than artificial hole, but as soon as she stepped past the energy curtain, her body weight returned as gravity asserted itself. Her suit's sensors indicated it was less than Earth's gravity but more than Earth's moon's; her step was a little more jaunty than usual, but she couldn't move in big, boisterous leaps.

Deeper into the tunnel she went, continuing to scan for any signs of life or technology. The only indication that she wasn't wasting her time was the continued presence of those dim lights, bathing everything in a sickly crimson. Had there been an emergency? Were these lights marking some escape route from whatever was at the end of the tunnel? And if everyone had escaped—had anyone escaped?—what had happened to Vakar?

Or maybe the lights are just red, Eva told herself. No need to assume the worst.

Eva was grateful that her isohelmet muffled her breathing, because to her it sounded as if she were panting like a hot puppy. While the lack of atmosphere outside had made her steps silent, inside every scuff of her boot against the dirt and rock seemed to echo until she couldn't believe no one had come out to investigate. Was the place really empty? Abandoned? Or were they biding their time, waiting for her to come closer so they could spring a trap?

With a snort, Eva stopped moving, loosening her death grip on her pistol. This is ridiculous, she thought. If someone is here, they know I'm coming. If no one is here, I don't need to try to sneak, which I'm totally failing at anyway. Acelera, ya.

Still wielding her weapon, she began to walk more normally. Nothing leaped out at her or attacked from a distance. Up ahead, a glow appeared and slowly brightened as she got closer. Unlike the red lights, this source of illumination was coppery, and grew increasingly rose gold as she approached its source. When she finally reached the end of the tunnel, she almost didn't notice, because she was so distracted by the unbelievable sight that awaited her.

An enormous cavern filled the core of the asteroid, easily the size of a whole neighborhood in Nuvesta. More astonishing, it teemed with luminous plantlike life: carpets of pale orange moss or fungus covered various surfaces, with larger yellowish things like anemones lifting clustered tendrils toward the ceiling. Mucus-like rock formations jutted from the ground, more undersea coral than stalagmite, and soft trees like giant pink dandelions glinted as if sprinkled generously with glitter. The sensors on her suit suggested it smelled sweet and sour, honey and vinegar with a hint of salt.

Most unbelievable, though, was the golden lake occupying the center of it all. Eva assumed it was a lake, though it was difficult to tell without touching it, to confirm it was filled with liquid and not something else. Her sensors had no idea what it was, and there was no wind to send waves rippling over its surface, no animals to—wait, that wasn't true. There was life everywhere, creatures she might have called insects if they were on a planet, drifting or flitting around between the plant tendrils, settling on the broad faces of mushroom-like clusters sprouting from the side of a rocky pillar. Larger things scuttled across the ground or clung to the thicker plant stalks, camouflaged by their own bioluminescence.

But the lake—how was that possible? What could it be made of?

A flicker of darkness in the distance caught her eye. She quickly sidestepped out of the tunnel's entrance and hid behind a glittery tree, then pulled up her isohelmet's zoom option to get a better look.

There was the robotic welcome she'd been expecting earlier: a drone slowly made its way toward the golden fluid from parts unknown. It flew down toward the lake's surface and extended a tube, using it to suck up a bunch of the liquid and store it in a translucent container hanging down from its butt region. Once the container was full, the drone stopped slurping and flew back to wherever it came from, disappearing into the terrain and foliage.

A pair of strong arms wrapped around Eva, restraining her own arms, lifting her off the ground and carrying her backward. She immediately grabbed the hands and tried to break the hold with her elbows, throwing herself forward to loosen the grip and get some leverage. Whoever had her just turned and dropped to the ground, pinning her facedown underneath their body. Because of the lower gravity, they bounced slightly.

"Eva, stop."

The voice was barely a whisper, heavily modulated, but every muscle in her body simultaneously sighed in relief and unclenched.

"Vakar." She wanted to roll over and look at him, but she had to admit the current position had its perks. Or it would if they weren't both wearing spacesuits. As soon as he seemed satisfied she wasn't going to continue fighting, he eased his weight off her, still caging her with his arms. She rolled over carefully, coming face-to-face with the metallic sheen of his Wraith armor. Her own isohelmet was opaque, and she kept it that way, in case someone else surprised them.

"How did you find me?" Vakar asked.

"Mari did."

"How did she find me?"

"Not a clue." She wished she could see him, smell him, because his questions were being delivered in a near monotone whose inflections were impossible to read. Memories flashed through her mind, of when they'd reunited after her year in cryo, and she hadn't realized it was him because he was doing his best impression of a smoothly efficient quasi-military secret agent. Which he was.

"Why are you here?" he asked.

That one was harder to answer. To make sure he was safe? To warn him about the monoliths? To beg him to come back with her? Because she missed him so much she couldn't handle their separation for another moment, and as soon as the opportunity presented itself, she'd run off like a complete and utter fool?

How had he managed for a whole damn year when she was in cryo? Barely any time had passed for her by comparison and she was already loca pal carajo.

"The monoliths," she said, deciding that was at least the most pertinent part of the truth.

"What monoliths?" he asked.

"No one told you?" She couldn't believe his bosses hadn't even sent him a message, a warning, anything. Or that he hadn't picked up on the broadcasts himself.

"I have not had any contact with anyone since my last transmission to my superiors. Total commlink silence was mandated."

"When was your last message?"

"Approximately twenty cycles ago."

Madre de dios, that was definitely before everything went to shit. Also not long after he'd last spoken to her.

He continued, "I presume if it were a significant enough situation, I would have been contacted. That I was not implies my mission is still a priority."

That pissed Eva off. "What's a bigger priority than the whole resingado universe being under attack?"

Vakar fell silent, then quietly got to his feet, offering her a hand up. She took it, rising less gracefully.

"I am waiting for a human named Smedley," he said.

"Smedley what?" Eva asked. "Or is Smedley his last name?"

"We are not certain." He turned away, scanning the cavern. "He is one of the remaining upper-echelon members of The Fridge, and we obtained intelligence that he inspects this location personally on a regular basis. It is the only firm lead we have on his whereabouts. If I can tag him for tracking, it will place us in an incredibly strong position for potential future information regarding Fridge movements and personnel."

That was a pretty solid mission, she had to admit, but she still thought hers was a bigger deal, all things considered. "Under the circumstances, maybe your buddy Smedley isn't going to make the rounds for a while yet. Or ever again."

"Explain," Vakar said, as if even the few moments he'd taken with her were an imposition.

Eva told herself he was being efficient. Also that if she hadn't spoken to anyone in three weeks, she was bound to be a little brusque, too.

"A few cycles ago, indestructible monoliths appeared in space near almost every Gate in a populated area," she said. "They're all broadcasting a message: surrender or die. It's enemy Proarkhe called Artificers doing it, and other Proarkhe are trying to stop them from invading or attacking or whatever their plan is, and our crew is out collecting giant mechs that are supposed to save the universe somehow."

Vakar turned back around. "Giant mechs?"

"They're . . . incredible. One is outside, if you want to see it."

"I cannot abandon my mission." He turned away again, but more slowly, as if reluctant. "If no overt aggressions have occurred yet, I may be able to finish here and then join you. Unless a new mission takes precedence."

What else could she say? He didn't sound like he wanted convincing. His work was important, and she'd certainly managed to cause enough problems for him already.

They stood silently together, for how long Eva didn't know. The strange creatures in the cavern moved about according to their own whims and needs, glowing softly, and the robotic drone flew back and forth from the lake again. How long had it been doing that? Would the lake eventually run dry? What was the stuff in it, anyway?

Before she could ask Vakar any of her questions, he said, "You should go."

After weeks of worry, of telling herself Vakar was fine despite her imagination insisting otherwise, of contemplating what bargains she might strike with the universe for the simple confirmation of his continued well-being, that brief statement hit like a sledgehammer to the wall of her self-control.

Eva began to laugh.

If she hadn't known her isohelmet muffled her voice, she would have been mortified at the prospect of attracting the attention of the local wildlife or worse, but even so she flipped the volume off completely after a moment to be safe. The laughter kept rolling out of her, though, in giddy waves, as uncontrollable as her extremely fool-ass decision to come here had been.

"I should go," she said. She repeated the words a few times, putting different emphasis on them, each iteration sparking another fit. Unable to catch her breath, she doubled over, resting her hands on her thighs. Forget going, she should never have come. She'd jeopardized not only Vakar's mission but her own, showing up like this and barging in like she owned the place.

And he was being so damn sensible about it. Standing there, calm and composed—no, he was looking at her now, probably wondering if she'd lost her mind. If she'd given away his position, made his weeks of comm silence irrelevant. He'd grabbed her, tackled her, questioned her, all in as neat and professional a way as one would expect of a Wraith.

No love, just business. Why had she expected otherwise?

Maybe because she had done something wildly unwise and, while blaming love was a convenient excuse, she had to admit it was mostly fear. Fear that something had happened to him, that he was too far away for her to help, that she'd never see him or smell him again.

With the fate of the universe allegedly resting on her shoulders, at least in part, had come a sense of power and agency she hadn't felt in years. And even when she'd been on Tito's crew, at her most brutal and incandescently cocky, part of her had always known she was only as good as her last win. She was only as strong as the strongest person she'd beaten. And you couldn't beat the unknown, not with fists and elbows and knees, not with a gun or a blade.

So here she was, scrambling for a sense of control over what had been, until a few minutes earlier, a gaping void of insecurity and worry and ignorance. Now she knew Vakar was fine, but it didn't make a damn bit of difference to her mission, except she'd wasted a bunch of time she and her crew didn't have, and put the whole universe on the line to fix her own feelings.

Eva heaved a breath and straightened, the laughter finally out of her system. "I really should go," she said, more softly this time. Not that Vakar could hear her, since she'd muted her isohelmet.

With as casual a wave as she could muster, Eva passed Vakar and headed back for the tunnel. She had barely begun cycling through various self-recriminations when she found herself pulled back into the shadows again, tucked against Vakar's chest. At least she was facing forward this time. Had he decided he wanted a hug? No, that didn't make sense.

Then she heard it: voices coming from the tunnel.

No way could she be so lucky as to show up just in time for Vakar to finally be able to complete his mission, after all this waiting. More likely, she had somehow triggered an alarm and whoever it was had come to check things out. Then again, this place was running so low-profile that maybe this really was good fortune.

Coincidence was just causality seen from inside the maze instead of above it.

The voices drew closer. One boomed, confident, the kind of person who spoke from the diaphragm and enunciated everything carefully. Eva hated him immediately. The other was oddly familiar. Grating, a little whiny, but also weirdly arrogant?

"Well, actually—"

Eva didn't hear the rest of whatever he said. The owner of the grating voice was none other than the inimitable Miles fucking Erck. He was inimitable because no one would ever want to imitate him, because he was a debatably sentient pile of crehnisk shit, with an ego whose mass rivaled a gas giant and was equally full of hot air. If she were forced to choose between being locked in a room with him for an hour or wrestling a needle-bear again, she would have to think about it, and she might even ask how big the needle-bear was.

Qué coño hace esta comemierda aquí? Eva wondered. She'd left Miles at a public transit station on the other side of the universe a few days earlier, after The Forge had respectfully declined to hire him on account of he fucking sucked.

The other man with him was stocky and muscular, or wearing a spacesuit designed to look form-fitting with a particular physique. Short dark hair, full beard trimmed neat and tidy, cheeks ruddy—from talking to Miles, maybe, unless that was their natural color. He held his head high, shoulders back, and he walked like someone who knew anyone walking toward him would step out of his way. Eva used to trip assholes like him for sport, because inevitably they were mucho ruido y pocas nueces.

He also seemed to be sweating profusely, given the sheen of moisture on his face, which was strange. Most spacesuits had built-in temperature controls that adjusted automatically.

A pair of guards trailed behind them, helmets dark. Their builds and height suggested they were truateg, but if they were mercs, they weren't wearing any identifying insignia. They were, however, carrying large plasma rifles, and probably a few other weapons in various sheaths or pockets.

Vakar's mission wasn't to stop them, Eva remembered. He had to tag one of them—Smedley, he'd said, presumably the human with Miles—and start tracking his movements. If he succeeded, he'd be allowed to leave.

Despite the presence of the most obnoxious human in the universe, Eva suddenly felt much more cheerful.

Vakar released her and flowed past her like water around a rock. A weapon had appeared in his hand as if by magic—no, not a weapon, a fancy long-distance DNA scanner. In her experience, they were easy enough to fool with the right tech, but maybe his bosses back at the quennian fleet had a new design that would bypass existing countermeasures. There also seemed to be a nanotransmitter attachment, one that would fire off a nearly undetectable tracking device, but it might not penetrate Smedley's spacesuit. Whether it did or not, he'd be more likely to find it later, especially once it sent out its first homing signal.

"—should still be inert," Miles was saying when Eva adjusted her sensors to hear him better. "Its feeding habits aren't as thoroughly documented as they could be, though."

"That's why we brought protection," Smedley said, gesturing at the mercs without turning. "They'll be with you at every moment. Real close. Good friends. Like butter and pasta."

Butter and pasta? Eva thought. What the fuck did that mean?

"Well, actually," Miles said, "I can take care of myself. I was at the battle on Pupillae, and the one against the Forge base in Suidana, you know."

He hid under a table and was locked in Eva's cargo hold for those two events, respectively. She rolled her eyes.

"That's phenomenal, really top-shelf," Smedley boomed. "I missed out on Suidana. I was getting my appendix replaced. Had them put in a new one, and add an extra one while they were at it. Always good to have a backup, I say."

Eva was glad they stopped talking for a few moments, because she had to replay everything he had just said in her mind. It made no fucking sense whatsoever. This guy was upper echelon at The Fridge?

Vakar had begun to creep forward, presumably to get a better shot, but Eva stayed put. Bad enough she had already made things harder for him with her presence, she wasn't about to wreck his whole mission by doing something foolish like stepping on a twig or whatever. Not that she noticed any twigs lying around; it was mostly the blobby, coral-like rock protrusions, some covered by glowing plants. One of the bug-creatures fluttered up, a kind of spidery dragonfly thing with two heads, and she resisted the urge to swat at it, even when it decided to land on her isohelmet and unload a mass of glittery waste.

Figures, she thought. I don't get shit on enough as it is.

In the distance, Miles was doing something to the drone that siphoned liquid from the lake. The mercs stood nearby, backs to the lake, scanning the perimeter, while Smedley had crossed his arms and periodically, for no apparent reason, dropped into a squat and then stood back up. He did it slowly, and at one point he kicked his legs out at the bottom of the squat like he was dancing, then rose again.

The surface of the lake moved. Eva almost missed it, watching Smedley, but it happened again a few moments later.

Had Vakar seen it? Should she warn him? No, she had to stay put. He was a dozen meters away already anyway, and it wasn't worth the risk, not when it was probably just some weird asteroid lake fish. She tuned back in to Miles and Smedley.

"This one will have to be replaced entirely," Miles said. "I can make it run for a few more cycles, but this part will keep decoupling without the proper lubrication."

"Too bad humans don't produce more natural lubricants, like the dytryrc," Smedley replied. "Great homeworld they have. Slides everywhere."

"Well, actually," Miles said, "Proarkhe lubricants have a different chemical composition, so using alternatives would potentially cause more damage."

"Right, right," Smedley replied. "What's good for the goose is bad for the gardener. Say no more."

The lake rippled again, more noticeably. Had an eyestalk briefly surfaced? It was hard to tell from so far away. She cycled through the various visual modes in her isohelmet, but none were able to penetrate the strange golden liquid.

"Almost finished there, champeen?" Smedley asked. "I need to see a man about a horse, if you know what I mean."

"You have to . . . use the facilities?" Miles asked, his tone more confused than usual. Eva could sympathize.

"No, no," Smedley said. But he didn't get to finish explaining himself.

A huge crablike creature erupted from the water, skittering forward on long, spindly legs, and lashed out with a claw three times the size of Eva. It grabbed one of the guards, waved it around wildly, then flung it away like a tantrummy toddler throwing a toy. The other merc reacted quickly, raising their plasma rifle and firing, but every shot they took rebounded off the critter's glittering gold carapace. Plants and moss and rock sizzled around them from the energy ricochets, sending up tiny plumes of coppery smoke.

"Qué coño," Eva muttered to herself. She started to retreat farther into the shadows, but an incredibly terrible and important thing caught her notice.

Vakar was barely a few meters away from the rampaging monster.

Chapter 10

LASER PARTY

Eva crept forward, trying to keep an eye on everyone involved in the mess by the lake. The optimistic part of her insisted Vakar could take care of himself, no problem, and she could continue to be patient and watch and wait for him to return to her side. The rest of her screamed that she needed to hurry, run, get over there already before the damn golden crab monstrosity grabbed her partner and shook him like a dog with a knotted rope.

She gripped her pistol, but if the merc's shots were any indication, it wouldn't do her any good. Every single one bounced off the crab's shell, and if the comemierda wasn't more careful, they'd end up hitting Miles or Smedley. All they seemed to be doing was making the crab angry, drawing its attention . . .

Maybe that was the plan? Buy time for the others to escape? Miles and Smedley had indeed begun to retreat, though they were doing it backward, which slowed them both down. Smedley even seemed to be taking pictures? He made right angles with his thumb and forefinger on each hand and held them up like he was framing, which made no more sense than anything he'd done so far.

Vakar, meanwhile, tried to get a clear shot at Smedley. Eva appreciated his commitment to the mission, but she also wanted to drag him to a safer vantage point. But she had to keep from being seen, or everything would be completamente jodido.

Miles finally got far enough away that he apparently decided he could safely run for it. He turned and started a bouncy sprint for the exit, weaving through the strange glowing plants and brushing aside the buglike creatures that got in his way. His form was a dark shadow against all the luminescence around him, making him easy to see, for her at least. Eva had no idea how the shiny crab-monster tracked its prey.

A cry signaled the inglorious end of the remaining merc, or at least their temporary and violent removal from the fray due to being repeatedly battered against a nearby rock. The crab didn't stop to savor its victory, though. Skittering sideways, it loosed a strangely musical noise, between a low note on a tuba and a bass guitar. Based on its trajectory, its target seemed to be Smedley.

Wait, mierda, if it got Smedley then Vakar's mission was a bust. But if she showed herself, then his mission was also a bust.

Or was it? If Vakar stayed in the shadows and Eva stepped into the light, Smedley would never know Vakar had been there. He'd know someone had, but not who—assuming he didn't figure out who Eva was—and he wouldn't know why, though he could guess. Then again, since this place was supposed to be supersecret, having anyone unexpected show up might start a mole hunt that would oust whoever had gotten Vakar's bosses this information in the first place.

So she'd try for secrecy but prioritize Smedley's escape. She wished she could coordinate with Vakar, but if he was maintaining strict comms silence, she wasn't going to break it.

Snaking her arm around a rock, Eva shot at one of the crab monster's eyestalks. She hit its carapace, and it slowed down and peered around. Smedley gained ground, though unlike Miles, he continued to move backward instead of sprinting away. Miles had slowed, too, clutching his side like he had a stitch, and glancing back to gauge how far he was from doom.

Get to the tunnel, comemierdas, Eva thought. The crab would be too big to fit inside, and they could meander all they wanted back to their ship or whatever as soon as they were safe.

But Smedley seemed to have no instinct for self-preservation. He picked up a random rock and tossed it at the creature, watching with interest when it bounced harmlessly off its shell. Eva shot it again, hoping to provide further distraction and perhaps encourage Smedley to speed up.

Instead, the strange, sweaty man grabbed the lip of what looked like a shelf of glowing oyster mushrooms and began to climb, aided by the lower gravity. Puffs of glittering spores rained on the ground and his spacesuit from the bottoms of the plants.

Eva had lost track of Vakar, but he must have a clear shot of Smedley like this. She hoped. Not that it would help if the fool became crab food.

Smedley peered around the cavern like he was looking for something. Or someone? Had he figured out he and Miles weren't alone? Was he trying to see where the mercs had landed? Her suit was already in ambient-temp mode, to trick infrared sensors, but that might not be enough. She was, after all, a dark shadow in a bright room, just like him and Miles. Aside from the glitter poop on her helmet.

The crab monster's legs sliced through the landscape, its gold carapace reflecting the other colors of the various plants and creatures. It seemed to have lost track of Smedley, but the utter maniac waved at it, and it made a beeline for him once again. He was going to die. What the fuck was wrong with him?

Eva reacted on instinct. Darting forward, she fired at the crab, then hid behind a pillar and started to climb, too. High ground would hopefully help, though getting underneath it might expose a soft belly that would be less impervious to attack. The joints also had potential. Then again, she didn't need to kill it, she just needed to distract it long enough for Smedley to get his head together and leave. Why the hell wouldn't he?

Smedley didn't even have a weapon, unless his copious sweat counted. Wait, was he talking now? She tuned him back in.

"Hello!" he shouted. "Look at you! You're great, just swell. Could I get you to come over so I can take a sample?"

Madre de dios, Eva thought. He wants a sample from the enormous killer crab-spider. Does he do this often? How is he still alive?

Eva's foot hit something that must have been a nest, because a swarm of neon-yellow mosquito-like critters the size of her fist rose from around her boot. A few smacked against her spacesuit ineffectually, while others hovered around her like she was trying to steal their honey.

It attracted the crab's attention away from Smedley, fortunately or otherwise. The long legs brought it toward her in a sideways rush that had her scrambling to get higher, while still staying on the far side of the pillar so Smedley couldn't see her.

The crab's claw shot out, snapping closed around Eva's perch and shearing it off. She leaped to the next closest one, catching the lip of a tentacle that might have been animal or plant. It immediately sucked up her hand and closed around it like a mouth. Biting back a scream, Eva tried to tug loose, only to find the sucker releasing her as the crab careened into the pillar it was attached to. Chunks of rock and plant-animal flew, and so did Eva.

She twisted into a shoulder roll as she landed, coming to her feet with her pistol extended. Worrying about Smedley was now low on her list of concerns, right under "don't get eaten by a crab-spider monster before you finish saving the universe." She fired a few more shots and continued putting as many obstacles as she could between her and the creature, but it mowed them all down mercilessly. There wouldn't be much left of the asteroid habitat if it kept coming like this.

The drone robot returned from wherever it had gone and began to siphon from the lake again. As soon as it touched the liquid's surface, the crab skidded to a halt and turned around, as if it heard or felt something wrong. As a test, Eva aimed at the lake itself and fired, the kinetic round from her pistol striking the surface and rippling out in a way that suggested something more viscous than water.

The crab-spider made that strange bassy noise again and took a few steps toward the fluid, then diverted toward Smedley, who still waved his arms and hooted like a demented owl. Did he want to die? No, more likely he didn't think he could. Some people would wrestle a needle-bear thinking they were getting a really spiky hug.

And some people would jump on the back of a crab-spider like they were at a space rodeo. Even though Eva saw Smedley do it, saw him jump and land on the creature's carapace and teeter precariously before hunkering down, for a few seconds she genuinely thought her imagination had taken over her vision. Surely no one would do something so unbelievably dangerous.

Smedley tried to stab the thing with what looked like a thick needle device. It must not have worked, because he did it three times and looked more frustrated with each attempt. Before he could go for a fourth, the crab bucked him off and he flew, away from the lake but in the general direction of the exit. He lay still, on his back with his arms spread.

Mierda, mojón y porquería, Eva thought. She raced toward him to check his vitals as best she could through his spacesuit, to see if the damn crab had killed him or not, but she was intercepted before she could reach him.

The crab-spider loomed in front of her, clacking its massive claws. Eva had a small explosive with a remote detonator, but if the thing's carapace was as impervious to explosions as it was to plasma fire, that would do her no good at all.

If she could use it on the lake, though . . . The crab seemed to be attracted to movement in the liquid, and an explosion would certainly cause movement. Maybe its house was under there? Babies?

Regardless, it might get the creature out of the way long enough for her to check on Smedley. And possibly get him the hell out, since he seemed to have no sense of self-preservation.

Eva opened the pocket with the explosive and fished it out, but before she could throw it, the crab charged. She once again leaped into a shoulder roll, but the creature caught her calf in a viselike grip and hauled her into the air. It flung her around a few times before releasing her, at which point she flew a dozen meters and landed on a surprisingly spongy surface.

Sadly, it turned out to be the center of a cluster of tube-tendrils like the one that tried to sucker her hand before. Several similar tubes waved at her, and one lashed out at her arm. Eva twisted away, struggling to her feet and staggering out of the thing. Pain lanced through her left shoulder and a few of her ribs, and her right knee protested her weight, even reduced by the lower gravity.

The lake was on her left, close enough that she'd be able to throw the explosive in it. To her right, the crab turned in a slow circle, as if looking for more prey. Maybe she could wait for it to get bored and leave on its own?

But what if it saw Vakar? No, she couldn't take the chance. Saying a prayer to the Virgin for luck, Eva drew her arm back and lobbed the explosive toward the lake. It arced beautifully, landing less than a meter away and then rolling the rest of the distance. As soon as it broke the surface, Eva pulled up the detonator routine on her commlink and triggered it.

The explosion sent golden liquid flying everywhere. It splattered on the shore of the lake, on nearby plants, even on a few hapless critters startled into flight.

The crab-spider freaked out immediately and raced back toward the lake, as Eva had hoped it would. Within moments, the creature disappeared entirely under the surface. Its huge bulk made the merest ripple, which was soon gone. The whole experience might have been discarded as some wild hallucination, except for the wide swath of destruction left behind.

Eva crawled behind the nearest cover as fast as she could, her injuries protesting. Smedley had probably seen her, and perhaps Miles as well, but with any luck they would assume one of the mercs had intervened. They might have survived, after all, though she wasn't in the mood to send out a rescue party. Let The Fridge handle their own people.

Leaning against a hard pillar of rock, Eva turned up the audio sensors on her isohelmet. She wasn't about to peek to see where the others were, but maybe she could at least hear them coming.

"Well, that was bracing," Smedley announced from somewhere to her left. He seemed to be stomping through the terrain with no regard for stealth, or fear of attracting the crab's attention. After a minute or two, he paused in his progress and said, "Hmm, what's this?" before continuing on his way. Eventually he reached the exit, where Miles awaited.

"Do you know what this is?" Smedley asked.

"Let me see," Miles replied.

"Look with your eyes, not your hands," Smedley said.

Eva's own eyes nearly rolled out of their sockets. Miles needing to be ordered around like a toddler was so typical.

"I remember something like this from a memo," Miles said slowly. "But why would it be here?"

"Where there's smoke, there's a cigar," Smedley said. "Let's take a look outside."

Alarms went off in Eva's head. What could they have found, and why would it prompt them to go outside to search for something? Her explosive was in the lake, and there shouldn't have been any shrapnel. Had she dropped something? She began to pat herself down. Her pistol was in its holster, snug under her arm. Her vibroblade was sheathed. The only pocket she'd opened was the one with the explosive, and—

"Eva," Vakar said, startling her into a defensive posture that made her injuries sing in terrible harmony.

"Vakar," she said. "Did you tag him?"

"Yes," Vakar replied. He hunkered down next to her, almost glowing from the reflections of the surroundings in his metallic armor. "Preliminary data suggests the mission was a failure, unfortunately."

"I'm so sorry," Eva said, hanging her head. "I tried to keep Smedley safe without letting him see me, but I thought the comemierda was going to get eaten by a crab-spider, and that seemed worse for your mission than staying put, and then . . ." Eva sighed. "I fucked up. I should have just stayed on my ship."

Vakar was silent for a few moments. "The mission failure," he said finally, "is because it seems Smedley tampers with his DNA. He is likely to discover the nanite tracker before it is useful, and is equally likely to alter his genetic code in a similar time frame."

"That explains why he's so hard to track," Eva said. "And probably why he was sweating like a sinner in church. I still should have stayed put, though."

Vakar wagged his head in the quennian equivalent of a shrug. "Your observations of Smedley suggest your choices were not entirely unreasonable. I was also surprised by his apparent willingness to engage in highly questionable behavior."

Eva snorted. "Bueno, that's one way of putting it. Even Miles fucking Erck had the sense to run. Are the mercs . . . ?"

"While I am uncomfortable with leaving them to their fates, I cannot risk my mission for their safety."

Eva nodded, finding an exciting new pain in her neck-and-shoulder assembly.

"How long should I wait before heading out?" she asked. She didn't want to take the chance of running into Smedley and Miles or any of their henchpersons, but she also couldn't stick around forever.

"A half hour at least," he said. "Longer if they send someone in to recover the mercenaries. I will escort you to the surface when it seems reasonable."

"Carajo," Eva muttered. She'd wanted nothing more than to be with Vakar for weeks now, but this was some monkey's paw, evil-genie-level mierda.

He sat down next to her, arms touching. This time he didn't speak, didn't move, to the point that Eva would have suspected he was sleeping if she didn't know quennians didn't. She wanted to hug him so badly, but felt weirdly ashamed to do it, like she hadn't earned it, didn't deserve it. Maybe later, once the mission was completely finished and behind them.

After twenty minutes, the mercs appeared, helping each

other limp toward the exit tunnel. The crab-spider remained wherever it had gone, whether at the bottom of the lake or some cave system in the belly of the asteroid. A half hour after the mercs left, Vakar stood and helped Eva to her feet. As soon as he realized she was injured, he swore under his breath and produced a quick-heal shot from a pouch on his leg, handing it to her and holding her up while she administered it.

The meds worked quickly, dulling the pain in her knee enough to diminish her limp. Her ribs still ached, and her shoulder, but it was more manageable. By the time they emerged from the tunnel, she'd almost started to feel like the whole trip hadn't been the massive disaster she'd thought.

"You're sure their ship is gone?" Eva asked.

"Ten minutes ago, based on the energy signatures," Vakar replied. "I am detecting something else, though, something I cannot identify."

"That's probably my mech," Eva said. "I'll show you around once we get there." She continued to talk as they climbed up to the nook where she'd hidden it. "It's pretty amazing, honestly. The interface takes some getting used to, but it's intuitive once you—" She froze, patting the pocket with the key.

"Once you?" Vakar prompted.

"No," Eva said.

"Once you no?"

The pocket—which had previously contained one mech key and one explosive device, recently detonated—was empty. And once she reached it, so was the place where the mech was supposed to be waiting. Eva stood in the dark, on the surface of an asteroid light-years from her ship, next to her confused partner, and contemplated how quickly feelings of power and importance could be reduced to dust on a solar wind.

Well, Eva thought, at least now I know what Smedley found.

Chapter 11

CRITICAL FAILURE

Eva huddled in the aft of Vakar's ship, spinning out one plan after another for how to find the mech and get it back. By the time she got to "put an ad on the q-net for a missing ancient device" she knew she'd run out of fuel. Not only did she not have the final mech, she'd lost one of the two she had already recovered, and to agents of The Fridge no less. To Miles fucking Erck and his amigo Smedley, who was impossible to find and whose professed intended whereabouts involved (1) a man and (2) a horse. Which made no sense, so the man was nothing if not consistent based on her extremely limited knowledge of him.

When she made it back to *La Sirena Negra*, she and Vakar received a mixed welcome. Everyone was happy to have him safely returned, but the cost . . . It was the worst-case scenario. Partly an accident, but she knew she should have aborted the so-called rescue attempt rather than leave the mech to proceed. But she hadn't.

She'd made the choice, and now the whole universe would suffer the consequences.

While she'd been expecting an ear-blistering lecture from Pink, what she got instead was exhausted disappointment, followed by a drunken bender that would have made even the reckless Eva of a decade earlier wary. And Eva had once gotten into a drinking contest with a meathead twice her size, ending it with a bar fight that led to her being banned from an entire star system.

Pink wound up on the floor of the sonic shower, fully clothed, cradling a bottle of bourbon from her stash. When Eva tried to help her get up, Pink shrugged her off, washed down a quick-sobering pill with the last of the booze, and stalked back to the med bay. She locked the door behind her.

Min wouldn't speak to Eva. Sue kept almost saying things, then shaking her head in bewilderment. Leroy threw a spare power coupling at the cargo bay door, breaking it irreparably, and Momoko led him to the crew quarters with a look of disdain that she'd no doubt deployed to good effect many times on *Crash Sisters*. Vakar stayed on his ship to debrief with his superiors. Even the cats snubbed Eva, turning away when she passed and flicking their tails and otherwise ignoring her as if she weren't there.

The only one talking to Eva was Joe, who had graduated from being tied to a chair to being confined to the passenger cabin.

"You don't mess up small, do you, Alvarez?" he asked when she checked in on him.

Eva struggled to summon up a smile, the scar on her face tightening. "You know me. All or nothing."

"I haven't known you for a long time," Joe said. He sat on the room's small bed, leaning his forearms on his thighs.

"Some things never change," Eva said.

"Some things do."

"Are you one of those things?"

Joe shrugged.

"You know your brother has been looking for you," Eva said.

Joe's eyes narrowed a fraction. "How did you know I have a brother?"

"I met him. We worked together on Garilia a few weeks ago."

"I'm surprised you went back there, after what happened."

Eva scowled, the scar on her face tightening. "It wasn't my favorite. Anyway, none of my business what you and Jei are up to. Just thought you might want to know, given . . ." She waved her hand as if a simple gesture could encompass the monolith mess.

Joe made a fist, then loosened the fingers one by one. "He thinks it's his fault I joined up with Tito."

"Is it?"

"No."

Eva crossed her arms and waited for an explanation.

Joe leaned back, head against the wall, and started to whistle to himself. It was an eerie sound, one that had always gotten on Eva's nerves. Clearly he wasn't interested in continuing. She left him there and returned to her own room.

Eventually, she called everyone to the mess for a meeting. She was still co-captain of the ship, and they had a job to do, even if she'd made it exponentially harder. Despite her stomach roiling from a surplus of shitty feelings, Eva forced herself to make at least some rice with fake eggs for protein. She was halfway through it when people started trickling in, and by the time she'd pushed the plate away and wiped her mouth, five sullen humans and a quennian who smelled like acrid incense were arranged around the table, staring at her in anticipation.

"We all know I fucked up," Eva said. "'I'm sorry' doesn't cut it, but I am. This is all our mission, not just mine, so the first question is: do you want me to back out and let you all take over running this?"

At first, silence replied, as well as expressions and smells ranging from dismay to incredulity to pensiveness. Pink slammed her fist on the table, then pointed at Eva.

"No," Pink said. "Absolutely not. You and I are in charge here. I had my pity party, and then I sobered up, and here I am. Sometimes you don't have the sense God gave a gnat, but you're not dropping this in our laps and walking away. This is your mess, and you're cleaning it up. This is your circus, and we are not your trained monkeys. You started it, and you're finishing it." She paused, then added, "Fuck that shit, you whole entire ass," leaned back in her chair, and crossed her ankle over her knee.

No one spoke up to disagree or add anything. Eva closed her eyes, counted to five, then opened them again.

"Anyone else?" she asked.

Momoko cleared her throat politely. "I know I'm only a temporary crew member, and I haven't been here for long, but I believe we all have our skills, our strengths and weaknesses. With such a major task to undertake, we should consider every tool at our disposal, even ones with . . . flaws."

Eva was deeply aware of her own flaws, but certainly everyone present had a few. Some had overcome them better than others, as a glance at Leroy showed. He nodded in agreement, then grabbed Momoko's hand and kissed it, rubbing his thumb over her knuckles as she favored him with a smile.

"You did get two of the mechs before you lost one," Sue mumbled. "That's not bad."

"Oh, honey," Min said through the speakers. "You're too nice."

Truly, Sue had a habit of seeing the best in people and situations, sometimes out of all proportion with reality. Her recent experiences with her brother and Mari had put a dent in that, but it was hard to get rid of it entirely.

Vakar was the only one who hadn't offered an opinion, directly or indirectly. Eva met his gaze and raised her eyebrow, then waited.

"I have not yet discussed your mission with my superiors," he said. "I may not be present for whatever you choose to do, given that I am awaiting their determination of my next course of action, and so I feel it reasonable to abstain from providing input."

Pink snorted. "Oh, come on. You've got tactics falling out of your ass, and you're sleeping with the fool in question. You at least get to talk, even if you don't want to vote."

Vakar's smell shifted to one he didn't put out often, one that reminded Eva of the orange blossoms on the trees in her abuelos' yard. Sheepish, her translators said. But still, an undercurrent of licorice came with it, and hints of jasmine and incense.

"Eva may utilize methods that are sometimes unorthodox," Vakar said. Eva bit back a smile, and Min giggled through the speakers, but he continued. "She is arguably the reason we are all here in the first place, and while she has flaws as previously mentioned, she also has useful skills. I am . . ." He paused again, the licorice smell growing. "I will take her with me, if you do not wish to keep her here. She is dear to me."

Eva's whole face went hot, all the way down to her neck and chest. She couldn't bear to look at him, because if she did, she would probably burst into tears. It had been that kind of cycle.

"We certainly know what Eva thinks of you," Pink said, her tone exasperated with a trace of affection. "She's been moping around here for weeks, and first chance she gets, off she goes to jump your bones."

Any protest Eva made would have been irrelevant at best, a lie at worst, so she pursed her lips and said nothing.

"Whether Eva helps us or not, what do we do now?" Leroy asked. "We have one mech, we lost one, and there's still one out there. Plus those monoliths are still broadcasting."

That was Eva's cue to wade back into the conversation. "We know where all of the mechs are, more or less," she said, ticking them off on her fingers. "We have one, like you said. Smedley and possibly"—her lips curled into a snarl—"Miles Erck have one. And one more is still waiting to be picked up. Since we don't know exactly where Smedley and Erck have taken theirs, or what they plan to do with it, I think we should go for the one we can locate, the one we have a key for, and worry about the other one later."

"Mercy," Pink drawled, "the lady can still think with her brain instead of her other parts. That's me agreeing, by the way."

Momoko half raised her hand. "Is there some method you could use to determine where the stolen mech has been taken? Any of us who have piloted one can sense the others once we're in close enough proximity, but the universe is big."

Eva gestured at Vakar, who shrugged in the quennian equivalent of a nod.

"The nanite tracker has already been disabled," he said. "He has not yet altered his DNA signature, and may not suspect we obtained it, but we believe it is only a question of when that will no longer function, not if. Meanwhile, his location is known to us."

"So maybe we should go after him, then," Leroy said. "Before Vakar's thingy stops working."

Min giggled through the speakers. "Hah, thingy."

"Please don't talk about his thingy," Eva murmured.

Vakar smelled briefly of grass, before the jasmine reasserted itself. "There are some problems with that approach. First, we cannot be certain Smedley will have the mech in his possession.

He may have left it with Erck or other Fridge scientists for research and experimentation purposes, and moved on to some other task. Second, there is every expectation that he—and the mech—will be immensely well guarded, making the prospect of catching him unawares highly unlikely."

"And," Eva interjected, "if they have it, Tito doesn't. He seems to be either tracking us somehow, or he has people watching for us at each mech location. The latter matches what Antimatter said about the Artificers, so it seems the most likely bet."

"Sounds like him, too," Pink said. "He never liked relying on chance or coincidences."

"You know what they say about coincidences," Leroy said.

Sue blinked at him. "What?"

Leroy paused, then rubbed his beard. "I forget."

"Regardless," Eva said. "It's fair to assume Tito doesn't know Smedley has one yet, so he'll have all his forces concentrated on keeping us from getting the last mech."

Leroy snapped his fingers. "I was thinking of assumptions, not coincidences. That's the ass, you, me one." He grinned, and Momoko shook her head but smiled back with her mouth closed.

Pink rolled her visible eye and turned to Vakar. "Can your people get any intel about what Smedley is up to, in a hurry?"

"They are attempting to do so as we speak," Vakar said, but he hesitated. "They may not share that information with me, however."

"Why not?" Eva snapped.

"I would prefer to discuss that after I am more certain of my position," he replied.

Eva didn't like the sound of that, but she put a pin in it and moved on. "So first, we vote on our next step. Do we try to track down Smedley and get the mech back from him, or do we go for the third one, then backtrack?"

Silence fell again as everyone considered their answers. This time, Sue spoke up first.

"I say we get the third mech," she said. "We know where it is, and we don't want Tito to get it first, and anyway he can't fly it without the key."

"Yeah," Min said. "And once we have two mechs, we can punch Smedley until he gives us back the one he stole."

Vakar smelled alarmed. "I do not think it would be advisable to punch a human with such an enormous fist," he said. "He would not survive."

"Who knows?" Eva muttered. "He jumped on the back of an invincible crab-spider and lived."

"The Lord protects drunks and fools," Pink said. "Anyway, I happen to agree. About getting the third mech, that is."

Momoko half raised her hand again. "Either approach seems reasonable," she said. "But if this Smedley will become difficult, or even impossible, to find once his DNA is changed, then he should be the first priority, isn't that so?"

"She has a point," Leroy said.

"She does," Eva said, tapping the table with her forefinger. "Vakar, any chance your bosses might be persuaded to send you off to tail Smedley?"

"It is possible," Vakar said. "And would be extremely convenient under the circumstances."

"And if they don't?" Pink asked. "Would you still be able to find out his location and pass it along to us?"

Vakar hesitated. "I do not believe so. Of the likely trajectories for me, only following Smedley would give me access to that information."

Eva didn't want to think of his other likely trajectories, because she had a feeling they sucked acid through a lead straw.

"How soon will you know what they want you to do?" Pink asked.

"I expect orders to arrive at any time."

Eva stopped tapping and flattened her palm. "So how's this: if Vakar gets sent to tail Smedley, we go for him and try to take back the stolen mech. If Vakar doesn't get sent after Smedley, we go for the third mech, since we won't have the intel we need anyway."

One by one, the heads around the table nodded, except for Vakar, whose shrug was the quennian equivalent. He smelled like vanilla and rosewater, his version of anticipation, laced with enough incense and ozone to make Eva's skin prickle with nerves.

"Get some rest, then," Eva said, slipping back into captain mode even though it felt more ill-fitting than usual. "Gird your loins, say your prayers, and be ready to reconvene here for more planning once we have a clearer picture of what's to come."

Before Eva and Vakar could speak privately, his superiors sent him a message and he had to go back to his ship to hear their verdict. Vakar hadn't used that word himself, but that's what it felt like. While Eva knew his record as a Wraith boasted plenty of successes, she also knew he'd gotten in trouble a few times—all of them, to her knowledge, related to her.

The tension between their two jobs had been the main source of problems in their relationship since they'd started having one. Managing their respective responsibilities was like juggling glasses, chain saws, and live grenades, and the floor was covered in its fair share of broken plates and worse. They did their best, but their whole experience with Garilia had been bad, and then the attack on the Forge base made it worse, and now this.

Eva didn't want to reach a point where harder choices would have to be made. But as her dad said, wish in one hand and shit in the other, and see which one gets full first. What she wanted and what she got often didn't line up.

When Vakar returned, Eva was lying in her bed, aching from the injuries that hadn't been fixed by his meds. At some point she would ask Pink for help, but at that moment she'd rather walk barefoot through a dirty cat box.

Vakar was out of uniform, which was nice for a change. It seemed like every time she'd seen him since well before he'd left on his mission three weeks earlier, he'd been wearing at least a spacesuit. It was easier to smell him this way, and unfortunately he was presently a perfume store on fire, all kinds of worry and anger and regret swirling around in her little bunk.

The fish didn't mind, as usual.

Eva sat up, then got to her feet, swaying a little as the rush of blood darkened her vision. She took all of one step toward Vakar before he swept her into a hug, tight but far more gentle and less violent than the bear hug in the asteroid cave. Licorice flooded her nose and mouth, and she resisted the urge to bite his shirt.

"That bad, mi vida?" she asked.

"I have been instructed to report to the Home Fleet for disciplinary action," he said.

Eva winced. Yeah, that was bad.

"This is all my fault," she murmured into his chest. "If I had just stayed here and kept going with my mission, none of this would have happened."

"Yes," he said.

A sad laugh escaped Eva. "You could sugarcoat it a little."

He ran a taloned hand over her hair. "I cannot dispute the truth of your statement, but consider the other potential timelines. If you had arrived earlier, you might have left before

Smedley arrived. Without your presence, he might not have survived the attack of the lake creature. If you had arrived later, you might have encountered him or his ship and waited until he was gone before approaching me, or you might have caused an altercation, and that could have ended in any number of outcomes."

"I'm not picking up what you're putting down." She felt a little better already, though, just being there with him.

"What has already occurred is immutable," Vakar said. "Unless the Proarkhe have somehow discovered a means of changing the past or traveling between timelines in the theoretical multiverse." A whiff of amusement escaped him.

"So I should focus on the present, or whatever?"

"It is certainly not practical to use your time constructing versions of alternative choices and outcomes when the choice was already made and resolved."

She could feel guilty, though, and ashamed, and generally shitty. Wallowing in it accomplished nothing; she had to take what lessons she could and do better next time, and meanwhile try to fix the damage she'd caused.

"I know I already said I was sorry," Eva said. "But I am. Not knowing where you were, not knowing whether you were okay, or . . ." She tightened her grip around his midsection, and was rewarded with a renewed burst of licorice scent.

"I am not unfamiliar with that sensation," Vakar said. "I was forced to endure it for much longer, and it affected my own choices in ways we are currently contending with."

"Cierto." When Tito had captured Eva and hauled her off to cryo storage for The Fridge, Eva had been missing for a whole year. Not only had Vakar not sat around patiently waiting for her to reappear, he'd gone back to the people he'd run away from, taken on the Wraith mantle despite never wanting it, all in an effort to find her. Or to get revenge, if she couldn't be found because the worst had happened.

If Tito had never grabbed her, she never would have gone missing, and Vakar wouldn't be a Wraith at all. Did that make all of this Tito's fault? The thought simultaneously enraged and amused her. Also pointless to consider, as Vakar had already noted.

Still, it all came back to choices. You made the best ones you could with the information you had. Sometimes you made shitty choices, because logic was a lie people told themselves, to ignore the sneaky fingers of emotion resting on the scales, skewing the weights of different alternatives.

Sometimes you didn't even pretend you were being logical; you flipped the scales and told them to fuck off and then set them on fire. At least that was honest, even if it amounted to the same thing in the end.

"So what are we going to do?" Eva asked. "Because if you turn yourself in and they lock you up somewhere, I might be tempted to take the other mech and see how fast I can crack open a quennian Home Ship." She'd be more than tempted; Pink might have to dump her on an empty planet somewhere to stop her.

Vakar took her face gently in his hands and nuzzled her forehead with his palps.

"We will proceed with the plan we all agreed upon," he said. "We will retrieve the third mech, and then we will find some means of locating the missing second one."

"That's our plan," Eva said, closing her eyes and enjoying the feel of him. "What's your plan?"

"My plan is your plan." He stroked her cheek. "When you walked out of the tunnel on the asteroid, I thought my faculties were compromised. Surely you could not be there. It defied reason. When I touched you, I told myself it was to prevent you from alerting unknown observers to my presence, to hasten you away so my mission would not be compromised. In truth, I was confirming that you were real."

It hadn't felt that way at the time. "You seemed . . ." A lot of words flashed through her mind, and none were quite accurate. Cold? Distant? "Businesslike," she said finally. "Or maybe super angry and holding it back. Like I was a problem and you were trying to get me fixed quickly so you could get back to work." She understood that; she had been a problem for him at the time, and sometimes compartmentalizing was the only way to get things done.

"I was concerned that if I touched you again, I would be unable to complete my mission." He smelled grassy, bashful, but there was also the metallic tang of shame. "I had to restrain myself. It was a great effort for me."

Eva rubbed the ridge above his hip. "Ready to jump me right there, hmm?" she asked jokingly.

"I will not deny that element was present," he said, his tone dry even as he teased her with a whiff of licorice. "I wanted nothing more than to leave with you. As convinced as I had been of the rightness of my assignment, of its importance in furthering goals you and my employers share, in that moment my conviction wavered."

"I'm sorry," Eva said. "I didn't mean to mess with your head like that. I was scared, and worried, and I . . ." She sighed. "You know I support you, whatever you decide to do. We're a team."

Vakar gently grabbed her arms and stepped away, putting space between them. "That is precisely why I belong here," he said, his blue-gray eyes clear and calm. "Once, I was unhappy being what I was not, but I persisted because others expected it of me. Then I was mostly happy despite hiding portions of myself in the hopes of achieving a measure of peace. Now I am unhappy again, dealing with constant scrutiny and orders that require me to become someone else entirely, someone I do not esteem, at the expense of the people I love." His thumb ran over her lips, followed by his palps. "Ultimately, they do not care for my well-being. You do. I would be a fool to prioritize those for whom I am merely an asset over those who love me so fiercely. If they want me, they can send someone to claim me. As I said, my plan is your plan. I am with you."

For several long moments, Eva stared at him, utterly breath-less.

"Alabao," Eva said finally. "That is the most romantic fuck-ing thing I've ever heard. How am I supposed to do anything useful after that?"

Vakar made a low, rumbling sound. "I am certain you will manage. You seem to have a limitless capacity for doing so."

She had her limits, Eva knew, but she wasn't about to argue with him. Not when there was a perfectly good bed right be-hind her.

"We need to get ready for the mission," she said, running a finger along one of his palps. "We don't have a lot of time."

"On the contrary," he said, the smell of licorice intensifying. "We have precisely as much time as we need."

He wasn't wrong.

Chapter 12

SARTÉN

The term "lava planet" had always brought to mind a mass of molten rock, churning seas of red and orange and yellow broken by the occasional volcano, which spit more fire into the sky and oozed superheated fluids. Yastroth had all that, but because it rotated extremely slowly, almost tidally locked to its star, it also featured areas where the ground cooled enough to solidify temporarily. This left smaller lava lakes and seas, like giant puddles, being rained on by superheated rock vapor drifting over from the other side of the planet like storms from hell. Instead of swirls and ridges of dark stone like whipped frosting, bluish glass covered the black-facing side, some of it wavy sheets but much of it cracked and crushed by earthquakes.

Eva had hoped the mech would be on the cool side—temperature cool, not existential quality. As usual, she was disappointed.

"We have to get in, get the mech, and get out fast," she told the people assembled in the cargo bay. "*La Sirena Negra* should be able to handle the heat, but Sue and Vakar are staying on board to make sure nothing goes boom."

Sue's pale face turned pink as everyone glanced at her. Vakar smelled like vanilla and rosewater, with the barest hint of tar.

"Our spacesuits aren't rated for more than about ten minutes of exposure to temperatures above 2500 K, and this planet has spots that go up to 3100." Eva sipped her espresso, forgetting to slurp properly and scalding her tongue as a result. She put the tazita down and glared at it. "If we can find the mech and stay level with it, I should be able to jump across from the cargo bay to the bridge of the unit without a problem. That's a lot less than ten minutes, and worst case, Vakar has an isosphere to make the transition seamless."

"And if Tito shows up," Leroy said, "Momoko will fight him off with the other mech." He grinned at her, and she smiled back.

"Right," Eva said. "You, Leroy, are on ship weapons, and Pink is on the bridge for captaining purposes and deploying the bag of tricks as needed." They still had some stuff after their recent Forge experience, but they hadn't been able to replace much, so the options were limited.

"Joe?" Pink asked, her expression neutral.

"Stays in the guest room, for now, if that's okay," Eva said. "I leave it to your discretion to let him out if you think he can help. And if he does something to fuck with us, neutralize him." It felt cruel to say that, after what Pink had been through and what Eva herself had done, but they still weren't sure of his loyalties.

"You want me to space him?" Min asked.

"I said neutralize, not yeet into the lava," Eva said. "Pink has tranqs."

Pink nodded, her visible eye narrowed.

"You keep an eye on him, too," Eva told Mala, who lounged in the middle of the mess like the room was her personal quarters.

"Miau," Mala said, blinking her hazel eyes lazily.

"You literally live here rent-free and do nothing but lick your own asshole," Eva replied. "No seas tan vaga. And tell your friends to help."

Mala radiated indignation but got to her feet and sauntered toward the cargo bay, tail flicking.

"Eva," Pink said, "you need to stop pretending you can understand the cats. It's weird."

"She can understand me fine," Eva said. "That's what matters." She stood, too, stretching her arms over her head until her elbow cracked. "We'll be there in under an hour. Everyone, get ready. We can do this."

We have to, she didn't add, because she had fucked up and lost them a mech already. But if they got this one, they could worry about finding the other. Maybe they'd get lucky, and Erck or Smedley would make the mistake of bringing the fight to them.

Eva didn't like to count on being lucky. The dice had a habit of rolling badly when you least expected it, the dominoes were high instead of low, and in real life you couldn't knock on the table and hope your next turn went better.

It was more difficult than they had anticipated to reach the mech once they got to the surface of the planet. Geysers of lava burst up unexpectedly, catching Min off guard once and spinning the ship into the air like pizza dough. Worse, the area immediately surrounding the mech was full of cyclones, like waterspouts but composed of vaporized, superheated rock, much hotter than the ambient temperature of the already-fiery place.

"We should go back up and try to come in closer from above," Eva said.

"I can do this, Cap," Min said. Then another geyser sprang up next to the ship and she flinched like she'd been burned.

"You can, but you don't have to," Eva retorted. "Just take us up a couple kilometers and—"

Alarms began to sound, and the ship rocked from a different kind of impact.

"Plasma cannon," Pink said. "That'll be Tito."

"Me cago en la hora que él nació," Eva muttered. She pulled up a visualization of the sensor readings; not one, but three ships came in from multiple angles, all of them firing.

Min didn't need to be told to take evasive maneuvers. She executed a series of dizzying loops and turns, threading a bunch of invisible needles and using them to sew fancy stitches. Every time she tried to gain altitude, though, the suppressing fire increased, driving her back down toward the surface. Leroy took his own shots at the attackers, but they must have been running fancy targeting scramblers, because all he seemed to find was empty air. *La Sirena Negra* had its own scrambling methods, but they were probably a decade behind anything Tito had in his pocket.

"I'm starting to think they don't want this mech after all," Eva said, after they took a few jarring hits to their shields. "Not if they're working so hard to shoot us out of the sky."

Pink snorted in indignation. "They'd definitely have trouble fishing the key out of the bottom of this lava ocean," she said.

That changed the whole situation. If Tito didn't care about the mechs, if he only wanted to prevent Eva from getting them, she had no leverage.

Eva opened a channel to Momoko, who'd been told to wait in orbit. "Empezó la fiesta," Eva said. "Come dance with us."

"Be right there," Momoko replied.

Min continued her wild flight, circling closer to the third mech's location despite having to work so hard to avoid Tito's attacks and the hostile terrain. Another alarm sounded, this time an alert to a hacking attempt. The automated cyberdefenses were already on it, but Eva had a feeling that wouldn't be enough.

"Vakar, I need you to get a bug out of our systems," Eva said.

His reply came a few moments later. "I am attempting to patch a—stinking wastehole!—a coolant leak."

"Which is it, a wastehole or a leak?" Eva asked wryly. Vakar didn't dignify her joke with a response.

Sue cut in. "I'll send Seventeen and Twenty-Two over, then you can work on the hacker. Hold on!"

A new alert appeared: something had exploded nearby.

"Got one for you," Momoko said over comms. Eva didn't ask how; the mechs featured a number of weapons, but she hadn't practiced as much as the others had.

"The third mech should be up ahead," Pink said, gesturing at a map she'd pulled up with the estimated location. "Hard to find it on sensors, so the key is all we've got."

Eva toggled the viewscreen on so she could see through the fore cameras. The motion of the ship sent a wave of nausea through her, but she swallowed it down and tried to make sense of what was out there. The cyclones were nearly invisible, though if she focused she could catch the different spin of the air like a heat shimmer against the fiery landscape. In the distance, there seemed to be a large, darker space, like an island amid the sea of lava—but there couldn't be an island, not with the temperatures. Was it protected somehow, like the strange floating planetary fragment that had held the first mech?

Moments later, her question was answered. It wasn't an island; quite the opposite. It was a giant caldera, a gaping hole in the ocean with lava falls pouring down the sides like curtains of red-orange flame. No mech in sight, just the same expanse of molten rock churning in whatever strange currents moved it, though why it hadn't filled this hole long ago, Eva couldn't imagine. Crack in the bottom, maybe?

"It has to be in there," Eva said. "I can feel it. Min, take us down."

"You got it, Cap," Min said, and in they went. The temperature readings rose slightly, as the air was enclosed on all sides like an oven, despite being open to the sky. After her recent experiences, Eva found it entirely too cavelike for comfort. Whoever had hidden the mechs hadn't cared much for making them easy to find, which Eva supposed was sensible. Even without the keys, the potential for study and reverse-engineering was too great.

"Incoming!" Min yelled, and spun them into a dizzying roll sideways.

A new ship appeared ahead, bearing down on them rapidly. The enemy Proarkhe, Kilonova, in their spaceship form—at least, Eva was fairly sure they were the one she'd seen, the one at the Forge's Gate and then again after they found the second mech. Why the jerk turned into a ship was beyond her, but apparently they had all the usual parts, because they began firing with at least three weapons, one on each wing and one in the nose. The energy that seared from those guns was like whatever Tito had aimed at her before, but closer to laser fire than plasma.

Min continued to evade, but the Proarkhe was nimbler than the other ships, and followed her moves with the grace and skill of a dance partner. They passed *La Sirena Negra* almost close enough to touch, then circled back around to fire at them from behind. Eva pulled up the rear cameras to get a visual, which didn't help since both ships were moving around so much.

"Momoko, how's it going up there?" Eva asked.

"I'm learning quickly," Momoko replied. "Two ships remain, but one is damaged."

"Leroy, get this resingado robot off our culo," Eva said. "Min, take a dive and see if you can chicken them into a swim in the hot tub."

As ordered, Leroy sent a volley of laser fire toward the Artificer pursuing them. Min dipped closer to the bottom of the caldera, trying to goad the enemy in, force them into a maneuver from which they couldn't recover. It didn't work. They played a game that had them almost skipping the surface like river stones, but neither of them sank, and none of Leroy's shots hit their mark.

In the distance, a mound of lava rose from the floor of the caldera.

At first Eva thought it might be a bubble or low-pressure fountain, some upwelling of gases from beneath, or internal pressure pushing magma from the interior of the planet to the surface. But its molten exterior solidified, darkening to a gray like hematite or coal, though parts of it remained a hot, sullen red. It looked like monsters Eva had seen in old holovids, read about in fantasy stories, a giant blob of sludge with long, ropy arms but no visible legs. Except this sludge was unbearably hot instead of stinky and gross.

"Qué rayo," Eva whispered. How could anything live on this planet? Then again, she'd just come from an asteroid where a crab-spider lived in a golden lake, so maybe her imagination needed to expand a little.

The lava monster lobbed a fireball toward *La Sirena Negra*, which Min narrowly avoided, shrieking. The Artificer was equally lucky, or nimble, and their chase continued. Another projectile followed, then another, trailing fiery liquid tails that arced past them, hit the ground and sank back into the pool below. Was the creature targeting their ship or the Artificer, or both, because they were so close to each other? Min couldn't shake the tail or speed up without taking them back up to the ocean and away from the mech.

Except they couldn't locate the damn mech. She could feel it in that caldera somewhere, presumably invisible like the others until someone got close enough with the key to reveal it. Unless it was underground? Madre de dios, was Eva going to find yet another access tunnel? Or worse, was the thing buried in the lava itself, or sunk to the bottom of the molten rock with no hope of retrieval without specialized instruments?

The ship approached the end of the caldera, so Min brought them around for another pass. As another fireball flew at them, suddenly the console in front of Eva flickered and went dark, and the ship began to fall.

"Min?" Eva yelped.

"I'm locked out!" Min shrieked. Her black eyes were wide and wild, her blue hair tousled as she sat bolt-upright in the pilot's chair.

"A moment, please," Vakar said over comms.

It must be the hacker, then. That meant Tito still waited out there, close enough to be jodiendo como siempre. Unless the Artificer was doing it? Didn't matter.

All that mattered was they were plummeting toward the lava.

The controls blinked back on, and with a muffled groan Min took control of the ship once again. They pulled out of the steep dive awkwardly. Before they could celebrate their success, a horrifying clang sounded from the rear of the ship.

The Artificer grabbed the cargo bay door and tried to wrest it open.

"No me busques," Eva said, and immediately slammed open the door to the bridge. "Pink, take the bridge. Min, get that fucking tick off." She raced toward the cargo bay, pulling her pistols out of their holsters, for all that her puny weapons would probably have no effect on the giant metallic creature.

Sudden acceleration sent her stumbling into the table in the mess before the ship's gravity adjusted to compensate. Min must have taken them supersonic, to try to shake the Artificer loose. Eva waited a few breaths, but the hull attacks began again, and she continued toward her destination.

"Sue, reroute all non-life-support power to shields," Min shouted.

The instant Eva reached the cargo bay, the lights winked out and the artificial gravity went with them. If they'd still been planetside, it wouldn't have mattered; local gravity was only slightly higher than Earth standard. Eva's feet left the floor and she drifted in the blackness. She flipped on her suit's illumination and checked below her for cats, then activated her grav-boots to secure herself to the floor.

A chorus of frenzied mewling began around her, along with waves of psychic distress, punctuated by bangs and groans as the Artificer continued trying to rip off the door. Eva's light revealed a half dozen cats floating freely in the dark room, frantically twisting in midair as they tried to orient themselves to the floor they weren't falling toward. The others seemed to have had the foresight to go into their container beforehand, and while a few were gently bumping against the top or sides, others clung to their pillowed bedding or scratching posts or the multitiered tower they liked to lounge on.

"Ay, pobrecitos." Eva resisted the urge to laugh. Hopefully Joe was having better luck in the guest room.

A sudden thrum of energy rippled along the length of the ship, more sound and sensation than anything. The noises of the Artificer stopped abruptly, and a few moments later, the emergency lights flickered on. The cargo bay glowed an eerie bluish-green, still filled with sad cats, as well as various spare parts and other clutter that normally littered the room. Sue's exosuit, Gustavo, and Min's fighting bot, Goyangi, were tethered to the catwalk but hovered above the floor like puppets on strings. If a cat were underneath one of them when the gravity returned . . .

As annoying as her feline tenants were, Eva did care about them. She couldn't let that happen.

"Min," Eva said, "did we lose our new friend?"

"For now," Min replied grimly.

"Momoko?"

After a few moments, Momoko replied, "Still chasing this shit-drip. I'm going to try the cannon."

Cannon? That sounded promising. "Sue, Vakar, status report?"

Sue spoke first. "Rusty buckets, Captain, I think we fried a converter. I sent my bots to grab a spare."

"I am soldering an additional cable to the auxiliary generator," Vakar said. "I should be able to force a manual reboot of the stabilizers once I have finished."

"Don't rush," Eva said. "I have a problem to fix before we get gravity again."

"Fix it fast, Eva," Pink chimed in. "We need to go back to the surface before Tito fucks us sideways."

Eva sighed and stomped over to the guest room, unlocking the door and sliding it open.

"Joe," she said.

"Alvarez," he replied. He'd used his belt to tie himself to the bed. Smart.

"It's Innocente," Eva said. "If I let you out, will you help me round up the cats? They need to be put back into their container before the gravity drops them like sad furry rocks."

Joe gave a low whistle. "That is one of the weirdest requests I've ever heard."

"Can you do it?"

He shrugged. "I can try. They can't claw through my spacesuit, right?"

She shook her head and gestured for him to follow her, trudging back to the middle of the room.

"Oye, gatitos," she yelled. "We're going to get you, just stop freaking out and hold still."

A couple of them continued to writhe and cry, but the others followed her orders and let themselves drift docilely.

Eva released her gravboots with a thought at the same time as she bent her knees and launched herself toward a cat. Joe joined her, and together they leaped and dived across the big, mostly empty space. Theirs was an awkward ballet of geometry and physics, angles and momentum, a new sport in which the balls were alive and deeply unhappy about the whole game.

Within minutes they had all but one of the sorry creatures safely tucked away: Mala, of course, who stubbornly insisted via psychic waves of disapproval that Eva take care of the others first. She may not have been their leader, but she acted as if she were in charge, and that often amounted to the same thing.

Not too different from Eva herself, sometimes.

"Get back in the cabin," Eva told Joe. "Gravity should be back soon, and then we have to take another spin at finding the mech."

"You sure you can't use an extra hand?" Joe asked. He flexed his artificial one and grinned.

"I just did," Eva said. "Thanks." Whether he'd helped to trick her into trusting him, or because he really could be trusted, she was still grateful.

Something slammed into the side of the ship, sending the

far wall flying toward Eva, suspended as she was in the gravityless space. She pivoted to take the impact with her boots,
checking to confirm that Joe had done the same. Mala had been
farther away, so she was now closer to the wall but didn't hit it.

"Min, what was that?" Eva asked. "The Artificer?"

"No," Min replied. "I'm not sure . . . Maybe another of Tito's
ships? They're not responding when I hail them. They hit us
with an immobilizer, but our shields were maxed so it dispersed
the impact."

Who would show up in the middle of Casa Carajo with an
immobilizer? Eva thought. Tito had just spent all this time trying to blow her up, not shut her down and try to board.

"It's a Wraith," Vakar cut in. "He tracked my ship to where I
left it by the Gate and has already disabled it. I've been instructed
to surrender or be apprehended."

Chapter 13

FUEGO

Me cago en diez, Eva thought. *That's all we needed now, one more comemierda trying to drag us deeper into some shit.* She closed her eyes for a moment and took a deep, calming breath as her skin prickled from a sudden rush of extra stress.

Next to her, Joe whistled. "I said it before, Alvarez," he said. "When you go out, you go all out."

"Cap?" Min asked. "What should I do?"

"I'm thinking," Eva said. Plans raced through her head, some more outlandish than others, and she sorted them in order of viability and odds of success. Ideally, they needed to get rid of all their pursuers at once, but it would take something drastic.

"Think faster, Eva," Pink chimed in. "We're not handing over Vakar, but this asshole is extremely puckered."

Even as Pink said this, Eva settled on the first phase of what needed to happen. They'd come looking for Vakar, but they'd found Eva, and they were going to be extremely sorry they had.

Vakar said, "Perhaps I should—"

"Don't even," Eva cut him off. "Vakar, leave the gravity off. Everyone, strap in or secure yourself to something." She pushed off the wall toward Mala, who desperately attempted to maintain a loaf position. Eva reached her in seconds, grabbing the cat and cradling her to her chest as she flipped to land feet-first against the ceiling.

"Miau," Mala said.

"You're welcome," Eva replied. She pushed off and sped toward the floor, once again tumbling to plant her feet firmly on the metal surface. Her gravboots kept her there, and she stomped over to the cat container, gently depositing Mala inside.

"Back in the room, Joe," Eva said. His expression soured, so she flashed him a grin. "It's for your own good, mijo. Remember that job on Enrion?"

Joe's eyes widened and he whistled again. "Your pilot can do that?"

"Of course. We go all out here, like you said." Eva began to walk toward the restraints on the side of the cargo bay. "Min, get ready to spiral."

Silence replied for a few moments. Vakar muttered a curse, perhaps forgetting his comms were active.

"Are you sure, Cap?" Min asked. "I haven't done a spiral in a long time. If I can't pull up—"

"We go for a lava swim," Eva said. "I know. Let's see if our Wraith buddy is willing to test his skills against yours. Aim for the caldera." It would be tight, like trying to swan dive into a puddle, but Min was the best.

Grabbing the emergency harness, Eva slid her arms and legs into the relative safety of the padded straps and impact absorber. She had a bad feeling she would need to exit in a hurry if they survived this maneuver.

"What's the plan when we get there, Eva?" Pink asked.

"Same as before," Eva said. "Find the mech and get inside."

"That's a goal, not a plan."

"We know it's in the caldera, we know there's a lava monster living there, and we know we've got at least three comemierdas who want us dead." Eva huffed out a breath. "We need to shake our tails before we do anything else. The spiral might help with one of them, so let's circle back when that's done and see what happens."

"Eva," Vakar said, "I would not wish for one of my Wraith colleagues to be killed on my account." She couldn't smell him, but she imagined it would be pained.

"That's their call, not yours," Eva said. "They can choose to disengage anytime." If they were anything like Vakar, they wouldn't, and they both knew that. But maybe they were a good pilot themselves, and maybe they'd refuse to take the bait and wait for another time to engage on better terms.

A person could drown in maybes as easily as they could in water. Dwelling on it was like holding your breath instead of kicking for the surface.

"Everyone ready?" Eva asked. A chorus of affirmatives replied.

"On three, Cap?" Min asked.

"Count it down and drop us," Eva replied.

Min counted, angled the nose of the ship down and flashed the sublight drive.

La Sirena Negra flew toward the planet's surface like a meteor, blazing into the atmosphere in a halo of fire. The cargo bay was dark by contrast, the emergency lights casting every angle into shadow, all the detritus that had been floating around before now plastered against the cargo bay door from inertia.

Min sent the ship into a tight spiral, and between that and the fall itself, Eva's stomach turned into a distraught cat. She swallowed spit and prayed to the Virgin that this would work. That Min wasn't too rusty on the maneuver, that some atmospheric or local weather quirk didn't interfere at an inopportune time, that Tito and the Artificer would assume the worst and stop chasing them.

So many variables, any of them potentially deadly. And she wasn't even on the bridge to see what was happening. If they hit the surface, she'd have no warning, just the impact and whatever came after. All Eva could do was sit tight and trust Min.

I can trust Min, she thought. I trust her all the time. This is no different.

A knot in Eva's chest loosened, and for a moment she felt like she was floating again, like a chunk of stress inside her had sheared off like a wedge of an iceberg and dropped into the sea, leaving her lighter than before.

With one last turn, *La Sirena Negra* leveled out abruptly, pushing Eva hard against the wall's padding. She yelled triumphantly, not caring whether anyone heard her, then prepared to slip her restraints and see what could be done about finding that mech.

"Everyone okay?" Eva asked.

"I am intact," Vakar replied.

"Rusty buckets," Sue said.

"I threw up a little," Leroy added, his voice strained.

Joe whistled an affirmative.

"We are never doing that again," Pink said firmly.

"Not until next time we have to," Eva replied. Pink huffed indignantly but said no more.

"The Artificer is back," Min said over the speakers. "And so is the lava monster."

Coño carajo, Eva thought. "And the Wraith?"

"Pulled out before we reached the caldera."

Eva sighed in relief. Maybe they'd be back, maybe they wouldn't, but now it was time to deal with their robotic buddy and the local fauna.

Was the lava monster sentient? Just because it tossed balls of lava around didn't mean it did so with any complex thought process. It could have been the equivalent of a dung beetle rolling shit around, a wild animal defending its territory. What kind of animal lived in a giant lava pit on a planet with temperatures hot enough to vaporize rock?

A thought occurred to Eva. A few related thoughts, in fact. Namely that as strange and diverse as the universe could be, as wild and wonderful, the odds were low that a lava creature would happen to be living in the precise place where their mech was supposed to be hidden. A creature with two arms who reacted with hostility to the presence of an enemy Proarkhe, just as Antimatter had warned it would if she approached.

"Alabao," Eva said. "I think the lava monster is the mech."

After a few moments, Pink replied, "That certainly is a theory. How are we going to test it?"

Eva's thoughts were hustling again. "I need to get close, with the key," she said. "Obviously we can't just pull up next to it with the Artificer up our culo, so I need another way."

"Could Momoko grab you?" Leroy asked.

"Only if she's finished with Tito," Eva said. "Momoko, you okay?"

"Yes," Momoko replied. "Whoever Tito is, I would be delighted to make his personal acquaintance." The acid dripping from her polite words could have burned holes in metal.

Eva snorted a laugh.

"Sorry, princess," Leroy said. "Don't let him stress you out, okay?"

"I'm going to play tennis with his spleen," Momoko said, then cut out.

"No Momoko, then," Eva said. "We need her to keep running interference for now. Min, stay loose and keep circling for a minute."

At the speed they were moving, it would almost certainly be deadly for Eva to take a dive out the back door. Slowing down meant exposing themselves to the Artificer's assault, even if the mech was trying to help on that front. Min could pull a fancy stop and the Artificer might not be able to match it, but Eva had her doubts; the cabrón seemed pretty nimble.

Eva's gaze fell on Gustavo and Goyangi. They were both combat rated, made from similar materials as the ship, so either or both of them could survive the external temperatures on the planet.

"Sue," Eva said. "Can Goyangi fly?"

"Cap!" Min exclaimed. "Not my bot!"

"Sue, can it fly?" Eva repeated.

"Um, yes," Sue said. "I haven't tested it in heat like this but . . . As long as you don't go into the lava, I think it would be okay?"

Eva activated her isohelmet and unstrapped herself from the emergency restraints, engaging her gravboots with a thought so she wouldn't stumble around while the gravitational stabilizers were inactive. As it was, the movement of the ship threatened to knock her over, weaving and turning to evade the pursuing Artificer.

"I need you to fly it for me, Sue," Eva said. "I won't be able to pilot and focus on opening the mech at the same time. Vakar, you're working solo now. Pink—"

"On my way with the key," Pink said. "You better not drop this one."

Sue emerged from a panel under the ship, her face covered in grease smudges, multiple tiny yellow bots trailing after her making irate squealing noises. She finally whirled on them, raising a finger.

"Get back in there and finish patching that pipe," Sue said. "Vakar is working his backside off, and he needs your help, so stop bellyaching and do your jobs!"

Whining and chirping sadly, the bots returned to the panel from whence they'd emerged, and Sue staggered up to release Goyangi from its restraints.

"You tell 'em, mija," Eva said.

Sue looked up at her, eyes wide with surprise. "Tell them what?"

Eva chuckled, but before she could answer, Pink arrived with the mech key. This one was a light amethyst cuff, wide enough that she'd have to slide it up to her forearm. Eva took it and tucked it carefully into a thigh pocket, then saluted and began to climb up the back of Goyangi. Bending her knees, she used her gravboots to secure herself firmly between what would have been the bot's shoulder blades if it had any shoulders. From her belt, she unspooled a thin length of cable, which she looped around its neck and reattached to herself. She grabbed the pieces of cable like they were reins on a horse, resisting the urge to flick them to make the bot go.

Giddyap, she thought. She'd never ridden a horse in her life. The closest she'd come was a skybike, or Antimatter in her vehicle form.

"Min," Eva said. "Get us close to the lava monster, then cobra and open the cargo bay door. As soon as we're clear, loop up and around and see if you can get behind the Artificer. Leroy, take any shots you can." To Sue, she said, "Once I'm outside, try to get me close to the monster. If I'm right, it should stop attacking and let me open the access door in its midsection. If

I'm wrong, it will attack me and you'll have to pull me back in a hurry."

Pink scowled up at her, swaying with the ship's motion. "If you're wrong, that thing's gonna swat you like a fly."

"Hope I'm right, then, for a change." Eva gave her a weak grin, then focused on the cargo bay door and waited for Min's signal.

Pink returned to the bridge while Sue strapped herself into the restraints Eva had used before, then activated Goyangi. The bot, whose last outside action had been a pit fight against a much larger foe, had been repaired and taken out to play a few times by Min for fun. It ran through various checks, stretching its arms and legs, flexing its weapons systems and retracting them like an animal showing off its frills or feathers. Goyangi took one step forward, then another, its heavy frame managing to stay stable more easily than the lighter humans. It stopped just in front of the cargo bay door, and Sue gave Eva a thumbs-up.

"Coming around, Cap," Min said a few moments later. "Please don't lose my bot, please." Her voice came through the speakers, thick with emotion.

"What about me?" Eva asked.

"You'll be fine," Min said dismissively. "You have more lives than the cats."

Eva snorted, continuing to wait, her fists tense from gripping the anchor cable.

((Be safe,)) Vakar pinged her.

((Love you,)) Eva pinged back. They both knew "safe" was the last thing either of them was.

"Brace for cobra!" Min yelled.

La Sirena Negra flipped up and braked in midair, its nose pointing at the sky. In front of Eva, the cargo bay door flew open, and Goyangi leaped out into the fiery planet.

For a few moments, Eva fell toward the floor of the caldera, her isohelmet darkened to let her look at the lava without hurting her eyes. Then the bot's boosters kicked in and it shot forward, parallel to the ground, before angling upward. Behind her, the ship's engines revved and launched it away, its ascent confirmed by a glance over Eva's shoulder.

But she couldn't watch it go, because in front of her loomed the massive lava monster, its eyes glowing bright red. The visible part of it was about thirty meters high; if it was the mech, presumably there was more below the surface of the liquid rock since it didn't seem to be hovering. Its arms glowed orange and red from being dipped back into the lava, but the rest of it was layers of rippling, cracked gray with streaks of red.

Goyangi flew closer. Eva prayed she wasn't wrong, because if she was, this would be a very short flight.

The monster grabbed another wad of lava, lifting the viscous fluid with a massive limb, and threw the steaming liquid at Eva.

"Coño!" Eva shouted. She pulled hard on the cable gripping Goyangi's neck, but thankfully Sue had already shifted it sideways.

A sound like a scream rang out behind her. The Artificer, hit squarely by the lava and writhing in a way spaceships didn't. They transformed into their bipedal form, brushing pieces of lava off, their metallic surface discolored and slightly warped. With what Eva assumed was the equivalent of a glare, they retreated, rising out of the caldera until they were beyond the range of the makeshift projectiles.

"Take me in, Sue!" Eva yelled into her helmet comms, and Goyangi moved closer to the monster. Eva reached into her pocket and carefully pulled out the key, slipping it onto her arm.

As soon as she did, the creature stopped and faced her, its arms falling to its sides. A red glow emanated from the cracks in the cooler lava, brightening as the gaps grew and widened. Within a dozen seconds, the layers of rock burst and crumbled away, leaving the more familiar form of a mech behind.

Its surface was, surprisingly, a similar gray to the shell it had just shed, with red accents at the shoulders and forearms. Its oblong head and elongated limbs were nearly the same as its counterparts, though about ten meters of its legs were buried in lava. The same door opened around its abdomen, and Eva released a breath she had absolutely been holding intentionally.

"Sue, can you get Goyangi back to the ship once I'm inside?" Eva asked.

"Of course," Sue responded after a moment. "Piece of cake."

"Don't eat your panetela before it's baked," Eva warned.

Goyangi reached the entrance, and Eva sighed with relief. All she had to do now was get inside and subject herself to the uncomfortable goo bath, and they'd be back to two mechs instead of one.

Before she could swap rides, something tackled Goyangi from the side. Together they careened into the mech, then began to fall. As quickly as she could, Eva deactivated her gravboots and detached her belt line. She rotated and turned her boots back on, flying toward the mech and latching onto its left hip.

Sue brought the bot back around and set it to hover in front of Eva, its optical sensors glowing, weapon-arms raised. Out of the heat shimmer came the Artificer who had been chasing them, still in bipedal form. Kilonova.

How had she forgotten they were so damn big?

"Human," the Artificer screeched. Eva wasn't sure what language they were using, but they—no, he—piped it into her head the way Antimatter had. It made Eva's teeth itch.

"Comemierda," Eva replied, not sure he could hear it.

His red eyes brightened. "My name," he said, "is Kilonova."

That confirmed it, then. Eva's suit quietly warned her that temperatures exceeded recommended levels. She couldn't stay outside for much longer. She took one sneaky step up toward the mech's door, then another.

"I am extending you a great honor," Kilonova said. He drifted forward slowly, like a stalking cat, if cats could fly. "In gifting you my name, you may know that it is I, the greatest of the Artificers, who have ended you."

That sounded like a load of crehnisk shit. But the mech's entrance was only a few meters away. Eva needed to keep him talking or find another way to distract him.

((Shoot him?)) Sue pinged at her.

((Hold,)) Eva pinged back. She'd have to time it carefully.

"Your paint job's looking a little burnt, Toaster," Eva replied. "Did you not enjoy your complimentary lava facial?"

He recoiled, his eyes narrowing in apparent shock. "You dare to insult me?" Kilonova shrieked. "When I have given your death meaning with my very presence?" His voice in her mind grated like gears that needed lubrication.

Okay, maybe insults weren't the best approach. "Discúlpame, Your Highness," Eva replied. "If I had realized I was in the presence of such amazingness, I would have bowed. I'll make sure to keep my pinkie out when the tea gets here."

((Now?)) Sue asked.

((Hold,)) Eva replied.

It took a few moments for Kilonova to detect the sarcasm, but once he did, he aimed his arm-weapons at her. "A pity Null Array will not witness my triumph," he said. "But at least I will enjoy watching you burn."

((Now!)) Eva pinged.

Goyangi rushed at Kilonova, missiles shooting from its arms. The Artificer gave an undignified squawk and engaged with this new target while Eva sped up as much as she could, given how gravboots functioned. Her suit continued to gently warn her that she was about to burn like a chicharron if she didn't get out of the heat.

Don't look back, she told herself, but of course she did. To her horror, Kilonova grabbed one of Goyangi's arms and wrenched it off.

Min's going to be so mad, Eva thought. She tried to move faster, but each step took time to attach, then detach. She was so close—

Goyangi's mouth weapon whined, then fired. Eva glanced back again to see what damage it had done.

None whatsoever. Kilonova was entirely unaffected. He used the arm he'd pulled off to whack Goyangi over the head, driving it down toward the lava like he was hammering a nail into a board.

Eva finally made it to the doorway, clambering awkwardly into the mech's bridge from her horizontal orientation. She rushed toward the piloting tube, which opened quickly and closed as soon as she was inside. Tapping her foot impatiently, she waited for her suit's sensors to tell her the tube was full of breathable air, then disengaged her isohelmet so she could suck in that vile fluid instead.

The lights overhead twinkled and blinked and finally, in a rush, Eva's senses were overlaid with the mech's controls and readings. She looked out its optical sensors at Goyangi and Kilonova battling in the blazing air a few meters away. Goyangi moved sluggishly, jerking and sparking from the damage it had taken.

Eva grimaced. If she tried to fire on Kilonova, she'd hit the bot.

"Sue," Eva said over comms. "Get Goyangi out of there."

Sue didn't reply, but Goyangi began to fly away from the Artificer. Too slowly, Eva knew, compared to how fast Kilonova moved. For a few moments, Eva hoped the bot would make it, that she'd get a clear shot, that something would happen to change the inevitable—some last-minute saving grace falling from the sky like a deus ex machina.

Instead, Kilonova grabbed Goyangi and threw it down into the bottom of the caldera, into the roiling surface of the super-hot liquid rock. Its remaining hand rose for a moment like it was waving goodbye, then it was gone.

The only machina left was Kilonova, who flew up to peer directly into the mech's optical sensors. His red eyes were as bright as stars, but his scuffed exterior proved he was no god.

"You will suffer for this indignity, meat," Kilonova said. He pointed at Eva, then drew his hand across his own throat and flew out of sight.

Where did he learn that gesture? Eva wondered. Then, more vehemently: Right back at you, cabrón. As soon as I get this mech out of this damn lava.

Chapter 14

GAME OVER

Once again, *La Sirena Negra* floated in the blackness of space near a distant planet, far enough from a Gate for privacy, close enough to jump in a hurry. This system, like a few others, had been stripped of its resources so long ago that by the time BOFA declared it inactive, the dark joke was that it had died of strangulation by red tape. But it was already empty by then, because some long-gone species had cared more about extraction than cultivation, had taken and taken until nothing remained to take, leaving behind only the crumbling skeletons of a worthless, unfathomable infrastructure.

There might as well have been a LOOK ON MY WORKS, YE MIGHTY, AND DESPAIR sign carved in mile-high letters on the nearest planet.

They'd vamoosed rapidly after realizing that Tito, the Wraith, and even the Artificer had staged a tactical retreat. They were safe, and they had won. It should have been a time for celebration, for taking their win and shouting it from mountaintops.

But they needed three mechs, and they only had two. The other one was missing and presumably in hostile territory, guarded by whoever or whatever The Fridge might feel like assigning to the task, which could be anything from mercenaries to battle cruisers. At least one Wraith had been sent to retrieve Vakar for what had to be more than a gentle reprimand if a highly trained secret agent was dispatched to help enforce it.

And Goyangi was gone forever. Min was despondent over the loss of her bot, which had been Sue's first and biggest gift to her. Eva took over flying the ship to give her and Sue some alone time in one of the mechs, while Leroy and Momoko kept each other company in the mess. Pink went to check on Joe, armed with the knowledge that he'd helped with the cats, if nothing else. Vakar hugged Eva briefly, tightly enough to reawaken her wounds, then returned to his repair duties since Sue was indisposed.

The cats resumed their normal shipboard activities, which mostly consisted of lying around and napping. Eva wished she could bounce back that quickly.

Because she had to. Because they didn't have the luxury of time, precious hours or cycles to plan and prepare so they weren't bringing guns to a nuke party. They needed the missing mech, and they needed it now.

The thing about time was, for all that it could stretch in strange ways while you jumped around the universe moving faster than light, eventually it would snap back. Like the finite, dwindling resources on a dying planet, it would run out.

A message came in for Eva, from Mari: "Check the feeds."

No more time. The invasion had begun.

· · · · · · · ·

Simultaneously, at every Gate with a monolith, a fleet of Artificer ships appeared. Some were larger than others, containing enormous fleetbreakers like the one Eva had managed to destroy, while others were primarily cruisers or smaller vessels. There were simultaneously fewer of them than Eva had expected and more than she could have imagined, given how many Gates there were.

How had the Proarkhe existed for so long, off in some other starless corner of the universe, without anyone ever realizing they were there? What the hell had they been doing, and how had no one run into them until now?

The universe was big, sure, but the sheer scope of it had narrowed for Eva the more she'd traveled and seen, the older she'd gotten. She'd put it in a box, neat and tidy, and suddenly she'd been forced to accept that the box was inside another box the size of, well, the actual universe.

All the Artificers were demanding unconditional surrender from the local officials, and replies began to trickle in based on the various news feeds and q-net traffic. So far, nothing had happened to the places that waved the white flag; they were told to stand by for further instructions.

There was also nothing occurring yet in the places where no answer had been offered, primarily BOFA-defended areas that had been told to sit tight and raise whatever shields were available. Representatives from those astrostates bunkered somewhere, arguing with each other about what to do. Some wanted to offer conditions because they couldn't believe the enemy would decline to negotiate, some insisted on refusing to condone any actions that would suggest weakness or reluctance to defend their homes and allies, and some demanded to know precisely what consequences awaited them if they told the Artificers to go fry ice.

Those particular consequences were, unfortunately, quickly illuminated when the gmaarg decided to attack one of the fleets.

The newest Glorious Apotheosis, in his infinite and infallible wisdom, had determined that his people would never be subjugated, and acted accordingly. From his absurd palace on his favorite world, he'd been one of the first to try attacking the monoliths, to no effect. Now he sent his fatherships and their vast groups of tiny fighters out, firing at will against the large and small Artificers alike. He expected a quick and decisive victory, adding more glory to his name, already respected and feared across the cosmos.

So far as anyone knew, none of the gmaarg ships had survived. And then the Glorious Apotheosis and his entire planet had been destroyed.

The only clue to what had managed such a colossally horrifying feat was a shaky holovid of what looked like a moon looming in the sky. Except that planet didn't have a naturally occurring satellite, so where had such a thing come from?

Like her understanding of the universe's size and scope, Eva had tricked herself into thinking their mission could be contained, limited, turned into a simple checklist and enacted with haste and precision. They would succeed, the mechs would do whatever it was they could do, and everyone would be saved without grief or bloodshed.

Now a whole fucking world was turned to space dust, every single life on it had been extinguished, and there wasn't a damn thing Eva could do to stop it from happening again.

Everyone on *La Sirena Negra* rushed to find out if their family and friends were okay. Comms traffic was clogged, despite authorities warning that it was probably being monitored by the enemy, so a few times they suffered painful waits before tearful good news could be confirmed.

Pink's family, big as it was, still lived mostly in a single settlement on a planet near the fringe of BOFA territory, and they were all present and accounted for. Their neighborhood had communally organized efforts to cook group meals and share food and other stocks, and their government engaged in similar action on a broader scale. While supplies weren't coming from off-planet, they produced enough locally to be set for a while. What they didn't have, fortunately, was a massive fleet at their proverbial doorstep, just a few of the smaller ships looming near their system's Gate. Pink's brother quietly put together evacuation plans, should they become necessary; while the planetary defenses were solid, no one had ever faced this enemy before, and intel was minimal. They'd all told Pink to keep her head down and be careful, and that if she and the rest of the crew needed somewhere to land, their house was open. Pink had told them the same, though it would be a tight fit in the cargo bay, and their own food supplies wouldn't hold out forever.

Min's family was scattered across multiple planets in a single system, and to Min's surprise, her estranged parents sent a tearful request for her to come home. They'd been enraged when she ran away years earlier, had cut off contact and support when it became clear she had no intention of apologizing and begging for their forgiveness, but apparently a universe-spanning catastrophe could break down even their stubbornly erected walls. At first, Min had refused to answer their message, but conversations with Sue and Pink helped her feel safe enough to politely turn them down while assuring them she was well.

Eva understood better than most how that kind of family rift worked, and how long it could take to heal, and how sometimes it never really would.

Sue's parents sent a message asking her to stay safe, wherever she was, but not to try to reach them because their home was on a planet that had surrendered immediately to the Artificers. Some people had left before the fleet arrived, while others attempted to escape through the system's Gate afterward. Those who didn't evade detection or outrun the blockade had been destroyed. For now, nothing else was happening, but everyone lived in fear of what demands or orders might be issued when the time came.

Vakar's sister Pollea had left her hab unit on the space station DS Nor with an early wave of people running away from the monoliths, since there were two Gates nearby. She had first visited their parents' Home Ship and then continued on to one of the outposts in a system without a monolith, plying her skills as a scientist and technician to help with whatever needs she could. The people there, too, were banding together to weather the trouble, hoping the conflict would pass in time and life could return to a semblance of normalcy.

Leroy's moms lived on Earth, which had garnered a surprisingly sizable fleet, given how scattered humans were across the universe compared to how many were left in their original solar system. As a BOFA member, the planet awaited the response of their far-off governing body, while residents and local politicians argued about whether to declare sovereignty and make their own choice faster. Not that it would be any easier, since they couldn't agree on that either. For all that humans had, by and large, learned to work together better over the millennia, especially on their various settlements, they still had nothing like a uniformity of purpose or method.

Momoko was secretive about her own family except to say they were fine and had offered sanctuary if she wanted it. She'd declined, preferring to stay with the mechs for now, for which Eva was grateful.

Eva asked Joe again if he wanted to get in touch with his brother, and Joe told her to mind her own business. She said fine, but that this might be his last chance to patch things up, so maybe he should take it. Maybe it was cruel to leave him with that thought, which she suspected he already had himself, but now wasn't the time to be coy about family without good reason.

Eva certainly had to reckon with her own.

Her mother, Regina, once again left a message telling Eva to proceed to a set of coordinates that would help her locate a safehouse, that her abuelos and tios and primos of all varieties were already waiting there. As an afterthought she added that Eva could bring her crew if it was necessary to convince her to go and stop being such a cabezóna. Eva sent back a message saying she was busy but fine.

Mari also left a message, that she was in meetings but would tell Eva if there was anything worth telling. She wanted to know about the status of the mechs. Eva didn't respond.

Pete didn't leave any messages at all. They hadn't parted on the best terms, but that was odd. Eva wondered what he was up to, and the paranoid part of her considered that maybe, just maybe, he was working with Tito. If he was, he would never confirm it, so it wasn't worth asking.

Eva sat in her room, on her bed, and watched her fish float aimlessly in their tank, going nowhere, doing nothing but existing. Simple. Straightforward. She envied that. A sudden, wild impulse gripped her, urging her to drop them into an ocean somewhere, let them swim free for a little while, even if it meant reality would snap its jaws around them. What had she been thinking, putting them in here in the first place? Had she imagined she was keeping them safe, that this was better than the alternative?

Someone knocked on her door, startling her out of her dark

thoughts. Eva opened it with a thought and Pink stood there, but didn't enter.

"Come on," Pink said. "We need to talk."

Eva got up and followed Pink to the mess, where a cup of water and a snack waited. Eva winced. If Pink was being aggressively practical about monitoring other people's self-care, that meant she was trying to avoid her own worries. Still, she sat down and dutifully ate the protein bar, savoring the chewy texture with the same nostalgia she felt for a few of her scars. The bricks of carefully calibrated macronutrients had become emergency rations once their cash flow started improving, when fucking with The Fridge was lucrative and Vakar's bosses were happy to subsidize their efforts.

Funny how fast things could turn around on you.

"Cuéntamelo, co-captain," Eva said, chasing a mouthful of mediocrity down with a swig of her drink.

"None of us are sure what to do now," Pink said, leaning back in her chair and hanging her elbow on the back. "Two mechs are a lot, but can we win this fight without the third one? Is it worth the risk?"

Eva shrugged. She hadn't figured out an answer yet herself.

"Me, I'm wondering if I might be more help on the ground somewhere," Pink continued. "Maybe Nuvesta, or some other crowded spot. My friend Pat is running a free clinic with his husband; he said he could use an extra pair of hands. Sue's thinking maybe The Forge could use an engineer, or at least a mechanic. Min doesn't want to leave her second body, but now might be the time for it."

Eva thought of Goyangi sinking into the lava and fought to swallow the chunk of food in her mouth. It lingered in her throat, a painful lump, aching all the way down.

"Leroy and Momoko are talking about running the blockade on Earth with the mechs," Pink continued. "Momoko isn't feeling it, but Leroy's real pressed about his moms."

"Seems like a good way to get a planet blown up, after what happened to the gmaarg," Eva said. "What about Joe?"

Pink sighed and rubbed her eye under the patch. "He says he has nowhere to go. He only went back to Tito because the *Crash Sisters* thing didn't work out, and he figured that was a safe bet compared to others." She stared into space, her features hardening. "He claims he regretted it as soon as he saw Tito's smugly face."

Eva hesitated, then reached out to lay her hand on Pink's. "Do you believe him?" Eva asked.

"I watched his vitals while I asked him about everything," Pink said. "He's either a really good liar, or he's not lying." She looked down at Eva's hand, as if trying to decide whether to move it. "Tricking tests like that isn't impossible. For some people, it's not even hard."

"But do you believe him?" Eva asked.

"I want to," Pink replied, her voice low and weary. "I really, really want to. I want to think he's like us, that he did what he did for his own fool-ass reasons, and he got tired of the bullshit, and he tried to get out but didn't stick the landing."

"Narrative disorder is a hell of a drug, though," Eva said.

"It sure is," Pink said. "Easy for some folks as lying, because in a lot of ways it's the same game."

They fell silent, and in that moment, Eva had the weirdest feeling. Like she needed to say something important, something enormously consequential, and if she got it wrong it would be like knocking over the first domino in a long, winding trail of them. And at the end of that trail, a domino would land on a trigger that would blow her whole life to pieces, and she'd never be able to put them all back together, no matter how hard she tried.

Before she could speak, her commlink jangled. A call on her secure line, so it could only be one of three people, all of whom were related to her.

"Don't move," she told Pink, and jogged back to her room. She hoped she wasn't making a horrible mistake in leaving things so unsettled.

The holovid projection from her closet showed a disheveled Pete Innocente, looking older and more tired than Eva had last seen him. His once-black hair was now a uniform gray fading to white, cropped short, and he sported a full beard that matched. His spacesuit collar looked smudged with grease or dirt, but the isohelmet was off, so presumably he was somewhere with breathable air.

Last time Eva had seen him, she had traded ships with him, leaving him with the one she'd christened *El Cucullo* during the brief time she'd flown it. She had no idea what he'd gotten up to since then, because she stopped talking to him again on account of how he stole her ship.

"Eva," Pete said. "Passcodes?"

"Of course." They exchanged the usual series of signs and countersigns that would seem bizarre to an outsider but were second nature to them, even now. Eva wondered if other families had this same level of paranoia every time they took a simple call; her mother didn't, but Mari had gone so far as to make Eva install various encrypted authorization programs on her commlink.

"So what do you need, Pete?" Eva asked.

"You assume I need something," Pete said, grinning. "Maybe I have an offer for you."

Eva was sure any offer would help him somehow, but she

held her tongue. She didn't feel like arguing with anyone, and she didn't have time to be diplomatic or evasive.

"What is it?" she asked.

"I've got a flotilla of ships together," he said, raising his palm to someone she couldn't see as if asking them to wait. "We set up our own flight path, traveling between a few of the Gates that don't have monoliths, taking it slow and skimming for fuel when we can't scavenge it."

"Scavenge" might also mean steal, but again, Eva stayed quiet.

"I know you've probably got your own plans," Pete continued, "but we can make space for you and your crew if you want to join us."

"I'll have to ask everyone else if they're interested," Eva replied. "What's the catch?"

"No catch, no conditions," Pete said. "We're just sharing resources, keeping each other safe."

Eva's suspicions rose like the hairs on her arms. "My ship isn't heavily armed," she said. "Are you stopping at places where you need guns or muscle?"

His expression went from friendly to serious. "A little bird told me you've got other options on the table."

"Which little bird?" Eva would wring its neck.

Pete waved a hand dismissively. "Staying out in the fringe means everyone is running out of supplies," he said. "At some point, depending on how things go, we'll need to start running the blockades elsewhere. With your experience and firepower, we could make a tidy profit transporting goods between places that have them. Whoever wants to barter will—"

"Are you serious?" Eva interrupted. "The universe is going to shit and you're thinking about how you can make money off it?"

"Not right away," Pete said. "We don't know how everything is going to shake out, but eventually we—"

"No!" Eva exclaimed. "I can't believe you! People are dead, and more people are going to die. Who gives a shit about money at a time like this?"

"People die every day, Eva-Bee," Pete said, frowning. "You want to pretend there weren't already cracks in the universe that folks were falling through before this happened? Did you care about them then? Don't get all high and mighty, little girl, just because there's a big wolf everyone can agree is bad. The universe is full of wolves, and if you're not a wolf, you're a sheep, and one day you're going to get gobbled right up."

"There are other options," Eva insisted. "Shepherds. Sheep-dogs."

"They eat the sheep in the end, too, kiddo. They're just wolves biding their time by pretending to be nice about it."

Eva took a deep breath to calm herself, because she didn't have the luxury of telling him to suck void when her crew's lives were at stake.

"I'll ask my people if they're interested," she said, as calmly as she could manage. "Do you want me to message you with my answer or are you going to give me a call back?"

"Message me," Pete said. "I'll send you the coordinates." He paused, then shook his head and plastered a smile on. "Take care of yourself, Eva-Bee. And that hunk of junk you call a ship."

"Back at you, Pete," Eva said. She couldn't bring herself to call him Papi, or Dad, or anything like it. Some habits died hard, and some never would.

The call disconnected, leaving empty space where her father's torso had been. Eva thought about what he'd said, about wolves and sheep; it was a cold way of looking at life, as if everything could be divided so starkly. As if people by nature had to kill or be killed, eat or be eaten. A binary that could yield only a one or a zero, a coin with only two sides.

People were people, not grotesque caricatures of reductive morality. When you told yourself every problem was a trolley problem, killing became a necessary part of every solution.

A coin had three sides, technically speaking, and one of them went on forever.

But Eva had said she'd make the offer to her crew, and she meant it. She couldn't decide this unilaterally, not even by withholding the option. They all had the right to consider every available avenue at their disposal, even the ones that might be difficult to accomplish. They'd done plenty of hard stuff together already; this was one more situation they'd figure out as a unit, one way or another.

That thought lightened her mood slightly. Before she could take it to the others, though, another call came in on the emergency channel. Pete again? Unlikely.

Eva answered, and this time Mari's face appeared, disheveled and frantic, eyes wide and lips half-open. A horrifying memory flashed through Eva's mind, of seeing this same expression when her sister had pretended to be kidnapped, except now it appeared to be genuine.

"Eva, don't say anything," Mari said, the words pouring out in a rush. "Just listen. I don't have much time, and they might cut me off." She took a steadying breath. "I'm on Earth, with The Forge, and we're working with BOFA in secret. Not even President Herrington knows what we're doing. The todyk used a superweapon here, millions of years ago, one powerful enough to destroy the Artificer flagship in this star system. It should be up and running in two cycles. But if they use it, the Earth will be destroyed, too. This will be the test case, and if it works, more of them will be made and used everywhere. Billions of people will die, trillions of them, to save the rest. You have to find the third mech. You have to—"

The call abruptly ended. Where Eva had previously stared at her closet and mused at her father's attitude in disgust and exasperation, now all she could summon was a vast, yawning chasm of horror.

This was the mother of all trolley problems, and Eva and her crew were the only ones who had even the slightest chance of stopping the trolley before it was too late.

Chapter 15

CONTINUE

When Eva told everyone about what might happen to Earth, what The Forge and BOFA were planning, Leroy went ballistic.

He punched the wall of the mess, then threw a chair that bounced off the table and nearly hit Sue. She managed to duck and flee, covering her head with her arms. Eva shouted at Pink to get a sedative as Momoko wrestled Leroy to the ground, but Pink just sat there, unmoving, her eye staring blankly at nothing. Vakar found the necessary tranquilizer but took a headbutt to the jaw when he tried to administer it. Momoko switched her leg lock to keep Leroy down, her muscles straining with the effort, and finally Eva finished the job.

The cats didn't even bother making an appearance. They'd learned the hard way that Leroy didn't respond to their efforts past a certain point.

Eva scrounged up an antigrav belt, which she and Momoko

used to get Leroy into the med bay, strapping him down on the chair so he wouldn't hurt himself or someone else when he woke up. It might have been the wrong thing to do—she knew how she would react to waking up tied down—but the person who'd know what was right couldn't be reached. That was next on Eva's punch list, no pun intended.

Pink still sat in the mess when Eva returned and lightly touched her shoulder. No response.

"Hey, Pink," Eva said softly. "Leroy is knocked out and tied up. Momoko is watching him. Vakar is fixing his own face. Sue is hiding with Min on the bridge. We need to . . ." She trailed off, biting her lip.

"We need to what," Pink said in a monotone.

"We need to make a plan," Eva said.

"Make a plan, then," Pink said. "Ain't nobody stopping you." She stood up slowly, as if her bones had gone arthritic, and walked out. Eva followed her to the crew quarters, but stopped and let Pink go inside alone and close the door behind her.

Vakar emerged from the med bay, smelling like a rusty fart. It wasn't a combination Eva enjoyed.

"How is Pink?" he asked.

"I've never seen her this fucked up," Eva said. "Losing the other mech was bad, the invasion was worse, but this? It's too much. I need to do something. I need to fix this." She fought the urge to punch the wall, like Leroy had.

"Then we will do something and fix it," Vakar said.

Eva blinked. "Just like that, huh?"

"I am well aware that the situation is extremely dire, and that everyone is experiencing intense emotional reactions." Vakar's smell shifted to incense, concern. "If it were my family members, my home, and predominantly my species currently being offered up as a sacrifice to the greater good, I would be in a similar state.

It is not, so while I am sympathetic and outraged on your behalf, I am better equipped to orient myself toward the goal of preventing such an undesirable outcome."

A laugh escaped Eva, and she slid her arms around him, resting her head on his chest. "Alabao," she said. "If you weren't here, I'd need another few hours at least to work myself up to doing anything useful. With you, maybe I really can start pulling together a plan instead of just giving up and joining Pete's fleet."

Vakar smelled briefly confused. "Pete, your father? He has his own fleet?"

"I'll explain in a minute." For that minute, Eva told herself she was allowed to hug her damn partner and do absolutely nothing, no matter what the writhing mass of stress in her stomach tried to tell her.

It barely lasted twenty seconds before Min interrupted. "Incoming fighters! Strap in, I'm going to run!"

No sooner had the words left the speakers than the ship shook from an impact to the aft shields, then accelerated as Min began evasive maneuvers. She had to account for the mechs, which were all tethered to *La Sirena Negra* with maglocks, trailing the ship like dogs on leashes. Eva and Vakar raced to the bridge, finding Sue there wearing an expression of alarm as Min, eyes closed, lay in the pilot's chair focused on flying. Mala clung to her lap, emanating concern.

Eva pulled up the sensors and examined the situation. Multiple attackers, varying sizes, weapons uncertain. The hit they'd taken suggested at least one plasma cannon, but kinetics were also possible if this was Tito—was it? She wasn't sure yet. It could be him, or his Artificer allies, or both. Or had the Wraith they brushed off staged a tactical retreat and come back with reinforcements? The quennians couldn't be that mad at Vakar, could they?

"Message for you, Cap," Min said, her voice strained.

Eva pulled it up. Audio only.

"Hey, Eva," Tito's cheerful voice said. "My amigos and I really appreciate you getting the mechs together for us. Super convenient. Give them up quietly and we'll let you leave, pero si no . . . Bueno, my guns are bigger than yours, mijita. Be smart for a change."

Eva gripped the captain's chair. That cabrón hijo de la gran mierda. How many of his ships had Momoko destroyed on the lava planet? And here he was, still high on his own farts.

Didn't matter. First priority was escape. Run away and live to fight another cycle and all that.

Except . . . This was another cycle, wasn't it? This was the moment. Things weren't going to get better unless they did something, and running away wouldn't accomplish anything. They'd be in another galaxy somewhere, licking their wounds, waiting for the next attack. The same scenario would repeat over and over as the enemy wore them down, until they'd make a mistake that would be too big to recover from, and that would be it. The end of the universe for them, and possibly for everyone else.

"No más," Eva muttered. "No me busques." But they had, and they'd found her, and she would make them sorry for it.

Sensors registered a half dozen smaller ships and a frigate—no, a destroyer. Alone, *La Sirena Negra* couldn't possibly handle something with that kind of firepower. But her crew had two mechs that were supposed to be phenomenal weapons by themselves. So what if the third was missing? That was a problem for later. Right now, the problem was firing on them as Min dodged and weaved, and they sure as hell were going to solve it.

"Sue," Eva said. "Get ready to pilot a mech and meet me in the cargo bay. We're not running. If these resingado comemierdas want the mechs, they're going to get them, and it'll be the last thing they ever get."

"Bloodthirsty," Vakar said, smelling like vanilla and rosewater.

Eva shrugged. "They came looking for a minnow, but they found a mermaid. And not the sweet, sexy kind. We're gonna crash their boat into some rocks and drown them."

Sue ran out and a haggard Pink walked in, her visible eye red-rimmed and bloodshot. Eva gripped her friend by the arm to steady her, and they stared at each other for a moment before Pink nodded imperceptibly. She wasn't better, but she was good enough for now.

"What's the plan?" Pink asked.

"Sue and Momoko use the mechs the way their makers intended," Eva said. "Sun's out, guns out. Min, keep evading. Vakar, keep us from losing shields or blowing up or catching fire. Pink, get Leroy conscious and working our weapons, or leave him sedated and you do it." She hesitated. "Or get Joe to do it. He's a good shot."

Pink's eye widened and she nodded, then left the bridge. She'd no doubt be back to barking her own orders and ideas soon enough, but for now, it was Eva's turn to be the load-bearing wall.

Vakar gave her one last hug, then left as well.

Eva scanned their current star system for a place they could stop long enough for Sue and Momoko to transfer to the mechs. It would be dangerous, and they'd need at the very least cover, otherwise two squishy humans would be vaporized before they had a chance to retaliate. If they could slow their pursuers down, buy some time . . .

There. One of the planets in this system had an ice ring that might do the trick. If Min could thread the needle through it for long enough, they could potentially lose their pursuers . . .

no, that wouldn't work, not with the mechs being towed along behind the ship. They were able to maneuver decently, but not to the extent required for something like this. Eva kept looking, her brow furrowed in concentration.

Nothing useful. Passive sensors would be able to find them anywhere in this forsaken system. They might be able to make it to a Gate and find a better place to engage, but they might end up losing their pursuers that way. While that appealed on some level, Eva wanted to fight. She wanted to win.

They did have one more option, though: they could play dead.

"Min, get us into that ice ring," Eva said, sending Min the coordinates. "Once we're in, we're going dark."

"Are you sure, Cap?" Min asked. "That's risky."

"It'll make us invisible to their sensors for long enough to get Sue and Momoko into the mechs," Eva said. "By the time they get a visual, we'll be back in action."

"If something goes wrong . . ." Min fell silent.

"Your body will be okay," Eva said gently. "Sue won't let anything happen to you, and neither will I. Stand by for my mark." She headed for the cargo bay to check on the cats. They all needed to be in their crate for this, or they'd be floating all over the cargo bay again.

She passed Pink in the hallway, coming out of the med bay with Momoko. Pink shook her head at Eva's quirked eyebrow. Leroy was out, then.

"Come on," Eva said. "Help me with the cats. Momoko, are you ready to fight?"

"I'm always ready," Momoko replied, smiling like the pretty princess she was.

This time, all Eva had to do was tell Mala what was happening, and soon all twenty of her feline tenants had scrambled in from their various hidey-holes and secured themselves in their crate. Unlike before, when the artificial gravity and stabilizers had turned off, going fully dark would mean that the engines were cut, the shields, the weapons systems . . . and most important, all life-support functions would be suspended. The ship's insulation would keep the temperature steady for a while, so they'd run out of breathable air before they froze or overheated.

If this trick didn't work, though, those would be the least of their problems.

"Isohelmets on, everyone," Eva said over comms. "Life support and gravity will be shut off in T-minus two minutes. Vakar, when the backups kick in, shut them down. No emissions, nada."

Pink joined Joe in his cabin to share the plan and get him plugged into the ship's weapons system for when they rebooted. Part of Eva still worried about him, whether he could be trusted, but this was as good a time as any for a trust fall. If he didn't catch them, they'd know for sure and could react accordingly—assuming they survived. At the very least, hopefully he'd care enough about self-preservation to work with them.

Momoko and Sue waited nearby, helmets activated. Sue looked determined but pale, nervous as she always was before a battle where she'd be fighting instead of fixing things in the guts of the ship. Momoko was calm and poised, or doing a damn good job of pretending to be—she was an actress, after all. Her fights had mostly been staged recently, and yet Eva got the impression that her past held a lot of action that wasn't so carefully managed and choreographed.

"Almost to the ice rings, Cap," Min said over the speakers.

"Bueno," Eva said. "Once you're in, maneuver as much as you can to get embedded and then power down on my signal." To Sue and Momoko, she said, "You'll have to use the emergency hatch, since the energy curtain won't be working and we don't want to let the void in. As soon as everything is dark, get out and get to your mechs. There won't be much time."

Sue and Momoko both nodded. What Eva didn't add was that there might be no time at all, assuming whoever was chasing them managed to find them despite their being invisible to sensors. If this didn't work, not only could these two get shot, the whole ship would be an easy target with no defenses whatsoever.

Eva opened the emergency hatch, gesturing for Sue and Momoko to climb in. Momoko went first, her face a mask of concentration, and Sue followed with a more determined look. Once they were inside, Eva closed the hatch and stepped away, back toward the hallway that would lead to the bridge, through the mess, and past the crew quarters and med bay and her own empty room.

For a moment, standing outside the door to the bridge, Eva closed her eyes and inhaled sharply. Then she activated her iso-helmet and pulled up the ship's sensor readings, along with the current views from the fore and aft cameras. They were about to plunge into the outermost ice ring, the planet itself looming large and deep blue in the background. Huge chunks of frozen rock tumbled through space, occasionally smashing into each other and breaking apart into smaller pieces. Min brought them in so they'd drift in the same counterclockwise direction once they cut power, hopefully hiding in the shadow of one of the larger pieces.

Besides being found and vaporized by Tito, the risk of being crushed by uncaring space ice loomed as the other part of this plan that could go very wrong, very fast.

"Setting a countdown, Cap," Min said over comms. "T-minus thirty seconds."

"Comm silence as soon as we go dark," Eva said. "Sue, Momoko, ping us when you're fight-ready and we'll move out."

"You got it, Captain," Sue replied.

"Let's do this!" Momoko added.

Eva grinned and stepped into the bridge, taking the seat next to Pink.

"Just like old times," Eva said.

Pink snorted, summoning up a weary smile. "It's not old times if it happens all the time, fool."

As usual, Pink wasn't wrong.

The countdown ticked away as the ship slid into the ice ring. Min dodged and weaved, over and around and under and even through the larger pieces, as nimble with *La Sirena Negra* as a dancer on a stage or a fighter in the pit. Eva had been in worse traffic jams, in vast airways or tunnels where vehicles crammed close together moving below supersonic speed. This had the same sense of density, the lack of order to the various movements aside from the general direction. Tiny flecks of debris hit their shields, and Eva hoped the empty wake they left wouldn't be so obvious that Tito could follow it straight to them.

A huge rock loomed, spinning and tumbling through the crowded field, big as a city block. It should be able to hide them, if they could manage to keep from crashing into it, or vice versa.

"That's our cover, Cap," Min said. "Decelerating and cutting power in five . . . four . . ."

Eva held her breath, even knowing it was unnecessary. Breathing stole her focus. Two . . . one . . .

The exterior views she'd been monitoring in her isohelmet disappeared as the control panel in front of her went dark. A moment later, the emergency systems tried to boot up, but Vakar cut them off manually from the guts of the ship. An eerie silence fell, broken when Eva finally sucked in a breath and exhaled.

Sue and Momoko should be climbing out of the emergency hatch now, pushing off the hull's exterior and floating toward their respective mechs. Eva's brain cycled through all the ways this could go wrong, until finally she started humming the *Crash Sisters* theme to distract herself.

The hull groaned. A patter of objects struck it, like hail on a metal roof, echoing through the empty cargo bay. Eva flinched and gripped the arms of her chair. Waiting chafed like a tight strap, especially like this, when she was powerless to do anything else. She had to trust her people, to believe they were competent and capable, and she had to trust her own plan even as she knew it was far from airtight.

Eva hated doing this, risking the lives of those under her command—voluntarily, to be sure, but her responsibility none-theless. If they died, it was her fault. This was her plan, but they were taking the brunt of the danger on their shoulders.

This part of being a captain never got easier. And in that moment she knew, too, that this feeling was one that Tito had never, ever experienced in his life. He wasn't afraid to lead from the front, but he loved himself, and he loved money, and that was the end of love as far as he was concerned. To him, every crew member was a tool, a weapon, an object to be used as needed and discarded when no longer useful.

To Eva, these people were life, and home, and love, and ev-erything she needed to keep safe. Theirs were the faces she saw every time she thought about the mythical greater good Mari was always flipping out over.

An eternity later, or possibly only a few minutes, Momoko pinged, ((Ready.))

Eva waited longer, her jaw locked tight enough to hurt.

((I'm in,)) Sue pinged.

Eva's breath hissed out of her like a leaky hose.

((Make trouble,)) she pinged back. By the time *La Sirena Negra* was up and running, with any luck, Tito and the rest of his little armada would be sucking void. Now they just needed to restart the ship and help the mechs do as much damage as possible.

Eva raised her comms again. "Min, power us up. The mechs are in play so we need to move."

"You got it, Cap," Min replied.

This locura might work after all, Eva thought. That would be a first. She waited, staring at the dark console in front of her, which would light up in a moment. Any second now. Definitely very soon.

"Uh, Cap," Min said. "We have a problem."

Right on cue, Eva thought. "What is it?"

"I can't get the ship to start. It won't even give me any error messages. The computers are totally offline."

"Me cago en diez," Eva said. "Vakar, what's happening down there?"

"Nothing is occurring because there is no power," Vakar replied. He sounded more testy than usual. "There is either damage to the power conduit between the starter battery and the computer systems, or the battery itself is depleted."

Eva groaned and tried to rub her neck, but couldn't because of her isohelmet. She fumbled to unhook herself from the chair's restraints, drifting upward as soon as she was free due to the lack of gravity.

"Eva," Vakar said, his tone brutally neutral. "Did you never replace the starter battery when I indicated it was no longer functioning properly?"

"I had Sue overload it so it would keep taking a charge," Eva replied. "It's been working fine since—"

"I told you that procedure was dangerous. The shock to the crystal accumulation can cause an explosion of poisonous gas that can kill everyone on the ship!"

"Well, it didn't," Eva said defensively. "I had her do it outside." She kicked off the back of her chair toward the door to the bridge, somersaulting forward to land on her feet, then launching herself down the hallway to the mess.

"Do you have a replacement battery?" Vakar asked.

"It's in the cargo bay," Eva said. "I think. I don't know where Sue keeps everything." And Sue was in the middle of a firefight, against a whole lot of ships, including a destroyer. And if Eva couldn't get their systems back up in a hurry, it would take only one missile or a nasty hunk of ice to end *La Sirena Negra* permanently.

The cargo bay was dark except for the dim glow of the cat container, illuminating twenty felines in various stages of emotional distress. Eva turned on her suit's light and activated her gravboots, stomping over to the cabinets where spare parts were normally kept. Sue wasn't as organized as Vakar, mostly because she kept her own internal inventory system relying on AR tags—which only required her to note where she had put something, not that it be a reasonable place for anyone else to find it.

Eva scanned the items through the doors, glad that at least she'd made everyone clean up and secure everything after their last antigrav incident. If this was going to keep happening, she might need to invest in fancier storage options.

Then again, she hadn't even replaced the damn starter battery, which had seemed perfectly reasonable at the time. Her dad had shown her how to boost them when she was still in her teens, and it had always worked before.

Focus, fool, Eva told herself sternly. You don't have time for this.

The battery should have been large enough for her to see it quickly, on one of the lower shelves where heavy items were kept.

And yet, nothing. Where else might Sue have put it? Eva considered the passenger cabin, but no, they'd emptied that out before they stuck Joe in there.

An impact rocked the ship with a loud crunch. It began to rotate more rapidly, as if whatever had hit them had also sent them spinning off into the ice ring. More pings and clangs struck the hull, echoing in the large room.

Without sensors or cameras, Eva couldn't know which direction they were moving in, whether toward the huge rock they'd been hiding under or away from it and into the stream of other ice shards. Either was bad, because crashing into an enormous solid mass would probably wreck the ship, but so would taking accumulated damage from smaller impacts, and if they ended up outside of the ring entirely they'd be much more likely to be picked up on visuals by Tito's fleet.

Eva pinged Sue twice in rapid succession. ((Starter battery. Where?)) Then she returned to scouring the cargo bay for it, hoping against hope it would magically manifest in front of her suit's light. Instead, Vakar appeared, startling a yelp out of her.

"Don't scare me like that," she said. "Help me look for the battery."

"There is an additional problem," Vakar said, grabbing a handhold on the wall to keep from floating around. "The power conduit is not damaged, but the control wires are extremely corroded. They must be cleaned or replaced before the new battery can be installed, and that takes time."

"So get cleaning, Cinderella," Eva said. "I'll be down there as soon as I find this cabrón pedazo de mierda."

"Cleaning these cables may degrade them beyond use," Vakar said quietly. "If we cannot replace them, the ship will never restart."

Eva hissed a breath out between her teeth as the ship continued to spin, the cats putting out tiny flickers of discomfort and fear nearby.

"We don't have a choice," Eva said. "No, that's a lie; there's always a choice, but I'm not going to choose to lie down and cry. Try to clean the cables, and if that doesn't work, I'll go down there with clamps."

"That could—"

Eva raised a finger to silence him as she stomped toward him. "A lot of things could happen. We could blow up literally any second. We could be space debris before I finish this sentence. I can't control any of that." She poked him in the chest, glaring up at his mirrored helmet. "What I can control is what I do right now, and the next thing, and the next. So go clean the cables, because if I can't find this battery, I'll be down there in a minute with clamps and a welder, and you can help me or you can get out of my way."

Vakar was silent for a long moment. "I had intended to say 'That could work,' but that was a very fine speech," he said. "I will see you again soon."

Eva snorted, watching him return to his work. Fuck, she'd missed him.

((Sorry, fighting,)) Sue pinged. ((Storage bin. Bottom left.))

One thing, then the next, Eva thought. She took a step toward the storage bin, and another, and another.

Chapter 16

POWERS COMBINE

By the time Eva and Vakar cleaned the cables and installed the new battery, Momoko and Sue had driven away the remnants of the attacking fleet. There had been at least two Artificers among the fighters, one of whom had reportedly become some form of crab or arachnid while grappling with Momoko; that was new, and creepy, but all that mattered was Momoko sent him packing.

The mechs sustained virtually no damage, which made Eva feel slightly vindicated for her risky choice, but also increasingly weirded out by how overpowered they seemed to be. Sue excitedly told her about how she used a giant blade to slice an engine off the destroyer before Momoko blew it up with an energy weapon, and Min screeched in delight and jealousy, demanding to have the next turn with the mech. As if they hadn't almost died, and the fate of Earth wasn't still a horrifying potential disaster looming ahead of them.

Then again, a win like this could do a lot to make the impossible feel like it wasn't.

Pink and Momoko retreated to the med bay with Leroy, who was slowly coming around with a lot of quiet care. There wasn't a plan yet for saving Earth, but there was at least intent, and that was the first step toward hope and away from despair.

Vakar threw himself into repairs, and Eva let him. He needed to feel control over something as much as she did, and it was frankly the most useful thing he could do until they had a firmer sense of what their next steps were.

Joe was back in his room. Eva almost would have thought Tito was using him to track their ship, except his access to Artificer intel was a more likely explanation. Antimatter had said they were either using the monoliths to monitor Gate travel or they had some way of accessing the Gate logs directly. And as plans went, hoping your sniper's ex-girlfriend would whisk him away during a firefight so you could have a mole on the enemy's ship? It was convoluted and not a little absurd to contemplate. That didn't mean Joe wasn't being used, but Eva continued to creep closer to trusting him.

Eva sat in the mess with a tazita of espresso, thinking. Their top priority had to be getting the missing mech back. That meant finding either Miles Erck or the mysterious and strange Smedley, who was so elusive that Vakar had been planted on a random asteroid for weeks in the hopes that he would eventually show up. Of the two, Miles was more likely to surface somewhere, or have left a trail Eva could try to pick up. She could start where she'd dropped him off before the trip to Brodevis, assuming Vakar and Min weren't able to find more recent information through their usual channels.

"Cap, there's someone outside looking for you," Min said over the ship's speakers. "I think it's the Proarkhe from before?"

"Antimatter," Eva said. "I'll be right there." She swallowed the rest of her coffee quickly, the burn worth it for the burst of caffeine that would hit her soon. She walked down to the cargo bay, pinging Vakar to meet her there in case she needed moral support. Before she opened the door, she glared at the cats sprawled across the floor.

"Oye, malcriados," she said. "Our guest is back, the one you all scared last time. Be nice or else."

Or else what? they seemed to ask, staring at her in utter disinterest or ignoring her entirely.

Eva pressed the button to open the door and folded her arms over her chest, waiting for whatever would come next.

It was indeed Antimatter outside, once again hovering in space with no consideration for the lack of atmosphere or the temperature. Proarkhe didn't need to breathe, apparently; they didn't feel hot or cold, or perhaps some invisible shielding and respiration technology did the job. She thought for a moment of Mari, poor Mari, who'd spent her life digging up Proarkhe ruins and writing books about them, and now they were standing here in front of Eva while Mari was in a whole other galaxy. Not to mention Leroy in the med bay, who'd devoured every rumor and conspiracy about the elusive ancient species, including Mari's own doctoral dissertation. And yet the Proarkhe near Mari were on a spaceship with weapons presumably pointed in her direction, ready to vaporize Leroy's family. Life really was a kick in the pants sometimes.

Had everyone else colonized Proarkhe space without realizing it, or had the Proarkhe been colonizers themselves? So many questions. Eva wished she'd written some down so she wouldn't be making them up on the fly, but then again, there were bigger issues to deal with than the history of a species that had disappeared for millennia.

Mari probably wouldn't agree, but maybe that was just Eva being judgmental.

Antimatter floated inside and landed carefully, compensating for the sudden gravity. "Hola," she said. "I'm sorry we couldn't warn you about the Artificers' timeline being rushed. We only found out ourselves when it was too late."

"You did what you could," Eva said, hoping it was true. This could all still be some elaborate con, but much like Pink with Joe, she didn't want to believe it. Couldn't believe it, because it would mean there was no hope of beating an enemy so many steps ahead.

"My leaders want to meet with you," Antimatter said. "Since you only have two of the three necessary constructs to complete the superweapon, they want to discuss the best strategy for how to proceed."

Eva raised an eyebrow. "So they don't trust me to come up with something useful?"

Antimatter blinked a few times. "No, but I understand why you would think that. They want to coordinate more closely since the situation has changed." She looked to Vakar, who surfaced from the ship's underbelly, smelling up a storm. "You can bring your . . . partner? Or if there is someone else—"

"I will accompany her," Vakar said, his scent enough like hot cooking oil to make Eva toss him a reassuring glance. He wasn't wrong to be suspicious, but broadcasting it might not be helpful.

"We're already suited up," Eva said. "Give us . . . ten minutes?" Vakar nodded and departed to put away his tools and grab whatever he wanted to bring along.

Antimatter studied Eva with slightly brighter eyes when she turned back. "What?" Eva asked.

"Sorry," Antimatter said. "I've spent some of my spare time learning about the ways your different species engage in certain . . . relations."

A flush crept up Eva's neck, but she grinned. "Are we talking friendships or mating rituals or what?"

"Both, but I was referring to the latter." Antimatter's glowing eyes narrowed, then widened again. "We have a surprising amount of overlap among my people, even though we don't reproduce in any of the ways life seems to here."

"You have, em, rituals though?"

Antimatter made a warbling noise that Eva took for a laugh. "Too sparking many, sometimes. Some of us like it slick and easy. Hook up for a while, decouple, and get back to work. Some of us prefer more serious connections."

"People here do hookups, too," Eva said. "Not always literally, but the tech exists. I've even known a few long-term relationships where the people never met physically."

"Same," Antimatter said. "The physical stuff can be fun, though."

Fun was part of it, Eva thought. Before Vakar, she'd been sure it was the only good part. It had taken her time and self-reflection to accept that she'd been doing all sorts of questionable stuff in her own brain that therapy was still trying to straighten out. But that was her problem, her trajectory, and other people had different ones.

"I should get ready to go," Eva said. "Be right back." Leaving her crew now, when things were so unstable, felt wrong, but maybe this would bring some of the stability back. Maybe she'd be able to help come up with the plan that would fix all the problems they faced.

It was hard to believe that, or even pretend to, but she had to. Her crew counted on her, and she counted on them. They all needed each other.

And now they knew the mechs were, indeed, a powerful weapon, so even without the third one, they could wreck some shit.

"Min," Eva said as she walked, "I'm going to meet with the Proarkhe. I don't know how long I'll be gone, but please . . . all of you, take care of each other. Hopefully I'll come back with good news."

"You got it, Cap," Min said. "Make sure you take holovids for Leroy!"

Eva ducked into her room and closed the door, grinning at the thought of Leroy flipping out over a selfie of her with a bunch of legendary people. Maybe when they got back, he would be chill enough to come meet with Antimatter himself.

At first, Eva assumed Antimatter had some way of turning into a spaceship that could transport her and Vakar to wherever they needed to go, but it turned out there was a more expedient method: the Proarkhe simply pulled them out into space with her, then opened a hole right there—a traverse, Antimatter had called it—and yanked them through.

It was as shocking as the first time it had happened to Eva, back in the Fridge lab when she'd been trying to get her ship back from Pete. A pair of devices had shot linked holes onto any flat surface, forming portable Gates that anyone could jump through at will. Eva had stolen them and hidden them, and to her knowledge no one had found them yet; one of them didn't work anyway, so they were of no use to her. It surprised her sometimes that the Fridge scientists hadn't bothered to re-create them yet, since she doubted Mari and her Forge allies had been entirely successful at wiping out all the data in the archives there. Hell, she was surprised Mari didn't already have Gate guns of her own, using stolen intel and whatever resources were available.

Maybe she did, and she just hadn't told Eva. Wouldn't be the first time.

So one moment they were drifting in space outside *La Sirena Negra*, and the next they were inside a tall, circular room lined with faint purple-pink lights. Eva glanced over her shoulder at the star-sprinkled blackness, which vanished in a blink, leaving only a large metallic ring in its place, like a miniature Gate. The ring was mounted on a raised platform with a ramp leading down, and off to the left an instrument panel rose from the floor, like the ones she and Vakar had found in Proarkhe ruins on Cavus what felt like ages ago.

Behind the panel, another Proarkhe stood, about a meter taller and broader than Antimatter. After a momentary lag, Eva's commlink supplied he/him pronouns but no name. He was a garish yellow compared to Antimatter's more muted tones, with bluish-gray limbs and a face like brushed steel. His shoulders were large and round, almost as if he wore armor, and his arms and feet were similarly oversized and plated. Turquoise eyes regarded Eva and Vakar, and he made a noise she could best describe as quizzical. Like with Antimatter when they'd first met, the sound came right into her head, accompanied by a sharp pain.

"Yes, this is her," Antimatter replied. "Use the language program and communicator, Drone, don't be rude."

Drone said something else in their language, a series of modulations and wince-inducing hisses of noise, followed by three loud chimes. Then Eva's translator nanites kicked in as he switched to something they recognized.

"Sorry," Drone said. "I thought I'd already run that subroutine. Welcome to the *Pathfinder*. The Radices are waiting for you."

Antimatter gave a startled whine. "Are we late? I thought we had time to show her around."

Drone's forearm plates fluttered briefly. "I was told to bring you straight to the meeting chamber. There's a lot to discuss, and we've already lost time in deciding to bring her here at all."

"Governing by committee?" Eva asked. That at least sounded familiar.

"The Radices are able to network and process things relatively quickly," Antimatter said.

"But when they can't reach consensus," Drone added, "that's when you get lag. Come on."

He led them out of the room, into a hallway that dwarfed most others she had encountered. Vakar, in his Wraith armor, moved closer to Eva as they came across more Proarkhe going about their business. They varied in height, some smaller than Antimatter while others were double her size or more, and their shapes ranged from gangly to tanklike. Some looked more armored, and some carried weapons similar to the ones Tito had sported when Eva first met him in the castle ruins. Different color combinations abounded, bright and muted, light and dark, solid or patterned, and Eva wondered whether it was natural—whatever that meant to them—or whether they chose it like hair dye or tattoos. Their eyes glowed in various colors, too, from white to amber to bright green or blue, all of them tracking their strange visitors as they walked.

"Do I have something on my face?" Eva murmured to Vakar over comms.

"I believe the mere existence of your face interests them," Vakar replied.

The hallway branched off a few times, but her guides didn't

turn, eventually arriving at an even larger open area like the interior column of a cylindrical space station. Instead of elevators, most of the Proarkhe simply flew between levels, as if they were all outfitted with natural antigrav; none of them seemed to be using boosters. Everything was covered in or composed of a metallic material, though some portions were translucent and some were energy barriers rather than physical walls or platforms.

There were no plants anywhere, no animals, nothing that resembled organic life in any way. Nothing that didn't look constructed rather than grown, not even crystals, and not a single grain of dirt or dust. Her suit's sensors told her there was no atmosphere, either, and certainly no water.

"Is this a space station?" Eva asked Antimatter.

"A ship," Antimatter replied. "All our space stations were destroyed, and eventually we stopped building them. When you're at war for as long as we've been, staying mobile starts to seem like the most reasonable way to live."

Sensible enough, Eva supposed. Vakar shrugged his agreement as well; various quennian cultures had adopted a similar position for much of their history, and he himself had been raised on a Home Ship.

"None of you ever want to settle in one place?" Eva asked.

"We are settled in one place," Drone replied. "The place just moves."

Eva could relate. She'd lived on one ship for years, and it was as much a stable home as anywhere else. No matter where it went, there it was. She might go to sleep in one place and wake up in another, but that was outside; inside, she was in her own bed, the same bed, with the same fish, and the same people sitting around the table in the mess.

On the other side of the vast room, a short ramp led up to a solid wall. Four Proarkhe stood at the top of the ramp, which seemed weird until Antimatter and Drone approached them. After they exchanged a few tones and hisses, the Proarkhe moved aside and the wall opened—a door, then, leading to a brightly lit place that was eerily silent. Eva and Vakar stepped inside, and the wall disappeared behind them as if it had never existed.

This new room was like a cross between a stadium and an executive suite. Its ceiling was at least fifteen meters tall, which made sense, given the sizes of the Proarkhe at the round table in the center of the room. Even seated, three of their heads had to be around four or five meters off the floor, which would make them probably double that height standing up. The others were shorter, and based on the chair arrangement, Eva guessed the larger ones were in charge.

Were they the bosses because they were bigger, or did they get bigger when they were made bosses? Did height make right?

Mari might appreciate that joke, or she might find it distasteful. As a short person, Eva couldn't decide. The longer she thought about it, the more she vaguely felt like she was dissociating, given the continued strangeness of her life and the stress catching up to her.

The occupants of the table turned to look at the newcomers, their eyes brightening and their bodies undergoing various small motions—plates flexing outward, sharp edges extending and retracting, and so on. One of the large Proarkhe stood, broad-chested and bulky, his head reminding Eva of old-fashioned suits of armor even more than Vakar's Wraith helmet. He was mostly red, accented with blue and gray, and his eyes glowed a pale blue that was nearly white.

"Welcome, new friends," he rumbled into Eva's head. "I am called Radix Unary." He gestured at the others flanking him. "Radix Binary and Radix Ternary are also present, though we are currently linked, and so I speak for them. Additionally, these are our valued advisers: Hotfix, Flashbeam, Dynamis, Zenith, and Skyrmion."

The Proarkhe barely moved as their names were called, making it harder for Eva to know which one was whom, but she nodded politely in their general direction.

"Mucho gusto," she said, almost wincing at herself. They should have sent a diplomat.

"We are honored to meet you," Vakar added. Eva tossed him a grateful smile. Better.

Radix Unary tapped the table, and a pair of Eva-sized chairs appeared on top of the table. "Please, join us to discuss our strategy. I would offer you energy replenishment, but we lack the necessary raw materials to create something compatible with your systems."

"We, uh, already ate, thanks," Eva said. How would they get up to the table? It was too high to jump, and there was nothing to climb.

As if sensing her question, Antimatter grabbed Eva around the waist and deposited her within easy reach of the chairs. Drone did the same with Vakar, and then the two of them retreated to stand by the now-sealed door. Without further ado, Eva sat down, back rigidly straight.

"We were discussing how we might best utilize the Ithorian soulless bipedal constructs in your possession," Radix Unary said. "We have records in the Archives detailing some of their abilities, but because they were constructed by the Ithorians to be used against us, we do not have a complete understanding of their potential. We hope you can assist us." His eyes were so bright, Eva couldn't look at them; they left dark afterimages, blurred shadows that persisted when she looked away.

"What did you have in mind?" Eva asked.

One of the other Proarkhe spoke, a red-and-white one Eva thought had been called Hotfix. "Our tactics since the beginning of this invasion have been primarily disruptive rather than overtly aggressive," he said. "In the past, we would obstruct supply chains, take over or destroy their energy extraction operations, even commandeer their ships when possible."

"With your constructs, we could do even more," another Proarkhe said—Zenith? She was teal and pale blue, with purple accents. "Their weapons capabilities and shielding make each of them formidable tools. Combined, they have might equivalent to, perhaps even greater than, a fleetbreaker."

Eva had been right, then, to think that they were still in the game as long as they had the mechs.

"Our priority right now has to be Earth," Eva said.

"We have located it in our records," Radix Unary said. "We knew it by another name. It was the site of a fierce battle long ago, between the Artificers and the ones called the todyk. The todyk used a weapon that pulled an asteroid from the belt between Mars and Jupiter, with a speed that shattered a fleetbreaker before it struck the planet. Its impact caused massive climate disruption and death, and the todyk who survived were forced to abandon the world permanently."

Coño carajo, Eva thought. She had hoped Mari was exaggerating the danger of the device, that her warning was more hype than reality. Not only did this confirm her worries were valid, it meant the Artificers likely knew about the weapon—and knew exactly what it could do.

"Some of our people still take todyk forms," the one called Flashbeam said quietly. "We honor their sacrifice."

Eva wasn't sure what that meant, exactly. Proarkhe that looked like todyk? If they could change into skybikes or spaceships, why not?

"Well," Eva said, crossing her arms, "someone found that ancient weapon and they're planning to use it again. I don't know what the planet was like when the todyk lived there, but billions of humans are there now. And if the weapon works, BOFA is going to make copies and use them in other systems." She left the implications of that unspoken, because she wasn't sure she could choke them out if she tried.

"That's unfathomable," Zenith said, her eyes wide and bright.

"A calculated risk," Hotfix said. "They trade some lives in the hopes of saving others."

Another Proarkhe chimed in. Skyrmion. They stared at Eva as if they could see through her. "What would you have us do about this?"

"We can't let the weapon be activated, obviously," Eva said. Maybe it was only obvious to her, though. "We have to get the fleet there to retreat, if nothing else."

"With only two of the constructs," Hotfix said, "engaging with the forces in the Sol system would be foolish."

"I agree," Skyrmion said. "We would have no choice but to attempt an all-out assault, which would overcommit our limited resources."

"But part of honoring sacrifices means trying not to repeat them," Flashbeam argued. "If we allow this—"

"It's not a question of allowing it," Hotfix interrupted. "How would we prevent it?"

Radix Unary raised a hand and everyone around him fell silent. "Do you know the location of the third construct?" he asked.

Eva reluctantly shook her head. "I know who took it, but I don't know where. Even if I did know, I'm not completely sure I'd be able to get it back without help."

"Help could possibly be arranged," Radix Unary said, eyes blazing. "What is your request?"

Eva pondered that for a moment. Her dad had trained her to ask for the galaxy and bargain down to the solar system when all you really wanted was a planet.

"We could use a few extra hands on deck," she said. "Access to your traverse tech would also be great, in case the Artificers are tracking our movement through the Gates or monoliths. Some of your fancy weapons couldn't hurt, either. Or could, I mean, that's the point of weapons. And is there anything you can tell us that will help make our current weapons or shields more effective against the Artificers?"

"Perhaps you would also like a fleetbreaker of your own," Hotfix said, his tone striking Eva as dry.

"If you've got one lying around, sure," Eva retorted.

"Your prudence is commendable," Radix Unary said. "However, we must be cautious. Access to our weapons or knowledge would jeopardize our own forces as well."

"And yet the enemy has already shared both knowledge and technology with their allies," Vakar said. "Withholding the same from us benefits them, while placing us at disadvantage."

"Exactly," Eva said, flashing a smile at Vakar. "I get that you don't want to help us and then have us turn our guns on you when this is all over. But if you don't help, we may not survive anyway."

"Your position has merit. We will confer." Radix Unary leaned back in his chair, and he and the rest of the Radixes—Radices?—went still and silent. Their eyes flashed as if they were processing, communicating without sound in a way that reminded Eva of the xana and their psychic links. No wonder their tech had integrated seamlessly with the Proarkhe stuff Josh Zafone had brought with him from his time working for The Fridge. But where the xana were organic, the Proarkhe continued to seem like machines—constructed, artificial, elaborate robots created millions of years ago . . . by whom? Or what?

But Antimatter and the others had referred to the mechs as "soulless," as if the Proarkhe not only had a concept of souls but believed they had them. Plenty of cultures across various species believed in similar things, and others didn't; Eva was agnostic, as far as that went, though she said her share of prayers even so. She wondered if all Proarkhe shared that belief or if it varied among them. What kinds of origin stories did they have? Religions? Gods? Saints? Demons and monsters?

Mari would be demanding a look at whatever passed for archives here, Eva thought to herself. She'd want to download every scrap of information about their history, ask a million questions that would spawn a million more. It's not that Eva wasn't interested, but it wasn't as if you could just walk up to someone and demand they tell you about their culture.

Well, you could, but they'd probably think you'd lost your mind. Eva would have told anyone who asked to search the q-net and leave her alone.

The three Radices moved again, their eyes settling to solid colors. The one to Radix Unary's right, Radix Ternary, spoke.

"We will provide additional assistance," Radix Ternary said. Dark-blue eyes gleamed in her rosy face. "Some of our people will be assigned to your vessel, and they will bring limited information you may use to craft weaponry and shielding. However, there is one additional complication."

"The fragmenter of worlds," Zenith said. "The star killer. We do not know how the Artificers managed to locate the subroutines to reactivate it, but they have deployed it once and will likely do so again."

"If they do," Radix Unary said, "then weapon or no weapon, the Earth may be doomed."

"Are you talking about the thing that blew up the gmaarg world?" Eva asked, leaping to her feet. "What more can you tell us about it? Is there any way to stop it?"

"We are still gathering information," Radix Unary said. "But the Artificers in the Sol system appear to be building a stellar traverse. They did the same just before the planet you allude to was destroyed."

"We had thought the making of such a thing was lost to memory degradation and intentional destruction of the plans," Flashbeam chimed in. "Unlike our personal traverses or the ones you call Gates, a stellar traverse is large enough to transport an entire star."

"Or in this instance," Radix Binary said, "a world." They were a deep reddish color, like dried blood, their eyes pale blue as thick ice.

"A world?" Eva repeated, feeling foolish. How could any Gate be that big?

"Indeed," Radix Unary said. His blue eyes blazed brighter. "This is a secret few outside this room are aware of, and so we hope to show our faith in this alliance by entrusting it to you."

Eva nodded, feeling out of her depth yet again.

"The weapon used against the gmaarg is located in the core of our homeworld," Radix Unary continued. "As you have already seen, it has the capacity to destroy planets. But if the Artificers have found the lost codes, they can do far worse: they can reduce entire stars to dark, empty shells, ending all life in those systems."

Eva remembered the black dwarf in the system where the first mech had waited, and the starless void beyond the Forge's Gate, where the mysterious mechanical planet had floated, and her blood iced over.

"Was that the Cataclysm?" she asked, almost not wanting to know.

"It was," Radix Unary said solemnly. "The appetite of our enemies was endless, and they scoured the skies until they were empty. And if we do not stop the Artificers now, it will happen again."

Chapter 17

YOUR QUEST IS OVER

Despite the Radix's grim pronouncement, nothing more substantial was achieved in their meeting, and Eva felt like she'd just gotten a taste of the nonsense politicians dealt with every cycle: arguments, concerns, apologies, and not a damn thing decided.

The Proarkhe couldn't commit resources to Earth, they couldn't be assured that reaching out to BOFA directly would yield anything useful in terms of coordination, and they were already doing more intel collection on their own than Eva could help with, given her limited knowledge and contacts. They wanted the mechs among their list of assets, to be deployed at will, and Eva refused as politely as she could, saying she needed to discuss the matter with her crew first.

She had no idea how she'd discuss anything with her people at this point, given they were still in a state of shock, barely mitigated by the sudden attack that had forced them to act and react instead of collapsing into heaps of organic matter. But the mechs wouldn't pilot themselves, so either her crew needed to do that work, or they had to give up the mechs to someone else who could pilot them, which wasn't the Proarkhe.

Given the threat to Earth and the possible deployment of a star-bursting weapon on that enormous machine planet they called their homeworld, Eva wasn't keen on giving away her only ace in the proverbial hole.

At the very least, she would have help finding and recovering the last mech, if that's what they chose to do. Antimatter had been assigned to accompany her for the duration of her mission, along with Drone and another Proarkhe named Ethervane, who was black with red and turquoise accents. They escorted Eva and Vakar back to the room with the traverse, where Drone operated the controls to open the way back to where *La Sirena Negra* waited.

And with them came information. Specifically, the Proarkhe gave her schematics for upgrading the shields and weapons on their ship, which would take time and parts they might not have. Not as much as Eva wanted, but something they could work with.

They had a lot to do, and it needed to be done with a quickness. But like she'd told Vakar: they had choices, and she wasn't going to choose to give up. Not while they still had a chance.

Galaxies spun around her, near and far, as Eva floated in the void between them, waiting for her time to shine.

As expected, Leroy absolutely lost his shit upon meeting the Proarkhe. He'd spent so many years chasing down every scrap of conspiracy about them, their origins, their inventions, their ruins, that seeing them in person helped him climb out of his pit of despair and start looking up at the stars again. Or in this case, at a trio of near-legendary life forms.

Unfortunately, despite being prepared in advance, the Proarkhe also lost their shit on meeting the cats.

Eva talked them down from the upper corner of the cargo bay's ceiling, which was a tight fit despite the fact that all of them had decreased their sizes—a trick that broke so many laws of physics, Eva was surprised the reality police hadn't rolled up to write some tickets. But since they hadn't appeared when the Pod Pals were doing the same thing, Eva expected they wouldn't start now.

The cats were equally appalled by their new roommates and wasted no time in being extremely vocal about it.

"I told you all to behave," Eva said to the assembled rows of furry freeloaders after she quieted their cries. "They're going to be traveling with us for a while, so you need to be nice to each other."

"Miau," Mala said coolly, but she emanated suspicion and displeasure.

"I know you didn't like the Pod Pals either," Eva said. "But those were robots and these are people. So get friendly or get in the box."

Some of them, to her surprise, did opt to hide in their container. The rest acted as if the Proarkhe weren't there, tails swishing peevishly as they returned to their previously scheduled activities.

Eva let Leroy talk the audio receivers off their new passengers while she and Pink conferred on the bridge.

"What if they're spies?" Pink asked, leaning against the console.

"Oh, they're definitely spies," Eva said, slouching in her chair.

"But as long as they're spies that help us out, we're good. It's not like they can steal the mechs."

"But they could stop us from using them."

Eva shrugged. "Why, though? Super elaborate setup for them to pretend they're the enemies of our enemies and help us out, then turn on us later. They could have just let us eat shit from the start and never have the mechs in the first place."

Pink pursed her lips and stared at the door. "They could want the mechs for something? You know me, I'm just trying to figure out their angle."

"I'm with you," Eva said. "Their story sounds legit is all."

Pink cocked her head to the side and gave Eva a look.

"Okay, it sounds wild, but it doesn't sound fake," Eva amended. "Millions of years of war is intense, but they're off in some other corner of the universe, when suddenly we're back on their scanners so they come in to see what's up. And the bad guys start trouble so they reach out to offer help that might help them, too. It sounds plausible."

"And it's not like they're the ones who showed up threatening every galaxy from here to the core," Pink agreed.

Eva nodded. "We've been screwed often enough that we start checking exits when we walk in a room. I think we're okay with these people, for now, and if they don't want to help us, they'll just leave instead of wrecking the party on the way out."

"So let's plan this party, then," Pink said, pushing off the console and heading for the door.

"Hey," Eva called after her. "Bring Joe, too."

Pink raised an eyebrow. "You sure?"

"Close enough for hand grenades," Eva replied. She grinned. "Besides, I like seeing you flustered for a change."

Pink tried to scowl, but she couldn't stop the smile that replaced it as she left.

•••••••

Even though everyone still stewed in their separate pots of emotional distress, Eva guided a productive conversation about next steps and got them on board with her plan—or her goal and the parts of a plan she had, anyway. As Pink would say, ingredients did not make a cake, but by the end of the meeting, they at least had a recipe.

Finding the stolen mech wouldn't be easy, especially with some star systems enforcing communications blackouts for safety. But there were always people breaking the rules, and plenty of places without monoliths or occupying forces engaged in brisk trade with each other, putting out messages about safe spaces and supplies that were equal parts lure and trap. Rumor mills turned gossip into gold, amateur journalists reported on first- and secondhand observations and experiences with varying degrees of accuracy and reliability, and official accounts from what officials were still accounting could at least be shaken down for the truth hidden in their pockets.

Vakar couldn't risk using his usual channels to monitor Fridge activity and gather intel because the odds of pulling some other Wraith in after him were too high, but he still had a variety of investigation skills he could work with. Leroy and Min knew the back alleys of the Freenet and weirder outlets where stories of giant mystery mechs were likely to crop up; they almost had fun scouring them together, sharing what they found and trying to separate fact from fantasy. Sue could reach out to her family and various supply channels and groups to see whether anyone had heard anything or been contacted to work on something strange and secret. Even Joe was willing to check in with people he trusted, who wouldn't rat him out to Tito, asking them to keep an eye out.

Momoko quietly said she would make some calls and disappeared into the passenger cabin. Eva wasn't sure what she meant but assumed it would be explained later.

Pink and Eva put their heads together about who they could approach, who might owe them favors or have tendrils in the right places that weren't wrapped around Tito's little finger—or Pete's, for that matter. Eva was loath to check in with Mari; too big a chance of Forge people finding out and trying to make a play for the mechs. Regina had stopped sending messages as soon as BOFA locked down, which didn't surprise Eva, given her mom's propensity for following rules. And after the ugly conversation with Pete, Eva would only talk to him again if she had no other choice. But there were a few business contacts, friends, and acquaintances she knew from old times and new, and she suspected at least a handful of them were finding ways to involve themselves in the shifting universal power plays.

Pink's close family was off in their quiet pocket of civilization, but her brother knew a few people who knew people who might be able to pass along information if something came up, and her extended family and medical colleagues and friends lived everywhere from Earth to Nuvesta to the farthest reaches of the fringe. They might come across only rumors or innuendo, but the more territory they covered, the wider the net they cast, the more likely something would snag in it.

Even the Proarkhe tried to help. Mostly they passed along anything useful from their own scouts. Some were watching the Artificers, but some were stationed near occupied Gates, and a few had spread out to the systems without monoliths as well. They also managed to scan the quantumnet surprisingly quickly, vast as it was. Unfortunately, they lacked the knowledge and context to parse what was useful from what was, say, fan fiction about a holovid series. Fortunately, Leroy and Min were more than happy to help with that, even if it meant occasionally interrupting Eva in the middle of writing a q-mail to inform her of some bananapants possible clue that turned out to be invented by a rogue botnet.

A few times, Eva wandered into the mess to make more coffee and found people at the table, chowing down on a meal or a snack as they discussed whatever they'd come across so far. Sue with Min sitting in her lap, an arm carelessly tossed around her shoulder. Leroy expounding on a theory while Momoko smiled, a cup of tea warming her hands. Joe whistling as he buttered a piece of bread for Pink, who sprawled in her chair, staring blankly at the wall, then treated him to a grin as he served her.

Lying on the floor of her bedroom, Eva gazed up at the ceiling, at the lights from the fish tank distorted by the water into ripples of paler and darker shades of blue. She tried to do some of the exercises Pink had taught her to destress, tried to take deep breaths and let intrusive thoughts drift away like clouds until the sky cleared again.

But over and over, she kept coming back to how they wouldn't be in this situation if she hadn't fucked up so badly in the first place by going after Vakar. This was too important to screw up, and she'd still done it. Actions and choices mattered, and if she kept making the wrong ones, she shouldn't be in a position where her choices could have such sweeping consequences. If—no, when they got the mech back, she needed to—

Vakar interrupted her thoughts with a tap on her door. She opened it with a thought and he stepped inside, smelling like so many different things her translator nanites lagged. At least the licorice was pronounced enough to pick out; Eva inhaled more deeply than her breath exercises had achieved, exhaling with a sigh.

"I was planning to call a meeting," Eva said, then chuckled

as a spike of fart smell conveyed his dismay. "I know, more meetings. I'm turning into a middle manager."

"No, you are a captain," Vakar said. "Your leadership style has evolved to include more discourse among your crew, which requires that you provide the framework to facilitate that discourse."

Eva snorted. "Stop making it sound like I know what I'm doing."

Another spike, this time vinegar and rosemary. "Your choices are not uniformly wise," he said, "but you are more competent than you believe."

"If I was really competent, I would have given the mechs to Mari," Eva muttered. There. She'd said one of the main things she'd been thinking, but didn't want to admit to herself. The Forge had more resources, they had plans, they had people who could do what Eva couldn't. For all of her grinding personal feelings about her family, for all she'd personally endured, she had to accept that some things mattered more than petty squabbles and vendettas. The universe was at stake, and Eva was, as usual, way out of her depth.

Vakar sat down next to her, running a clawed hand over her short hair. "You still could," he said. "If you genuinely believe that would be the best course of action."

"I think it's too late now." She closed her eyes and sighed again. "They're embroiled in their Earth plan, and if I gave them the mechs, they'd probably use them to facilitate that instead of as an alternative."

He moved his hand to her arm and stroked that. "And why do you believe they would not have done the same if they had obtained the mechs sooner?"

"Because they would have been able to stop the Artificers without messing with that locura." But she fell silent, because

she knew that wasn't a certainty. The Forge had shown themselves to be a group that had contingency plans for their contingency plans, lettered all the way from A to double-Z. They
almost certainly would have done both, and probably were
doing other equally questionable things somewhere in case the
asteroid weapon failed.

So why did Eva think she had a chance? Why had she ever
thought that? Even if she got the mechs, that might not stop
The Forge and BOFA and whoever else was involved. She was
just one person. What the hell could she do?

No. That was fear talking, and guilt, and she didn't have time
for it. Mistakes were made, and maybe she'd figure out a suitable
punishment for herself, and maybe the universe would figure it
out for her. Maybe the best punishment was atonement, busting
ass to make things right instead of wallowing in the past and
burning her own future to ash before it happened. She wasn't
powerless, and she wasn't alone. She had a crew of dedicated,
skilled people ready to fight for themselves, their families and
friends, and the rest of the universe, and she would help them
succeed.

Right now, the most important thing she could do was get
off the damn floor and keep going.

Vakar was already standing and offering her a hand when
Eva opened her eyes. She took it, stood up, and gave him a kiss
before putting on her game face and heading for the cargo bay.

The information everyone brought to the table was scattered
and disjointed, but they laid it all out like pieces of a huge jigsaw
puzzle and started looking for corners and edges.

Reports circulated of mercs with strange new weapons, suggesting that Tito didn't care to keep his Artificer toys a secret,

or that more people were playing with fancy fire than Eva would have liked. Regardless, the mech hadn't come up in those stories, except as a thing the mercs were asking about, so it was mostly an interesting rumor and a sign that Tito was just as spaced as Eva when it came to intel.

A holovid recorded by a lone beacon operator on an otherwise abandoned planet in the Trabbert System might have been the mech, blurry and distant and engaging in targeted destruction of the remains of a city that had been stripped of useful parts a century earlier. It also might have been one of the Artificers letting off steam, literally or figuratively, or a convincing fake made by someone with nowhere to go and too much time on their hands. The supposed "battle robot" was far enough away that it was nearly impossible to make out any details. If true, though, anything they could dig up about Fridge activity in the area might lead to another clue.

One of the most useful weak points, as suspected, was Miles Erck, who had a propensity for comiendo mierda that rivaled some species that literally ate their own shit for sustenance. He had some extremely convoluted secret message group, a holdover from his days as a bot fighter, where he bragged about his exploits, making himself out to be much more heroic and awesome than he was. Why he hadn't been corralled and shut down by his employers, Eva had no idea; she suspected they either had some use for his nonsense, he'd genuinely managed to bypass their security, or their tendrils no longer extended as far as they once had.

Regardless, from his shit-talking they discovered that he had allegedly piloted the mech, whose capabilities were still being researched, but that he was furious about losing access due to his employer's "stupid fundraising plans." What those were, he didn't say, and his location was surprisingly hard to pinpoint.

When that bit of data was revealed, Momoko's lips curled up

in a small, satisfied smile. "I believe I may know where the mech will be in the next two cycles," she said.

Leroy whooped and grabbed her in a hug, spinning her around and then depositing her on the floor, his cheeks pink. "Sorry, Princess, I got excited," he said, rubbing his chin. Momoko blushed as well, apparently still not entirely used to his excesses of public affection.

"Spill," Pink said. "What you got?"

"An auction," Momoko said. "It's being held at an old factory on Zeslov, with the Chela group handling security."

Eva knew of the place, and the group; their name had stuck at first because it was spelled like her great-aunt Graciela's nickname, but pronounced "kee-lah" instead. It was a fancy word for claw or talon, and as security went, they were the best—and most expensive. Each of them was basically a super-Tito, and had their own unique approaches to busting heads and asses and tentacles. Zeslov was their base of operations, neutral territory where enemies conducted business when they wanted assurances that violence wouldn't be tolerated.

After a few moments of mental meandering, Eva's brain replayed what Momoko had said, and she winced.

"They're going to sell the mech?" Eva asked. "Qué rayo?"

"I'll forward you the information I found," Momoko said. A moment later, it dinged into Eva's commlink.

"A rare and extremely powerful weaponized device . . . The perfect centerpiece for any offensive or defensive arsenal in these contentious times," Eva muttered. No further details, no images or schematics, but considering what Erck had said about fundraising plans, this was a solid lead. The listing had more exclamation points than any sane person should use—Smedley's handiwork, she assumed. Then she read the terms and the entry deposit and her jaw dropped.

"That's just to get in the door?" Eva asked. "Guao . . . I mean, ño, qué caro." She knew the rich traveled in entirely different orbits from everyone else, but there was a difference between knowing it and getting whacked in the face with it.

"This will have been distributed to a very select group of people," Momoko said. "I can get some names, but you can be sure anyone with enough credits will be there, if only to see the item up close."

Eva had no earthly idea how to begin infiltrating a party like that. Maybe if she managed to get a line on who was catering . . .

"How did you find out about this?" Sue blurted out.

Momoko fell silent, then looked at Leroy, who shrugged. "Up to you," he said. "I trust them."

Momoko cleared her throat and raised her chin. "My family received an invitation," she replied slowly.

Eva's thoughts hit the air brakes as she turned all her attention to Momoko. "Qué?" she asked.

Pink rolled her eye. "I think what she means is, you wanna get a little more specific about that?"

"My real name is Mihara Keiko," Momoko said. "My father is the CEO of the Matsutake Consortium. My mother serves on the board of directors, and nearly everyone else in my family is at least a shareholder, if not an employee."

"What?" Joe exclaimed, and everyone's attention turned to him at once. He shrugged. "We were all thinking it."

Pink barked a laugh. "Surprised it came out of you, though. Usually Eva is the one with a direct line from her brain to her mouth."

"Are you, um . . ." Sue trailed off, her face pink.

"Superrich?" Min finished.

"Yes," Momoko said. Just the one word, no elaboration.

Eva raised her hand to stop anyone else from chiming in.

"Let's keep the intrusive personal questions to a minimum," she said. "If Momoko wants to tell us anything else, she can. Otherwise, we need to figure out how to confirm this is the mech, and how to use this information to get to that auction and get it back."

"Getting past Chela won't be easy," Pink said, leaning back in her chair. "They'll do background checks on everyone who breaks atmo, at a minimum."

Eva grimaced. "I can try to get us something that will pass muster, but in two cycles? And with the way comms are jodido? I'd have to try Pete." Which she didn't want to, but she would if it made this possible instead of a pipe dream.

Antimatter made a soft whistling noise. "Perhaps we can be of assistance," she said. "We could open a traverse to the location if you can get us precise coordinates."

A portable Gate. With that, a bunch of them could step straight through onto the planet, grab the mech, and be gone before anyone realized what had happened. They'd have to be extremely fast and perfectly coordinated, though. If something went wrong, they'd be left dealing with the most skilled, powerful security company in existence, plus whoever else had showed up trying to buy the mech. They wouldn't be happy to have their potential new toy stolen out from under them.

"We can definitely get Gate coordinates," Eva said, "but we'd need someone on the ground for anything more precise than that."

Drone hummed. "That would only put us in the system. Not close enough for a targeted extraction."

Eva sighed. Back at square one: how to get someone on the planet in the first place, without a solid cover story, which would potentially take too long to fabricate with the universe in disarray.

"There is a simpler option," Momoko said. "I could pay the deposit and bring Leroy as my escort."

"Qué coño?" Eva exclaimed.

Pink snorted. "Brain to mouth," she said. "Not even a little hop first."

Eva made a moue and stared into Momoko's eyes. "This is gonna sound rude, but are you sure you can afford that?"

Momoko shrugged. "It's just money," she said. "What am I going to spend it on if the universe is destroyed?"

"That's the most sensible thing a rich person ever said," Pink muttered. "Never thought I'd live to see the day."

A tiny smile teased up the corners of Momoko's lips. "Don't worry," she said. "I'll let my fists do the talking from now on."

Pink laughed, and Leroy joined her, and the tiny hope Eva had kindled in her chest grew into a roaring flame. She'd spread that hope around until it burned down every asshole between them and saving the universe, and then she'd roast a celebratory lechón over their ashes.

With the point of entry settled, the plan to retrieve the mech came together quickly. Calls were made, credits were transferred, and people yelled at each other across the ship or sent terse pings as needed. Time moved in jumps, with very little happening until suddenly a lot happened all at once.

"Did you make sure Leroy's background is clean?" Eva asked Vakar as she pressed his face into the mat during a friendly sparring match.

"I confirmed it, yes." Vakar got an arm behind Eva's knee and flipped their positions so he was on top. "His employment history was linked to the shell corporation you and Pink established when you first obtained this ship."

"And that's linked to my Victor Cecil alias," Eva said. "That one's as airtight as I could make it, and I've never used it for anything illegal. Worst case, someone might find the agency where I hired Leroy, but not me." She grunted and slapped the mat, acknowledging the pin.

Vakar ran a hand up her hip as he released her, smelling smugly of lavender. "The people at *Crash Sisters* seem to have done additional work to ensure his reputation is clear of scandal."

"Ugly scandal anyway," Eva said. "I'm sure they love to manufacture juicy stuff for ratings." She wiped sweat off her forehead and caught her breath as she stared up at the ceiling. "So if Chela won't find anything when they check on him, Leroy's good to go with Momoko to Zeslov."

"So it would seem," Vakar said. "Now they simply need transportation."

From the other end of the cargo bay, Momoko paused her own exercises, dropping the straps she'd been using for pull-ups. "I've rented a ship for us," she said. "A Puissance Vingt."

Eva leaned back on her elbows and whistled. "Ño, that's fancy. Where and when do we pick it up?"

"I already sent the information to Min," Momoko said. She stretched up, touched her toes, then executed a perfect back handspring. Yes, Eva could definitely see what Leroy liked about this woman.

Not to be outdone, Eva kipped up and launched a spinning roundhouse kick at the patched and refilled heavy bag. "Let me know when your tickets are confirmed," she said. "We'll go over the plans and work out any last kinks."

Momoko nodded and returned to her routine, under the watchful eye of various bored cats and the Proarkhe, who were currently networked and handling their own part in the mission.

Vakar leaned in, smelling like a candy store. "Are there any kinks we need to work out privately?"

Eva grinned. "Abso-fucking-lutely. Who's showering first?"

Freshly cleaned and then freshly sucia, Eva took a well-earned nap while Vakar continued to handle his other mission tasks. When he woke her a few hours later, she made a cortadito for herself, an Americano for Momoko, and a pot of green tea for whoever wanted it, then called yet another meeting, this time in the cargo bay so the Proarkhe could attend without shrinking themselves down to the size of humans. She had no doubt they could do it, but it was still a little unnerving.

Sue rigged a portable holographic projector, which Eva used to display a visual of Zeslov from orbit, controlled by her commlink.

"We've got old schematics for the building, thanks to Vakar," she said. With a mental flick, she zoomed in on the planet until she reached the auction location. The architectural model showed the different levels, interior doorways, and exterior access points, with layers for electrical, plumbing, and HVAC that could be pulled out separately. "We don't know if this is all still accurate, but it's better than nothing."

"A rousing endorsement," Vakar said dryly, still smelling mostly of cinnamon.

"That's not our only unknown," Eva continued. "We don't know where the mech is exactly, and we don't know where the key is. We need both, or we're spaced."

"Another problem is the guest list," Momoko said. "I managed to get a few names, but the auction is being handled with extreme discretion and privacy. Everyone there will have money, otherwise they couldn't get in the door, but people can obtain money in many ways."

"Like what?" Sue asked innocently. Min snickered through the speakers.

"Ay, mija," Eva said. "We'll have a long talk about the vultures and the wasps later. The main issue is, we could be dealing with Forge members, criminal conglomerates, who knows how many mercenary groups, maybe even Tito himself."

"Rusty buckets," Sue said, hugging her knees more tightly.

"Not that those folks are worse than anyone who made bazillions of credits doing stuff that's legal but unethical," Pink said dryly. She and Joe cleaned their respective sniper rifles in eerie unison. "It just means they're more likely to be plotting something shady, like trying to steal the mech themselves instead of paying for it."

"Así es," Eva said. "Even if we had a chance to outbid everyone and get the mech in a quasi-legit way—"

"I don't have that many credits," Momoko said, wincing.

"It's still unlikely that we'd be able to just take our win and leave without getting jumped."

"There is also the possibility that this is all an elaborate ruse by The Fridge," Vakar added.

"And they'll end up trying to keep the mech for themselves." Eva sighed, spinning the holo with a finger. "Miles Erck at least seems to think the sale offer is for real, but I don't expect his superiors to keep him up to speed about whatever they're actually planning. If anything, I'm shocked that his total inability to keep his damn mouth shut hasn't landed him in a morgue, or on a slow trip to a star without a spacesuit."

"So what's the plan?" Pink asked, staring through her rifle Anthia's empty barrel.

"Plans," Eva said. "I'm not taking chances. Plan A: as soon as Leroy and Momoko are inside the auction and have eyes on the mech, they find somewhere private and send their coordinates to Antimatter, who opens a traverse. Vakar, Sue, and I slide in, fast and quiet, and we use the tracking program Drone made to find the key. We steal it, get to the mech, and escape."

"Should we stage a distraction?" Momoko asked.

"I'm good at being distracting," Leroy said, grinning and rubbing his bright-orange beard.

"Only if you have to," Eva said. "Sue will fly the mech out with me and Vakar as passengers, plus you two if you can't get back to your rented ship. We head for the system's Gate, meet up with *La Sirena Negra*, and salpica."

"Solid," Joe said, passing an oily rag to Pink.

"And what's Plan B?" Pink asked.

Eva took a sip of coffee and swallowed. "If there's no way to send the mech's coordinates, Plan B is for Momoko to find the key and steal the mech herself."

"And then I get to distract them?" Leroy asked.

"Again, only if you have to," Eva said. "You might need to keep Momoko from getting nabbed by Chela."

Leroy grinned evilly at the thought.

"Are those all the plans?" Antimatter asked, her blue eyes irising wider.

"Hell no," Eva replied, holding up her fingers as she ticked more off. "If Leroy and Momoko send the coordinates but something else goes wrong, Plan C is for you to storm the castle and be distracting while Vakar, Sue, and I find the key and steal the mech."

"The construct will probably activate to attack us as soon as we're detected," Drone said.

"It would be chaos," Ethervane added.

"Exactly," Eva said, grinning. "If Plan B goes wrong, we'll have no way of knowing, so Plan D is basically Plan C but with the starting point at the system's Gate instead of on the ground. Absolute worst case, we go all out and fly in with the other two mechs, but I'd rather not risk them unless we have to, and that might make it harder to find the key for the third one."

"Chela will no doubt be guarding that carefully," Vakar said. "If they suspect they will be unable to repel an attack, they may attempt to move it off-world."

"Which would put us back where we are now," Eva said. "The absolute worst case would be if we went to all this trouble and someone else got to the mech first. We can't let it vanish again." She didn't add that if they lost it and couldn't locate it in time, the Earth could be destroyed. By the looks on most faces, everyone was already thinking as much.

"So that's it?" Pink asked. "Get in, get the mech, get out?"

"How's that for a cake?" Eva asked, grinning.

"You still have to bake it," Pink said, raising an eyebrow. "But at least this time you have a recipe."

"And there's room to improvise," Eva said. "Come on, my little sous chefs, fire up the oven and let's break some eggs."

"Miau?" Mala asked, poking her head out from behind the cat container.

"Not this time," Eva said. "You all stay here and keep the ship safe."

Mala chirruped and radiated mild indignation, flopping down on the floor and licking her butt vigorously. Eva rolled her eyes and went about her business. She didn't have time to deal with cat feelings; she had too much work to do.

She was counting on the fact that they had the ability to find the key, which prospective buyers and thieves might not know about. Her people also knew how to pilot the mechs already, so they'd have an edge in terms of getting in and out quickly, even if everything else went completely wrong.

But as everyone hustled to get ready, she did some more thinking, and then some talking to Vakar and Pink, and she quietly made a Plan Z that she hoped would work even if all the rest failed.

Once that was set in motion, Eva did the thing she most hated to do: she waited.

Chapter 18

WE PRESENT YOU A NEW QUEST

Zeslov had once been a lovely kyatto settlement near a space-port, with tiered houses made of platforms in subdued shades of pink and blue and yellow, the roofs covered in sun-loving plants to serve as cozy resting spots while keeping the interiors cool and comfortable. Almost every abode had a central room with a circular window in the roof, which allowed a spot of warm light to move across the floor as the planet rotated, as well as a porch wrapping around the walls for outdoor lounging in sun or shade.

The buildings were inhabited by a broad mix of people now, fewer than had lived on the planet when it was used for legitimate trade instead of the more clandestine variety. Eva didn't know the full history of what had changed—gone wrong, depending on one's perspective—but now the residents catered to visitors in various ways, from sustenance to starship repairs. It was almost like a fancy resort, in that all the guests were people with a lot of money, but they also happened to have a penchant for murdering each other about it.

The auction was being held in an abandoned factory. It had previously been used to distill and distribute an alcoholic beverage called Ligma, whose name was due to a translation mix-up and the fact that each container included small boba-like balls. The place had a large central room that used to contain the bottling equipment, a subfloor where the distilling had taken place, offices and a break room for the employees surrounding that, a warehouse for storing and packaging the product, and a loading dock where packages were transferred to delivery vehicles to be taken to the spaceport. Open lifts granted access between levels, large enough to move a group of people or large quantities of—Eva snorted a laugh—the ball-filled Ligma.

The surrounding neighborhood contained a mix of houses, eateries, and storefronts for local services. It was a mess, tactically speaking: narrow roads curved and intersected like tangled yarn, dead ends and bottlenecks abounded, and snipers had plenty of spots to set up on rooftops and terraces. That was presumably part of the benefit to the Chela mercs, who could stake out the best chokepoints and lines of sight, and knew the area so well they could herd their quarry easily if it became necessary.

Which it usually didn't, since few people were convinced enough of their own skills and invincibility to stage a test.

"You sure we can't just nuke it from orbit?" Min asked, idly stroking Mala's back as she lay in the pilot's chair.

"You got a nuke somewhere you haven't told me about?" Eva asked from the captain's seat. Min giggled, and Eva continued. "Someone tried that once, if the stories are true. One of the Chela mercs hacked the damn thing and sent it back at the sender. Debris for light-years."

Min's grin faded. "And you're sneaking Sue into the middle of that?"

"I know." Eva sighed. "Trust me: if I could, I'd do it alone, with the rest of you safe in here. But I can't."

"If you hadn't gone after Vakar in the first place . . ." Min scowled. "I would have done it for Sue, though."

Eva snorted and rose. "Well, don't. Trust your girlfriend. She's little but fierce, and she's probably going to save all our asses."

"She is pretty fierce." Min's smile returned, and as if summoned, Sue entered the bridge. Eva left the two of them to say their goodbyes, hopefully temporary ones, and went to the cargo bay.

The Proarkhe waited there, fidgeting every time a cat moved. Drone stood with his arms crossed, occasionally burbling something quietly. Ethervane did a slow, tight kata with a wicked-looking blade, not moving more than a meter from her starting position. Antimatter sat with her back against the cargo bay door and her legs stretched out, eyes closed, emitting a low hum like she was running too many processes at once. Or maybe that was how Proarkhe snored.

The hum stopped. "Do you have the coordinates?" Antimatter asked, one eye irising open slightly.

"Not yet," Eva said. "Should be soon, though, so I figured we should wait in here."

Antimatter's arms rippled. "Bueno. Be sure to contact me immediately if the proximity sensor doesn't function as intended."

"Since we need that key, I won't have much of a choice."

Vakar walked in, his Wraith armor different from its usual mirror finish. It took her a few moments to realize the color had dulled to a darker gray, like hematite.

"Ready?" she asked.

"Of course," Vakar replied. He nonetheless methodically

checked through the weapons he'd secured in their various holsters and sheaths and compartments.

Eva did the same, though she wasn't packing as much as he
was. Vibroblade, garrote, sonic knuckles, a pistol on each thigh.
She'd even dug her submac out of storage and prepped it, then
tucked it into the small of her back. None of the fun tricks Vakar squirreled away in his belt—acid balls and EMPs and smoke
bombs and flash-bangs and so on—all she had left was a couple
of paint capsules and a gumball she didn't remember putting
in there.

Sue arrived last and was the least decked out, with one pistol
and a backpack full of her robot friends. Eva had told her to
take as many as she could, to have strength in numbers, but Sue
opted for a mere dozen, insisting she didn't want any to get left
behind or lost. After what had happened to Goyangi, Eva didn't
blame her.

Pink sauntered in and put her hands on her hips. "Remember when we just delivered cargo?" she asked, a sad smile touching her lips.

"No," Sue replied brightly. "I haven't been here that long."

Eva laughed. "I don't remember either," she said. "I'm getting
too old."

"Be cautious," Drone chimed in. "Memory degradation can
be dangerous. I once lost the capacity to speak for a millennium."

"He could only communicate in musical tones," Ethervane
said, feinting a thrust. "Extremely annoying."

Eva's humor seeped away. "Don't worry," she said. "I remember more than I would ever want to."

Pink walked up to her and they exchanged hand slaps and
hip bumps. "Remember this," Pink said. "Stay safe and get your
ass back here in one piece."

"I'll come back with the same number of ass cracks I left with," Eva said, smirking.

"Cap," Min said over the speakers, "the coordinates just came in. Sending them over."

Eva received the ping and passed it along to Antimatter, who stood and flexed her arm spikes.

"I can only keep the traverse open briefly," Antimatter reminded her. "Get through it and move away for safety before it closes."

"Claro que sí." Eva remembered all too well what had happened to one of Sue's bots with the Gate guns, and also the Artificer ship when she'd cut the Gate's power.

Vakar, Sue, and Eva lined up, ready to jump quickly. Antimatter raised her arm, and in the center of the cargo bay, an opening appeared. The other side of it looked like a tiny room with gray walls, something white and rounded just visible at the bottom.

Without a word, Vakar stepped through, reaching back to help Sue in after him. Eva climbed over the edge of the traverse and winced as she stepped into something concave and hard. She had just enough time to make sure she cleared the opening before it vanished.

"There is not much space here," Vakar said, pressing against the wall.

Eva glanced around and stifled a laugh. "That's because we're in a bathroom stall." She lifted her gravboot, which was literally inside a toilet, and hoped the components hadn't been damaged again. She didn't need more malfunctions.

It would have been nice if Momoko had chosen a slightly less awkward spot, but Eva had to admit, it was private.

"Get the cameras," Eva told Vakar. "Any other monitoring equipment between here and the mech?"

"Yes," he said. "Motion and temperature sensors. Their systems are quite sophisticated, but I should be able to manage them in—" He stopped, tilting his head slightly. "Someone has already tampered with the cameras and the motion sensors."

Mierda, mojón y porquería. That could mean a few things, but one was most likely.

"Someone else is trying to steal the mech, too," Eva said. "Either they missed the temperature sensors or they didn't have to worry about them."

Who was it, and how had they gotten in? A mystery to solve another time, if ever. For all she knew, it was Tito and his merry band of comemierdas. She doubted he had the cash to pay his way in, but he could have found a sugar daddy and used one of his hundreds of carefully crafted aliases.

Or his Artificer friends had managed to do the same traverse trick to get them inside. Bet he didn't land in a toilet.

"So, um," Sue said quietly. "Can we get out of the stall now?"

Vakar opened the door into a bathroom that had been redesigned to accommodate the sanitary needs of multiple species. Each stall was labeled accordingly, as well as the accompanying sterilizer options. The yellow light overhead cast warm shadows on the bare blue floor, which sparkled like terrazzo and was surprisingly clean, given the number of people reportedly present. Presumably the auction was about to begin or already had, since they were entirely alone; Momoko had left as soon as she sent the message, so they wouldn't be discovered together and their backup plans could go off as needed.

Eva activated the proximity detector Drone had rigged up to let her find the mech's key. She'd been told it would alert her to the direction of the object, and the signal would strengthen as she got closer. What she hadn't expected was that it would feel like she was getting jabbed in the side of the head.

Proarkhe tech was less a double-edged sword and more of a *Crash Sisters* surprise container. Maybe you got a glow knife, and maybe you got a face explosion.

"It's that way," Eva said, pointing to the upper-left corner of the room. "Must be on this floor because it doesn't feel higher or lower."

"Feel?" Sue asked. "How does the—"

"Later," Eva interrupted. "Vakar, take point. Sue, stay between us."

Vakar eased around the wall that created a doorless privacy entrance to the room, peering out at what Eva hoped was the hallway on the blueprints they'd reviewed earlier. He gestured for them to follow, so Sue trailed after him and Eva took up the rear.

There was indeed a hallway, branching to the left and straight ahead, with the same yellow lights at intervals between flat panels that likely held some of the sensors Vakar had mentioned. The walls were bare and pale blue like the floor of the bathroom, as if the painter or builder had slapped the one color all over the place because it was cheap in bulk. Two pairs of thick metallic doors broke the monotony of the surfaces on either side. Vakar moved quickly but smoothly forward, stun pistol at the ready. Sue also had her weapon raised, two of her tiny bots sitting on her shoulders and more clinging to her belt, silent for a change.

If the key was on this level, it would either be in the distillery in the central core of the facility, to their left, or on the outer portion somewhere past the end of this hall. It felt close, but not too close; she had a suspicion it was in the interior but not accessible from this hallway. They'd have to go around until they found the right door.

Eva continuously glanced back toward the bathroom, watching in case someone came out of a room or around the corner and spotted them. No one did. That their luck was holding thus far only made her feel like her other shoe was about to drop into a different toilet.

Vakar reached the T-junction at the end of the hallway and glanced in both directions. Eva gestured to the left; he shrugged assent and proceeded down the left corridor, Sue trailing after him. The sensation of the key's location stayed on her left, but shifted angle slightly, and moved about ninety degrees by the time Vakar stopped at the next corner.

With his mirrorlike hand, Vakar checked the area to their left. He held up two fingers and made a C with his thumb and forefinger. Chela guards. Which made sense, because the poking sensation in Eva's head had definitely strengthened, indicating the key was nearby.

Eva gestured at Sue, who nodded and pulled one of her tiny robots from her backpack, then placed it gently on the floor. She then pulled out a small tin can and put it on top of the bot. When it stood up, its tiny feet were visible; when it crouched, it disappeared entirely into the can.

Slowly, silently, the bot walked away and turned the corner. Eva got as close as she dared and listened.

"So I said to Gary, I said, 'I don't care how many times you offer me one of those things, I'm not trying it,'" one of the guards said.

"What did he say?" the other guard asked.

"He said, 'Fine, more for me,' and finished the whole box."

"The whole box?"

"The whole box. I heard the doc say he'd be out of isolation in a few cycles, but half his guts had to be regrown."

Eva made a disgusted face, wondering what poor Gary had eaten.

"You hear something?" the first guard said.

They both fell silent. Eva held her breath, even though her

isohelmet suppressed any sound it might have made. Would they notice the can? Vakar raised his stun pistol.

"Don't get jumpy," the second guard said. "We already took care of two groups of thieves. What are the odds of more showing up?"

"You're right. Probably someone coming down to piss again. I heard they have some fancy caterer upstairs with an open bar."

"How did they get food and drinks for so many different species with the blockades at all the Gates?"

"A shipment came in a few cycles before everything went bad. For that Smedley guy, the one doing the deal."

Smedley. So he was involved. Why would he sell it, though? Did he need the money more than the mech? Had his Fridge associates agreed to it, or was he running this operation solo?

Wait, had they said two groups of thieves already tried for the key? Maybe they meant the mech, too? Either way, that didn't bode well.

Vakar held up his hand again to check the bot's position. The reflection showed the tiny can slowly edging toward the guards and the door between them. Eva stifled a laugh at the absurdity of the robot sneaking up on two large, armed, and armored mercenaries, imagining it bursting out of its hiding place and slapping them senseless with a chancleta.

"How much longer until Tweak and Fuzz replace us?" the second guard asked.

"They're not replacing us," the other guard replied. "Their job is to get the item and take it upstairs to whoever wins the auction. Boss doesn't want anyone else in the vault."

"When, though? I've needed to purge my vapor sacs for an hour."

"Shouldn't be more than five, maybe ten minutes. Auctions tend to go fast when there's only one item."

Less time than Eva had hoped. She exchanged a glance with Vakar that suggested he'd heard the fuse get lit, too. They had to hurry or this would explode right under their asses.

Vakar held up his hand again. The robot was almost to the door, and the mercs still hadn't noticed it. They might actually have a chance. All the little bot had to do was get close enough for Vakar to relay through it and disable the door security. Then he could open the door a crack, just enough for the bot to get in, steal the key, and get back out without triggering any alarms.

A loud clank startled Eva, who tightened her grip on her pistol.

"What the—is this a can?" the first guard asked. "Did you drop some trash?"

"Why would I do that, do I look like Gary? I know where the waste disposal is."

"Well, I doubt it just walked over here by itself, Edotora."

Please don't pick it up, Eva thought, but she made eye contact with Vakar and held up three fingers. When he shrugged, she started to count down. Before she reached one, another noise intruded.

"Stop, this area is restricted!" the second guard exclaimed. A moment later, a pair of soft thuds signaled that something quietly violent had occurred.

"Quickly, the bidding slows," a gruff voice said.

"Well, actually," another voice replied, "it won't matter as long as we get the key. They can't use the mech without it."

Eva didn't need Vakar's hand signs to tell her who now awaited them. Not Chela, but Miles fucking Erck. Eva sighed and gestured for Vakar to hand her his stun pistol. A new clock was ticking, since the guards had been knocked out or killed, and they couldn't let these sinvergüenzas get the key first.

Vakar shrugged agreement. Eva leaned around the corner,

raised the stun pistol, and fired at Miles's guard. The snotty jerk wasn't even wearing a helmet to hide his identity, and he was so focused on cutting a hole in the door with a laser borer, he didn't even notice the thud of the unconscious body hitting the floor.

"Hey, Miles," Eva said. "Qué bolá?"

Miles let out an unholy squeal and dropped the laser, raising his hands defensively. "You!" he snarled, hands clenching into fists. "How are you here? Are you trying to steal the mech, too?"

"Your buddy Smedley stole it from me, so yeah," Eva replied.

"A fool like you doesn't deserve such a powerful mech," Miles said. "I'm the only one with the experience and vision to wield such power."

Remembering his stint as a bot fighter, Eva snorted derisively. "What's your plan, comemierda?"

"Well, actually," Miles said, "first, I'm going to get revenge on everyone who ever crossed me. Then, I'm going to conquer the universe!" Miles gestured expansively, as if he had a larger audience than Eva, her companions, and a bunch of unconscious people.

"Am I on your vengeance list?" Eva asked, suppressing a smile he couldn't see through her opaque helmet.

"Of course," Miles replied. "You're near the top, actually."

"Why would he just tell you that?" Sue whispered.

Eva tapped the stun pistol against her thigh. "Here's the deal, Erck. You get one chance. Walk away now."

"Or what?" Miles sneered.

"Or—uh-oh," Eva said, pointing behind Miles.

"What?" Miles asked, spinning to look.

Eva punched him upside the head, knocking him into the door. He bounced off and landed on the heap of bodies with a groan.

"Vakar, get the door," Eva said.

Vakar laid a hand on the sliding panel, and within a few seconds it opened. The small room inside looked more like a broom closet than a vault. A single bare light illuminated the space, casting the corners into shadow. Several shelves lined the walls, but most were currently empty, except for one that contained a suitcase and another that held a large barrel.

The key was on a far shelf, near the top, not even inside a box. It had been tagged with an inventory code, but otherwise it was untouched.

"Alarms?" Eva asked.

"Negative," Vakar replied. "Miles or his associate appear to have disabled them prior to assaulting the Chela guards."

"Traps?"

"Give me a moment to investigate," Vakar said.

"Too slow." Eva grabbed Miles by the legs and pushed him into the room, angled toward where the key was kept.

Nothing happened right away, but after a few seconds, he was targeted by nearly invisible lasers, followed by multiple stun shots that set him twitching.

"Investigation complete," Eva said. She turned to Sue. "Send the bot in. It can climb over Miles."

"Will the traps get it, too?" Sue asked nervously.

"Not likely," Eva said. "It's smaller than a pizkee, and those sensors tend to have a size threshold. Use the can again if you want to be sure."

Sue replaced the can on top of the bot and sent it clambering over Miles. As Eva had expected, nothing happened. She glanced up and down the hallway; no one else had arrived yet. The back of her neck itched, but she couldn't scratch it with her isohelmet up. The longer this took, the more nervous she felt.

The bot discarded the can when it reached the shelf, so it

could climb. It slid down a few times, but finally made it to the top and grabbed the key, giving a shrill, delighted sound. It leaped off, engaging a tiny parachute, and drifted back down to Miles, then raced for the door. Sue knelt down to pick it up, cooing praise at it, and took the key. Instead of putting it away, she immediately slid it onto her finger, ready to pilot.

"We need to go," Eva said. "Before someone comes to check on these comemierdas." She gave Miles one last nudge with her toilet-dirty boot, then flushed him out of her brain like the turd he was.

Not knowing where the mercs were concentrated, she couldn't predict which direction someone might approach from, but their best bet was still to make for the lift near the mech. It was a simple matter of going back down the hallway they'd come from and continuing past the T-junction until they reached the end. Vakar led the way, Sue behind him, Eva once again at the rear.

Vakar and Sue turned the corner, and Eva had enough time to think they might pull this off before kicking herself for tempting fate, which immediately kicked back.

"Don't move!" someone shouted before she could duck behind the corner wall. She turned her head slowly to regard the approaching merc. Chela this time. Just a grunt, though, with nice armor and an assault rifle.

Eva smiled at him, raising her arms. "Tranquilízate, papito," she said. "We're in a security detail for one of the guests up top. We caught some naughty pups trying to bust into your storeroom. You can go collect them if you want."

Unless he came closer, he wouldn't be able to see Sue, pressed against the wall around the corner, or Vakar, with his stun pistol locked and loaded. He raised a hand and tapped his helmet, then held up two fingers; the merc had called for reinforcements over comms. If Chela decided to run biometrics on them, at best she and Vakar and Sue would get locked up until they could hitch a ride elsewhere. At worst, they'd be shot and tossed into a trash incinerator.

Vakar started rummaging through his belt.

"Stay where you are," the merc said. "No sudden movements."

"Sure, no problem," she replied. "You mind if I chew some gum?"

"Gum?" The merc's face wasn't visible, but Eva could picture his incredulous expression.

Vakar pulled out a small capsule, and Eva's smile widened.

"Yeah, you know, gum. Chicle." She raised her eyebrows. "The candy? Sweet, sticky, loses flavor after a few minutes. It's in my belt but I don't want to get shot over it, I just have a craving. Trying to quit smoking, you know."

"You smoke?" His tone was disgusted.

"Sometimes," Eva said. "Like now."

Vakar's smoke bomb bounced off the wall and landed between Eva and the merc. It exploded into a hot, gray cloud, completely wrecking visibility through the infrared spectrum. Eva leaped toward Sue and Vakar, rolling to her feet as gunfire riddled the area where she'd stood a moment earlier. She tapped Vakar and grabbed Sue's arm, pulling her into a run toward the lift that awaited them at the end of the corridor. Vakar dropped another smoke bomb behind them as they went, and one in the adjoining hallway for good measure.

They reached the lift, but a shimmering wall of force separated them from their exit to the outer world. Eva cursed under her breath and examined the edges. Depending on the type, there were a few ways to—

Vakar pointed at a spot on the wall. "There," he told Eva. "Hit it hard."

"As you wish, mi vida." Eva holstered her pistol and activated her sonic knuckles, pummeling the thick concrete like it was a heavy bag.

A thump came from where they'd just left, then shouting. It didn't sound like Chela. More mercs? Did the truateg have backup? Didn't matter. Once the smoke cleared, her team would be easy targets, so they had to hurry.

Eva punched faster, harder, the golden glow of the force weapons increasing. With a final grunt, she broke through the wall, and whatever electronics had been safely protected inside sparked and sputtered. The barrier in front of the lift vanished.

Sue went in first, followed by Vakar and Eva, hiding themselves behind the narrow parts of the conveyance that were covered by the concrete. Shots rang out, their impacts rattling against the far wall and ricocheting wildly. Vakar shielded Sue with his armor even as he overrode the lift commands to get them up to the higher level.

The floor started to rise. Through the circular opening above them, a translucent overhang was visible, the pearly material tinting the violet sky to lavender. Once they were up, it should be only a dozen meters between them and the mech. Twenty steps, give or take. A lot could happen in twenty steps, and they'd lost the element of surprise, but Vakar still had more tricks on his belt, and Sue had her bots. They didn't have to fight, or win, they just had to move fast and get inside the mech. The platform reached the surface with a gentle click.

A crowd of surprised, confused, and angry faces greeted Eva and the others from rows of seats arranged in front of a small podium. Smedley stood nearby, wearing a disturbingly gleeful expression, and several Chela mercs raised their weapons in unison. The mech loomed in the loading area beyond, like a statue of extremely inappropriate proportions for the relatively small space. Apparently the auction had been held very close to the prize indeed.

Eva raised a hand in greeting and smiled. "Is this the Fernandez quinceañera, or are we in the wrong abandoned warehouse?"

Chapter 19

FIGHT FOR THE FUTURE

Smedley began to clap, his strange, plastic face a mask of joy. He wore an old-fashioned three-piece suit with a bright-purple shirt and cream-colored jacket and pants, which made his skin look like bread smothered in orange marmalade.

"Incredible!" he exclaimed. "This is just great. Super. Everything was going so calmly, I was getting worried that no one really grasped the value of this little beauty." He gestured at the mech, and Eva wondered how he could call the thing "little" even as a joke.

"It's more valuable to me than to anyone else here," Eva said. "And technically, you stole it from me, so I'm reclaiming my property."

Smedley laughed, a deep belly laugh that somehow sounded fake. "That was you on the asteroid! I knew someone was there, but you never said hello. Well, finders keepers, possession is nine-tenths of the law, so on and so forth." He gestured at the Chela mercs positioned nearby. "Would you mind taking them alive? I have so many questions."

"Listen, please," Eva said, cranking up her isohelmet's speakers and summoning up every ounce of rhetorical skill she possessed. "The universe is in trouble. If I don't get that mech, every star system with an occupied Gate could be taken over and subjugated, or destroyed. Earth could be wiped out. I need that mech to save not only everyone here, but your families and friends, and people everywhere who are innocent and deserve to live their lives in peace. And even when I have this mech, I'll need all the help I can get, or we may all have to suffer through a long, painful, and unnecessary war that could end life as we know it permanently."

She gazed at the sea of faces, forcing herself not to linger on Leroy and Momoko, who were doing their best to seem as distant as everyone else there. Some expressions showed shock, some interest, but most were merely annoyed or upset.

"You could all make a difference," she continued. "You could help save so many people, and all you have to do is let me have that mech."

"Nice speech," Smedley said. "It didn't sound like you practiced it, which is a shame. Just doesn't work as well off the cuff, you know? Anyway, good to meet you, can't wait to interrogate you with a knife later, bye now!" He shot his cuffs and walked away with a wave, toward some long tables loaded with food on tiered trays.

The Chela mercs began to close in on Eva, Vakar, and Sue, who stood back-to-back with their own weapons raised. Those twenty paces to the mech seemed like a kilometer now.

Suddenly, a traverse opened to Eva's left. The first one through it was Tito, his face masked by his helmet, but she'd recognize his swagger anywhere. Four mercs flanked him, all armed with their fancy new Proarkhe weapons. Eva could practically feel his feral grin.

"Tito," Eva growled.

"Beni," he said, his voice distorted by the helmet mic. "I'm surprised you got an invite to this fancy fiesta and I didn't."

"They met their asshole quota already," she replied, her finger twitching to slide to the trigger of her pistol. "How's your shoulder? I'd say I'm sorry Pink shot you, but I wish she'd aimed a little higher and to the side."

Tito laughed. "Unlike you, I can afford a real doctor. But hey, I'm glad you're here. It makes my life a lot easier. I get the mech, or I kill you and bury it under half the planet so you don't get it. Either way, my last payment clears and I throw my own party." He raised his weapon. "Sorry, Beni. Just business."

A shot from nowhere took him in the side of the head and Tito staggered. His mercs immediately shifted to a defensive position, aiming toward where the shooter had to be positioned.

"Qué carajo?" Tito asked, then another shot hit him from the other side, driving him to one knee. He pivoted and fired, his cannon blowing a huge chunk of parapet in the distance to rubble.

Eva smirked. "I can afford a doctor and a sniper, cabrón." Pink and Joe had joined the party. Now they just had to finish the job.

Around her, a pearly glow sprang up as Vakar activated his isosphere, safeguarding them from most weapons right before everything went to hell.

The auction crowd leaped to their assorted appendages or maneuvered their hoverchairs in a race to evacuate, none of them armed per Chela protocols for the event. Shields sprang up to cover their exit, though Smedley seemed disinclined to follow, instead taking a plate piled high with snacks and sitting in the front row a few meters from Eva. Leroy and Momoko followed the group, though Eva knew they'd peel off as soon as possible to circle back in case they were needed.

A pair of Chela mercs descended on Tito's crew like avenging angels, clearly team heavies instead of the grunts Eva had dealt with down below. A pale redhead in black armor shot a plasma ball at the merc to Tito's left, which he rolled to dodge. On the other side of the group, a silver-armored man fired projectiles that struck the ground underneath two mercs, imploding with a gravity charge that collapsed everything in a two-meter radius and pulled the targets in with painful-looking force.

Tito's mercs were well trained and armored enough to handle the situation. They accepted they were stuck, at least temporarily, and began firing back, the purple-pink energy beams from their weapons sizzling in the crisp air. The silver Chela man dodged and retreated, raising a barrier that the Artificer beams penetrated as if it weren't there. He was struck on the shoulder and leg, spinning from the impacts before falling to the ground.

A dark-skinned man in jump boots landed nearby, raising a rocket launcher to his shoulder and firing. This time, the blast knocked everyone away from each other, one of Tito's mercs bouncing off Vakar's isosphere and landing on his back. She kipped up and fired a brace of miniature missiles at the Chela merc, but he disappeared into his own isosphere and the projectiles detonated harmlessly on the surface. When she stooped to retrieve her Artificer gun, he dropped the shield and launched another rocket, which she barely avoided by throwing herself into a leaping roll.

Tito had also moved away, engaging with no one Eva could see at first. Then the air seemed to smoke as a new Chela merc became visible, wearing a mask painted like a skull and wielding a massive pair of shotguns. He unloaded both on Tito, who was already out of the way and retreating for a better shot.

"Ready to join the party?" Eva asked.

Sue nodded gravely, and Vakar shrugged assent. Beyond the melee, the mech loomed, sturdy and immobile.

"Get Sue to the mech," Eva told him. "I'll watch your back." She readied her submac, pulling a paint capsule out of her belt. Given what she'd seen already, she had a few ideas for how to use it.

Vakar deactivated the isosphere, dropping all of them to the ground. Eva leaped sideways, and as soon as she was clear, Vakar reactivated the shield around Sue. He had to tow her along instead of her being able to run with him, but it was worth the inconvenience to keep her safe. She had the key, she could pilot the mech and get everyone out, so she was the most important person there.

The fight continued around her, Chela mercs facing off against Tito's people. In the hopes of signaling her allegiance, Eva fired her weapon at the merc who'd launched the tiny missiles from her bracer. Taken by surprise at being flanked, the woman flinched at the patter of impacts, swiveling to point her Artificer weapon at Eva.

She never had the chance to fire, because a sniper shot took her in the side of the head and she crumpled. Given her armor, she wasn't likely dead, but the concussion she'd end up with would suck plutonium exhaust.

Vakar and Sue were fifteen meters from the merc and moving slowly. With all the chaos around them, Eva briefly suffered from the vague hope they might be able to push through unnoticed.

Sadly, that hope was quickly concussed.

"She's got the key!" Tito shouted, gesturing at Sue. "Dale, desgraciados!"

His remaining mercs coalesced on Vakar, who hid behind the isosphere as best he could, taking shots around the side with the pistol in his other hand. Eva fired at them as well, trying to draw them away, but they ignored her. She threw her paint capsule at one, covering his helmet and obscuring his vision. He had to stop to wipe his ocular sensors clean—a small delay, but better than nothing.

Worse, a glance at movement out of the side of her eyes indicated Tito's mercs weren't the only ones interested in the key. Chela security had staked their reputation on keeping the mech safe and transferring ownership at the completion of the auction, which was now on hold, possibly permanently. And others, like Miles Erck and the truateg they'd taken down earlier in the hallway and the teams that had already fallen, had apparently planned their own thievery attempts and were now swarming around the mech like bees around a hive.

Eva slid her submac into its holster at the small of her back and raced toward the concussed merc, sliding like a baseball player to grab the Artificer weapon that had fallen nearby. She had no idea how to operate it, but it seemed simple enough; instead of a trigger pulled back with a finger, there was a grip with a button where her thumb naturally rested.

Tito fired his own weapon at Sue, and the isosphere shuddered and vanished before blinking back into existence a moment later. Eva's stomach clenched. If his gun could shoot through an isosphere, their plan was suddenly less solid than she'd hoped.

With a prayer to the Virgin that she got it right, Eva pressed the button and waited for the weapon to fire.

Nothing happened.

The red-haired Chela merc aimed her arm weapon at Eva, who barely managed to jump sideways. The merc was shot from above, and Eva flashed a salute in what she hoped was Pink or Joe's general direction.

With a scowl, Eva felt around the front of the Artificer weapon, trying to see how Tito and the others were holding theirs. Ah, yes, there was another spot in the front, and another button . . .

As soon as she pressed it, a huge ball of energy erupted from the thing, colliding with one of the random newcomers jockeying for position. He screamed and fell to the ground, his armor smoking like he'd been hit with acid. Eva didn't want to imagine what might be happening where she couldn't see.

But that, at least, had gotten Tito's attention. Despite his helmet being shaded, Eva could practically feel the glare he leveled at her.

They fired simultaneously, their aim equally perfect after years of training together. The force of the energy balls crashing into each other caused an explosion that knocked back everyone who'd been close enough to get caught in it. Some people stayed down, while others scrambled to their feet and retreated to more defensible positions. One of the Chela mercs had a rocket pack, which he used to get to higher ground atop the roof above them. Several others used the mech as cover and fired from behind it.

Eva glanced at Vakar, who had managed to get Sue another few meters closer to the mech. She hoped Sue would be able to activate the damn thing soon; she should already be within range with the key. This was easily the most frustrating payload delivery she'd ever handled.

Vakar tossed a smoke bomb to the other side of the isosphere and it burst into a cloud that briefly obscured him and Sue. Unfortunately, the Chela merc with the gravity charges dropped one in the center of the smoke, and it immediately sucked the entire cloud up like a vacuum. Eva cursed and fired at him; he dodged and the shot simply kept going, hitting a section of the distant roof. It didn't so much collapse as disintegrate, leaving a round hole behind.

In the distance, Eva glimpsed Leroy and Momoko wading into their own battle. While *Crash Sisters* might be at least partly fake, their skills were extremely real. Momoko wore a perilously poofy dress with a matching parasol, which she wielded like a club. Her skirt was loose enough to allow her freedom of movement, and her long opera gloves did nothing to hide the muscles in her forearms and biceps. Leroy had gotten ahold of serious liquor and used it, along with a small torch from his spiked bracelets, to breathe fire at anyone who got close to them. If someone made it past the fire, he simply punched them into the ground, where they tended to stay.

The Chela guard with the rocket launcher aimed it at Vakar. Everything seemed to slow down as the projectile streaked forward. Vakar angled the isosphere to take the brunt of the impact, but he succeeded only in having it detonate right in front of him instead of striking him directly. He flew backward and skidded along the ground, dropping the isosphere generator. The shield around Sue winked out, leaving her completely exposed.

Sue yelped and ran. Ten meters should have been nothing, a mere few seconds of sprinting. Eva fired wildly as cover, moving closer to Vakar. She hoped the damn mech would do something, anything to protect the small spacesuit-clad woman with the key to saving the universe. Vakar, still prone on the ground, pulled out both his pistols and added to the fire.

A familiar figure leaped from the nearby roof and landed between Sue and the mech. Eva's hope evaporated.

Nara Sumas, merc extraordinaire, had arrived. Eva hadn't seen her since Garilia, when she'd left her employers behind to escape from BOFA forces. Her towering form loomed over Sue, sunlight glinting off her black armor. A scream rose in Eva's throat as Nara lifted her arm cannon.

And fired at one of Tito's mercs, behind Sue. Eva exhaled sharply. Whose side was Nara on?

As if in answer, Nara grabbed Sue around the waist and jumped straight up. Sue screamed and struggled, but Nara held on to her, scaling the mech in quick bursts until she reached the door that had opened in its midsection. She shoved Sue inside, then turned and shot at the rocket-boosted Chela merc, who flew sideways and returned fire.

Eva wasn't about to look a gift crehnisk in the anus. She closed the distance to Vakar and helped him to his feet. They pivoted to stand back-to-back, weapons up.

Now all they had to do was get out alive.

They started shooting, his weapon dispensing round after round of projectiles while hers fired giant balls of energy more slowly. One step at a time, slow and steady, they moved closer to the mech. Occasionally, Vakar holstered a pistol and smoothly pulled something from his belt—an EMP, which he threw at two Chela mercs who'd been stealthed near each other. An acid ball at one of Tito's goons. A flash-bang behind Eva. Then he'd grab his gun again and keep firing, despite the shielding and armor of their enemies making his weapon the equivalent of killing someone with pinches.

A testament to their skills, Pink and Joe were undetectable, but occasionally someone would jerk sideways from an impact that could only be from their sniper weapons. Leroy and Momoko had staged a tactical retreat when Sue got inside the mech, hopefully to their borrowed ship. And Sue . . . what was taking her so long to jack in?

"Innocente," Nara said, her voice magnified by her suit. "Need a boost?"

"Take Vakar," Eva replied.

"I will not—" Vakar began.

"I'll be right behind you," Eva said, knowing how feeble it sounded.

Despite the way she imagined his palps twitched in dismay, Vakar allowed Nara to grab him and leap up the leg of the mech. He kept his arms extended around her bulky form, continuing to fire all the way up to the mech's entrance, which opened to allow him inside. Nara leaped away, shooting as she fell, then delivered a jaw-shattering punch to the red-haired Chela merc as she landed.

Eva's attention was distracted long enough that she didn't see the attack coming. The shadowy Chela merc swirled into view and unloaded both his shotguns directly into her stomach, launching her backward across the courtyard. She crumpled, pain turning her insides into lumps of lava. Her suit had absorbed some of the impact of both the shots and the fall, but there was only so much it could handle.

Get up, she told herself sternly. This isn't over.

Her body curled into a ball and mutinously refused her orders. She fumbled for the stims on her belt with her left hand, her right arm underneath her still cradling the Artificer weapon. Her vision blurred. Did she even have stims? Their supplies were so low—

To her horror, the scene around her blinked, the various combatants suddenly in an entirely different position. She'd blacked out. For how long? She moved her left arm and found she gripped a stimshot. Gasping from the pain of lifting it, she jammed the end into the socket at the neck of her spacesuit.

Someone walked toward her, their stride full of swagger despite the chaos swirling around them. Eva knew that shoulder-swaying look, had seen it in real life almost as much as in nightmares. Tito.

"Beni," he said, looking down at her. "Qué lástima. I always knew you'd go down fighting, but this is sad."

Was he going to shoot her? Did he think she was dying? Was she? No, the stim flooded her system with more adrenaline, numbing her nerves to let her make poor life choices, since her actual injuries weren't affected. She groaned.

You don't have to win, she told herself. You just have to get out alive.

"I'll be sure to tell your dad what happened," Tito said, nudging her butt with a booted foot. "Not the part where I double-tapped you in the head, just the dying part." Now he did shift his weapon, smooth and sure. Eva stared down the barrel at the purple-pink energy pulsing inside.

Something distracted Tito, and he swung the weapon around, firing at someone Eva couldn't see. It didn't matter. What mattered was this chance, maybe a last chance, to get rid of him.

Eva rolled onto her back, her own weapon rising so the barrel was level with Tito's waist. Before he could return his attention to her, she shot him.

At point-blank range, the weapon's effect was immense. Tito flew backward, arms and legs flung limply forward. He landed hard and didn't move, smoke curling up from his armor.

Eva slowly, wearily rolled onto her side again, using her weapon and her off-hand to rise to her feet. Her pain ebbed, faded, but the darkness at the edges of her vision suggested she would need a lot of help from Pink before the cycle ended.

A dark-haired Chela merc came out of stealth next to her. Without breaking stride, Eva punched the woman, who stumbled into a truateg trying to shoot a human in Protean armor. The

Chela merc snapped her fingers and the portable, segmented armor all but leaped off the person and clattered to the ground. The human screamed and tried to cover their suddenly defenseless body.

Still, Eva kept walking until she reached Tito. She kicked his weapon out of his hand, which twitched reflexively. For years, she'd worked for this man, following his orders and trusting they were acceptable until she was forced to confront his lies—and acknowledge her own complicity in them, her own foolishness and willful ignorance. Even then, she hadn't completely severed ties, blaming her father in large part because he'd been the mastermind behind it all. Tito was just his employee, after all.

But that was bullshit. Tito made his own choices, like she had, and his were made with a lot more information than she'd ever possessed. When she thought back to her life as one of his mercs, Eva felt a cold anger at her past self, but more than that, she was disgusted by the ways he'd messed with everyone, the sheer glee he experienced at committing violence and destruction.

Everything was a game to Tito, and the rules didn't matter as long as he won.

And now, here he was, trying to help the Artificers, who were occupying the universe and threatening to subjugate it or blow it up. Why? For money, for power, for fancy weapons and whatever disgusting sense of satisfaction he got from being an asshole.

But Eva could end it—end him—assuming he wasn't already on the verge of taking a quick Gate trip to the afterlife from his wounds. She'd be doing the universe a favor. Potentially saving future lives. And he'd tried to kill her moments earlier, hadn't even paused to think twice. No, his only delay had been to gloat about it, to taunt her. He wanted her to suffer before she died.

So why was she hesitating? Why was she waiting instead of pulling the trigger?

Because murder was shitty. It couldn't be taken back. Once someone was dead, they could never change, never be rehabilitated, never make amends for the wrongs they'd done in the hopes of achieving some small measure of redemption. There was a point in her life when Eva hadn't been much better than Tito, when someone standing over her with a gun would have been justified in engaging in their own moral calculus and finding the weight of her soul to be too heavy.

No, that wasn't fair to her: killing had never delighted her the way Tito seemed to revel in it. She'd liked the satisfaction of a job completed, the praise from her fellow mercs and from Tito himself. Even those feelings had lost their luster eventually, and the shine had never come back.

Eva stooped down and picked up Tito's weapon, cradling it under her left arm. She kicked him in the head, because she wasn't a murderer, but she wasn't a saint either. And with that done, she turned to walk away.

She didn't get far. The mech came to life, ignoring the random shots ricocheting off its plating. It didn't take a step, because it would have crushed a half dozen mercs, and Sue wasn't one for wanton killing. But it bent at the waist, and its huge hand reached down to offer Eva a lift. She climbed aboard its palm, hunkering down as best she could, the echoes of her pain singing like music with the volume turned down. A few Chela mercs tried to come after her, but she held them off with her new weapons until they pulled back to regroup.

The door at the middle of the mech opened. Vakar and Nara Sumas awaited her inside, already securely seated. Another chair appeared, and Eva collapsed into it with a groan.

"Now what, Captain?" Sue asked from inside her floating pilot tank.

"Stick to the plan," Eva said. "Rendezvous with Leroy and

Momoko's ship at the Gate and we'll get back to *La Sirena Negra*." She hedged on sharing the rest of what they intended to do, on the off chance that their new ally was being paid to do something nefarious now that she'd gotten on board the mech.

"Are you well?" Vakar asked as the mech launched itself into the sky. Eva couldn't smell his concern, but her imagination supplied the requisite whiff of incense.

"I'm alive," Eva replied.

"That is not a satisfactory response." The sheen of his armor dimmed further, and Eva gestured dismissively. It wasn't as if either of them could do anything about it at the moment.

"Sumas," Eva said, turning her attention to the mercenary. "Why did you help us?"

"I was paid to," Nara said.

Eva blinked. While that was certainly the most reasonable answer, it was incredibly unexpected.

"Can you say who your client is?" Eva asked.

"Sure," Nara said. "It was Pete."

Pete? Eva's dad? The breath left her in a rush. That wasn't what she'd expected either.

"How did he afford you?" Eva asked. "How has he ever afforded you?" Nara had been part of his crew when he stole *La Sirena Negra*, and she never did anything for free. Plus, she was one of the most respected and expensive bounty hunters out there.

"Technically, I owe him," Nara replied. She deactivated her helmet, revealing her bright-green hair pulled into a high ponytail. A few strands stuck to her tan face, which was covered in a fine sheen of sweat.

Eva closed her mouth, which had fallen open. "How did you end up owing him anything?" she asked incredulously. Pete had a lot of friends and favors all over the universe, but this was a story she had to hear.

"Ask him," Nara said. "I won't tell if he won't."

Eva swallowed a laugh. She hadn't intended to talk to Pete again, not after their last disastrous conversation. But he must have somehow found out what she was up to . . . unless . . .

"How did he know to send you here?" Eva asked.

"He didn't," Nara said. "He found out about the auction and had a feeling you'd try something, so he had me attach myself as security to one of the bidders."

"Who?"

"Captain Orlando Baldessare."

Eva grimaced. "That pirate . . . Did you get paid?"

Nara smiled, more shark than human. "I always get paid. I would have gotten you into this monstrosity sooner, but I had to make sure he reached his ship safely first."

Of course she did. Even if the other job was only a cover, Nara's reputation would suffer if she didn't execute her orders flawlessly.

"We'll reach the Gate in a few minutes," Sue announced. "Pink and Joe are on the ship with Leroy and Momoko, and some Chela forces are in pursuit, but they shouldn't be a problem."

Eva didn't doubt it; Sue was probably spoiling for a fight. And once they got back to La Sirena Negra, they'd be prepping for the biggest fight they'd ever been involved in.

The stims started to wear off. Eva's pains seeped back in like the tide on a world with oceans and moons. Some of her ribs were bruised if not broken, and her right elbow and knee had escalated from asking to speak to the manager to throwing bricks at the building. She couldn't remember whether Pink still had any quick-heal nanites left, but if she didn't, Eva would have to take whatever temporary fixes she could get and live on stims until the universe was safe.

The shivers and nausea that came with the pain rolled in next, but Eva took careful breaths and tried to ride it out. This would all be over soon, one way or another. She bit down on the anxiety that made her want to scream, telling herself Pink would have something for that, too. She'd be a walking pharmacy before the hour was up.

"And we're through!" Sue exclaimed. "Now we do a couple of bounces and we'll be back home before you can say 'sister Suzy sipped a soup' ten times fast."

Eva didn't think she could say it one time fast in her current condition. Not that she would have tried.

"Wait," Sue said. "Something's wrong."

Of course. Nothing could be easy.

"Qué pasó?" Eva asked.

"Momoko is rerouting the Gate to somewhere else. The coordinates she entered won't work."

A chill shot down Eva's back that had nothing to do with her injuries.

"How is that possible?" Vakar asked.

"Tell her to go straight to *La Sirena Negra*," Eva said. "Forget the jumps. Just get us back, now."

"Sure, Captain." Sue continued to float serenely in the piloting goop, her black hair feathering around her head.

Eva resisted the urge to hold her breath, especially since doing so made her ribs hurt more. She had an extremely bad feeling about this. If they couldn't get back to her ship, where the other mechs waited—

"We're here!" Sue announced. "That was close. I wonder what—"

"Cap!" Min's frantic comms connection interrupted whatever Sue had been saying. "This is bad, this is really bad!"

"What happened?" Eva asked, wincing as she sat up straighter.

"It's the Gates," Min replied. "They've been shutting down. All over the universe. It's lucky you got back here, because we weren't sure how long this one would work."

There it is, Eva thought. The sound of the other shoe dropping, straight into the toilet.

"What about the Gate to Earth?" Eva asked.

"It's dark," Min said. "We have no way to get there now. We're stuck here, unless the Gates come back online."

Chapter 20

BLACK AS THE PIT

Eva stared at the ceiling of the med bay, the machines above her drifting in and out of focus. The needle secured to her arm delivered a steady stream of the medicines Pink had decided were necessary—painkillers, sedatives, whatever else she'd rattled off to a half-listening Eva before leaving.

She hadn't come back yet.

A gentle beep nearby both broke the silence and called attention to it, like a coin tossed into a well revealing its depth even as it assured the existence of the bottom. This certainly felt like bottom. Like Eva had been handed a shovel and told to dig her way out of a pit, but had only succeeded in burying herself more thoroughly.

Without bothering to run the calculations, Eva knew there was no way to make it to Earth in time to do anything. It would take years to even reach the Milky Way galaxy, much less the Sol system. They didn't have enough fuel to get that far, and they certainly didn't have enough food to survive the trip.

Across the universe, trillions of people were no doubt grappling with the same despairing thoughts. The monoliths had been bad, the invasion worse, but this? This meant no one could even try to run a blockade to get necessary supplies to places in need. It also meant—and this was nearly beyond all comprehension—that all communications that relied on the Gates were gone. Without access to this one ancient and barely understood technology, everyone was cut off from each other. Within a star system, people could still travel and communicate and resupply to whatever extent their surroundings allowed, but beyond? Nothing. The vast emptiness between worlds once again loomed as an impossible barrier.

At some point, a half dozen cats gained entrance to the med bay despite Pink's usual prohibition. They spread out around the room, mostly lying on the floor, but Eva had one cat on each thigh in complete defiance of her injuries. One of them wasn't even facing her; the other was Mala, whose half-lidded hazel eyes periodically offered Eva a slow blink before dismissing her as if she were furniture.

"Why aren't you more worried?" Eva asked the cat.

"Miau," Mala replied.

"You're right," Eva said. "Why would you worry? You're a cat. You have no fucking idea what's going on right now."

"Miau," Mala said, but this time a wave of indignation washed over Eva.

"What do you think?" Eva asked. "You think I'm going to magically pull a Gate out of my ass?"

"Miau," Mala replied, her tail swishing.

Eva scowled. "There would have to be a Gate in my ass in the first place for me to pull one out, tonta."

Mala didn't say anything, just slowly blinked at Eva as if her human was being particularly dense again.

Which she was, Eva realized. Because she couldn't pull Gates out of her ass, but she knew someone who could.

"Pink!" Eva bellowed, then realized she was being ridiculous. ((Come here,)) she pinged at Pink. ((Please,)) she added. As tempting as it was to dramatically tear the line out of her own arm, it would hurt a lot and probably cause more damage she didn't have time to deal with.

In under a minute, Pink burst through the door.

"What?" Pink asked breathlessly. "What happened?"

"Where are Antimatter and the others?" Eva asked.

"In the cargo bay," Pink said. "Why?"

"Because they can open portable Gates," Eva said.

Pink stared at her, eye widening as a grin spread across her face. "Eva," she asked slowly, "did you just remember this right now?"

"You already knew," Eva said.

"Of course we did," Pink replied. "We've been trying to figure out logistics the whole time you've been in here. How did you forget?"

"Because everything just exploded—again—and I'm stressed as hell from doing unbelievable shit on a steady diet of stims and no sleep?"

Pink shook her head, her braids swaying gently. "Girl, take a nap."

"Not a chance," Eva said. "Unhook me and let's get down to business."

Antimatter, Drone, and Ethervane stood or sat in the cargo bay, regarding Eva with unreadable expressions when she limped into the room, leaning on Vakar. Her knee still wasn't fully functional, but at least it wasn't shrieking in agony anymore. And this conversation couldn't wait.

"Can you open a traverse to Earth?" Eva asked.

The three Proarkhe exchanged glances, their various surface components shifting or fluttering as they did.

"We already explained this to your co-captain," Antimatter said.

"We can do it, if you have the coordinates," Drone replied.

"But it would not be large enough to allow one of the constructs to travel through it," Ethervane added.

Eva's sudden feelings of hope deflated, but she tried to pump some more helium in.

"Can one of your ships do it?" she asked.

"No," Antimatter said. "We use the same stabilized traverses you were using. Shutting them down is a tactic that has been employed occasionally in the past, but we've managed to work around it." She idly tossed a ball toward one of the cats, who chased it with gusto.

"How?" Eva asked.

Antimatter's arm spikes flared. "It depends on the nature of the situation. Sometimes we send crews to reactivate individual traverses. Other times we infiltrate the Artificer systems and reverse their deactivation codes."

Eva's hope stopped sagging and puffed up a bit. "So this isn't something permanent. You've dealt with it before."

"Many times," Drone said.

Behind Eva, Pink loosed a sigh loud enough to startle a cat, and Vakar smelled like vanilla and rosewater. Eva was relieved as well, because that meant they had options, assuming they could get aboard an Artificer vessel.

"Do you have any way of tracking the Artificer ships?" Vakar asked.

"Sometimes." Ethervane's shoulder blades moved her back protrusions, making them look like wings for a moment. "It depends on whether we have a spy embedded onboard, or someone shadowing them."

"Please," Eva said. "Contact your superiors or associates or whoever would know. We need to get at least two Gates up and running: the one nearest to us, and the one in the Sol system near Earth." Once that was done, the mechs could be brought through and the original plan to save Earth could proceed.

Antimatter stood, her head almost brushing the ceiling. "I will return shortly," she said. "Could you please open the door?"

Eva used her commlink to open the cargo bay door instead of stalking over to the manual release. She was still injured, after all, and every step she took was a reminder. As soon as the door creaked open wide enough, Antimatter leaped out and floated away. She opened a traverse a few moments later and disappeared, presumably into the ship Eva had visited previously.

Closing the door again, Eva sagged into Vakar's side and turned back to Pink, who stood nearby with her arms crossed.

"We can talk about our next steps in the med bay," Eva said.

"Took the words right out of my pocket," Pink replied. "After you."

Eva walked slowly, gingerly, back to where the relief of pain meds awaited, leaning heavily on Vakar. She didn't know how long Antimatter would take, but she acknowledged that resting was probably the most useful thing she could do now. She hated it, but qué sera, sera.

Sue stood outside the bridge, a tiny robot perched on her shoulder. Her dark eyes were ringed with fatigue, her hair disheveled.

"We're going to fix this," Sue said. "Right, Captain?"

Eva plastered on a grin that was only partially bravado. "Claro qué si, mi cielo."

Sue's face lit up like a star. "Good," she said. "That's good. I knew you'd have a plan. I'll go tell Min." And with that, she retreated into the bridge.

How had she known Eva would have a plan? Eva herself hadn't known until moments earlier, and even now it was still nebulous.

Trust was a strange phenomenon, weirder than a lot of the weird shit Eva had seen in her travels across the galaxy. It wasn't tangible, but it was still quantifiable; it had to be earned or granted, and once it was lost it was extremely hard to regain. But it seemed that once you had it, even the direst circumstances couldn't completely disintegrate it.

"Come on," Pink said, grabbing Eva's other arm. "Let's get you hooked back up, and then you can tell me what cake ingredients you think are gonna bake into something this time."

"Maybe we can make a flan instead," Eva said. She let herself be led, her mind already in motion, drunk on hope and trust and a hundred other emotions she couldn't quantify.

Antimatter returned less than an hour later, her agitation visible in her rippling metal skin. Eva once again met with her in the cargo bay, this time sitting in a chair Leroy had scrounged up from some ignored corner.

"At present," Antimatter said, "we have few options."

"Dímelo," Eva replied.

"We have agents on two ships," Antimatter said. "One of them would not have the capacity to reactivate the Gates outside the local system, but the other should." A sudden impression of locations hit Eva like a blow to the head, and she winced. The Proarkhe method of information as blunt-force trauma wasn't her favorite.

"So we put a strike team together," Eva said. "Get in, get the Gates back up long enough for the mechs and *La Sirena Negra* to get to the Sol system, then retreat."

Antimatter's eyes dilated and narrowed. "Unfortunately, by the time we managed to complete that mission—assuming we succeeded—the Artificers on our home planet would easily be able to override the command and reverse it. The window of time might be too small for the operation to proceed without casualties."

Eva remembered how she'd sliced the Artificer ship in half by deactivating the Gate it was passing through, and shuddered. The last thing she wanted was for *La Sirena Negra* and any crew left on board to suffer the same fate.

"Is there another option?" Eva asked.

Antimatter hesitated, then raised a fist. "We can infiltrate the home planet itself and attempt to take over the Gate controls there."

Eva slumped in her chair, crossing her arms over her chest. Her ribs protested slightly, so she shifted to accommodate them.

"How feasible is that?" Eva asked.

"About as feasible as the alternatives," Antimatter replied. "The odds are not ideal."

But they weren't impossible. That's all Eva needed to know.

"So if we get onto the home planet, we can bring up all the Gates for long enough to get everyone to Earth?" Eva asked.

"Yes," Antimatter said. "If we can hold the position. The main system controls are there, so they cannot be overridden as long as we keep the Artificers out of the room."

Something tugged at Eva's memory, something important.

She closed her eyes for a moment and let her brain fish around until it hooked what it was looking for.

"The home planet," Eva said. "Your superiors thought the Artificers might be planning to move it to the Sol system. Is that still accurate intel?"

"I was not updated on that," Antimatter said, shifting in a way that Eva would have read as uncomfortable if a human had done it.

"So it's still possible, but we won't know until we get there." Eva huffed out a breath. If that was part of the Artificers' plan—to use the so-called star-killer kept on the homeworld to blow up Earth or its star—then Eva might be able to stop that from happening, too.

"How heavily guarded is this home planet?" Vakar asked.

Ethervane emitted a squeal that might have been a laugh. "Not as heavily as the flagship, but there are substantial enemies present. We maintain our own strike force there that fluctuates in size, engaging in various sabotage tactics when and where it is feasible."

"Control of the planet has changed hands many times over the course of the war," Drone added, moving his arm in an arc. "Sometimes we declare a truce and attempt to rebuild, until we are betrayed again and the conflict resumes. Sometimes we drive the Artificers out, only to have them return like cog rust."

Eva didn't know what that was, exactly, but it sounded unpleasant.

"See if you can get an estimate on numbers," Eva told Antimatter. "We may not be able to bring the mechs through, but if enough of us can get in and get to those controls, we can at least take away this one advantage. And then we can keep going with the rest of our plan from before."

"What about Plan Z?" Pink asked.

Eva shrugged. "We can try again once we get the Gates up. I never managed to get firm commitments, so I don't think we can count on it." The thought made her angry, remembering her encounter with Tito, but those were feelings she could deal with after this was all over. Plan Z was a last resort, anyway, and if it came to that, it might just be a really foolish way for people to die quickly in a blaze of glory instead of slowly from starvation.

Sometimes, having a choice in how you went out was the best you got. Eva was happy to offer that choice, but she had to accept that not everyone would take it.

"I hope you're ready for your investment to pay off," Eva said.

Antimatter hesitated. "An investment is . . . something related to the credits you use in exchange for goods and services?"

Eva sighed. "Never mind. Do you have any maps of your home planet we can study? This plan needs to be as airtight as we can make it."

As Antimatter complied with her request, Eva once again settled in the chair provided for her. A few moments later, she found herself petting Mala, who had flopped onto her lap without even a polite purr.

"Will they be involved as well?" Drone asked, his eyes warily widening and narrowing at the cat.

"Sí," Eva replied. "If nothing else, they're moral support."

"Miau," Mala said, and began to purr in agreement.

It was fortunate that the Proarkhe could move freely between *La Sirena Negra* and their own ship, and moreover that their comms weren't down because of the Gate disruption. That meant no delay in the information Eva had requested, which continued to kindle the weak hope that had flamed to life in her chest.

As previously noted, it wouldn't be easy, but infiltrating the

Proarkhe homeworld was by no means impossible. The currently embedded strike force would need to get into position, then send their coordinates to Antimatter so a traverse could be opened to their location. From there, Eva and whoever accompanied her would need to get into the place with the Gate controls, override them to turn all the Gates back on—or at least the ones that would let the mechs reach Earth—then retreat back to *La Sirena Negra*.

In the meantime, Sue, Momoko, and Leroy were taking the mechs out for a spin. Min was intensely jealous about it and kept trying to convince Momoko to pilot *La Sirena Negra* instead. Pink and Joe seemed amused by the power struggle, but unfortunately neither of them could fly, and they weren't inclined to take over the mechs, either. Instead, they spent a lot of time sitting together quietly in the mess, drinking sweet tea and jasmine tea, respectively.

Nara Sumas was the odd person out, having been accidentally acquired in the escape from Zeslov. While the Proarkhe had said they might be able to open a traverse if she could give them coordinates, she politely declined. Her mission wasn't complete yet, she claimed. Once Eva gave up trying to persuade her to leave, she climbed up to the catwalk near the ceiling of the cargo bay and proceeded to nap.

As for Vakar, well.

"I will go with you," Vakar said without preamble as he let himself into Eva's room.

"Claro que si, mi vida," Eva said. She barely glanced at him as she lay on her bed, wearing only her underwear, going over the maps and schematics Antimatter had jammed in her mind like a fork in a coffee grinder. The planet was like a massive building, riddled with elevators and corridors and side rooms and all sorts of nooks to hide in, but also incredibly annoying to navigate. The place they had to reach was, of course, frustratingly defensible, with only a few access points unless they somehow managed to tunnel through meter-thick walls made of a nearly indestructible metal.

Vakar's smell made her look up at him: relief with a tang of orange blossom for sheepishness.

"What?" she asked.

His palps twitched at her. "I had expected you to attempt to dissuade me from joining you."

Eva furrowed her brow and sat up. "Why would I do that?"

"To protect me and risk only yourself in this endeavor." He sat down next to her on the bed, his weight shifting her closer to him.

With a quiet chuckle, Eva pushed away thoughts of infiltrations and gunfights and rested a hand on Vakar's leg.

"I can't do this alone," she said, looking up at his blue-gray eyes. "I'm one person, not an army. I'll have the Proarkhe, but we're going to be fighting our way through who-knows-how-many shapeshifting killers. We need all the help we can get, and you're a lot of help."

Now Vakar rested his claws on Eva's bare thigh, which elicited a tingle of anticipation in her gut that she told firmly to simmer down.

"Thank you," he said. The smell of licorice permeated the air now.

"For what?" Eva asked.

"For valuing my contribution. For accepting my assistance." He brushed his forehead against hers. "For not compelling me to stay here while you rushed into danger without me."

She kissed his face. "Pink is the only other person I trust to watch my back as much as I trust you. Besides, if I leave you here, I can't watch your back, and that will just stress me out more."

Vakar made a low, gravelly sound, the equivalent of a quennian laugh. "It is charming how you pretend all your motives are selfish."

Eva considered that. Was she pretending? Probably. Mostly she was worried about getting the job done, and saving Earth, and if that meant putting herself and Vakar in danger, she was willing to take the risk. The math might suck, it might be only a variation on the same ugly trolley problem that always came up when lives were at stake, but at least in this version she was willingly throwing herself in the path of the runaway vehicle.

She thought of her father, how he'd told her not to be a hero, to take her crew and run as far as she could, as fast as she could. To keep them safe, because they were her responsibility as the captain.

But responsibility was a strange thing. Some people had more of it, some had less. Some people needed to worry only about themselves, and some were in a position where every choice they made would lead to consequences that would affect a hundred other people, or a thousand, or a billion. Some people's actions were a stone dropped in a pond, some people's were a boulder.

Right now, Eva's choices were neutron bombs.

Of course she wished she could stick her whole crew—her family—in an isosphere somewhere far from danger and leave them all there until the whole universe was safe again. But they'd never really lived safe lives, and the last couple of years had been less safe than most for them in particular.

And now here they were, about to embark on a plan that would either save the entire cabrón universe, or damn it to whatever fate the Artificers intended. The Earth would be preserved, or it would be destroyed. Billions of lives would continue to play out in their wild cosmic dramas, or they would be snuffed out like a star collapsing into a black hole.

Eva didn't have to do anything. No one was forcing her but herself. And yet, that was enough. Maybe she couldn't stop the myriad horrors that occurred across the universe every cycle, like Pete had said, but she could try to stop this.

All anyone could do was take whatever sliver of control they'd been granted by the cosmos, even if it was just a tiny splinter, and jam it into God's eye until he blinked.

"Thank you," she said. "For believing in me. For trusting me as a leader." She flashed a grin at him, her scar tightening on her cheek. "I'd honestly been wondering if I was as bad as Tito."

"How could you think such a thing?" Vakar asked. The vinegar and rosemary scent of his incredulity was briefly overpowering.

"Mari said I was," Eva said, looking down. "I might have given her a little concussion about it."

He brushed his palps against her forehead. "Good."

Eva thought of Tito lying on the ground, all but dead. Should she have killed him? Would he show up to spoil their plans now? Would she regret her mercy at a critical time? Had her foolish sentiment inadvertently doomed one of the crew she loved in his place?

It wasn't worth obsessing about. She couldn't see the future; all she could do was make choices that felt right in the present, and hope they didn't come back to bite her in the ass. That was life in a nutshell. But speaking of asses . . .

"I just took a shower, you know," Eva said conversationally.

Vakar's head tilted to one side, the scent of licorice flooding the room. "I have discovered through research that not all humans consider hygiene to be a prerequisite to intimacy."

Eva leaned backward on the bed, resting on her elbows. "You don't need to research human intimacy," she said, her lips curling up in a smile. "The only human you need to research is me."

His licorice smell filled her mouth as he leaned over her. "Let us continue our experiments, then," he said.

Eva set a timer for fifteen minutes, since they had to get moving on the infiltration plans. She could be goal-oriented, too, when the situation demanded it.

She hit snooze on the timer only once.

Chapter 21

TOWER OF POWER

Everyone gathered in the cargo bay to see them off. Eva gazed at their faces, stoic or scowling or brow-furrowed, and tried to tell herself it wasn't out of fear, it was out of love. But they were all afraid, every single one of them—well, she wasn't totally sure about the Proarkhe, but only because she didn't know them as well and they were less squishy than everyone else. Being afraid was easy, natural, especially in the face of unpleasantly skewed odds with so much at stake.

Eva felt compelled to deliver a rousing speech for the occasion, something that would give her nervous crew a boost of confidence and willpower and whatever else would keep them going until the situation was resolved one way or the other.

"Bueno," Eva said, drawing out the *e* sound. "We'll be back. Be ready to hustle when the Gates come up."

"That's it?" Pink asked, eyebrow raised.

Eva shrugged, her mouth quirking up in a half-smile. "What do you want me to say? Everything is completamente jodido? Everyone is depending on us? We're not alone because we have each other? We're going to get out there and we're going to win?"

A moment of silence followed, everyone continuing to stare at her.

"Well, yeah," Sue said finally.

"It might be nice to hear it," Leroy added.

"Okay, fine," Eva said, putting down the heavy Proarkhe weapon she'd been holding. "The whole damn universe is up to its eyebrows in mierda and trying to dig itself out with a spoon. Right now we've got the biggest fucking spoon, so we're the ones who get to dig the most. Pinch your noses and get ready, and when we get back, maybe we can set some of this shit on fire and throw it at the comemierdas who started it."

Another moment of silence replied.

"Bless your heart," Pink said. "That was awful."

"You did ask," Joe added dryly.

"Ay, jódete," Eva said.

Antimatter and Ethervane stared down at her impassively. Drone was staying behind, to serve as a communications relay since the Gates were down. The Proarkhe could speak to each other without a problem, but everyone else relied on either entangled comms—which Eva didn't have—or Gate relays. If the Gates went back up, theoretically Eva could get a message out in time to let Min move La Sirena Negra and the mechs through to the Sol system. But Drone might be faster, and if something went wrong, they'd need a backup plan.

Drone was already part of an existing backup plan, but Eva didn't want to deploy that one unless it seemed necessary. It was extremely dangerous, and while experience suggested it would work, it might also be a horrible, messy failure.

"You still don't have to come," Eva told Antimatter again, tapping the barrel of her fancy new Proarkhe weapon against her thigh.

"Technically, you're the one who isn't necessary," Antimatter replied. "Any of us could bring the traverses back online more easily than you. That said, a stealthy approach is wise, and to say you're unexpected is an understatement. But if you run into trouble, it will be much harder for you to run out of it alone."

Eva shrugged, the motion reminding her neck that it had been recently injured. Pink's painkillers were doing a lot of heavy lifting, and she didn't want them to drop their loads before the mission was complete.

"Let's get this over with already," she said. "I've got a date at Club Cama, and I don't intend to miss it."

The last time Eva had seen the home planet of the Proarkhe, she had been falling toward it slowly, inexorably, caught in its gravity well after careening through an open Gate from another universe. She'd never reached the surface, thankfully, because Vakar had swooped in and saved her from certain death. Her memories were of metal rising into peaks and falling into chasms, with glowing purple-pink lines forming what could have been roads or rivers or energy grids. No atmosphere, no sphere of sky rounding the hard edges of the land, just the planet itself floating through the endless black.

Not a single star visible anywhere in the sky.

The terror of that had only begun to penetrate through the layers of other things she'd been freaking out about at the time, but ever since, the more she thought about that aspect of the situation, the more anxious and sick it made her. How could a place exist anywhere in the universe without even the faintest glimmer of a far-off light in the distance? How had a planet been formed so far from what human scientists had always conceived of as one of the most vital components to the formation of life? How had it survived if every star around it had gone through its natural life span and then utterly burned out? Or had the planet been moved there from somewhere else entirely?

Or worse, as Antimatter had suggested: had every single star within sight been destroyed? Consumed, obliterated, nullified by the technology of a species for whom war was the single constant in their effectively endless lives?

If the whole damn Proarkhe planet somehow appeared anywhere near Earth, Eva didn't even want to imagine the consequences. The Gmaargitz Fedorach had been an asshole, but that didn't make genocide acceptable.

But it wouldn't come to that. Any of that. Eva and her allies would succeed in turning the Gates back on, the mechs would make it to the Sol system in time to stop the suicidal weapons test. And if the Proarkhe planet was on the move, Eva would send it back to where it came from.

Firmly telling herself things like that had never magically manifested them before, but there was a first time for everything. Eva shoved the tangled mess of her feelings into a sealed cargo container in her brain, focusing on the task at hand.

From the surface of the planet, it looked remarkably similar to any other city-world, even Nuvesta. The broad spires of buildings rose into the endlessly dark sky, their walls occasionally lit by the glow of whatever powers lurked inside. Gaps in the floor under her gravboots led down into other levels—skyscrapers in reverse, hanging like stalactites, mottled with the same gentle, sporadic glow. The geometry of it seemed to have some order, but in the way a person's body was orderly, which was to say it only made sense if you already knew what you were looking at.

Otherwise, the logic of why a kidney floated around in a back, or a cloaca was somewhere near the chest, didn't necessarily come easily to mind.

"It's in that one?" Eva asked, gesturing with her fancy new Proarkhe weapon at one of the towers about a hundred meters away.

"Yes," Antimatter replied. The glow of her eyes flickered. "The controls are on the forty-second level. There shouldn't be too many Artificers guarding the area, since they have no reason to expect an attack."

Eva sent up a prayer to the Virgin that she was right. They needed every scrap of helpful odds they could get.

"Vakar, take point," she said.

He raised a fist in response, and the dim mirror of his armor all but melted into the darkness. She followed him, grateful that the lack of atmosphere on the planet meant her footsteps were effectively silent. Perhaps the Artificers would detect the vibrations of her footfalls, or her spacesuit's efforts to mask her heat signature and other signs of life would be useless against some technology Antimatter wasn't aware of, but all she could do was keep going and watch for enemies.

An empty area surrounded the building; Eva would have called it a plaza if it were a human structure. The strange sheets of ridged metallic material that comprised the ground spread out like a patchwork quilt, the shades of gray more varied than she had noticed at first. Objects were arranged at the edges of the area, like benches or chairs, even a light sculpture whose form resolved into one of the Proarkhe as she approached from a certain angle. It suggested motion, transformation, not only for the subject but also for the viewer.

What did such art say about a species whose life spans were measured in eons?

A flicker of electricity caught her eye, and in a smooth motion Eva trained her weapon on what turned out to be a hovering drone. But it had also been dealt with, apparently, and the spark she'd seen was a sign of its impending drunken spiral to the ground.

"Vakar?" Eva asked.

"No," Vakar replied. "I would like to know how to manage that, however."

Antimatter's arm spikes rose and fell. "Perhaps another time, I'll show you."

They continued into the building, which reminded Eva of the Proarkhe ship. Same structure, with a central core rising to the top, dizzyingly far away, and various rooms around it. Most of the place was dark, like the outside, but a few rooms here and there spilled dim light onto the landing platforms in front of them, visible even from where they'd entered. Whether their enemies were on those floors was uncertain, but it drew the eye if nothing else.

"What do you all do in here?" Eva asked. "Or what did you do before everyone left?"

"Administration," Antimatter replied. "A combination of data collection, report discussion, decision-making, and actual actions taken in whatever ways were possible remotely."

That the Gate controls were located in the equivalent of some boring governmental edifice made Eva snort. Of course the kill switch for the entirety of civilization was in the place where people made spreadsheets. In the same way that crablike creatures kept popping up across the universe in various forms, so did bureaucracy. There were words for "pivot tables" in almost every known language.

"Up we go, then," Eva said, and activated her antigrav belt. Since the Proarkhe could all fly, they didn't have elevators or stairs or the equivalent; they just went to the middle of the building and jumped up and kept going.

This, as Eva was painfully aware, made them extremely easy to see and attack. All she could do was hope their incursion hadn't been noticed.

They made it about five floors up in a single leap before the flash and sizzle of an energy weapon shot past her face.

They retreated, finding cover where possible on the periphery of the center shaft. Eva scanned the upper levels, cursing the entire mission, which reminded her of Garilia more than she wanted to admit. It was the same ugly climb, the same vulnerability to attacks from above, and as everyone knew, the high ground was the more strategically advantageous.

Advantages could always be countered, though, and she was here to do her best on that front.

"Flash them," she told Vakar, who grabbed an EMP off his belt. He activated it and tossed it upward, where it hovered briefly before exploding into a sphere of technological nullification. According to Antimatter, such a device wouldn't directly harm a Proarkhe, but it would give them the equivalent of a bad allergic reaction.

Eva used the distraction to gain a few levels, taking them one at a time and retreating to cover when she did. The splash damage from their enemies' weapons was ugly, like being hit by a wind hard enough to bruise. The building itself was impervious to much of the impact, only shuddering or spraying a few small bursts of damaged particles rather than disintegrating the way other things had when they'd been hit by the purple-pink energy. Presumably the Proarkhe had enough experience dealing with their own mierda that they could work around it.

Had employees kept toiling in this building even in the midst of different factions attacking each other? Eva wondered.

It was wild to consider it, but then again, Earth's history had its own bizarre moments, so who was she to judge? Normalizing extreme experiences was another universal constant.

Vakar crouched across the core from her, aiming up at something she couldn't see. He fired and, despite the eerie silence, was rewarded with a flash followed by an Artificer plummeting past them to the ground floor below. Apparently it was hard to fly when you'd been hit by whatever the hell their energy balls were.

Antimatter and Ethervane flew past them, gaining elevation faster but engaging in the same jump-and-hide tactics. They were still in bipedal form, which may have been their preference—Eva didn't know how Proarkhe shapeshifting worked. She wasn't even sure what Ethervane changed into, or if they could choose more than one body style. Might have helped to take that into account during planning, but she wasn't used to accounting for allies who could become vehicles or animals or whatever.

Focus, she told herself. Shoot now, ask questions later.

The glint of moving metal caught her eye, so she leaped into empty space and fired toward it. The Artificer didn't fall dramatically like Vakar's target had, but they staggered away from the platform's edge and into the darkness beyond. She took the opportunity to make another leap up, gaining two levels at once, then flinging herself sideways to avoid an incoming attack.

Slow and steady. They didn't have to get rid of all the Artificers in the building; they just had to turn the Gates back on long enough to get the mechs to Earth. And if they could keep the Gates open beyond that, well, Plan Z might come into play.

Eva didn't want to count on that. She'd been disappointed too many times. But hope was a weed, and it grew in a lot of weird cracks, so why not this one?

((Incoming,)) Vakar pinged; he'd gotten well above her at some point. Eva hid behind a pillar, wishing she had more than motion sensors and visuals to guide her. Thanks to the lack of atmo, she could only hear her own breath, coming fast.

The proximity alert on her isohelmet tagged someone behind and to her left. Eva pivoted with her weapon, already firing in that direction before she cleared her cover. A good idea, as it turned out, because at the same time an enormous fist slammed into the place she'd been hiding.

She ran for the central core and leaped again, twisting to fire behind her as she did. That Artificer didn't immediately come for her, but another one appeared below her. The sizzle of its attack made her suit's sensors protest, so Eva turned the alarms down. Not like knowing she'd almost been turned into carne asada would help.

The Artificer who tried to punch her rose to hover in front of her as she landed. Kilonova. The scuffs he'd received from the lava-covered mech were cleaned up or buffed out or whatever the Proarkhe version of healing was. His eyes glowed, angry and red.

"You again, human," Kilonova screeched into her head. "How fortunate that I will have the pleasure of ending you at last."

Eva dodged laser fire from the weapon on his wrist, sliding behind what might once have been a desk.

"How's your ass feeling?" Eva asked. "Still recovering from the spanking I gave you on Yastroth?"

"Your insolence is disproportionate to your potency," Kilonova said. Eva's isohelmet showed him stepping forward slowly.

"Mucho ruido y pocas nueces, mijo," Eva said. She retreated farther into the level, staying behind half-walls taller than her. A rare benefit of being short for a human, and tiny for a Proarkhe.

Kilonova made a sound like high-pitched static. "You may have eluded me before, but I knew you would come here to foil our final conquest of your pathetic species."

"I'm definitely predictable," Eva said. Moving away from the core was a tactical mistake, because now she had to find another way to get to the next level. She jumped and activated her gravboots, clinging to the wall halfway up so she could shoot at Kilonova over the top. He dodged and retreated, then fired back, but she was already moving.

The map in her head showed a small exterior access down a hallway, if she could make it there. But then she'd have to go outside the building, climb to another floor, and find her way back in. If Kilonova caught her outside, she didn't think it would end well.

This must be what fish in a coral reef feel like, she thought. Weaving in and out of holes to avoid sharks. One wrong move and chomp.

Eva stopped running and activated her gravboots again, letting them pull her along the floor toward the far wall. The surface was smooth enough that she didn't even bounce. She deactivated the boots before she landed, twisting and using the momentum to plant her feet and vault over another piece of furniture. The deeper she went, the darker it got, forcing her to rely on her isohelmet's overlays to keep her from running into something.

Finally, the access point loomed in front of her. It looked like the equivalent of a doggy door—Antimatter had explained earlier that these were used for drones, mostly. Eva sprinted for it, weaving as she went in the hopes of avoiding an attack from behind. Her breath quickened even as her artificial heart continued to pump in its smooth, beatless fashion. With a final leap for the opening, she almost made it out safely.

Almost.

The shot hit her square in the back, launching her farther out than she intended. Instead of a controlled dive, she tumbled through the open air—or vacuum, since there was no atmosphere.

If it hadn't been for her Proarkhe-enhanced shielding, she had no doubt she would have been utterly wrecked. As it was, she fought the pain lancing through muscle and bone to position herself so her gravboots would pull her back to the side of the building.

Her boots absorbed the brunt of the impact, but her teeth still clacked together from being clenched too tightly. She had to move fast, before Kilonova joined her and hit her again. Crouching, she deactivated her boots and pushed herself up at an angle in one swift motion, her antigrav belt helping her stay afloat. Boots on, she flew back toward the building, continuing in awkward leaps toward the next window.

A bolt of energy sailed past her, her sensors jangling. Eva glanced down at Kilonova, who had somehow shrunk himself to get through the opening. A moment later, he transformed in midair.

Even though she'd seen him and other Proarkhe do it, and the small Pod Pals that had been based on their technology, the process gave her simultaneous jolts of admiration and unease. How could someone go from being a giant robot to an angular spaceship in the span of a few seconds? What did it even feel like to shift forms?

Eva leaped again, narrowly avoiding a flurry of shots from weapons at the end of each wing. This was every bit of badness she had imagined and then some. The next access point was still about five meters above her. Why couldn't this damn building have more windows at regular intervals?

"Hold still, meat!" Kilonova shouted.

"Jódete, cabrón!" Eva retorted, jumping again.

A streak of movement lit up her sensors. Ethervane landed on Kilonova's back, driving him down several meters from the force of her impact. Kilonova let off a few shots, but they sprayed wildly, nowhere near Eva or the attacking Proarkhe.

Unfortunately for Kilonova, Ethervane produced a wicked-looking energy blade from her arm, then stabbed him directly in the center of his body.

His screech reverberated through Eva's head. She froze against the side of the building, eyes closed, trying to force the sound out of her mind so she could continue to climb. As long as he and Ethervane were fighting, Kilonova wasn't paying attention to Eva.

He could still shoot at her without looking, though, and that's what he did. Spinning wildly, his shots ricocheted off the building, the ground, and soared off into the black, starless sky. Focused as she was on trying to move and not get hit, Eva didn't see when he changed back into his bipedal form. Ethervane's sword flashed bright magenta in the dark, while Kilonova had drawn a pair of the same weapons, blazing orange. They appeared to be evenly matched, but Eva wasn't well versed in swordplay; there was a big difference between her brand of back-alley fistfighting with occasional stab wounds, and these two huge fencers swinging and parrying and darting around each other in a dizzying aerial dance.

Eva reached the access point and climbed into the building, glancing back at the battle one last time. She hoped Ethervane came out of it the winner, or at least alive.

Racing back toward the central core, Eva resumed her climb toward the room containing the Gate controls. Antimatter and Vakar were nowhere in sight, but at least with Vakar that didn't mean much. He was sneaky when he wanted to be.

The flash of weapons fire above her a few moments later illuminated Antimatter, who darted across the open space and took cover on the other side of the building. Eva directed some suppressing shots toward where the enemy appeared to be hiding, and was rewarded by their attention being redirected at her.

The impacts of the energy beams shook the wall she hid behind, but thankfully it didn't break or melt.

A series of flashes at the Artificers' location ended with a lightly smoking figure careening past Eva toward the ground. The style reeked of Vakar, no pun intended, but Eva didn't want to jump to conclusions. She jumped across the core instead, reaching another level.

This continued for what felt like an eternity: leap, hide, shoot, wait, shoot some more, leap again. Eva's injuries began to protest through the previously comfortable armor of painkillers and healing nanites, but failure wasn't an option. Earth, and maybe the rest of the universe, depended on getting the Gates back up.

Finally, a million years later, Eva reunited with Antimatter and Vakar on the level that housed their objective. All that stood between them and success was a long hallway.

Also about a dozen Artificers with big guns.

"Any chance of backup?" Eva asked Antimatter.

Antimatter's eyes flickered, then dimmed. "No," she replied. "Our local contacts are pinned down in another quadrant."

"Anyone on your fancy flagship with free time?"

"None that my superiors are willing to spare."

Ethervane appeared behind them, her external plating scarred and singed in places, and one of her arms didn't seem to be functioning quite right. "Kilonova ran away," she said. Eva still wasn't up on Proarkhe tones, but she sounded simultaneously pissed and pleased.

"Fools!" came Kilonova's grating head screech from the other end of the corridor. He had retreated to join this fight, then. "How have you not managed to get rid of these barely autonomous vermin yet!"

"It's because Null Array put you in charge!" Antimatter

broadcast to everyone there, earning a stuttering squeal that Eva assumed was a curse.

Me cago en diez, Eva thought. Outnumbered, outgunned, and at a distinct strategic disadvantage. Even now she hesitated to enact her backup plan. One of the worst parts about being a commander when violence was your mission—putting other people in danger, even if they fully supported it.

"It's time," Eva said to Antimatter. "Tell Drone to send in the G Team."

Antimatter's eyes brightened, but she gave a thumbs-up.

"Should it not be the C Team?" Vakar asked.

Eva grinned. "Not in Spanish, mi vida."

A portal opened behind Antimatter, revealing the cargo bay of La Sirena Negra. For a few moments, nothing seemed to happen. No one moved as every combatant waited for either a retreat or a renewed assault.

"What nonsense is this?" Kilonova shrieked.

"It's evolution, baby," Eva said. "Some people are scared of spiders, some are scared of snakes, and some . . ."

A small, furry figure wrapped in a form-fitting energy shield strolled into the hallway.

"Miau," Mala said. Then she charged.

Chapter 22

EL GATO VOLADOR

More cats poured through the open portal behind Mala, racing down the corridor toward the Artificers like a tiny riderless cavalry unit. Eva held her breath, hoping she hadn't made an enormous mistake, that she'd read the situation correctly, given her previous interactions with Antimatter and the other Proarkhe.

For once, the universe was on her side.

The Artificers freaked out and scattered. Some made high-pitched noises and ran or flew away, while others shifted into inert forms like large cubes or other solid shapes. Not a single one of them attacked the cats.

"Go!" Eva shouted, sprinting toward the room with the Gate controls. They couldn't waste their chance.

Antimatter and Ethervane thundered past her, quickly outpacing the cats as well. Vakar brought up the rear, more slowly because he kept checking to be sure the Artificers hadn't recovered and that all the cats were accounted for. Eva caught up with Mala and scooped the feline up with one arm, ignoring the wave of psychic indignation that emanated from her.

The door at the end of the corridor slid open, revealing an octagonal room beyond. Eva followed the Proarkhe inside, waiting pressed against the wall as Vakar herded all the cats in and then followed them. Ethervane closed the door and Eva turned to survey the area more carefully. It was equipped with a Gate—traverse, she corrected herself again—big enough to accommodate one of the larger Proarkhe but still much smaller than the ones built for spaceships. There was also a similar control center to the one Eva had seen on the Proarkhe vessel, a tall table-like contraption with translucent panels.

Behind it stood another nightmare that had plagued Eva for months. The Proarkhe she'd helped Vakar remove from a cave full of horrible flesh-eating shape-stealing things, only to have Fridge agents bust in and take over. The one she had unintentionally awakened in the Fridge facility while trying to take it back, who had transformed in front of her, opened a traverse and escaped.

Now she knew how the Proarkhe felt when they saw a cat. Eva froze, unable to move, the proportions of the giant entity larger than she remembered. Their dark plating rippled, and their bright yellow eyes turned to her with an expression she couldn't fathom. All she could do was stare, a gun in one hand and Mala in the other.

"Oscillator," Antimatter said venomously. "I should have known you'd be here, too."

"Aligning yourself with meat again," Oscillator replied. "Your predictability is laughable." The static of their voice tore through Eva's mind, spiked with what felt like malice despite being utterly monotone.

"Get out of the way or we'll disassemble you," Ethervane added, the limpness of her arm not affecting her snarl.

"With what, your army of tiny mammals?" Oscillator didn't move, and if the cats concerned them, it didn't show.

Eva's stiff muscles began to loosen as anger overcame fear. This comemierda was the only thing standing between her and completing her mission. She was tired and frustrated, and a lot of people had already died over a war that had nothing to do with them and everything to do with a bunch of assholes who'd run out of toys to play with and decided to find new ones.

She couldn't shoot the Artificer, because she'd probably hit the controls, which would be a huge problem in terms of mission success. So either they needed to move, or the controls had to be manipulated remotely, or both.

((Gates,)) Eva pinged at Vakar. She didn't care if the Artificer could hear, or if they understood.

((In progress,)) he replied.

Breaking into a completely foreign system was a challenge even for Vakar, but at least he'd had some practice and upgrades thanks to Drone and Antimatter. Now what he needed was a distraction.

"Oye, mijo," Eva said, stepping forward. Mala bristled under her arm, radiating hostility.

"I do not speak to meat," Oscillator replied.

"Yeah, well, this 'meat' pulled you out of a fucking cave," Eva said, continuing to advance. "When this 'meat' found you, you were a box of scraps waiting for someone to reassemble you. How long were you there, by the way, you miserable pile of spare parts?"

Antimatter warbled a laugh.

"What happened to you?" Eva asked. "Did you switch to

sleep mode but forget to plug yourself in to recharge your batteries?"

Oscillator continued to ignore her. "What do you hope to accomplish here, rebel?"

"I'm enjoying this story about how Eva found you in a cave," Antimatter said, eyes brightening with amusement. "Did you forget to bring an energy supply?"

"Oh, that's the best part." Eva glanced at Ethervane with a grin. "That facility was manufacturing that energy source you all use for everything. You probably could have snacked on that at any time if you had to, so the only way you could have ended up bricked like an old commlink is if somebody managed to knock you out."

Antimatter's eyes flashed. "What do you think, Ethervane?"

"It must have been an organic," Ethervane replied. "I saw the intel. They were using small captives to operate the harvesters, under threat of nanovoid replacement."

"Is that what you call the stuff that turns creatures into creepy inky copies of themselves?" Eva asked.

"Yes," Antimatter said disdainfully. "We don't use them, but the Artificers find it expedient as both encouragement and punishment."

Eva was only a few meters from Oscillator now. They had, she noticed, moved backward a fraction. Mala growled deep in her chest and they shifted away a bit more.

"You know what I did to one of your nanovoid puppets?" Eva asked, staring at Oscillator.

"I do not care," they replied. The fact that they responded suggested otherwise.

"I fed it one of your energy blocks," Eva continued. "And then I vaporized it."

She feinted tossing Mala at Oscillator. They flinched, moving sideways faster than she expected for someone their size. But now they were away from the control panel, and Antimatter had a clear shot, which she took without hesitation.

Oscillator crumpled, folding in on themselves until they were a long rectangular block rather than bipedal. But as they did, an alarm began to sound, and Vakar stumbled, clutching at his isohelmet.

Eva rushed to his side. "Are you okay?" she asked.

"That was deeply unpleasant," he replied. "I was disconnected before I could complete the Gate reboot."

Ethervane slid behind the console where Oscillator had stood, motioning with both hands for a few moments, her injured arm still stiff. Her fingers seemed to elongate briefly, and possibly multiply? It was hard to keep track.

"We've been locked out," Ethervane announced. "The entire system needs to be rebooted before we can do anything."

"Mierda, mojón y porquería," Eva muttered. "How long will that take?"

"It cannot be done from here," Antimatter said grimly. "We would have to infiltrate the central core of the planet, which is completely impossible right now."

"No," Eva whispered, a wave of emotion washing over her. This couldn't be a failure. They'd come so far, gotten through so much. It couldn't end like this. There had to be a way.

Vakar's hand rested on her shoulder and Eva looked up at him, her mouth half-open as she sucked in one breath after another.

"We'll figure something out," Eva said. "We have to. We can't give up. Not now, not ever."

She looked around at the faces in the room: Vakar, his armor a mirrored mask showing Eva only her own warped image.

Antimatter, her blue eyes dim and narrowed. Ethervane, staring down at the console, her hands still as they hovered over the glowing surface. And the cats, sitting in neat rows like students or soldiers, faces turned up toward Eva with anticipation as they began to purr in unison.

"There is a way," Antimatter said quietly.

"No," Ethervane immediately replied. "It's too dangerous."

Eva's mechanical heart didn't skip a beat, despite feeling like it was somewhere in her throat.

"Whatever it is, I'll do it," Eva said. "Tell me."

Antimatter's eyes widened and brightened. "It's not for you to do," she said. "One of us can immerse ourselves in the data core and attempt an override."

"What could go wrong?" Eva asked.

Ethervane's shoulders spasmed. "The data core is immense," she replied. "Locating the requisite functions could take petacycles. Whoever attempts it could effectively be lost, irretrievable, for a very long time. Especially if their physical form were moved."

A frantic banging on the door suggested staying in their present location wouldn't be easy. Eva's hand reflexively gripped her weapon more tightly. She didn't want to think about what "a very long time" meant to a species that could live for millions of years.

"It could be worse," Antimatter said wryly. "Whoever does this could be effectively disintegrated and absorbed, becoming one with the core for eternity."

Like a raindrop in an ocean, Eva thought. A chill rippled across her skin.

"Some of us believe that's what happens eventually anyway," Ethervane muttered. "Doesn't mean we want to rush it."

"Is there a best-case scenario?" Eva asked hoarsely.

"Best case," Antimatter said, "we locate the necessary functions quickly and we're out of here in the equivalent of a few of your seconds."

A few seconds or what amounted to forever. There was a lot of space between the two ends of that spectrum.

"Is there any way to remove you from the system after a certain time period?" Vakar asked. "A predetermined escape parameter of some kind?"

Ethervane's shoulder gears shifted. "Perhaps," she said. "But we haven't resolved whether we're going to do this, and if so, which of us it will be."

The banging on the door intensified. Eva had no doubt the enemy would attempt an override soon, if they weren't already. And if that didn't work, probably some kind of siege weapon . . .

Eva huffed out a sigh. "I can't expect you to agree to something this dangerous," she said. "You already helped us infiltrate this place—"

"And our own destruction was always a possible consequence of that," Ethervane said.

Antimatter's forearm spikes rose and fell. "The automatons you collected are the best hope we have, both of saving your vast plurality of civilizations and of turning the tides of our own war."

War, Eva thought bitterly. She knew peace didn't mean an absence of conflict, that the ebb and flow of power and circumstances had a tendency to make war feel inevitable, primarily to people insulated from its consequences. But she also knew that for the arc of history to bend toward justice, sometimes it had to be nudged, and sometimes it had to be shoved with a gun in its back.

"Is there anything we can do to help?" Vakar asked.

Antimatter made a whirring sound. "Hold the door," she said. "For as long as you can."

Eva nodded and raised her weapon. "Let's get the cats out of here first, though. I don't think that trick will work twice."

"Miau," Mala said, as if offended.

Eva squatted down and offered the cat the back of her hand. "You did great," she said. "You scared the coolant out of those comemierdas."

"Miau," Mala replied, slightly mollified. After a moment, she trotted over to Eva's hand and rubbed it with the top of her head, then returned to her place with the other cats.

A few moments later, a traverse opened back into *La Sirena Negra*. Pink stood inside just beyond Drone, her hands planted on her hips in her usual fashion. Eva gave what she hoped was a reassuring smile and wave as the cats filed back onto the ship. Pink shook her head and returned the wave, her tension and sarcasm evident in the clipped motion. Presumably Drone was keeping her filled in on the latest developments as they were being conveyed to him, but Eva couldn't know what the Proarkhe were telling each other and what they might be holding back.

The traverse disappeared after the last cat was safe, leaving Eva and the others once again cornered in a building full of hostiles. That Drone could pull them out if necessary was only slightly reassuring; they might live to fight another day, but failure would mean the fight would be that much harder to win. If this new plan didn't work, their next option was a suicide run on an Artificer flagship, and Eva definitely didn't want to think about trying to hold that door even if they managed to get inside in the first place.

"Bueno," Eva said, taking a deep breath and turning back to Antimatter and Ethervane. "Which of you is going to do this thing?"

Antimatter's eyes flickered as she tilted her head to one side. "I am already in." She slipped to the ground without a sound.

"Coño carajo," Eva said. She was surrounded by big damn heroes.

Ethervane squealed and ran to Antimatter's side, cradling the other Proarkhe's unmoving form in her arms. She launched into a series of noises that Eva's awkward understanding of the language parsed as mostly cursing, phrases occasionally separating out into things like "sodding scrapheap" and "molten slag" amid what might have been the equivalent of groans and sighs.

"Vakar," Eva said, grabbing his arm. "Can you do anything?"

Vakar shrugged a nod. "Their systems are massively more complex than the ones I have dealt with in the past," he said. "But the principles are not entirely dissimilar. I believe I can craft a kind of beacon for her to use as a means of returning to her body."

"And that will work?" Eva asked.

"It could," Vakar replied. "This is not something I have experience with, as I said. If nothing else, the existence of a foreign entity within their core may serve as an anomaly that would naturally attract the attention of internal programming."

"Like drawing a crowd to a bar fight," Eva muttered. "Well, do it. We have nothing to lose." Except Antimatter, and the rest of the universe, she thought, but saying it out loud felt like bad luck.

The racket at the door stopped. Eva didn't like that one bit. It suggested they were planning something, that they'd regrouped and were bringing reinforcements or working on another way through. She expanded the sensor range of her isohelmet as much as possible, but the construction materials made everything either impervious to her tech or fuzzy at best. The vibration sensor was definitely picking up something from outside. Something big, moving closer.

"Ethervane," Eva said. The Proarkhe didn't respond, still clutching Antimatter as her external plates spasmed and shifted.

Eva closed her eyes, her breath loud in her otherwise quiet isohelmet. Grief could be so different across various cultures, but some parts often overlapped. The denial, the anger, the bargaining . . . Eva had always been one to grasp for control, making plans even if they only extended to the next few minutes, choosing to believe she was more than a piece of flotsam launched into the void whose trajectory was dictated by the laws of physics. She could act and react, and she wasn't about to wait for things to happen to her unless she had no other recourse.

Pink had told her once that if Eva were left alone in a room for fifteen minutes with a choice between waiting patiently or giving herself a mild electrical shock, she'd take the shock out of sheer boredom. Eva had to acknowledge that Pink wasn't entirely wrong.

She couldn't wait for Ethervane to process her grief, so maybe it was time for a shock.

"Ethervane," Eva said more loudly. "Antimatter is busy, not dead. Cuddling her isn't going to change anything. Vakar is trying to help her. Either help him, or help me figure out what the hell is coming toward us, because I doubt it's friendly."

The latter part at least seemed to penetrate the miasma of emotion. Ethervane turned her head to stare at the wall, her eyes widening and brightening past their usual size and intensity. She gently laid Antimatter on the floor and stood, flexing her limbs in a way that looked more deliberate than reflexive.

"It's a coalescence," Ethervane said. "I'll inform our local allies."

"What's a coalescence?" Eva asked.

"I will explain in a moment." Ethervane's eyes narrowed and dimmed again, then began to flicker.

Annoying. Eva stepped back over to Vakar. She hated how his reflective armor made it impossible to judge his appearance or, more important, his scent.

"Any luck?" she asked.

"The beacons I create are removed quickly," Vakar said. "The system is not particularly intuitive, I must confess, but it seems to have its own intrinsic equivalent of an immune system—"

"And you're a virus," Eva said. "As long as it can't physically hurt you, keep trying."

Ethervane's eyes stopped flickering and became solid again. "It can, unfortunately, hurt him physically. Along with the rest of us."

Eva tried to smack her forehead, but her isohelmet took the impact instead. "Cuéntamelo," she said.

"The coalescence is part of the planet's defense system," Ethervane said, stepping over to the door. The banging still hadn't resumed.

"And the planet is defending itself against us?" Eva asked.

"Correct." Ethervane pressed a hand to the door, then opened it, revealing the empty corridor beyond. She then turned and stared down at Antimatter as if trying to make a hard decision.

Eva didn't like that look. "What is the coalescence exactly?"

"It's—"

Before Ethervane could respond, the far wall burst inward like a punched piñata. The lack of an accompanying explosion or other concussive force confused her for a moment, until Eva realized the metallic surface had, in fact, been punched by a fist bigger than her.

"A very large Proarkhe," Ethervane finished. "Part of the planet itself, in fact."

"Madre de dios," Eva murmured.

Through the new hole in the wall, an enormous face appeared, colored in shades of blue and gold. Their glowing orange eyes stared directly at her.

A wave of psychic noise assaulted her, resolving into something like "Intruder alert."

"Are they after me, or Vakar?" Eva asked.

"Not sure," Ethervane replied. "But they're definitely the planet's manifestation, not an Artificer construct."

Eva had only moments to guess, calculate, and act. She couldn't run and leave Antimatter here alone, and she couldn't risk opening a traverse back to her ship if a giant fist might go through it. That left one option.

"Keep working!" she yelled at Vakar, then ran toward the gaping hole and leaped through.

She didn't have far to go, since the giant Proarkhe was only a few meters away. Before she could blink, Eva found herself clinging to their metallic exterior, her comparatively small hand gripping a protrusion on the lower part of their chest. Given how high up she'd been in the building, that meant this particular security guard had to be over fifty meters tall.

Carajo, she thought, the dim voice of her mother in the back of her head yelling about looking before she leaped.

A hand moved in her peripheral vision. Eva had only a moment to push herself upward before the appendage smacked the place she'd just been. Another hand came flying toward her, so she continued to jump and climb, wishing she had rocket boots instead of gravboots and an antigrav belt. She didn't bother trying to use her weapon; the Proarkhe was probably too heavily armored for it to do anything but mark her as an aggressor.

The plates she'd been gripping abruptly rippled and moved, turning her handholds into something between quicksand and a meat grinder. With a yelp, Eva shoved her weapon into the shifting surface, then used it as a platform as she tried to figure out her next move. She didn't get much time before it was propelled out of the body of the Proarkhe, forcing her to jump up and float in the air like a target at shooting practice.

She found herself once again level with the enormous, orange-eyed face. How could anything be so huge? She used to think todyk were too much. Ah, the good old days.

"I'm not an intruder!" Eva shouted. It occurred to her belatedly that this was pointless, because why would this giant machine-person speak her language?

A hand whipped up again and she used her gravboots to pull her toward the Proarkhe's body. It had stabilized enough to give her a solid surface to land on, but she didn't stay long, once again jumping up and away. For all the times she'd told Min to make like a flea, she'd never expected to be doing it herself, literally. The only difference was she had no bloodsucking tendencies. Certainly she could be squashed as easily, though a flea could be tougher than expected.

Distantly, she hoped Vakar was making progress, that maybe Antimatter would be back soon. The alternative was unthinkable. And the notion that she herself might not live to find out was not worth contemplating.

Another leap took her above the Proarkhe, looking down on their massive form. They were easily the size of her ship. They reached up to grab her and she used her gravboots to zip down toward their head. Another jump and she barely avoided being hit, but to her bitter amusement they slapped their own forehead and staggered backward a few steps.

Too bad I sent the cats away, she thought. I wonder if Super Proarkhe are afraid of them, too.

The Proarkhe's hand once again swept toward her. She shot

down, but before she could jump away, a metallic cage enveloped her. Massive fingers closed around her feet, nearly crushing them, and she howled in pain as her boots disengaged.

The hand tightened around her until she doubled over, her arms pinned, her helmeted head forced between her bent legs. This wasn't how she had ever imagined she would die, but then again, she'd never had the best imagination.

This must be what a ship in a recycler feels like, she thought, and wished she'd at least been able to kiss Vakar goodbye one last time.

((Love you,)) she pinged at him. If those were her final words, at least they were true ones.

Abruptly, the Proarkhe's hand stopped closing, leaving Eva uncomfortable as hell but not quite dead. She couldn't move her head to figure out what might be happening, couldn't do anything but take shallow breaths and try to ignore the pain in her feet and ribs.

A burst of agony lanced through her brain. She might have screamed, but her teeth were gritted together too tightly to move her jaw. Images of her life flashed before her eyes, important memories and formative experiences, but also disconnected moments of thought, things she'd read once and immediately forgotten, things she'd seen but not paid any attention to at the time. Restaurant menus for places she couldn't afford, commwall ads for things she wouldn't buy, spam q-mail subject lines and the labels on boxes of expensive nutrition replacement bars. A fight with her sister over who could watch a holovid. The antiseptic scent of a sterilized spaceship. Her first spacewalk. Birds singing in a poinciana tree. Blood on her hands. The taste of her abuela's albondigas. Shame and fear and selfishness and regret, so much regret, but also love—deep love, full love, love that she would kill for and die for, love as bright and hot as stars, hard love and hopeless love and love wrapped in thorns trying to keep a sweet flower from being cut.

Through it all, the smell of licorice grew until Eva thought she would drown in it, and she supposed that was all right, too. She hoped Vakar and the others would be okay, and would forgive her for this like they'd forgiven her for so many other things, even when she didn't deserve it. She hoped they would find a way to succeed where she had failed. She had to believe they would, for the sake of everyone and everything she had ever loved.

The pressure on Eva's body suddenly vanished. For a moment, she assumed she'd finally died. Then she realized she couldn't be thinking that if she were dead, except maybe she could? A brief existential crisis led to her noticing her feet still hurt, along with many other parts of her, which seemed unlikely to carry over into an afterlife unless the god or gods responsible had particular views on how such transitions should go.

Eva looked up into the huge orange eyes of the Proarkhe holding her. They had loosened their grip, but she still sat on their palm, knees bent, back hunched.

"Your species is not known to us," they said.

It took a moment for Eva to get her breath to respond.

"Human," she said. "We're pretty new compared to you."

"State your purpose," they said.

Eva hesitated. "For humans in general, or do you mean why am I here right now?"

"The second."

Alabao, that was a lot to sum up. Eva opted for the direct approach. "I'm trying to reactivate the . . . traverses? That your people created and placed around the universe. Someone turned them off, and that's harming my species, along with many others. We need to get back to the Sol system before the human home planet is destroyed." Now that they were talking instead of playing flea tag, she found herself wanting to keep babbling, if only so they wouldn't go back to crushing her.

The giant Proarkhe's eyes flickered, which was oddly comforting, given how similar it was to the way the smaller ones seemed to process things. Finally, they spoke again.

"Who is inserting anomalous code into my core systems?" they asked.

"My partner," Eva replied. "He's trying to help someone find their way out of your, em, core systems? If possible."

Their eyes darkened slightly as if growing distant. "It is an eternity within," they said slowly. "We have not been compelled to stir for eons. We have been . . . contemplating fundamental conflicts."

Eva had no idea what that meant, but it didn't seem wise to pry, so she clamped her mouth shut.

"We must return to our processing," they continued. "Do you intend to cease your disruptions once the traverses are functional?"

"Yes," Eva said, hope kindling in her chest.

"It is done." They paused, turning their gaze back toward the building. "We will ensure the traverses remain open for a time. We have escorted our lost progeny back to their individual form as well. Does this satisfy your requirements?"

"Yes," Eva said breathlessly. She wasn't even sure if she said it out loud or simply thought it.

"Go, then. Promptly. We have work to complete."

They moved their hand toward the hole in the building, allowing Eva to limp back inside, where the others stood or lay frozen in shock.

Antimatter shifted and staggered to her feet. "What did you do?" she asked.

Eva shook her head. She didn't even know how to begin to explain.

"Ask Drone to open a traverse as soon as they're in the Sol system," Eva said. "The Gates should be up now."

After a moment, Ethervane squealed in astonishment. "You're right, they are. How . . . ?"

Eva thought of her childhood, of catching errant insects or reptiles who had snuck into her abuelos' house and quietly escorting them back outside. She could have killed them, but she never did. They hadn't done anything to her but exist; they were simply in the wrong place at the wrong time. Maybe it was harder to deal with them that way, but it had always felt better to her. She didn't think her actions had somehow stored up karma for this moment, but she had a sudden feeling of kinship for all those creatures whose lives might have gone very differently if some other random person had come along instead of her.

"I was lucky," Eva said. "And honest. Mostly lucky."

Vakar wrapped her in a hug that threatened to strain her already-crushed torso, but she welcomed it. A few moments later, the traverse opened, showing the inside of her ship and the variously delighted and serious faces of her crew. This wasn't over. They still had a whole battle to win elsewhere, and time, as always, was running out.

Chapter 23

ROBOTS IN THE SKIES

Eva's most immediate concern, on returning to her ship, was getting medical attention.

She hated having to dump herself on Pink again, when she had just been patched up from the debacle with Tito and Chela, but it was either that or collapse on the floor of the cargo bay in a very uncaptainlike fashion. So she quietly signaled to her co-captain, walked briskly toward the med bay, lowered herself gingerly onto the exam table, and closed her eyes and tried not to scream or vomit.

Pink, a professional who had known Eva for many years, did not blink or question this. She got to work, and within minutes Eva was once more hooked up to a machine pumping something useful into her body. That it was likely the last of whatever they had on hand did not escape her notice, but she let Pink do whatever she wanted, because Eva was not a doctor.

She also, despite any protests she might have wanted to make, desperately needed both drugs and rest. The latter she couldn't afford much of and the former was in low supply, but now was the time for both.

"Pink," Eva said, once she felt capable of speech again. She opened her eyes to find Pink leaning against the countertop, arms crossed.

"Vakar filled me in," Pink said. She looked grimmer than usual, given the stakes.

"I won't waste time, then," Eva said. "How's everyone?"

"We're in position to start an assault on something," Pink replied. "Sue and Momoko are already in two of the mechs. We just need a third pilot."

Eva took as deep a breath as her unhappy ribs allowed and exhaled. "I think Min should do it, and I'll take over here."

"Agreed," Pink said. "Given Min's experience and background, she's the best bet. It's not like you weren't piloting *La Sirena Negra* before Min joined up."

"And this is a job for the mechs now," Eva said. "All we have to do is stay out of the way and offer support if it's needed."

Pink flipped her eye patch up to give Eva a two-eyed stare. "That sounded downright thoughtful," Pink said after a moment. "I had to make sure you weren't possessed or something."

Eva huffed a laugh, wincing at the pain in her ribs. "Come on," she said. "I haven't been the worst captain."

"You haven't," Pink agreed. "We're all still alive, after all."

"For now," Eva said, then immediately regretted it.

"Now is all anyone gets," Pink repeated quietly, resting a hand on Eva's arm.

Eva closed her eyes, inhaling the sharp tang of disinfectant and Pink's coconut lotion and the fake-cherry undercurrent of one of the salves rubbed on her bare skin. Every time she made it back alive from their latest dangerous outing, it felt like a gift rather than an inevitability. Not a surprise, but a relief.

"You good?" Eva asked. "I mean, you know." She gestured at everything, because what was good right then, even?

"Yeah," Pink said. She uncrossed her arms and pressed her hands into the corners of the counter behind her.

Eva let Pink collect her thoughts, listening to the soft beep of machinery.

"We've been at this a long time," Pink said finally. "Some cycles I thought I'd go bugfuck crazy on Tito's ship, dealing with all the shit he got us into. But your fool ass kept me laughing it off."

Eva snorted. She'd been more sarcastic then, harder and sharper even when she cracked jokes. Trying to prove she was a badass to everyone, including herself. What a waste.

"We made this," Pink said, looking around her med bay. "I know you wouldn't have taken this ship as a payoff from your dad if it hadn't been for me. You'd probably be drinking yourself to death in a bar on Earth, or hustling in some space station out in the fringe."

"Omicron, maybe?" Eva asked.

"Lord, who knows?" Pink replied. "Armida might have let you bust heads for her back before you turned her into a flaming fart."

"Yeah, I really burned that space bridge," Eva mused.

Pink barked out a laugh. "See? You can't turn your mouth off."

Eva's smile faded. "But where would you be without me, hmm? Probably working in some fancy clinic somewhere, making bank. You were always the better of us." I dragged you down, Eva thought, unable to say it out loud.

"I made my choices," Pink said, arms crossing again. "You know that. Growing up out in the sticks, being tied down to one place on one planet . . . You think I would have jumped on Tito's ship if I hadn't been desperate to see the universe?"

"He was lucky to have you," Eva muttered.

"Too fucking true," Pink said. "I'd say he was lucky to have you, too, but you were a pain in his ass half the time, so." Her gaze turned distant, inward. "We were both smart enough to get out when we did. It's been tough, but it's been ours."

If Eva's heart weren't mechanical, she imagined it would have swelled with love and pride. As it was, the damn thing kept chugging along silently.

"And now look at us," Eva said. "What the actual fuck are we doing right now?"

"Fuck if I know." Pink smirked. "You're the one who agreed to save the universe. I was just here minding my own business."

Eva laughed again, trailing off into silence. She couldn't help but fill it.

"Tell me off if I'm being a metiche," Eva said, "but what's Joe planning to do, you know, once . . ." Eva wasn't sure how to finish the sentence.

"Well," Pink said, looking down at the floor. "If we all flame out and explode, there's nothing to talk about."

"We won't," Eva said.

Pink ignored that bluster. "We might, you know, give it another try maybe. See how it goes."

"Does he want to stay on board?" Eva asked. "It's getting a little crowded, but Leroy and Momoko will be back to their own business, and we could squeeze in."

Pink hesitated. "I could ask him. Not now."

"Why not now?" Eva asked. "You chicken?"

Pink shot her a glare like a laser. "Don't test me."

Eva held up her hands in mock surrender, wincing as her muscles protested. They fell silent again, surrounded by the sounds of the machines ticking off Eva's vitals. This time, Pink spoke first.

"One for the road, Eva-Bee?" Pink asked, gesturing at the cabinet containing her secret stash of bourbon. "Just for old times. I'll make sure you stay sober."

Eva grinned and shook her head. "It's not my thing anymore," she said. "I know I'm not an alcoholic, but I said I wouldn't after Omicron, and I don't want to break the streak. Though maybe you could send Vakar in here?"

"Oh no," Pink said, shaking her head for emphasis. "Every time I tell you two to take it easy, you just sneak better. Stay here, take twenty, and thank your Virgin I still have enough stims to keep you truckin' after all this."

"Fine," Eva said sullenly. "I have to make some calls anyway. Twenty minutes should be more than enough time."

Pink gave a mock salute. "I'll have the others suit up. Min will hang back until you can get to the bridge."

"What, you don't all want another inspiring speech before the shit hits the air filters?"

Pink didn't even look back, just raised her middle finger as she walked out the door and closed it behind her.

Eva gave herself exactly one minute to rest, then pulled up her commlink and started to make trouble.

Nineteen minutes later, Eva dragged her aching self into the bridge. She hadn't gotten ahold of anyone, but pieces were laid out on the Reversi board and she hoped some would flip and make a difference.

With a groan, she settled into the pilot's chair. It smelled like Min, a barely-there aroma similar to jasmine. It was strange to be in her place, like borrowing her clothes or sleeping in her bed.

Not wrong or bad, just odd. When Eva considered that *La Sirena Negra* had essentially been Min's second body for years now, it felt more invasive, but she tried to remind herself that this was temporary and consensual.

It didn't help, especially not when Eva worked herself up to jacking in through the plug on her neck. She knew it had to be done, to ensure the fastest possible response times, but she hated how it made her taste peaches. She'd never liked peaches.

Vakar poked his head through the doorway, already suited up. "I was told in no uncertain terms to avoid exacerbating your injuries," he said, his voice altered by the helmet.

"You got that lecture, too, huh?" Eva asked, grinning just enough to stretch the scar on her face.

He stepped farther inside, standing at attention, watching her prep for the direct ship connection. Eva knew it was more practical for him to wear his Wraith armor at a time like this, but she was struck with a sudden bout of nostalgia for years past—before The Fridge had stormed into their lives and wrecked everything, back when they were just a captain and an engineer on a small cargo ship trying to make ends meet. He'd worn a generic spacesuit then, nothing fancy. They used to spar for fun, and Eva didn't ask where a mechanic learned to fight, and Vakar didn't ask why her whole crew was full of people who were uncomfortably good at being violent while also trying to avoid it as much as possible.

And here they were, about to do violence on a massive scale. Saying "the other people started it" felt immature at best, but it was true, and now Eva's crew—her family, her friends, allies new and old—were going to end it, one way or another.

Eva paused right before jacking in, casting a hesitant glance at Vakar. "Can I . . ."

"Can you what?" he asked.

Bashfully, Eva cleared her throat. "Can I smell you for a second?" she asked. One for the road, Pink had said. Eva didn't want to go against doctor's orders, but one sniff couldn't hurt.

Before she could register the movement, Vakar was on her, wrapping her in his arms and pressing his face to hers. For a moment, her senses were overwhelmed. He was strangely warm, the slightly rough texture of his scales stimulating instead of abrasive. His palps brushed her cheeks, her lips, her neck, like feathery kisses.

But the smell. Oh, the smell. She wanted to roll around in it, to pump it straight into her isohelmet every time she felt lonely or sad. Like a bakery making anise-flavored cake, vanilla and rosewater and licorice smothering an undercurrent of incense, that slight wisp of concern a reminder that they weren't about to make a quick trip to the nearest space station for supplies.

Eva kissed him back, shoving every fear and worry into a locked box in her mind and then spacing it. Breathless, she rested her forehead against his.

"Pants party," she said. "You and me. Later."

Vakar's dry rumble of amusement stroked up her spine. "I am told one does not wear pants long at such events."

"Half the fun of wearing them is taking them off," Eva said.

A polite cough from the doorway signaled that Pink had arrived. Eva sighed and released Vakar's neck, allowing him to straighten and back away.

"Go on," Pink said gently, an amused smile teasing her lips. "Get to your station. We'll let you know if anything needs fixing in here."

Eva's pants could use some fixing, but that was not to be. With a wag of his head, Vakar went to his post in the bowels of the ship, to keep an eye on the usual problems.

"Everyone's ready?" Eva asked.

"And raring to go," Pink replied.

"Bueno," Eva said. "Vámonos."

She connected the ship's jack to the plug in the back of her neck. Data and sensation flooded into her mind and body, extending her awareness into every corner of *La Sirena Negra* within seconds. There was Pink, standing next to her in the bridge, and Vakar, still making his way through the mess. Leroy was hooked into the weapons systems, strapped into the emergency seat in the cargo bay, while Joe was on standby for whatever fires might need to be put out. Nara Sumas still rested on the catwalk, while below her, twenty cats were tucked into their crate, safe as they could be under the circumstances. Min, Sue, and Momoko were piloting their respective mechs, which felt like strange satellites to Eva's enhanced senses, separate bodies that were nonetheless familiar and welcome to the friend-or-foe programming. The Proarkhe had returned to their own ship with the promise that they would enter the fray with allies if there was a useful way for them to do so.

And beyond that, all the small pieces of the ship itself, the temperature readings and hull integrity data and operational indicators, all flitted through her consciousness as if she were aware of every organ in her body, every vein and artery, every nerve ending and axon, all feeding information to her brain. Most of it was automatic, but sometimes a flag would go up, something that required her direct attention and instructions, and she would send an order along as if this were another crew rushing about to ensure everything went smoothly.

Eva's voice came through the speakers now, as Min's usually did. "Adelante, amigos. Let's go piss off some assholes."

Shrieks, cheers, and various other noises replied. Through the bridge cameras, Eva could see Pink smirking, her visible eye gleaming with anticipation.

The Artificers had fucked around, and now they were going to find out.

The battle wasn't going badly, exactly, but Eva had hoped for better.

Much as she wished she could get a visual on the fighting, she had to settle for long-range sensors, moving around to keep *La Sirena Negra* from being targeted. From her vantage point at the edge of what she called the engagement zone, on the Martian side of the asteroid belt in the Sol system, Eva studied the actions and reactions of the different groups involved in the scuffle—namely, the mechs and the Artificers. By numbers alone, this should have been a total wipe: three giant robots against hundreds, maybe thousands, of metallic people who could change from bipeds to various ships and weapons and even animal forms, plus their actual spaceships with their respective weapons. The flagship in particular had multiple smaller-beam guns and a huge fuck-off cannon that fired bolts of purple-pink energy.

Every miss was a future hit on something, somewhere, eventually, thanks to the laws of physics. Eva had never been fond of laws.

Despite all that, the mechs were holding. They had their own energy blasters and blades and missiles, along with other individual tricks each pilot had discovered while practicing. Min had a sonic cannon, while Sue could cloak her mech to render it invisible to the enemy. Momoko had two swords instead of one, which seemed to suit her perfectly, given how she danced around, cutting through everything within reach.

The Artificer ships at least were at a disadvantage for close-range combat, their weapons designed like those of most spaceships to attack from a distance using sensors and math. Their shields held the mechs at bay, until they didn't; the blades were designed explicitly to tear through the damn things. It was like watching someone with an old-fashioned seam ripper dig into a dress and pull it apart, except the next step was to jump through the hole and start murdering everything inside.

Analogies had never been Eva's specialty. She preferred to stick with punching.

One problem was, there were a lot of enemies. However many there had been to start with, the Artificers were smart enough to realize shit was hitting air filters, so they kept bringing in reinforcements. The more individuals threw themselves against the mechs, the more the mechs had to slow down their big ship-breaking attacks to focus on the equivalent of hand-to-hand combat or small-group melee. Eva thought back almost fondly to the *Crash Sisters* fight a million years ago, when the worst thing that could happen was missing out on a free vacation.

Now, instead of punching people, all she could do was call out information to the mech pilots in the hopes of keeping them alive.

"A dozen new friends come to play," Eva told them. "Coordinates sent."

"Got 'em, Cap," Min replied. Moments later, her mech was among the group, shooting and slicing and driving them back if she didn't blast or cut them into pieces.

Another annoying thing about the Artificers was that, possibly due to the way their bodies worked, they didn't always stay down when damaged. While Eva knew of robots that could keep going depending on where and how they'd been hit, the Proarkhe had an uncanny ability to pull themselves back together and keep fighting. Even healing nanites needed raw material to work with, to repair cellular damage; the Artificers seemed to instead discard anything inoperable and remake themselves into a slightly different form that didn't need whatever had been lost.

Eventually they'd run out of bits or get hit somewhere vital and drift off into the black, but until then, the mechs were trying to empty the ocean with tazitas. Pretty soon, they would need either more cups or a much smaller ocean.

There had to be something she was missing, something she was forgetting. She pulled up another line to Antimatter, hoping the Proarkhe was available.

"Hola," Antimatter said. "If you're looking for reinforcements, believe me, I've been telling people to stop being such rustfuckers ever since I got back. They're not budging."

Rustfucker. Eva liked that. She filed it away for future use.

"Much as I'd love the help," Eva said, "I actually wanted to ask you about the mechs."

"What about them?"

Eva tried to figure out how to frame the question. "When we first met," Eva said, "you said the mechs were a weapon. Later you said they weren't quite what you expected, and you blamed the differences on memory degradation."

"Right, the information I'd been given was clear and accurate in some ways and strangely wrong in others. It didn't seem particularly significant."

"I think it might be, though." Eva flicked coordinates over to Momoko with a thought as more Artificers appeared on sensors. "What was wrong with them?"

Antimatter paused as if scanning her memories. "The reports I was referencing made it sound like there was one weapon, not three. That each construct was part of that weapon."

Something was on the tip of Eva's brain, something extremely important, like a person wildly waving their arms to get her attention while she was looking in the wrong direction.

"It reminded me of merging," Antimatter continued. "Some of us can learn to combine our forms with others to create a single larger entity, but it's dangerous. Networking our minds is one thing, but our bodies? Pulling them back apart can be tricky."

"Interesting," Eva said, shoving her dirtier thoughts sideways. "I'll see if I can figure it out."

Eva manifested the mech's instruction manual in her mind. The whole thing being dumped in there at once had given her a strange subconscious awareness of how to work the mechs, how to pilot them and make weapons appear and so on, but it wasn't the same as if she'd been trained little by little. And because it was basically a chunk of memory rather than an actual manual, finding answers wasn't as intuitive as it could have been.

She tried to search through the mech protocols, but there was too much happening for her to focus on that, too. Distantly, she was aware of the strain on her physical body, still recovering from injuries and lack of rest and all the emotional upheaval of the past week. Despite the temperature controls of her spacesuit and the way her artificial heart smoothly pumped her blood through her veins, she was sweating profusely and clenching her jaw so tightly she'd have a headache any minute.

"Leroy," Eva said, "I need you to do me a favor."

"Anything, boss," Leroy replied immediately.

"You've got the mech instructions in your head. Look for anything there about a big weapon or a special group tactical maneuver."

"Will do, boss."

Eva almost laughed. She hadn't been his boss in ages. Some habits died hard.

"Do we have any hints from the Proarkhe?" Leroy asked.

"Antimatter thinks maybe it has to do with the mechs combining somehow," Eva replied.

"Oh wow," Leroy said, with barely suppressed glee. "Combining mechs. That's so cool."

"It's not definite," Eva warned. "Might be something else entirely. Poke around and see what you find."

A call came in over the emergency frequency. Her humor faded. Eva shifted her attention away from the battle and pulled up comms.

"Qué coño estás haciendo!" Mari shouted at her.

"Hola, Marisleysis, mucho gusto, como estas," Eva replied.

"You're insane! Loca como una chiva!"

"Y siempre chivando," Eva said. "But as long as my people are out here doing this, we keep the flagship occupied, and your fool-ass buddies can't use their Earth-killing weapon, can they?"

A strangled laugh replied. "I'm on the flagship, comemierda."

Eva was dimly aware that the hairs on her human body's arms and neck had stood up.

"The fuck?" Eva asked. It wasn't really a question.

"Did you seriously think I would stand around comiendo mierda while a bunch of suits decided to murder billions of people?" Mari asked.

"You sold me out less than two years ago for the greater good," Eva said. "Of course I fucking thought that."

Mari sighed. "Bueno, now I'm stuck in some Proarkhe equivalent of a broom closet with my team, trying to figure out what we can do to salvage our plan."

Eva's sensors tracked another incoming squad. "Hold on, Mari." Despite the squeal of protest, she switched over to Sue. "Five more on the approach."

"Rusty buckets," Sue grumbled. "I don't think we can keep this up forever."

She wasn't wrong. Slow and steady might win the race, but

this wasn't a race. It was perpetual attrition, a grind where the enemies kept respawning.

"What was your plan, exactly?" Eva asked Mari.

"You put me on hold!" Mari exclaimed.

"No jodas, just answer the question!"

Mari hesitated. "We stowed away on a merc transport. We were going to find their reactor core and detonate it, take out the flagship and any vessels in range."

Eva assumed someone at The Forge had gotten intel about how the reactor core worked on an Artificer ship, but maybe that was overestimating them. "So, a suicide mission," she said.

"Better a half dozen volunteers than a few billion victims," Mari snapped.

Across Eva's sensors, the mechs continued their dance of destruction, flying and shooting and slicing through their enemies. The occasional small explosion signaled the end of a life, or a larger one suggested multiple casualties. Endless blackness with bursts of light that burned brightly and briefly. It was all so pointless and stupid.

"Just to be sure I'm on your page," Eva said. "The todyk weapon was proof of concept to get rid of the invaders, as either an attack or a threat intended to make them back up."

"Right."

"And this is your alternate proof of concept, showing that you know enough about their ships to get inside and blow them up without incurring mass casualties."

"Sí."

Eva scowled. "But how did you expect the other teams to get on the ships? I doubt they all have mercs coming and going."

"We were . . . we're working on that. There are a few potential options. We had hoped they would be intimidated enough to retreat and—"

"Fine, never mind, forget I asked." Eva sighed. She had to get Mari out of there, if possible, before the flagship blew up. "I don't suppose you had an escape plan?"

"No," Mari replied sourly. "We were expecting to die either way."

"Well, I have good news: our mechs are tearing through your shit so you'll probably go out in a blaze of glory, even if it's not yours." Except the mechs weren't making as much progress as they'd hoped . . .

Eva's sensors alerted her to a more pressing issue just before Sue's frantic voice reached her.

"We're surrounded!" Sue yelped.

"She's correct," Momoko said. "They're going to suppress us with sheer numbers very soon."

"What do we do, Cap?" Min asked.

Whatever advantage surprise had given them was gone, and now hundreds of the Artificers—if not more—were getting ready to swarm the mechs like a school of piranhas. What had been many separate points of light to her sensors was now a series of arrows, a coordinated strike by at least five different squads with supplemental units incoming from other directions.

This kind of strategy wasn't Eva's specialty. It was too big. Too much. But she couldn't let her people die because she was busy feeling intimidated by her own inadequacies.

And yet what could she do? The blips that were the enemy moved closer to the mechs by the moment. Their only chance, given the circumstances, was to pick a direction and try to punch through. That would leave all the other Artificers to chase after them, and where would they go? Would they pull back or bring in reinforcements? So far they were doing the latter. Might that mean the other occupied places across the universe were being left alone? Could they all do something now, while attention was focused on this one location, this one battle?

Eva hoped some of them might take a chance and succeed.

"All three of you," Eva said. "The smallest incoming force is here." She sent a location ping. "Break through that squad and then separate in different directions, and you can regroup here." Another location ping, farther away from the various forces, but not far enough to be safe from the flagship's weapons.

At best, they'd get a short breather. She had to figure out their legendary mystery weapon in the meantime. Whatever would make them such a danger that it would drive the Artificers back to their corner of the universe to lick their wounds, hopefully for good.

She needed something to buy her time. A distraction. Eva had hoped—but what was the point of hope? It was a lie you told yourself to keep going, to stop you from giving up when the odds seemed impossible. She'd almost made herself believe she could do more than she already had, but she had to accept the situation as it was rather than as she wanted it to be.

They weren't losing. They had expected this to be hard. It just would have been nice if it wasn't quite such a long shot.

Eva realized she still had a line open to Mari when someone mumbled something and her sister replied, "That's impossible, how did they get past the asteroid mines?" More alarmed mumbling followed.

Suddenly, an alarm went off in Eva's mind—no, it was her ship, alerting her to an anomaly. An extremely large anomaly, uncomfortably close to the fighting.

"By the Ancients," Antimatter whispered.

"What now?" Eva asked.

Before Antimatter could answer, Mari's voice cut in. "Eva, please tell me you're responsible for this."

Eva still didn't know what "this" was yet. The sensor readings made no sense, unless—

"Cap?" Min asked. "Why is there a whole new planet here all of a sudden?"

"It's the Proarkhe homeworld," Eva replied, her hands clenching into fists. "The one with the planet-busting weapon."

"It's moving toward Earth," Antimatter added. "I'm sorry."

Mierda, mojón y porquería, Eva thought. Defeating an armada was one thing; how did you stop a whole planet?

Chapter 24

YOU'VE GOT THE TOUCH

Pink's voice cut through the vast noise that seemed to be rushing through Eva's senses. "Eva."

"Pink," Eva replied, her own voice coming through the bridge speakers rather than her mouth.

Despite Pink's calm tone, she gripped the sides of her seat so hard her forearms trembled. "I know you're using sensors instead of cams, but I hope you're getting a good look at what's out there."

"I also have, like, five different people yelling about it in my head," Eva replied.

"All right, good." Pink paused. "Just so we're clear, this ship ain't attacking a whole planet."

"Claro que no."

"Cool."

"I already attacked that planet once. It kicked my ass."

Pink sighed and hung her head, but she was smiling, too. "How are you still alive?"

"Fools and drunks, mija."

An old joke, but it was also said that gods helped those who helped themselves, and Eva was doing her best to make that happen.

The Proarkhe planet had been transported to this galaxy, this star system, and it now advanced toward Earth at a speed that shouldn't have been physically possible, given its mass. If the Proarkhe could change shape and invent Gates that stayed functional for millions of years and sprinkle them across the universe, what couldn't they do?

They're people, Eva told herself sternly. Don't mythologize them. Your crew is out there busting heads and other assorted parts of their bodies, and the Artificers are dying just like anyone else. The thought was only vaguely comforting, because killing people sucked plutonium exhaust.

She ran down her current list of problems: The mechs weren't making enough headway. Mari and her team were stuck on the Artificer flagship and needed help or rescue or both. Fools on Earth were planning to destroy the flagship in a massive martyr move that would kill billions. And now, even if Eva prevented that, the Proarkhe homeworld would do the job anyway.

So she and her allies had to defeat the Artificers, save Mari and friends, stop the weapon from being activated, and send a whole planet back to the galaxy from whence it came.

That wasn't a to-do list, it was a cruel joke. Even Hercules had something to work with when he got saddled with seemingly impossible labors. But maybe Eva could find one more god in a machine to save them all.

Then again, last time she'd hoped for that, Goyangi had ended up sinking to a fiery lava doom.

As Eva tried to shake off her doom feels, a message chimed its arrival, and she swore if it was spam she'd find the sender and yeet them into a star. Instead, it was a brief recording, from a long shot she hadn't expected would reply after their last encounter. At the time, they'd both been entangled by The Fridge, though at least Eva had managed to help them with that particular problem by rescuing their kidnapped relative.

The face that greeted her was as green as an emerald, eerily eyeless, with a layered head ruff like a cloth headdress around a narrow skull. The overlapping folds of their mouth were like the petals of a flower bud, barely moving as they spoke.

"Captain Innocente, good wishes are extended to you in this time of trouble." The whisper-soft voice of Pholise Pravo, Eva's former Fridge handler, came through the ship's comms. "Apologies are offered for the delay in responding to your request. While official assistance cannot be rendered at the present time due to the uncertainty and instability of the unfolding situation, the intelligence provided by you was received gratefully."

Eva's brief burst of hope fizzled and sank. Well, at least Pholise had responded instead of leaving Eva in the dark.

"In the interests of securing a positive resolution," Pholise continued, "authorization has been granted for a volunteer diplomatic force to meet with your vessel. Should the force be intercepted aggressively by any other faction, self-defense would be seen as justified."

Eva's scowl turned into a smirk. Of course they wouldn't want to start a fight, or join one, but if the fight happened to come to them . . . And a volunteer force made sense; instead of a clear military presence, they'd send a bunch of supposed ambassadors who were probably as armed as the tuann could make them. Which was a lot; the tuann had been running the arms race with the quennians for ages—no pun intended, since they didn't have arms.

But would they arrive in time to help?

"This message was sent to coincide with the imminent arrival of the diplomats," Pholise continued in their quiet tones. "Direct contact will be made shortly." Their head ruff rustled as they shifted position slightly, almost as if looking directly at the recording device. "No matter the outcome, your continued efforts in this and other situations are to be commended. You are deserving of gratitude, and it is hoped you receive it."

The message ended, leaving Eva's eyes suspiciously watery. Gratitude? That wasn't one she heard a lot, and frankly she didn't think she'd done nearly enough to deserve it, but as Pink would remind her, that wasn't her call to make.

And not something she could dwell on, regardless. Moments later, another new set of blips appeared on her sensors, and the gentle combined voice and text comms from the allegedly diplomatic corps informed her that they were under attack and would be returning fire.

"Go for it," Eva said. "If you can make it to this point, the mechs are pinned down and could use help." She sent the coordinates and received a quiet affirmation that they'd do their best.

It was something. Her Plan Z had felt like notes in a dozen bottles thrown into the ocean, containing the intel Antimatter had been permitted to give her about the Proarkhe history and weapons and defenses. She'd been waiting since the Gates came back up, since the flurry of calls she'd made while in the med bay, hoping to hear good news from the messages she had sent out, but until Pholise, only silence had replied. Maybe, if one group was willing to help, others wouldn't be far behind.

Eva took a deep, steadying breath and checked on all her

people, one by one, assuring herself they were okay. Then she offloaded as many piloting processes as she could, to give herself space to consider her options.

A minute later, she got back on comms and started doing one of the things she did best: talking to people until they either helped her or hit her.

"Mari," she said, "not that I'm supporting your suicide run, but why did you hide in a broom closet and call me instead of just doing it?"

"Our plan was predicated on intel about the typical ship habits. Crew locations, standard procedures—stuff we found out from mercs who'd been on board for a while." Mari huffed out a breath. "It was incomplete data to begin with, but now that they're fighting you, it's gone from somewhat predictable to entirely chaotic."

"And I'm guessing you don't have the firepower to shoot your way through," Eva muttered.

"We can try," Mari said. "But the odds are worse than the stealth approach we'd initially planned. We'd need a few more people and better weapons."

"Hold that thought." Eva shifted to another line. "Antimatter, quick question. What if I could get you inside the Artificer flagship?"

"What?" Antimatter replied. "How?"

"My sister has people in there right now. She could pass along the coordinates."

Antimatter gave a whistling squeal. "That might get my superiors to act, yes."

Eva grinned ferally. "The team on board thinks they have a way to blow up the ship from the inside. They were planning on going out with a bang, but could you use a traverse to get them all out safely instead?"

"Maybe," Antimatter said. "If I can get my superiors to agree, and if we're lucky and everything goes well." She paused, then said, "Even if they don't agree, some of us might want to help. Might be only two or three, because we'll be in a mess of trouble if we survive, but—"

"Mejor que nada," Eva replied. "You probably have a better idea of how to get around the ship than this team does, and where to stick the bomb."

She switched back to Mari. "Good news. I may have found you backup, a tour guide, and a way out." She explained briefly, including that the numbers were conditional on chain-of-command approval.

Mari didn't answer for a few long moments, and when she did, her tone was surprisingly gentle. "Increíble. We had almost given up and decided to set the charges wherever we could. How did you do that?"

"I haven't done anything yet but talk," Eva replied. "That's the easy part."

And that left the problem of the mechs and the planet. The tuann ships were helping, but the mechs were still fighting their way out of the net tightening around them.

"Eva," Pink said, "we have more reinforcements coming through. Momoko's family mobilized their personal fleet along with some mercs, the Conelians sent a squad of fighters led by Vixen Nimbus, and the todyk were apparently inspired by the history lesson you sent them and decided to defend Earth for the honor of their ancestors."

"How many ships total?"

"Thirty-four."

Eva's eyes flew open, then closed as the sight of the bridge overlaid on her ship senses disoriented her. She wasn't as good at handling the load as Min was.

Thirty-four ships? Added to what the tuann had sent, their group was slowly becoming a ragged fleet. They were still vastly outnumbered by the Artificers, trying to kill an elephant with mosquito bites, but it was better than three mechs against the entire enemy force.

Given what had happened to the gmaarg armada, they might all be cannon fodder. Since Eva had called them in, their deaths would be on her conscience.

The flagship had yet to do more than fire a few pointless warning shots, since the mechs were too small and fast to be usefully targeted by the giant ship-killing weapons. That might change, she realized, if any more backup happened to arrive. It's not as if she expected a dreadnought; if anything bigger than a corvette appeared, she'd be shocked.

"Set up a secure channel for everyone, please," Eva said. "Tell them to stay clear of the flagship and focus on the Artificers in ship form, or the ones inside actual ships."

"The glamorous life of a captain," Pink replied dryly.

Eva grinned but didn't respond. Her body was getting twitchy from being still for so long, especially her bladder, which was regrettably full of Cuban coffee.

"Leroy," she said, shifting to another of her many spinning plates, "did you find anything about the weapon?"

"Sort of?" Leroy paused. "There are all these things about a 'final form,' except they don't actually explain what the final form is. Like the pilots should already know, I guess?"

Mierda. That didn't help. "What can the final form do?"

"It has four multi-bladed melee weapons, some kind of serrated clamp or crushing tool, a couple of giant guns, and a massive energy cannon."

That sounded underwhelming compared to what the mechs

could already do, but presumably the cannon was the main attraction. If that could wreck the flagship faster, they needed to figure out how to get it working.

"Keep chasing that lead and get back to me," Eva said.

"Will do, boss."

Eva's ship senses tracked him pacing across the cargo bay. She returned her attention to the virtual map of the battlefield, noting that their new allies were flitting around the different squads bullying the mechs. If the numbers shifted again as more Artificers were pulled in from other places, the situation could devolve quickly. Those mechs needed to get free and get out.

"Eva," Vakar said, interrupting her thoughts, "they're coming."

It took a few moments for her to parse what he was saying. Who was coming? How would he know? By the time it sank in, a new bundle of lights had appeared on her sensors, flying in a tight formation straight toward the mechs.

The Wraiths had sent help.

After how they'd treated Vakar, she hadn't even wanted to speak to them, but Vakar had convinced her it was for the ever-elusive greater good. Assholes they might be, but giving them the option to provide an assist outweighed the harm they'd caused.

"They have the intel we sent?" Eva asked.

"Yes," Vakar replied. "They have modified their vessels accordingly. They intend to help draw the enemy away from the mechs unless you have a preferred objective."

"No, that's perfect." As she spoke, the mechs finally managed to punch through the net of Artificers closing around them, then began the evasive maneuvers she'd suggested. They'd come a long way in no time at all, and she was so proud of them she could yell.

The net followed them, splitting into three groups smoothly, as if they'd expected that approach. But now with so many additional ships circling that net, it was harder for the Artificers to recover and re-form their ranks.

Al fin, parió Catana, Eva thought.

Watching a battle from so far away was a strange experience. It was one thing to see combat up close, to punch your enemy in the face and get their blood or viscera on your hands, even to shoot them from near enough that you had to watch their body crumple. Out in the starlit darkness, there wasn't much to see, even if you were in a dogfight. Ships might be barely visible if you were close enough to the local light source, or if they were glowing by some other means, but mostly you relied on your instruments, your sensors, whatever visualization method your own ship used to show you the shape of what you were trying to kill.

Eva understood how captains and generals and admirals up the chain of command could stare at a bunch of moving lights in a holofield and make dispassionate choices about whom to send where and why. Those lights weren't people anymore. They were numbers. Assets. Pieces on a game board.

It was bullshit and she hated it.

The mechs continued their flight to reconvene at the coordinates Eva had sent, but that would only move the location of the battle. As long as they were caught up in the equivalent of single combat or small melees, they weren't dealing with the flagship, or the planet now looming as an even bigger problem.

"Captain." Antimatter reappeared in Eva's comms, sounding nearly breathless for a species that didn't breathe. "I've got a team of six, armed and standing by. Send me the coordinates for the flagship entry point."

"Will do," Eva replied. Hopefully Mari was either still in the same place or had moved to a better staging area. She doubted six Proarkhe would fit in a broom closet or its equivalent.

Mari didn't answer the first comms attempt, or the second, but the third time was the charm. "Busy," she snapped at Eva. "Qué quieres?"

"I have six Proarkhe who want your number," Eva replied. "Can they call you, maybe?"

"What?"

"Get somewhere big enough to fit them, then give me your coordinates. They're going to open a portal to your location and help you."

Mari laughed, but it had a maniacal edge. "Of course. Yes. That will make a dozen of us against, what, a hundred or so?"

"Doubles your odds of reaching your target," Eva said. "Plus they can, you know, actually get you out instead of you all having to explode and get your bravery medals in the afterlife. You can thank me later with pastelitos."

Mari said something that sounded like "jódete, cabrona," but it was drowned out by a proximity alert. Someone was approaching *La Sirena Negra* in a hurry, and it wasn't Sue.

Eva was about to hustle out of the way and figure out a new intercept point when she was hailed on comms. Not just any channel, but the secure one, which meant it was one of two people, and both of them had contributed genetic material to her.

"Captain Innocente," said Regina Alvarez, her tone entirely businesslike. That she was using Eva's title and current last name rather than Eva, Eva-Benita, or Eva's full name suggested she was speaking in an official capacity rather than as Eva's mother, no matter which channel she'd used to call.

"Speaking," Eva replied, trying to match the tone. It was tough to do while simultaneously tracking mechs, allies, and enemies and flying a whole damn spaceship. And needing to pee.

"My name is Regina Alvarez," Regina continued, as if Eva didn't know. "Your request for assistance in your unsanctioned attack against the local enemy fleet was received. As a representative of the Benevolent Organization of Federated Astrostates, I've been asked to order you to stand down immediately and remand yourself into the custody of law-enforcement authorities."

Eva stifled a laugh. "And if I refuse to comply?" she asked.

"A warrant will be issued for your arrest, effective immediately," Regina replied. "However." She paused, either for effect or to figure out how to carefully phrase what she had to say.

Eva waited. It was easier to be patient with all the other background processes she was engaging in.

"At the present time, our officers are not permitted to engage in any actions that may be construed as acts of aggression against the invading forces," Regina said. "The warrant will be served immediately upon your entry into BOFA space after cessation of present hostilities."

So Eva was a fugitive once she helped end the war. Lovely.

"And my crew?" Eva asked.

"They are presumed accomplices unless evidence suggests otherwise."

That meant they were all criminals as of right now. Why the hell was her mother telling her this? To get her to stop fighting? That would be incredibly unwise. Also, it wouldn't work.

"Is this a private call on your end, Ms. Alvarez?" Eva asked.

"This conversation is being monitored and recorded," Regina replied.

"Perfecto." Eva inhaled deeply. "Please tell your superiors to disable their resingado todyk weapon instead of pulling the flagship to Earth and killing billions of people. Tell them they can't have the mechs, they can't have me or my crew, and I will not let them commit genocide no matter how fucking brilliant they think that idea is. Tell them they can keep comiendo mierda until their eyes are brown, but I'm not going to stop fighting, no matter what."

After a long pause, Regina sniffled and cleared her throat. Her voice took on a hoarse quality. "Anything else, Captain Innocente?"

Eva hesitated, too. "No, eso es sufficiente."

"One last thing, then. A contingent of now-former BOFA agents is approaching your location. They are not acting with the support of the Federation and will also be arrested once hostilities have ended. There should be forty ships in total. They are armed and dangerous."

"Good for them. So am I."

"That's all then, Captain Innocente," Regina said. After a moment, she added, "Que Dios te bendiga," then cut the connection.

Eva wished she could fight the headache suddenly pounding behind her eyes as easily as she could a person. Talking to her mother was difficult on a good day, but this had taken a lot of energy she couldn't afford to expend.

"You okay?" Pink asked, peering down at Eva with her eye patch flipped up.

"Siempre," Eva replied. "More good news. BOFA sent us another forty fighters, though I don't know what kind they are."

"BOFA did what?"

"They're playing it off as naughty rogues. That was my mom, giving me the cover story."

Pink snorted. "Could have just left it a secret and not said anything. They must have black ops for this shit."

"Their black ops forces may not be available, or they may be doing something else, who knows?" Eva shrugged. "Not looking this gift crehnisk in the asshole. If they call, send them the mechs' current coordinates."

"Wish we had a bigger tactical display."

"We never wanted to be tactical. We wanted to be fast and sneaky and not get shot at. We just can't fucking help ourselves."

Pink's belly laugh made Eva grin. She needed to do more than grin, though. She needed to figure out that damn final-form supreme-weapon thing.

Eva set the ship to coast and delved into the mech's operating information, wishing the organizational structure made more sense. But if wishes were spaceships, then beggars could fly. She tried to clear her thoughts, then focus intently on the question of how to make the mech stronger, more powerful, but that didn't get her anywhere. She thought "weapon" and ended up with a general notion of all the available weapons, with no clear idea of how to summon or use them. Chasing that rabbit led her down a hole with more specific information about each weapon's energy output and shot capacity and so on, but still nothing about how to induce the final form, whatever it was. The query "how to achieve final form," which seemed fairly straightforward, achieved a vague feeling similar to when Eva, in rare moments, wanted a hug, which was infrequent enough that even the received sensation made her pull away from her perusal with a frown.

A gentle tapping attracted her attention. Mala had emerged from the crate and jumped onto her chest, staring at her and batting a paw against her chin.

"Miau," Mala said.

"Qué miau?" Eva asked. For all that she had conversations with the cat, her interpretations were mostly just that. Usually if she was way off, Mala hit her with a spike of disdain, but for some reason they seemed to be on a wavelength most of the time.

A wave of emotion washed over her. With it came a sense of togetherness, unity, like cats piled on top of each other for warmth or companionship, bathing each other and rubbing faces and napping. Eva had no idea what to make of it.

Mala put her forehead against Eva's and purred. Eva closed her eyes and tried to channel what Mala was feeding her, telling her. What did it mean? What was the cat trying to say? She let those ideas and sensations merge into the mech instructions, almost as if she were lazily flicking through a book or q-net node looking for a phrase to catch her fancy, letting herself follow tangents and links and drift through guided entirely by feel and whim.

Show me this, Eva thought. Show me hope and love and family. Show me a tangle of cats.

As if a key had been turned in a lock, suddenly Eva knew what the final form was. She knew everything about it: how it functioned, what it could do, and most important, how to make it happen.

"Sue," Eva said, her face still centimeters from Mala's. "I need to get inside your mech. Set a course for my position and I'll meet you halfway. Then we need to reach Min and Momoko, now. Min, Momoko, meet us . . . here." She sent coordinates over.

"Are you sure, Cap?" Min asked. "That's right in the middle of the fight, near the flagship!"

"I'm positive. Stay mobile, but be ready to go there on my order."

"What are you up to?" Pink asked.

Eva ran a hand over Mala's furry head. "Not me. Us. We're going to end this, all of us together."

Chapter 25

LEAP OF FAITH

Eva didn't hesitate. She grabbed Mala with a free hand and pushed the ship into the fastest sublight she could manage without overshooting the rendezvous location. From her seat nearby, Pink protested the sudden motion, which briefly jarred everyone on board despite the artificial gravity's quick compensation.

"Why do you need to be in Sue's mech?" Pink asked. "Are you going to take over?"

"Nope," Eva said. "She has to keep flying it, but we need to get a second pilot in there."

Pink hissed through her teeth. "That means you or Leroy, and you're busy."

"I know what needs to be done, though," Eva said. "I'm not sure I can get Leroy up to speed in time." Over the speakers, she said, "Everyone, prepare to abandon ship."

A chorus of confused voices replied.

"Pardon my language," Pink said, "but what the fuck?"

"It's the best option," Eva said. "Right now, the mechs are a lot safer than this ship."

"The mechs," Pink said, her tone flat. "The ones scrapping with all the bad guys out there."

"Yes," Eva replied. "Besides, Vakar is the only one who might be able to take over from me as pilot anyway. We both know he's not as good at flying this hunk of junk as I am."

And if they didn't get Eva or Leroy into the mech, they'd lose this entire fight for sure. It didn't matter how many extra ships people threw at them—or rather, it could, but the rest of the universe wouldn't come around in time for it to help. The mechs were the secret weapon, the unstoppable force meeting the apparently immovable object and pushing it back. They could afford the loss of Eva's ship—even Eva herself, if Leroy could make the final form happen—but not the mechs. Not a single one of them.

Not that Eva was eager to toss her life away. Mari might be able to handle that, but Eva was extremely attached to existing. Maybe they had pastelitos and specific adorable quennians in the afterlife, but Eva didn't want to find out the hard way.

"Reach out to our new fleet, amigos," Eva told Pink. "See if they can keep the space around us clear."

"On it," Pink said.

"You're the best, as always," Eva said.

"Keep telling me that. It never gets old."

Nobody would be getting old if this didn't work. Eva told herself not to be morbid, but as usual, she didn't listen.

It took her a few precious moments they could ill afford to collect herself. "Here's the plan," Eva said. "We'll rendezvous with the mech in a minute. Vakar, switch energy to shields once we stop. Leroy, you get in the mech first, more orders to come.

Pink and Joe, push the cat crate over. Nara, help them or stay out of the way. Understood?"

"Yes, boss," Leroy replied.

"If you say so," Joe said.

"Better there than here," Nara added.

The delay for Vakar's answer compelled Eva to search for him, on his knees in the bowels of the ship. He rested one claw on the floor, his forehead pressed against the hull. She couldn't smell him, but the ship's sensors did the work for her and she translated in her mind. Fart, rusty copper, and something else, something almost sulfurous. Dismay and regret and pain. The last, she imagined, was probably what she was feeling.

Sadness. Deep enough to drown in.

"Vakar?" she said quietly, directly to his comms.

"I will only leave if you do," he replied.

"Claro que sí, mi vida." She wasn't sure she could move that fast, but she had every intention of trying.

"Very well." Vakar fell silent again, but Eva knew he was getting ready to do what she'd asked.

"Once you're inside," Eva told Leroy, "I need you to search the mech manual for the feeling you get when you hug Momoko. Or your moms. You think you can try to focus on that instead of words?"

"Sure thing, boss," Leroy replied, but his voice told her he thought she'd sprung a leak.

Through the cargo bay cameras, Eva could see Leroy unstrap himself from his seat and activate his isohelmet. His solid footsteps sent minute tremors through the floor, which Eva received as a strange combination of sensor data and something like a faint tapping against her skin. The longer she stayed jacked into the ship, the more she merged with it in subtle ways.

"Almost there, Captain," Sue said. The mech was invisible to standard sensors, but Eva could feel it nearing.

"Vakar," Eva said over comms. "Stand by for engine cutoff."

"I am prepared," Vakar replied.

Each person would still have a few moments out in the open as they transferred to the mech—that couldn't be helped—but they could keep *La Sirena Negra* protected in the meantime, and hopefully draw fire away from them. This was worse than the damn ice-ring maneuver, because at least they'd had the benefit of being invisible to sensors. Now they'd be a nice little target for not only the Artificers in pursuit, but any larger ship that might have been keeping an eye on them from farther away.

Pink snorted derisively in reply. "How are you planning to get out?"

"I'll try the same trick as last time," Eva said. "Once you're out, I cut power and let it drift. Hope they ignore the ship because they can't see it on sensors."

"And if they blow it up?"

Eva closed her eyes again, letting her consciousness flood her home for the past eight years. Her means of achieving freedom from her father and Tito. Min's second body. She'd lived here and loved here, hired people who became friends and then family. She'd staged the infiltration of a Fridge base to get this ship back, for herself and her crew. The idea of abandoning it now was sickening, stifling, like swallowing unfiltered water or breathing the air of a planet unfit for human habitation.

"It's just a ship," Eva said softly.

The silence in the bridge was so profound that Eva opened one eye to get a look at Pink. Her co-captain and best friend stared at her with the serious expression usually reserved for medical emergencies.

Then Pink smiled ruefully. "Gimme that cat of yours. Moving them is gonna be a pain."

Eva rolled her eyes. "At least they're in a crate with antigrav. The fish, unfortunately, are out of gas."

Pink gently picked up Mala and cradled her. The cat gave a perfunctory whine and then settled. They headed for the cargo bay, where Pink began to wrangle the box of cats with Joe and Nara's help. Leroy stood in front of the door, clenching and unclenching his hands, tossing glances over his shoulder as if he wanted to help but knew he had other orders.

Distantly, Eva realized she was crying. She sucked in a breath and told herself firmly that *La Sirena Negra* wasn't gone yet, that it might survive once they were out, because why bother blowing up an empty ship? But she knew if it were her, she'd probably take no chances and ensure the enemy had nowhere else to go. It was the prudent thing to do.

She slowed the ship down as they closed in on the mech. Unlike Min, she'd never quite perfected the slide to a stop, so she settled for a gentler halt that wouldn't send everyone flying into a wall. Once Eva cut engines, Sue tethered the mech to the back of the ship. As soon as she did, the shields flared, the normally invisible field around the ship glowing a faint indigo. Vakar's work was done. Now it was her turn.

Eva opened the cargo bay door, and Sue positioned the mech's stomach for an easy jump from one place to the other. The ship didn't move when Leroy leaped out, but Eva still felt the shift, the moment when the cargo bay suddenly became slightly lighter, and Leroy's vitals left her sphere of awareness. Her cameras tracked his motion, traversing the short distance between doors, and then he was inside the mech and she released the breath she'd been holding.

"Eva," Pink said. "Who's next?"

"Let Nara jump so she can catch the cat box," Eva said. "Hurry."

The Artificers would be there in moments. Not good. Pink and Joe might not be able to get the cats across, much less themselves. And that would still leave Vakar, and Eva herself . . .

The seconds kept ticking down. Farther afield, the various clusters of fighters allied against their enemies held their own, trading fire and chasing each other around. Two units had peeled off to approach *La Sirena Negra*, but they probably wouldn't make it in time to be much help.

A few moments later, Pink and Joe moved along with the cat crate. Eva once again held her breath as they flew toward the mech's door, Pink entering first. For an awkward moment, the gravity inside the mech asserted itself, leaving the container half inside and half out with Joe clinging to the back end, flopping around like a hooked fish as Newton's laws got ridiculous. Eva couldn't see what happened exactly, but presumably Pink and Nara pulled from the other side, and soon they were all on board.

That left only her and Vakar. Wait, where was Vakar?

The instant she asked herself the question, she knew the answer.

Eva's eyes flew open. "Qué coño?" she yelled, glaring at him.

"I will not leave without you," Vakar replied coolly. He stood in front of the instrument panels, their lights flashing behind him to warn of the lack of engine power.

Eva closed her eyes again. How did Min manage to walk around the ship while flying it? "At least get to the cargo bay," she said.

"We will go together," he said.

The curses that rolled off Eva's tongue didn't faze Vakar in the slightest. He stood in front of her, unmoving, like a silver-coated statue in his Wraith armor.

It didn't matter. Time was up. The Artificers had arrived.

Five of them circled *La Sirena Negra*, observing but not firing. She quickly closed the cargo bay door before they could decide to fly in. They seemed more interested in the mech, though.

Ice shot through her veins. Were her people safely inside?

The Artificers stopped moving, as if conferring with each other. Eva resisted the urge to tear her jack out and run.

"What's happening?" she asked Pink. "Is everyone okay?"

"We're all fine," Pink responded. "Waiting on backup, and you."

"Has Leroy figured out the final form yet?"

"Nope, so don't get any fool thoughts about hunkering down."

Mierda. She and Vakar had to get over there. Powering down the ship wouldn't help at this point. The Artificers were right outside; they could see the damn thing with optical sensors, or whatever they called their eyes. Might as well let it stay in its bubble until the fuel ran out.

"Bueno," Eva said. "Vámonos. Time to go."

Reaching up to the back of her neck, Eva disengaged the cable jacking her into *La Sirena Negra*. The shock of losing her extra senses, all the varied data inputs and perceptions linked to the ship itself, left her unsettled, diminished, hollow. Like she'd been spread out in a huge bed and now she was stuffed into a cot, or she'd had a case of the hiccups that had suddenly stopped and she kept waiting for them to start again.

Vakar helped her stand, and together they left the bridge, Eva struggling to shake off the last of her ship-mind. Her legs wobbled more than usual, requiring extra attention to make them do what she wanted. The taste of peaches faded, though the memory would linger for a while yet, and the other scents of the ship flooded in, stronger than usual. Pink's coconut oil, the last round of espresso Eva had made, the disinfectant Sue's bots used on the floors.

The thought of leaving it all behind was a worse emptiness and ache than the physical disconnection from her ship, her home. Eva didn't have time to mourn, and it made her want to scream.

Don't cry over milk that hasn't even spilled yet, she told herself. One thing at a time. She could still access the ship's readouts through her commlink, at least, even if she didn't have a wireless jack like Min did. Shields were at full power; none of the Artificers had fired yet, and the fuel reserves were holding for now.

"Should we utilize the cargo bay door?" Vakar asked.

"No," Eva replied after a moment. "Let's go out the escape hatch. Less obvious." She was glad for the strength of his arm under hers, his clawed hand on her waist. Even if her spacesuit dulled her senses, his presence and solidity were still palpable.

With every step, a little of Eva's control returned. Vakar released her to open the hatch, hesitating for a moment.

"You should go first," he said.

"No me diga," Eva replied. She pursed her lips. Then again, that meant she'd be the first one to get hit if the Artificers saw them.

Before she could accept, Vakar seemed to figure out the same thing, and started climbing down so she couldn't stop him without making more trouble for both of them. She smirked. Her own fault for not thinking faster.

It took Vakar a few seconds to turn around so he faced the exit hatch; the perils of artificial gravity. Once he had, he cautiously opened the aperture and poked his head out, doing a quick survey of the ship's surroundings. Not much to see out in the vast black of space, even with Artificers nearby.

Vakar continued up and out, gripping the handholds on the exterior of the ship to keep from drifting away or knocking himself loose. A belt line would be safer, but not if they had to jump in a hurry. Eva followed him as quickly as she could, then closed the hatch behind her.

The mech floated just beyond the cargo bay door, still tethered so it stayed with the ship. Sue had closed the opening in its abdomen; they'd have to time their approach carefully if they didn't want enemies to start shooting inside. Meanwhile, all she and Vakar had to do was not get shot, jump through space, and not miss their target.

Naturally, that meant an Artificer appeared in front of them, just beyond the ship's shields. And it was Kilonova, currently in all his bipedal glory. Eva groaned and rolled her eyes.

"How is it that you persist?" Kilonova shrieked into Eva's mind.

"How have you not been smothered to death by your own ego?" Eva replied.

"Human psychological concepts such as ego are primitive and—"

Eva sent him the mental equivalent of a prolonged fart noise and gave him the middle finger. Antagonizing him was probably a bad idea, considering she and Vakar were only protected while Kilonova was outside her ship's shields, and even those would withstand only so much damage before vanishing.

"We cannot reach the mech unless he moves or the mech does," Vakar said over comms.

"Working on it," Eva said. "Do you have any ideas?"

"Not presently."

Why wasn't Kilonova attacking? Eva checked the ship's sensors; the other Artificers were converging on his location. Wonderful.

"Were you the one who sent the planet after me before?" Eva asked. Maybe getting him to talk would buy them time. As it was, the mech had already rotated past where they needed it to be, so they'd either have to wait or do something else.

"You triggered the defenses yourself, meat," Kilonova replied. "How you managed to escape is inconceivable."

"I bet a lot of things are inconceivable to you," Eva muttered. To Vakar, she said, "If we can get a solid jump sideways, I might be able to use my gravboots to pull us to the mech."

"We would have to be completely clear of the enemy," Vakar said.

And he could quickly shift to block them, at which point Eva would be stuck to him feet-first. She suspected that would make her even easier to hit, even if he risked hitting himself.

The stars in the distance shifted minutely as *La Sirena Negra* spun, the lack of gravity making Eva's insides churn. She was less than ten meters from her destination, but it might as well have been ten light-years. With the other Artificers approaching rapidly, there would soon be a wall of guns and fists between them and their goal.

"I will enjoy dismantling you," Kilonova said, his red eyes flaring more brightly.

"That's cute, coming from a talking teakettle," Eva said. "All shrieking and hot air." But he definitely had the high ground, so to speak. She and Vakar should probably climb back inside and try to find another way to deal with the mech situation.

She was about to tell Vakar as much when something appeared on her ship's sensors. An anomaly, a glitch, something she'd programmed the system to spot because her dad had told her about an old trick some ships could use to stay invisible. An emissions flutter that usually registered as interstellar background nonsense. She'd asked him why it wasn't standard for sensor software to look for it, and he'd said some things weren't worth the hassle and cost to account for officially, given how infrequently they were exploited. People on the edge of legality would know how to deal with it; people who had to submit forms in triplicate to wipe their ass deserved whatever they got.

The question was, who was running that exploit and why were they here?

She didn't have time to care. She had to figure out how to get back inside fast, because she had a feeling as soon as she and Vakar started moving, Kilonova would manifest his fancy gun and shoot to kill.

"What are you waiting for?" she asked him. "An invitation?"

"I have been ordered to apprehend you," Kilonova replied. Something about the way he said it suggested the idea was extremely distasteful to him.

"Why?" Eva asked, before her mouth could catch up with her brain.

"You are clearly someone with authority in this sector, and yet our sources have had difficulty obtaining information regarding your history," he replied. "What we have found strains credulity. We assume you are a covert agent with vast resources and we intend to exploit your knowledge and abilities."

Eva snorted, then laughed. Once she started, she couldn't stop. This was not the time for it, but it bordered on hysterical, and soon tears were leaking from the corners of her eyes.

"Are you well?" Vakar asked quietly.

"Madre de dios," Eva said. "They think I'm some kind of government superspy. Vast resources . . . no puedo." She wheezed, her lungs filling with air and then immediately seizing as she struggled to overcome her fit. She couldn't do this. She had to move, to act—

A sudden comms call interrupted. She was still connected to

La Sirena Negra, and she would have let it roll to voicemail except it was the private, secure channel. One of three people. Any of them could be a nightmare or good news.

Let's find out, she thought, and answered.

"Eva-Bee, something wrong with your boat there?" said the excessively cheerful voice of Pete Larsen, Eva's dad. She honestly hadn't expected to hear from him again until after the Artificers were defeated, if ever, given their last conversation.

"Pete, slumming it in the Sol system?" Eva retorted. She assumed the invisible ship was related to him somehow. "I'm a little busy," she continued, her gaze still locked on Kilonova. At least she'd managed to stop laughing.

"I heard there was a big party going down and figured I'd see what the fuss was about," he replied.

Eva blinked. The ship was him? No, ships; there were at least six of them.

"You weren't invited," Eva said.

"You sent me a message."

"Right, and the message was 'Keep your people away from the Sol system, you fucking coward, or they might get blown up. I'll see you in hell.' Something like that, anyway."

Pete chuckled. "That sounds more like a taunt than a warning, don't you think?"

Of course he would think she was playing mind games with him. What a fucking narcissist.

"I'm a little busy," Eva said. "One of these cabrones is trying to kidnap me."

"Which one, this one?"

Kilonova disappeared in a cloud of bright pink flames. Eva sent a quick mental command to her isohelmet to darken it, but her vision was already streaked and spotted from the afterimage.

"Warn me next time, comemierda," Eva told Pete over comms.

"Stop using opticals on your helmet, Bee," Pete replied. "What are you, twelve?"

Fair enough. Not that she'd admit it to him.

Sensors showed the distraction had worked, though. Kilonova and his band were moving toward Pete's squad now, though they were off just enough that she assumed the emissions trick worked on them, too. She doubted it would last; the Artificers seemed quick to see through such things.

"Adelante," she told Vakar.

"What was that?" he asked.

"Pete doing something useful for a change," Eva replied. She eyed the direction of the mech as compared to the ship and mentally calculated the necessary trajectory. Once she was satisfied, she held out a hand to Vakar.

"Do you trust me?" she asked.

"Of course," Vakar replied, gripping her wrist with his claw.

"Then jump!" Eva shouted, leaping into the void.

Chapter 26

BY YOUR POWERS COMBINED

For a few moments, Eva and Vakar flew, weightless, through the star-sprinkled darkness. In retrospect, she realized she should have given him more warning, but thankfully Vakar's reflexes were up to the challenge of following her lead. His hold on her was firm, solid; she reached her other hand out and he took it, turning their wobbly path into a wide twirl. In the distance, the faint glow of energy weapons and occasional explosives flashed enough to be distinguishable from the broad scar of the Milky Way farther beyond.

All was silent, almost serene. Now that Eva wasn't monitoring sensors and yelling into comms, it was only her and Vakar with their legs splayed out behind them like a pair of skydivers. Not the most useful form, but maybe the judges would give a few extra points for style.

Eva activated her gravboots. She and Vakar were yanked

toward the mech, landing somewhere on its hip rather than at the door. Unlike the rest of her crew, she could walk the remaining distance instead of being bounced back into space. It was awkward going with Vakar oriented vertically above her, drifting back and forth like a stalk of seaweed, but they'd been through worse, together and separately.

Any time they weren't being shot at counted as pretty good, on average.

They reached the door and Eva flung Vakar inside first, then grabbed the edge of the doorframe and crawled in after. Her guts settled thanks to the return of gravity, but the disorientation persisted through several deep breaths as she lay on the floor, staring up at the unfamiliar ceiling. A shadow fell over her: Pink, crouched next to her with her eye patch flipped up, scrutinizing Eva with her cybernetic eye.

"What's up, Doc?" Eva asked.

"Your adrenaline levels," Pink replied. "You're gonna crash for a week when this is over."

"Bold of you to assume I won't be dead," Eva said.

"That's just my cheerful bedside manner." She finished her examination and stood up. "You're not dead yet, so get your ass in gear."

Eva sat up, gazing around at the mix of grim faces sitting or standing nearby. The cats' box was wedged into a corner, taking up an uncomfortable amount of space, since the room was smaller than the cargo bay. Sue had also brought her little robots with her, so they were running around or sitting in groups or hiding inside her big backpack peering out at the newcomers.

Eva checked in with Momoko and Min. They were both engaged in ugly hit-and-run fights with Artificers, staying roughly in the area Eva had sent them to.

"Momoko, Min," she said over comms. "We're on our way to you. Keep fighting and get ready to be amazing."

"Okay, Cap," Min replied.

"Absolutely," Momoko said.

The various squads of fighters were scattered around the area, losing ships but still fighting. Eva couldn't take on the challenge that was about to come and stay on top of them, too.

"Vakar," Eva said. "You and Pink work on a battle plan for our allies, especially once we get the mechs into their final form. Loop Pete in, but don't let him try to boss you around."

"As if he could," Pink replied dryly.

"As you wish," Vakar said.

Her last call went to Mari, who took just long enough to answer that Eva's chest tightened at the thought that her sister might be beyond her reach for good.

"Ahora qué?" Mari snapped.

"Did your reinforcements arrive?" Eva asked.

"Sí, and we're busy trying to reach the main reactor core."

Eva suppressed her desire to get more details. "Any luck keeping the Earth squad and their death tractor beam from starting their comemierdería?"

"I haven't been keeping abreast of the situation," Mari said, her voice strained.

"If your breasts get any messages, let me know." Eva ended the call, torn between frustration and relief.

The mech suddenly pitched sideways, sending everyone sprawling. Eva was already sitting down, but her isohelmet banged against the floor as she fell sideways. Pink and Joe landed in a heap, him on top, while Nara lurched into the cat container. Leroy stumbled sideways and fell, skidding toward Eva on his shoulder with a muffled yelp. Vakar did a full backward somersault, landing in a crouch.

"Sue?" Eva asked immediately.

"The flagship fired on us," Sue replied. "Systems are working to repair the shields, but it wasn't good. Diagnostics are still running. Starting evasive maneuvers."

Have to hurry, Eva thought as everyone righted themselves. They might not be able to take many more hits, and the Artificers were likely to send reinforcements their way any moment.

Eva straightened up and walked over to Sue. She stopped about a meter away, raising her hands to waist level with the palms facing down.

A podium rose out of the floor, stopping when it reached just below her hands. The surface was covered in the same sparkling lights as the interior of the pilot cylinder, and when she touched them, her entire body felt electrified, energized, like she'd gotten a rush of serotonin and dopamine and was ready to take on the universe.

"What are you doing?" Sue asked, her voice awed. "Whatever it is, it's amazing. It's like . . . I feel so . . . big."

"Yeah," Eva said. "Like you could fistfight a god."

Eva was dimly aware that everyone else in the room had fallen silent. Her skin glowed, and so did Sue's, a pale blue like the color of the sky on the planet where she was born. Her hair floated around her head, too; not like static, which would have had it standing on end, but like she was underwater, even though she wasn't inside the cylinder or surrounded by fluid.

"Eva," Vakar asked, "are you well?"

"I'm fucking awesome," Eva said, smiling widely at him. She couldn't feel everything about the single mech the same way Sue did, but now she could access a variety of systems. The interface was different, more sensing directions and distances than seeing them on a board, but the result was the same. Eva knew where all the nearby ships and Artificers were located, and she could track how Sue dodged and weaved around them to reach the place Eva had designated for the meeting of the three mechs.

Momoko fought half a dozen swarming Artificers. Her spinning two-bladed dance registered to Eva almost like the sure knowledge that someone on the other side of a room was getting physical, like some form of ancillary muscle memory coupled with impressions of air displacement and the sounds of motion as opposed to visuals. She knew what Momoko was doing, knew each swing and shift and strike, even though the style was nothing like her own.

It was no stranger than being plugged into her ship, yet different in a way Eva couldn't articulate. Like finding a new set of senses she hadn't been aware of, or had taken for granted until now.

Min was more accustomed to fighting one person at a time by herself, tagging in and out of a bot battle, but she and Momoko synced with each other as if they'd been a team for ages. One moved and the other followed. One ducked and the other fired. One punched and the other swept a leg. It was almost dizzying, and faster than anything that big should be able to move.

But hitting the Artificers where it counted wasn't easy, and so while some retreated or were killed, others continued reassembling themselves to attack. They weren't making progress so much as treading water, and time was running out. The homeworld would reach Earth, the doomsday weapon would be fired, and billions would die.

Almost there, Eva thought. A few more seconds. Then we can start taking back this system, and with it, the universe.

The instructions were clear, but something could still go wrong. And yet, this had to work. But if it didn't, they'd keep fighting, keep pushing, because there was enough death in the

universe on a daily basis. If they could do even one thing to reduce the body count, it was worth it.

Sue dove into the fray, immediately positioning herself as
the third side of a triangle of destruction. But that wasn't what
needed to happen, and now Eva had to figure out how to con-
vey the next step. She considered the mechanism of achieving
the final form and decided the simple approach was probably
easiest.

"Min, Momoko, Sue," Eva said. "I need you all to group hug."

None of them responded for a moment. This did not surprise Eva, given the circumstances.

"You want us to what?" Momoko asked first.

"Did you say 'hug,' Cap?" Min added.

"I heard hug, too," Sue said. Her brow furrowed in confusion.

Eva laughed. She felt too good to do otherwise. "Just do it,"
she said. "First Min and Momoko, then Sue on the outside. And
then just . . . concentrate on how you feel when you get a really
nice hug. From each other, or your partner, or your family. Whoever you like hugging."

"What if I don't enjoy hugging?" Momoko asked suspiciously.

Eva considered this. "If you don't, think of the thing you do
like from other people, even if it's being left alone. Being in the
same room but not talking. Being apart but knowing they're
thinking about you. Whatever makes you feel safe and comfortable and loved."

She didn't know how she knew that was the key, that sense
of intimacy and belonging, no matter how it manifested. Even
"love" might be the wrong word for this, but it was as close as
she could get. She wasn't a poet; she was a brawler, a pilot, a nobody spaceship captain from a small star system in one tiny corner of an enormous universe, and if this worked, she was about

to do the biggest thing she'd ever done in her life. Not alone, never alone, but she was a part of it, and it was fantastic.

The allies in their fleet took over harrying the enemy as best they could. Each mech disengaged from whomever they were fighting, disabling them or driving them backward enough to buy a few moments of breathing room. Min and Momoko slid their arms around each other—awkwardly at first, as if they had forgotten how hugs worked. Sue wrapped her mech's arms around both the others' torsos, and they stayed in that huddle for too many heartbeats.

Distantly, Eva felt more than heard Min say, "That's not right," then change positions. She pulled one arm free, then moved the other to be wrapped around the other mech's back, under the arm with a hand at its waist. Momoko mimicked this, and Sue raised her mech's arms so its hands were gripping opposite shoulders, almost like they were all posing for a holograph.

"Something is . . . oh!" Sue exclaimed as a renewed rush of nearly manic glee flowed through Eva. The chamber around them rumbled, the green light returning more brightly than before. In their container, the cats began to purr in unison, their eyes flashing with the reflected glow.

"What in blazes?" Pink asked. "Are we moving up?"

Eva tossed her a grin. "Final form, Captain Jones. Enjoy the show."

She pulled up visuals from the optical cameras, enhanced by other sensors, and set them to appear on one of the glowing walls. They showed the starfield surrounding the battle, along with the contingent of a dozen Artificers who had been attacking the mechs, and were now either retreating or attempting to fire, their shots harmlessly striking the cocoon of shields around the transforming trio of mechs.

"Why can't they hit us?" Nara demanded.

"Defense mechanism," Eva replied. "The change takes time, and it's not meant to be used unless it's absolutely necessary."

"How do you know that?" Joe asked.

Eva shrugged. She just did. It was buried in the instruction manual, a series of thoughts and impressions and warnings.

"It will be finished soon," she said. "And then . . ." Her grin widened. "I would say the Artificers won't know what hit them, but they will definitely know." Some of them might even have memories buried in their software or hardware or wherever they kept that stuff stored, which would potentially make all of this even more deeply satisfying.

The green light faded again, replaced by a brilliant rainbow that cycled from red up through violet, then turned a dazzling white. The room's occupants yelped or cried out, temporarily blinded. Spots danced across Eva's vision, but instead of being annoyed, she closed her eyes and let the other sensations flow through the controls beneath her hands.

The cycle completed and the light disappeared. Sue's pilot cylinder rippled with bubbles, her hair now standing straight up where before it had simply floated around her head.

"Everyone, buckle up. This is about to get funky." Eva used the controls to manifest seats, which rose out of the floor. The chamber's passengers, aside from the cats, scrambled to sit and secure themselves.

Outside, the protective bubble around the mechs popped. The Artificers, who could have taken advantage to attack, instead backed away, some of them fleeing entirely.

"Ladies," Eva said. "Let's pounce."

The mech—now singular—darted forward, swiping at one of the retreating enemies. They split in half, the purple-pink core of power at their center dissipating into nothingness. Their eyes flickered and went dark, and the two parts of their body started drifting away from each other.

"I'll be damned," Pink said.

"Not today," Eva replied. "Satan can get behind me and kiss my ass."

The mech moved again, from one Artificer to the next, dodging weapons fire as if it were blinking out of the way, then neatly bisecting one after the other. It was faster, stronger, and bigger by an order of magnitude. Eva had almost always been shorter than her foes, training to use her lower center of gravity against their height, but now she towered over these assholes who had tried to take over the place where she lived. It felt fan-fucking-tastic.

The flagship had to be the priority, though. Get rid of that, and the Earth was one step closer to safe.

"Let the rest run," Eva said. "Time to play with the big toy."

She didn't even have to pull it up on the sensors. It was as if the mech knew where it was and leaped to reach it. Within moments, claws raked the side of the enormous fleetbreaker, causing muted explosions as the ship's power conduits broke or overloaded from rerouting. There was no atmosphere to vent, nothing to fuel ongoing fires, so the damage was mostly limited to whatever was caused directly.

Eva was good with that. She had a lot of aggression pent up and ready to unleash.

Leroy had figured out how to control the optical-sensor output, so everyone in the chamber could watch the action unfold on the viewscreen Eva had brought up. Awed silence was occasionally interrupted by muted cheering or a whispered "Yeah, fuck 'em up." A few Artificers tried to engage, but most of them had drawn back, running or hiding inside the flagship. Some had gone to smaller ships and launched themselves toward the planet, which still proceeded Earthward at an uncomfortably fast rate.

"Is it time?" Sue asked suddenly.

As soon as she did, Eva knew exactly what she meant. Their new single mech had a weapon that would rip through the flagship like a vibroblade through paper. How could they not have known this? But no, whoever had designed these mechs did their best to leave instructions behind, and help, and guidance. They couldn't have known exactly what to expect of their potential future pilots. No UI survived contact with users, as her father used to say.

"Wait," Eva replied. Something important nagged at her. Something she'd forgotten in the thrill of tearing through her enemies, the ones who'd threatened her people, all people everywhere . . .

Mari. Antimatter. They were still on board the flagship. They had to get out, now. And everyone else had to get out of the blast radius.

"Keep fighting," Eva said. "We need to get our allies on the ship clear before we destroy it. Pink?"

"Yeah?" Pink replied.

"Tell all the other support vessels to pull back. At least a light-minute. There's gonna be a big boom soon, and then they can come back in and clean up whatever's left."

"Okay, I'm on it."

Eva couldn't see Pink behind her, but she knew everything would be handled. With more effort than she expected, she pulled up her comms and called her sister. The wait for Mari to pick up on the other end was nearly torture. It was like trying not to scratch an itch, or blink, and this was almost certainly the warning about this form—it wanted to move, to play, to fight.

Eva understood that sentiment profoundly.

"What?" Mari snapped. "This ship is full of hysterical Proarkhe and I'm trying to shoot them."

Eva couldn't stop the laugh that burbled out. "You sound like me," she said.

"Then I guess I should say adios, because I'm probably about to die. Again."

"Get off the ship now."

Mari paused. "We're almost to the reactor core. We can end this if we—"

"The mechs are fully activated," Eva interjected. "Get out before we blow your ass up. Dale. Salpica. Now."

"Are you sure?" Mari's voice was tight with emotion. "If we leave now, we can't come back to finish this. You have to do it, or Earth is doomed."

"Nobody's doomed today except these sinvergüenzas."

"Are you sure?" Mari repeated.

Eva's voice softened. "I've got this, hermanita. Vaya."

A conversation ensued between Mari and Antimatter, though Eva could only hear the one side of it. Antimatter seemed to have the same concerns as Mari, which Eva could understand; they'd had a plan and ditching it now seemed ludicrous, unsafe.

"Can Antimatter get you onto the planet?" Eva asked. "Someone needs to fix that problem, or the flagship won't matter anyway."

"Good point," Mari said. The conversation continued, and this time it sounded like Antimatter grudgingly admitted that might be a better option.

Meanwhile, the mech continued to batter the ships around it, to Eva's delight. Survivors limped away, while more and more simply avoided the engagement entirely. She shouldn't be enjoying this so much, she knew, but sometimes people started shit and got hit, and justice was delicious.

A message tried to intrude, technically over comms but with the strange originating address that Eva knew meant it was one of the Proarkhe. Probably one of the Artificers, given that she'd already spoken to Antimatter and knew what that felt like.

"Cuéntamelo," Eva said.

The connection drove into her mind like an awl, but she was ready for it. This wasn't anyone she recognized, though. They felt older somehow, more malevolent. Almost hungry. She got an impression of a huge figure with bone-white plating and blood-red eyes.

"Captain Innocente," a gravelly voice said. "I am Null Array, leader of the Artificers."

Eva grinned. She got to talk to the big boss now, eh? Funny how fast someone could graduate from meat to worthy adversary.

"Mucho gusto," Eva said. "Hope you and your amigo Kilonova are enjoying this spanking."

"This altercation is foolish and unnecessary," Null Array replied. "Why are you defending a worthless planet swarming with useless specimens?"

"It's a nice place," Eva replied. "A lot of people have worked pretty hard to keep it running. Fix the climate, clean up the environment, you know."

This seemed to confuse Null Array, who hesitated. "Your weapon would be a powerful addition to our cause. Why do you choose to defend those who are inferior to you? Why would you not assist us in cleansing the universe of those who do not conform to your will?"

Eva laughed. Not from amusement, no. Her laugh was as bitter as sugarless espresso and twice as dark.

"Conform to my will?" she asked. "Let me tell you what I will. I've spent years trying to build a business from scratch with my friend, busting my culo all over the damn universe. I've fought mercenaries, bounty hunters, emperors, psychic gases, parasites, battle robots, giant crab-spiders . . . I'm sure you've got millions of years on me, bro, but let me tell you, even if I lived until the heat death of the fucking universe, all I would will is to chill out with my crew and punch comemierdas like you until you cry and piss your pants." She paused. "What I'm saying is, jódete cabrón, go fuck yourself, then turn into a spaceship or a gun or whatever and fuck yourself again in whatever new hole appears, then throw yourself into a star and burn, because the only thing you're good for is slightly prolonging the existence of a life-giving celestial body, you resingado pedazo de mierda."

After a moment, Null Array said, "I will enjoy shattering your bones."

"Surrender or explode, fucker," Eva replied.

The call ended. The choice had been made.

"Who the hell was that?" Pink asked.

"Future space dust," Eva said. "Mari, are you out yet or what?"

Ten seconds later, Mari responded. "We're now on the surface of the planet. I'm not sure precisely what you think we should do, but—"

"Try hacking into the local network and putting up a sign," Eva said. "Something like, 'The Meat Is Back and Wants You to Stop Moving,' maybe."

"Eva, what does that even mean?" Mari sounded genuinely bewildered.

Eva took pity on her, but there wasn't time to explain. "Just do it and see what happens. Gotta go, love you, adios!"

With a happy sigh, Eva returned her attention to the flagship. "Ladies," she said. "Let's end this."

The mech renewed its assault, shredding through the enemy vessel with reckless abandon. Strips of metal sheared off into space. The hull, through the optical sensors, looked like a tree used for stress relief by a bear. It was still operational, though, still filled with people who wanted Eva and trillions of others across the universe to shut up or die.

Not for much longer, she thought.

"Time to bring out the big gun," Eva said. "Ready?"

"Yes," Sue replied.

"For sure, Cap," Min said.

"On your mark," Momoko added.

"Draw back to a safe distance, then hit it here." Eva tapped a location on the flagship to mark the target.

All it would take was a single penetrating hit with their weapon. While Mari's plan might have worked, if they'd managed to get their explosive device to just the right spot and triggered it at the right moment, this was a guaranteed winner.

For them, anyway. The Artificers were going to have an ugly time of it. But Eva had given them plenty of chances, and they'd made their choice.

"Count of three," Eva said. "One . . . two . . . three!"

A blast emanated from the mech, so bright that the optical sensors showed only white light for a few long moments. A flash of pinkish-purple followed, so massive it seemed like a new star was suddenly born in front of them. Gasps of shock and discomfort came from the passengers behind her watching on the viewscreen. Despite being relatively far away, the shockwave from the explosion still washed over them shortly after, pushing the mech backward like a boat in a storm. If it hadn't been shielded, Eva wasn't sure they would have survived.

"Sweet merciful heavens," Pink said.

"Yikes," Leroy said. Then, a moment later, "Did we win?"

Eva checked the mech's sensors. The opticals faded back to black as the dim glow of distant stars returned to visibility. The other readings were more important, though. Relying on visuals was like hoping to glimpse a loose screw at the bottom of the ocean.

According to the mech's readings, all that remained of the flagship was a debris field.

"We won," Eva said. "No, wait, one more thing."

Before she could call Mari, though, her sister buzzed in on comms.

"Eva," Mari said. "I have no idea why your incredibly weird message worked, but it did. The planet has stopped. Earth is safe."

Eva's senses seemed to dim as soon as she heard that. Her hands pressed down harder into the panel, and the rush of information from the mech's sensors flooded through her. Min and Sue and Momoko had realized the flagship was destroyed—how could they not?—but they all waited like cats staring at prey in the distance. There were more Artificers to round up, more enemies to subdue, and then what? Then they could take their new mech to other solar systems in other galaxies and . . . play.

She wanted to. The urge was so strong, nearly primal. Hunt. Chase. Pounce. The others felt it too, she knew, still linked up with them as she was. They were strong now, and they wanted to use that strength.

This was the danger and the responsibility that came with the great power they had been granted. Because once used, the temptation to keep going was huge. Eva could face down a BOFA fleet with this mech, could urge her crew on to one battle after another until they shaped the known universe into whatever form they deemed worthy. As long as they were inside this mech, they were nearly invincible. They could hold one government after another hostage and demand whatever they wanted.

They could do what the Artificers had attempted, and they could succeed.

"Captain?" Sue asked. "Orders?"

They could be liberators. Tyrants. But it would be wrong. It would be trading one form of despotism for another. Democracy was a shit system, but it was better than the alternatives, and she was in no position to declare her crew the new masters of the universe. Bad enough that anyone who knew they were involved in this mess would probably be gunning for them after this, trying to get the mechs.

That thought sobered Eva enough for the thrill of victory to recede. It was time to put the toys away.

"Let go," she whispered to the other mech pilots. "It's over."

They resisted initially, but with a collective sigh that bubbled into each of their tanks, they disengaged. The mech was once again encased in a protective field, and more slowly than it had combined, it began to come apart. First Sue's mech disconnected from the others; the pilot chamber moved back down to the abdomen of the bipedal form, eliciting a startled gasp from some of the passengers at the sudden motion. Then Min's and Momoko's mechs separated and changed, reshaping themselves until they were the same as they had been when they were first found.

Eva was able to watch it on the viewscreen this time, and it was arguably more unsettling than when the Proarkhe did it. Their transformations were fluid, while these were more stilted, robotic, perhaps because they were machines rather than people. Legs separated, the arm that had twisted into a body cavity became an arm again, the head tucked into the chest popped back up and settled into place. Eventually, finally, the three mechs were themselves again, humanoid and long-armed and individually colored.

"Wait," Leroy said from behind Eva. "What did the mech look like when it combined?"

Eva laughed. "I'll show you later," she said. "First, let's go see if *La Sirena Negra* survived the explosion."

Even if it hadn't, they'd still won. That would have to be enough.

Chapter 27

GOD'S IN HIS HEAVEN

Eva walked down the central corridor of *La Sirena Negra*, feeling a hundred years old.

Everything was exactly as she'd left it, to her astonishment. She had expected, if only because the whims of causality were cruel, to lose her ship to the Artificers as soon as she left it behind. But everything was fine, more or less. The temperature inside was a bit low, and she'd need to refuel if she wanted to get farther than Pluto, but otherwise . . .

The cargo bay was as clean as it had ever been, which wasn't saying much. The passenger compartment stood ajar, and the catwalks near the ceiling were draped with the straps Sue used to hang Gustavo and poor, melted Goyangi. The cat container had not yet been returned to its corner—she should clean the floor while it was moved, Eva thought ruefully.

The mess was eerily quiet, the food replicator sitting on the counter and all the dishes put away, chairs arranged around the table as they usually were, except for one that had fallen over at some point. The cafetera called to her, but she resisted. There would be time for it later.

The doors to the crew quarters and head were closed, and so was the one to Eva's room, where presumably her fish still swam in their enormous tank. The med bay was open, all the instruments and machines inside tucked into their respective places. A bottle of bourbon sat on the counter, flanked by two shot glasses.

The bridge was empty. The pilot's chair that normally contained Min and Mala was dark, the cable Eva used to jack in flung carelessly across it since she'd left in a hurry. The instrument panels glowed or blinked the way they always did, revealing the inner workings of the vessel to any who could understand their unique language, even as the data was streamed to Eva's commlink for convenience. Right now, several alarms gently attempted to attract her attention, primarily regarding energy outputs and shield capacity.

Repairs needed to be made, sure, but nothing they couldn't handle. Like them, the ship had survived. Now came the hard work of living.

Footsteps echoed behind Eva, and she turned to meet Pink's eye. With a smirk, Pink leaned against the frame of the door to the bridge, crossing her arms.

"Well," Pink said. "We did it again."

"Qué?" Eva asked. "What specifically, this time?"

"Saved a lot of asses and ended up in a different kind of trouble." Pink shook her head and stared down at the floor. "What the hell are we gonna do with those mechs?"

"No sé," Eva said. "Take them all back to the floating space castle, maybe."

"The Fridge knows where that is, though," Pink said. "And Mari's people."

Sadly true. "We'll find a place," Eva said. "Or we hold on to them for a rainy day, if there's nowhere safer to stash them."

Pink sucked her teeth. "That's painting a big ugly target on us, but I guess we already did that as soon as we picked up the first one."

"No 'we' about it," Eva muttered. "I did it without asking any of you. I should be the one to deal with the fallout."

"Don't start that again," Pink said, rolling her eye.

Eva shrugged. "I could take them and go. Disappear for a while, maybe die on the record even. Come back when the radiation settles."

Pink didn't bother to reply, just snorted and raised her eyebrow.

She wasn't wrong, Eva thought, collapsing into the captain's chair. Radiation had a half-life way longer than Eva's whole life, and so would this.

"Do you trust anyone else with the mechs?" Pink asked.

"Fuck no," Eva replied instantly. "Do you?" She leaned over the side of the chair to look at Pink.

"Nope. So that's it then. We keep them." Pink raised her hands in a dismissive gesture and turned to walk away.

"You're good with that?" Eva asked.

Pink paused and tossed a smile over her shoulder. "I'm a doctor. My whole life is about helping people. We can help a lot of people with these things, so yeah. I'm good."

"Who's gonna help us?" Eva mused.

"We are," Pink replied, and walked away.

Eva grinned. They were fucked, truly, but at least they would get to negotiate some of the terms of their fuckening.

She sank further into her seat, her injuries and aches seeping through the pain meds and stims she'd been using for days. Was it really over? Would the Artificers be back with reinforcements from somewhere? Antimatter insisted they wouldn't, that the destruction of the flagship was a setback from which they wouldn't recover quickly. Their corner of the universe was safe for now, and enemies were likely to hesitate before trying another attack when this one had ended so badly for them. But it wasn't a guarantee.

Antimatter had implied there were scarier things out there than the Artificers, though she hadn't been specific. Eva hoped she'd never come across those things.

On top of that, every government in the 'verse was likely to be after the mechs. They were too powerful. BOFA had already issued a formal call for surrender; how they managed to put together a message like that so quickly when they spent weeks sitting on their thumbs over a whole fucking invasion, Eva did not know. Presumably they expected she and her crew would be more of a pushover than the mystery monolith makers, despite everything they'd done.

Bureaucracies, Eva thought. They talked the house of shit and hoped you didn't notice the smell.

With a sigh, Eva forced herself to stand and walk back to the cargo bay. Everyone had unloaded from the mechs, including the cats, and were milling around uncertainly. Leroy and Momoko were wrapped around each other like a pair of tangled electrical cords, while Sue and Min held hands and stared soulfully into each other's eyes like lovesick kids. Pink and Joe stood next to each other, legs barely touching, until suddenly Joe put his arm around Pink's waist and tugged her closer.

There weren't enough rooms on the damn ship for all the post-battle hormones flying around, Eva's included. She met Vakar's blue-gray eyes from across the room, and within moments he closed the gap between them, the air filling with the scent of licorice and relief. But instead of reaching out for her, he stopped and inclined his head. They'd already said everything that needed saying before, and would say more soon. Right now, Eva had to be a captain.

"Escúchame," Eva began, using her Cuban party voice. All faces turned toward her, and she took a deep breath.

"It's been a weird week," she said. "Hell, it's been an intense month. Year? Madre de dios, I don't even know anymore. Who gives a shit. We're not getting paid by the cycle anyway."

"I am," Nara said from her spot near the passenger cabin.

Eva gave her the finger and went on. "Assholes from another part of the universe busted in here and tried to take over. We could have sat around and let someone else solve that problem, but we didn't. Any of us could have walked away at any time, but we didn't. We worked our asses off, and we almost died—"

"A lot!" Leroy yelled with a grin.

"So many times, Cap," Min added.

"Yeah, yeah, back to therapy for all of us." Eva shook her head, smirking. "The point is, we just kicked some serious asses, didn't we?"

A chorus of agreement and gleeful shouting replied. Eva waited for it to die down before continuing.

"I wish I could say it was over. I wish we were heading back to Brodevis for the fancy vacation I earned by knocking that guy down." Eva gestured at Joe.

"I was still standing," Joe said coolly. "And so was Kroko."

"Not for much longer, mijo," Eva replied. "But anyway. The point is, we have these mechs now. We used to be low-level freelance ass-kickers, but now we can blow up any dreadnought in BOFA's fleet, just like that." She snapped her fingers, the sound sharp in the silence that followed.

The conversation she and Pink had shared on the bridge seemed to slowly dawn on everyone in the group, though Eva couldn't know precisely what parts of it each person was coming to understand. They would all have different needs and concerns and questions, but she had to keep them focused.

Sue broke the silence first. "Rusty buckets," she murmured, eyes wide.

"The rustiest fuckbuckets we've ever had," Eva agreed. "We need to keep the mechs away from all the people who are going to come after them. At best, right now, we might have some time, because nobody will want to fuck with us to our faces."

"And because BOFA moves as slow as molasses," Pink said.

"Cierto," Eva said. "But we have to make plans, for when the universe we just saved gets its shit together and decides we're the new hotness that needs to be iced."

Momoko cleared her throat. "Perhaps I may be of assistance."

Eva raised her eyebrow.

"Not me specifically," Momoko said. "My family is quite adept at negotiating business arrangements, as you may know. In some sectors, we have effectively signed treaties with local governments in order to operate according to our own needs and specifications."

Leroy grumbled something under his breath that sounded like "corporate overlords" and scowled. Momoko's skin reddened as she glared at him, earning an apologetic kiss to her head that somehow managed not to be patronizing. Maybe because Leroy was red, too, and because Momoko immediately stroked his arm reassuringly.

"You have lawyers," Pink said.

"Of course," Momoko replied, as if it were the most normal thing in the 'verse.

Eva looked over at Pink, and the grin they shared could have lit up the room.

"Your brother," Eva said.

"He knows every settlement law on the books," Pink said. "He could have papers ready for us in a blink, declaring us a sovereign nation or some shit."

"If he worked with Momoko's team of sharks—"

"We wouldn't have to worry about running forever."

Eva squinted at Momoko. "Are there strings attached to this offer, by any chance?"

"No!" Momoko exclaimed, looking offended. "That is, I am not sure what we will do now, and the mech . . ." She flushed again. "I very much enjoyed piloting it."

"We can table that for the moment, then," Eva said, raising an eyebrow at Leroy. He hugged Momoko more tightly, his grin replaced with a thoughtful expression.

Pink pursed her lips. "That still leaves The Fridge and The Forge."

Eva narrowed her eyes in thought. "We might be able to negotiate something with Mari's people, but The Fridge? Not likely."

"We should keep fighting them," Min said. "They're jerks."

"At this point, we could probably get rid of those cucarachas for good." Eva thought of Smedley's wild laughter and bizarre fixations and suppressed a shudder.

"We don't want to run around with a hit list," Pink said. "We help people. We're not bounty hunters. No offense," she added, gesturing at Nara.

"Some bounties help a lot of people," Nara said, her face hidden behind her glossy black helmet.

"Ya, basta," Eva said. "We're going to vote on a bunch of stuff, right now, before the universe comes knocking on our door. First, are we keeping these mechs, selling them, or giving them to someone else?"

"Keeping them" was the unanimous response.

"Bueno," Eva said. "Are the mechs for hire or are they our personal protection?"

That gave the crew pause. Gears turned in heads, with Leroy's ears practically steaming.

"I say they're not for hire," Pink said. "We only use them when we think it's the right thing to do."

"We might think it's right to use them on a job," Eva said.

Pink snorted. "What the hell job are we gonna do now anyway? The quennians have ditched us, so it's either Fridge-spanking or cargo delivery."

Vakar's smell shifted to jasmine as he grew thoughtful. "The quennians may be more willing to discuss revised terms than you might think, now that the efficacy of the mechs has been demonstrated."

"We might have scared them into being friendly?" Eva asked.

"That is one way of describing the situation, yes."

Eva clapped her hands and rubbed them against each other. "You know what? Fuck it. I changed my mind."

A half dozen pairs of eyes and Pink's single one regarded her with a mixture of curiosity and concern.

"Eva," Pink said, her tone full of warning.

"No, listen," Eva continued. "All of this? It's a big decision. We're going to have people up our asses trying to make us pick sides or whatever. We need time to figure out our shit, but more importantly, we need to rest."

Once again, Pink broke the silence that followed.

"You're not wrong," Pink said. "Running on stims and existential fear for this long isn't going to help us make smart choices."

"But where will we go?" Sue asked.

Where indeed, Eva thought. They needed somewhere that no one would find them, or if someone did, they wouldn't be bothered. It couldn't be in BOFA territory; they'd get tagged immediately. They'd either have to resupply on the way or pick a spot that wasn't wrecked by supply-chain disruptions. That narrowed their options considerably.

A slow smile spread across her face. "I know exactly where we're going," Eva said. She winked at Pink, whose mouth fell open.

"No," Pink said. "Really?"

"Why not?" Eva asked.

Pink choked on a laugh. "You are nothing if not consistent, Eva-Bee. All right."

"Where are we going, Cap?" Min asked, her eyes slightly unfocused as she started prepping the ship for transit.

Eva held up a finger. "Give me a few minutes. I need to dig up the coordinates." She walked back toward her cabin, leaving her curious crew and tag-alongs behind.

The amethyst sky of the planet Neos made the whole place seem constantly bathed in twilight or dawn, an effect compounded by the local star being permanently fixed on the horizon in the location she'd told Min to land. The area was known for its perpetual sunrise or sunset, the local name translating to a word that meant both "cusp" and "respite." Few people came by this outpost despite the natural beauty of its coastal forests and rocky shorelines, because a power-plant incident during its first settlement year had increased the radiation levels to well beyond natural tolerance for any sentient species who appreciated the view. While the native vegetation was incredibly resilient and had long since recovered, food crops couldn't be eaten without extensive processing, and the trouble and cost of importing everything from off-planet meant the corporation that funded the initial venture shut it down rather than clean it up.

Someday the radiation levels would drop enough for Neos to attract its share of tourists, and the random ecologists and holovid enthusiasts who braved the toxic territory would have to fight for hotel space. For now, though, there were plenty of other places on other planets out there in the black, all of them equally pleasant to look at without requiring a spacesuit.

Hard to get a tan or feel the wind on your face like this, but some trade-offs were worth it.

Most important to Eva and her crew at the moment was the isolation. Neos wasn't a member of BOFA, was barely occupied except for a person older than Eva's parents who had inherited their position from their own parents. They liked the quiet, they said, and in exchange for being allowed to stay on an abandoned corporate world, all they had to do was maintain the testing sites scattered around the place and field comms requests. Requests like the one Min made to get them landing access and a quiet place to wander unmolested.

Eva stood on top of a boulder overlooking the sapphire sea. The dim glow of the star below the horizon gave the tips of the waves an occasional twinkle, and with her isohelmet's noise filters turned off, the roar of the water crashing against the rocks below her was almost loud enough to drown out her inner thoughts.

Vakar clambered up next to her, intentionally making enough noise to keep from startling her. With their helmets up, she couldn't smell him; one of these days, she'd get the suit upgrade for it. *La Sirena Negra* was nearby, though, and they could always head back if she wanted to roll around in licorice for a while. Not yet, though.

"I could become accustomed to this version of peace," Vakar said, staring out across the water.

"Part of me always wanted to retire to a place like this," Eva said. "Human psychology experts say being near water and trees is good for your brain."

"Where did the other parts of you desire to go?"

Eva grinned. "I think I'm past being landbound. It's nice to visit, but I belong up there." She gestured at the sky, at the stars beyond it, already feeling the pull of it, like the void had its own gravity stronger than what was underneath her feet.

"That does seem to suit you better," Vakar said.

"Y tú?" she asked. "What kind of forever home are you looking for?"

Vakar shook his head in the quennian equivalent of a shrug. "My home is with you," he replied.

Eva's smile softened as she blinked back tears. "Sentimental stinkbug," she murmured. He wrapped an arm around her shoulders and she leaned into him, as much as she could with both their helmets up.

In the distance, two mechs rose from the water and began to splash each other vigorously. Sue and Min, saviors of the universe, fooling around with deadly weapons in a way that would probably give Mari heart palpitations. Eva could practically hear them giggling.

Despite their bonding during the near-end of the Sol system and the known universe, Eva and Mari hadn't reconciled, precisely. There was still too much hurt between them, and maybe there always would be. But they'd declared a truce, at least, and were giving each other space and time. More important, Mari had quit her position at The Forge and been tentatively accepted as a sort of exchange student by the Proarkhe. For all the disdain

Antimatter had treated her with before, fighting together seemed to have forged a bond they were both interested in exploring.

Eva hoped they had a lot of fun telling each other about their respective cultures. Nerds.

Nara Sumas decided to hitch a ride with Pete, who tried to convince Eva that his efforts in the final battle meant she should work with him going forward. She thanked him for his contribution and turned down his very generous offer. As if showing up at the last minute somehow absolved him of all his prior offenses. If he wanted to be a wolf so badly, he could be a lone one.

Back at the outpost, Pink was giving the planet's solitary local a full physical in exchange for their silence, unless she'd already finished and was out hiking through the forest with Joe. He had said something about calling his brother while Pink worked, so that might be ongoing, too. They had packed their rifles and some target drones for after, but Pink had also mentioned heading back to the ship early for some privacy. Eva had taken the hint and discreetly passed it around to everyone else in the form of an order to stay outdoors for a minimum of a half cycle.

Leroy and Momoko had wandered down the shoreline in the other direction, toward a small inlet with a pair of skimmers abandoned by the long-gone residents. They were planning to race each other along the coast for a while—nowhere near the rambunctious mechs, though their waves would probably make for choppy going. She and Vakar had been invited along, but Eva found water travel unpleasant, all the rocking and unsteadiness underfoot too chaotic for her tastes, even at the most neck-breaking skimski speeds.

Besides, she needed a break. Too much action and not enough relaxing. Part of the allure of Neos was that she didn't have anywhere to be, nothing to do. Everyone could look after themselves for a while, and the universe could get its shit back together without her.

Vakar pulled away slightly, looking down at Eva. "I had intended to ask you something previously, but had forgotten."

"What?" Eva asked.

"What was the appearance of the combined mech form? We were only able to perceive what the optical sensors were receiving."

The mech couldn't look at itself, of course. And it's not like there was a mirror out in space.

Eva chuckled and pulled up the schematic from the place where the mechs had dropped the information into her memories. It was much easier to find now that she knew where and how to look for it. A bit of finagling with her commlink and she had a memcap, which she sent over to Vakar. She wished she could smell his reaction, but watching his face was enough.

Vakar's palps twitched and his eyes narrowed. "Are you—is this a joke?"

"Nope," Eva replied, grinning.

"But how?"

Eva shrugged. "The more I think about the place we found the mechs, the more I wonder about the people who made them. Antimatter didn't have great data, so we'll probably never know more than we do now. It's pretty funny, though."

"Do you intend to tell the other crew members?"

"If they ask, sure." Eva squeezed his waist. "Just don't tell Mala. She's already got an ego the size of the Milky Way."

Vakar squeezed her back. "What makes you think she is not already aware?"

He was probably right. Mala had been the one to help Eva figure it out, after all. But how had she done that? How had she known?

Eva went back to resting her helmeted head against Vakar's chest. Together, they faced the horizon, the dawn twilight of the local star painting the moment with a timelessness that made imminent decisions seem more distant. It was like the whole universe had paused so they could take a breath, and hold each other, and just exist for a little while.

As with most of Eva's silences, this one didn't last for long.

"Wish I could have seen Mari's face when her people showed her footage from the battle," Eva murmured. "She must have lost her shit when she realized her baby sister helped save the universe with a giant robot cat."

ACKNOWLEDGMENTS

Here we are, at the third (and possibly final) adventures of Eva and the rest of a crew who deserve a soft epilogue. I'm sure I'll forget someone who deserves to be thanked for supporting me along the way, and if you are that person, I'm truly sorry. I hope I get the chance to thank you personally someday.

Humble and sincere thanks to:

Eric, my husband, for gaming with me and taking over parenting and household responsibilities so I could work. This book wouldn't exist without you.

My agent, Quressa Robinson, for her tireless advocacy and diligence and thoughtful guidance.

My editors, Tessa Woodward and David Pomerico, and everyone else at Harper Voyager for letting me take this story to all the weird, wild places I wanted to go.

My mother, Nayra, for always sending me stuff I need and can't get on my own. Te extraño mucho, Mamita.

Jay Wolf, for reminding me not to apologize so much and for holding my head above water every time I walk into the sea.

Matthew, Rick, and Amalia, for flying casually with me in the void as we all scream.

My Strange Friends, for your support on and off camera. I can't wait to see where our future adventures take us!

My Isle of Write friends, for sharing in my triumphs and tribulations, and for continuing to help me rehome brain weasels to a nice farm in the country.

Clint, Clarissa, Sean, and all my other Twitch friends, for coming along on all my side quests. We'll get to the main quest someday!

The denizens of the various Slacks and Discords I haunt daily, for answering my anxious questions and listening to my ramblings and giving a hand up when needed. I hope I can repay you in kind.

My NaNoWriMo folks and Twitch writing streamers, for sprinting with me so I never had to work alone.

My sister Laura, for yelling with me about politics and life. We deserve all the wine.

My family-in-law, Aimee and Luis and Vanessa and Ashley and Erik and Nate, for your warmth and kindness and help in raising my kids to be excellent humans.

My dad, Keith and stepmom, Jackie, for encouraging me and hand-selling my books to more people than I have.

My siblings and stepsiblings, Tasha and Kirk and Jennifer and John, and all their spouses, for your love and support. See you in the stars, Pat.

My many other friends and family, for buying my books, for sharing my posts, for coming to my panels and readings, for sending me cat pictures, and for helping me feel less alone during endless quarantine.

And finally, to all my readers, for coming along on this epic journey! I hope to see you soon for more shenanigans, space cats optional.

ABOUT THE AUTHOR

VALERIE VALDES's work has been published in *Nightmare Magazine*, *Uncanny Magazine*, and the anthologies *She Walks in Shadows* and *Time Travel Short Stories*. She is a graduate of the Viable Paradise workshop and lives in Georgia with her husband and children.

READ MORE FROM
VALERIE VALDES

CHILLING EFFECT

"Jam-packed with weird aliens, mysterious artifacts, and lovable characters . . . a tremendous good time and an impressive debut."

—*Kirkus Reviews* (starred)

A hilarious, offbeat debut space opera that skewers everything from pop culture to video games and features an irresistible foulmouthed captain and her motley crew, strange life-forms, exciting twists, and a galaxy full of fun and adventure.

PRIME DECEPTIONS

"Eva's personal growth and the found family aboard *La Sirena Negra*—including the crew's psychic cats—will draw readers in and delight series fans."

—*Publishers Weekly*

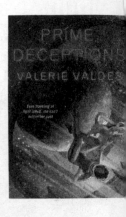

The lovably flawed crew of *La Sirena Negra* and their psychic cats return in this fast-paced and outrageously fun science fiction novel, in which they confront past failures and face new threats in the far reaches of space.

FAULT TOLERANCE

The hilarious new novel about the adventures of Captain Eva Innocente and the crew of *La Sirena Negra*.

With the crew of *La Sirena Negra*, a score of psychic cats, a feline-phobic robot, and a superweapon she has no clue how to use, Eva prepares to battle the unknown. But first, she has to defeat the known mercenary Tito Santiago, whose idea of a clean fight is a shower before kill time. His mission is to ensure Eva doesn't succeed at hers.